THE BAG

A NOVEL

ARUP KUMAR DUTTA

olive turtle

NIYOGI BOOKS

Published by
NIYOGI BOOKS
Block D, Building No. 77,
Okhla Industrial Area, Phase-I,
New Delhi-110 020, INDIA
Tel: 91-11-26816301, 26818960
Email: niyogibooks@gmail.com
Website: www.niyogibooksindia.com

Editor: Vibha Chakravarty Kumar
Design: Shashi Bhushan Prasad
Cover: Misha Oberoi

ISBN: 978-93-86906-54-0
Publication: 2018

Printed at: Niyogi Offset Pvt. Ltd., New Delhi, India

In fond memory of
Late Rajkumari Kaul (Aunty),
and Late BN Kaul

CONTENTS

PROLOGUE

Lahiri's Civet

Prior to the moment when he first detected a touch of grey upon his well-trimmed moustache, Senior Inspector Lahiri of the Special Intelligence Branch of the Assam State Police Department had imagined the world to be a wad of putty he could pat into better shape. But by now he was the converted cynic; his altruistic ideals had decamped bag and baggage a little after the ripening of his moustache and quite many years after he joined the State Police Department—so it was easy for him to be wry. However, his short stature, slight build and non-descript features were a convenient camouflage, as were the outsize spectacles through which peered seemingly unintelligent, kindly eyes. Perhaps, deep down in his subconscious, he despised his diminutive ordinariness, and thus, the dashing moustache; his thin voice enhanced the involuntary disguise so that his colleagues, friends, or family members never suspected he was capable of humour. None of them knew he chuckled constantly though inwardly at contrasts, contradictions, and paradoxes detected through sharp, all-seeing but seemingly bewildered, bespectacled eyes; the glut of ironies within the constricted circumference of his one tiny life (amongst a trillion-zillion) metamorphosed almost involuntarily into unuttered jocularity in his razor-sharp brain, articulated silently only by his internal organs.

Thus now, at this meeting of Unified Command, though remaining outwardly grave, he bubbled with inner laughter at perceived incongruities. For one thing, he was too small a fry to be participating at such a 'high level' sitting—to his surprise the Director General of Police (DGP) himself had called up early in the morning and instructed him to attend, he had not the faintest idea as to why. He was, of course, deeply involved at the grass-roots level of the anti-insurgency operations...that might be a reason, but surely the old coot had something more up his sleeve! Perhaps, he wanted Lahiri to get a feel of the goings on at the highest level by attending this meeting of the top tier of the three-tiered Unified Command (set up by the Assam state government to coordinate and monitor anti-insurgency operations in the state) before broaching the idea to him.

For another, it appeared to him that the Unified Command was in reality an Un-unified Command! He sat invisibly at the most unimportant end of the long and rectangular conference-table, with a laughing liver and a kidney which just would not stop chortling, as the big fries—the State Home Minister (SHM) standing in for the Chief Minister (CM) and representing the political component, the State Home Secretary (SHS), the bureaucratic, the Lieutenant General (Lt. Gen.) of the 4th Corps, the Indian Army, the DGP, the State police, top officers of the Research and Analysis Wing (RAW), the Central Reserve Police Force (CRPF), the Border Security Force (BSF), the Seema Suraksha Bal (SSB) and half a dozen others of gradually diminishing importance—went hammer and tongs at each other. Yet there was no real passion in their hearts or voices; passion of the kind possessed by those poor idealistic fools who were the reason for the formation of the Unified Command and the subject of this morning's discussions; they tore into each other with civilised dispassion, tried to one up on each other, shifted the blame onto someone else for committed errors of judgement, and patted themselves on their own backs for seeming successes; and, above all, strove to ensure that the meticulously maintained minutes of the meeting, sent as high as the Union Home Ministry, mirrored positive traits so their superiors could fabricate positive annual reports on them. Make no mistake—despite the bellies of each being pregnant with egos, despite their high professional status, each had his or her superior, even the SHM!

And that, according to Lahiri, was the biggest paradox—one keeping his innards rumbling for over an hour now—he was no doubt the smallest fry in the gathering, yet he appeared to be far more passionate (though it was a deliberately enkindled, coerced and pastiche 'passion') than the rest of them. Passion seemed alien to those present at the meeting. Dispassion had been the key to their professional success; if they had risen relatively high in their careers it had been due to their adroitness at off-loading passion early on; to have been able to trample upon others without shame or remorse and adapt to requirements of their respective vocations—politics, bureaucracy, army, police, paramilitary services, et al. They were, therefore, in a sense perfectly dewormed for professional success—the non-dewormed ones (like Lahiri, for instance), those who had failed to dismantle self-erected ivory towers, had fallen by the way side, fated forever to sit at or preside over less important meetings. Of late, Lahiri himself was sometimes (during bouts of solitary self-introspection) uncertain as to whether despite considering himself to be passionate, he, too, was actually dispassionate; his conversion to cynicism had simultaneously enkindled within him a tired consciousness of the futility of it all—the ephemeral nature of life. And the certainty that those stone gods were just that and nothing more—absolutely the right kind of existential posture for the self to slowly stoop into dispassion. No, not the dispassion of the Unified Command bigwigs but of a deeper, more philosophical kind. Yet Lahiri was intelligent enough to recognise it to be the surest route to perdition; perhaps also towards the moral stupor his middle-class upbringing had conditioned him to despise, even though involuntarily. So he had willed himself into passion; fought off the monsters born in the tragic wombs of extraordinary IQs and summoned up every erg of energy to focus passionately on a goal—an objective—on a single pin-prick as it were, tiny enough to be cosmically invisible, non-existent even.

And, at that very moment, sitting invisibly with his invisible goal at the unimportant end of the long and rectangular conference-table and constantly taking off his outsize spectacles, rubbing them with a handkerchief before putting them on again while half listening to the members of the Unified Command, flashed into his mind the memory—of those two eyes, twin burning coal-embers in the dark, and bared fangs ivoried by the beams of the kerosene-lantern light. As yet not distanced by time although it was a memory of a time long past, their 'Assam-type' house in the semi-urban settlement—the granary, pond, cattle-shed, firewood-shed, duck-coop and patch of plantain in the backyard—he as a child sent late in the evening by his mother to get some wood from the shed for the kitchen fire. Till this day he could not tell who had been more startled—the *hepa* or he. What on earth had the civet cat been doing in the firewood-shed? Perhaps, disheartened by its inability to claw its way into the duck-coop, it had entered the wood-shed sniffing for rodents. Its eyes had glowed ember-red as soon as young Lahiri pushed open the bamboo-door of the shed, and then the glow dulled in the light of the lantern; it bared its ivory-white fangs even as he stepped back terrified. Finding a gap, the *hepa* had streaked off.

Lahiri understood why that civet of his childhood had scurried into his mind in the middle of a meeting of the Unified Command… Consciousness was the most fickle thing in the universe, flipping like a struck ball on a bagatelle-board from one thought to another as associations constantly shifted. The very instant when the bleak humour of dispassion being forcibly transmuted into passion had touched his mind, the feral image was triggered; for Lahiri's civet was Lahiri's passion! The goal, the objective, the self-induced obsession—which seemingly imparted to his life an immediate, exigent 'meaning', gave it the transient direction and purpose, making it all seem worthwhile (for the time being, of course, since he would have to switch to another 'passion' if and when this was over!). An existential determinism since other passions had dissolved; his wife was no more the passion of his middle-aged life, nor were his two sons; both had gone out of Assam in quest for greener pastures, the elder to Bangalore to work in a computer firm, the younger to Delhi for intensive tutoring at a coaching centre so he could pass the All India Civil Service Examinations. This was the pattern of many middle-class families not only in Assam but also the entire North-East region of India—*in this stagnant, sterile soil no opportunities grew.* Thus, those who could afford it dispersed to alien climes for education or work; favoured centres like Delhi, Bangalore, or Mumbai were filled with bright sparks from the North-East who had left behind yearning men and women in lonely apartments who would dutifully join their offspring for a few weeks at least once each year. Thus, the fabricated obsessions…thus, Lahiri's fabricated passion, eyes which glowered ember-red in the dark, fangs ivoried in the lantern-light.

He tugged at his mind to make it refocus on his surroundings. He knew he would not be uttering a word in this Unified Command sitting. But the DGP had instructed him to meet him at his office at four o' clock this afternoon, and might seek his opinion as to the discussions, so he needed to concentrate on what was being said. Also, the inspector—being privy to the latest intelligence on the insurgency situation in upper Assam—suspected that his superior would primarily be dwelling on Lahiri's civet, though no one apart from the inspector himself referred to him as such (silently, of course). Lt Gen., who headed the army-operations against insurgent outfits in Assam, had the floor at that point of time. Figuratively speaking, of course, for he actually sat at one far end corner of the important side of the long, rectangular table, half-facing the SHM who sat alone at that end of the table upon a chair resembling a throne; the SHS sat around the corner on the SHM's right opposite to Lt Gen., who sat on the SHM's left. Such details were important, for the functioning of the entire administrative mechanism was dependent on constant and symbolic iteration of the pecking order. 'Don't mollycoddle the buggers,' Lt Gen. was speaking forcefully into the microphone before him. 'Treat them as the criminals they are, not bloody freedom-fighters!' He did not punctuate his words with 'sirs'; the SHM had never liked this but could not summon up the nerve to express his dissatisfaction, nor to request the hardened army-man to not use expletives. Lahiri could make out that everyone in the room—even the equally hardened commandants of the BSF or the CRPF—acknowledged that Lt Gen., being an officer of the Indian Armed Forces, belonged to a different world; that he was, in fact, a different species altogether. Members of the Indian Armed Forces, both officers and jawans, thrived in numerous island-like colonies in different parts of the nation; talked, walked, ate, shat, and farted different from the rest. Some, like Lt Gen., had aped the gait and mannerism of their British counterparts and become brown-sahibs. To insulate the Armed Forces of free India from the common multitude, there had been a continuation of the tactics used by the British in insulating their sepoys from the natives—'Stop the buggers from fraternising with the rabble and picking up politics'—a stratagem as relevant today as it had been in the days of the Raj.

'What's your point?' the SHM politely asked.

'*Operation All Clear* in December 2003 broke the ULFA's back. Since then we've kept the heat on them, and have had them on the run. But I hear you civilians contemplate holding talks with them. That's illogical! Don't give them a chance to get up on their feet. Keep kicking them so the bastards stay down.'

Then, seeing the looks of disapproval on the faces of the SHM and SHS, he continued, 'I'm not alluding to a ring-fight, obviously, but a street-scrap, so to speak. . .with no quarter given, where no rules operate...in those jungles with thick undergrowth, where you take one false step and you're dead!' Not that he was exaggerating. A veteran of counter-insurgency—Sri Lanka, Kashmir, Nagaland, Manipur—you name it, and he had been there. It was the reason why he was now heading the army-led operations against the insurgent outfit which called itself the United Liberation Front of Assam (ULFA). Moreover, Lt Gen., a strapping six feet two inches-tall *Jat* from Haryana and a hard-headed realist, was not given to exaggeration.

'We're more inclined towards a political settlement,' the SHS was intruding.

'That's because you sit at a bloody table in an air-conditioned office,' the abrasiveness in Lt Gen.'s voice was a deliberate challenge he knew would not be taken up. 'Let me repeat. The army has got them down, and will keep kicking them down.

No concessions. They've offered a cease-fire—nothing but a ruse to buy themselves time—to let the heat cool off. So they can re-group, find new hideouts, set up bases elsewhere, and repair their disrupted intelligence network. So, no cease-fire!' He paused for a moment, then continued, 'We continue to press home the advantage; keep digging them out of their rat-holes. Your government is considering giving safe-passage to them during this *bihu* to meet their families. In the bloody hope that it will induce some to stay back and turn over a new leaf. Bloody insane! Will merely give the buggers time to re-strengthen their intelligence network amongst the people—the network we have so effectively infiltrated and destroyed.'

'The general's absolutely right,' the CRPF commandant was saying. He had not needed to switch on his microphone since his voice carried across the entire hall. 'This is not the moment for offering concessions but to maintain the full offensive. As the general has pointed out, *Operation All Clear* had broken the ULFA's back. Their camps in Bhutan totally destroyed; they've been on the run for the last couple of years. Their self-styled commander-in-chief currently operates from a make-shift base in Bangladesh…'

Lt Gen. was cutting him off sharply, none too pleased at the intrusion. 'We go after them with all we've got,' he was saying. 'Wipe the buggers out within Indian territory. Reinforce vigil on the Bangladesh and Myanmar borders so they cannot sneak in... Patrol river routes more stringently. Have Delhi put on diplomatic pressure to deprive the outfit of shelter outside. I repeat—no cease-fire, no safe-passage, no peace talks. On the contrary, to enable us to clear Indian territory from the ULFA's presence, the army and Paramilitary Forces need greater leeway—shoot at sight rather than capture must be made the primary option.'

Unheard guffaws erupted from Lahiri's innards. The Lt Gen. was neither a politician nor a diplomat; simplification was his forte, shredding off complex layers of flesh with bestial ease to reveal bare bones. Though comfortable with complexities of army logistics, the complexities of politics eluded him. In other words, he could not see beyond his own nose. Moreover, neither he nor the CRPF commandant had been touched by the history which had accumulated through the centuries in the collective consciousness of the people of this region; these two came from different climes with different histories and different ethos; they could neither sense the claustrophobic sentience of a community that had once been armed with wings, nor feel the bonding warmth of kinship even between seeming enemies. Lahiri could almost pre-guess what the SHM would be saying.

'Your point of view is noted.' The SHM laid special emphasis on the phrase 'point of view'. 'But the entire issue is more intricate. Perhaps the state home secretary would like to put forward his opinion?'

Yes, thought Lahiri. An intricate issue! Years and years of ceaseless strife, destroying what had once been the most peaceful region of the Indian nation and ushering in an ambience of mindless violence and terror. Lahiri had seen it all, as it were, from the box-seat. Midnight raids on slumbering villages, bomb blasts, encounters laden with gun-fire and gore. Violence—of the State and of those who opposed the State, both to blame—and a society caught in the middle, hostage to an unforeseen collective destiny, trapped between the devil and the deep sea. SHS was shifting through some papers in the file before him as if to refresh his memory. He actually did not need to do so; all he had to do was clear his throat and switch on the play-button of the tape-recorder implanted there, and blurt out the 'official position' arrived at through prolonged deliberation with officials of the

Union Home Ministry digitalised upon his larynx. 'True, sir,' the SHS was saying, 'the issue is far more complicated than the lieutenant general has made it out to be. It's not merely a matter of us versus them. There are socio-political ramifications—these cannot just be wished away—or solved by simplistic means such as shoot-at-sight orders or denial of safe-passage.'

'Kindly record my dissent,' Lt Gen. was intruding gruffly, his dispassion masquerading as anger.

'Recorded,' SHM said with an air of benignity designed to further infuriate Lt Gen.

'Will you please hear me out?' SHS was resuming, words directed at Lt Gen. 'Military action is merely one component of the over-all thrust.' Then, as if posing a question, but to no one in particular, he was asking, 'When was the ULFA formed?'

No one bothered to reply, for it was a rhetorical question which SHS himself was expected to answer. This was his style—ask a question and answer it himself. 'On 7 April 1979... When the entire Brahmaputra Valley was in the grip of a mass-movement, protesting against alleged illegal migration from Bangladesh. Why was it formed? Because a small and extreme section of the agitators gave up peaceful protest and took up arms, declaring their goal to be an independent Assam. Let me repeat, 7 April 1979. It is December 2005 now, so over 25 years ago. For the last quarter of a century there has been sustained military and paramilitary action against the outfit. But has it been crushed?'

No, it has not, the answer popped into Lahiri's head even before SHS could follow up his question with the customary answer. A long passage of 25 years—a quarter of a century! Had it been so long back? Lahiri had been through it all from the very inception. He could trace with his mind's fingers the contours of a community's recent past as though it were something solid—the by-election in Mangaldoi—the catalyst to the mass-upsurge, sometime in 1979. Lahiri could not recall the date and month; around three years after he joined the State Police Force and found his probationary slot in the intelligence wing. The voters' list in Mangaldoi constituency in lower Assam had been found to be full of illegal infiltrators from Bangladesh—45,000 by a conservative estimate out of six lakh names in just one single constituency—clear indication that lakhs of Bangladeshis had stealthily sneaked into Indian territory and fanned out all over the state. The indigenous people of the Brahmaputra valley, panic-stricken that they might be finally outnumbered and lose political power, had risen as one in protest. Indifference of Delhi, ham-handed police action by the State government, lathi-charges and firings—the placidity which marked a laid-back, easily satisfied, complacent community had vanished for ever even as the corpses in hospital morgues piled up. Delhi, in connivance with the State government, had tried without success for six long years to suppress the upsurge, when a mere drop of understanding could have resolved the situation the very moment it had started. Only in 1985 some sort of accord had been signed between the Union government and leaders of the mass-movement. But, by then, State repression had led to violent reprisals by a section of hot-blooded youth—the ULFA had fed on fear and hatred towards the Armed Forces, and had gone from strength to strength, bleeding the tea-industry dry and running a parallel administration.

'No, it has not,' SHS said. 'You all may remember *Operation Bajrang*—the biggest of the initial offensives against the ULFA. When was it launched? On 28 November 1990. Naturally, the Union government's hands were forced.' The SHS added, 'The ULFA was gaining in popularity and the State government headed by the regional party Asom Gana Parishad (AGP) seemed helpless to combat it. So, earlier that year, Delhi dismissed the AGP government, imposed President's Rule as well as the Armed Forces Special Powers Act 1958, giving the Indian Army and Paramilitary Forces sweeping powers of arrest and detention without trial. Do any of you recall what the Lt Gen. heading the anti-insurgency operations had predicted before the commencement of *Operation Bajrang*?' Immediately, he answered himself as usual, 'That he would get rid of the ULFA within six months! His troops swept into ULFA camps in the Arunachal-Myanmar border areas. But what did they find? Abandoned camps, vacated by the insurgent cadres days before *Operation Bajrang* was launched. Such had been the effectiveness of the ULFA intelligence network throughout the Brahmaputra valley, that they had been alerted to the operation way ahead.'

After a pause, he said, 'Oh yes, the army did raid numerous Assamese villages and effected a number of arrests, giving the anti-Indian elements the opportunity of calling it a reign of terror. Six months! It's almost 14 years since *Operation Bajrang*. Has the ULFA been gotten rid of?'

It has not, of course—thus, the Unified Command, and thus, Lahiri's civet! *Operation Bajrang* had been the first in a series of Indian Army operations—in a limited sense *Operation Rhino* of 1991 was a success; a number of top ULFA leaders had been killed; no less than the self-styled deputy commander-in-chief of the outfit had been shot dead. That had been the phase when the army had been given a blank cheque, of the type Lt Gen. wanted again. The Armed Forces Special Powers Act 1958—a modification of the Armed Forces (Special Powers) Ordinance 1942—framed by the British to be used against Indian freedom fighters, and first enacted by the Union government of independent India to crush the call for secession by Naga nationalists, was then in operation in Assam. It was a blatantly anti-democratic Act which invested extraordinary powers of arrest, detention, and search without warrant to the Paramilitary Forces, even as it authorised shooting of suspects during encounters. At the same time it protected army and paramilitary personnel from prosecution by civil courts, thereby providing them immunity against charges of rape, torture, and murder. Yet, though this draconian Act led to numerous assaults on the democratic rights of the people and served to alienate them further, it proved to be of little help in destroying the ULFA.

Even *Operation All Clear*, launched with the strategic help of the Bhutanese authorities, had not been able to totally obliterate the insurgent outfit. No doubt the ULFA suffered heavily, yet it had been able to shift base to Bangladesh to carry out its struggle. Lahiri's innards chuckled inaudibly at yet another irony—the very same Lt Gen. who had proclaimed prior to the launching of *Operation Bajrang* that he would wipe out the ULFA in six months was currently the governor of Assam—as also the complementing irony that despite the 'power' vested in the office of the governor, a bureaucrat had dared to mention his inglorious and unfulfilled prophecy in an official meeting!

'Please get to the point,' the SHM said, merely for the record, since he had no objections to SHS's droning. After all, it was his own tape which was being played!

'Right, sir. As I'd said, there are socio-political ramifications a hard-line approach can't tackle. Let me quote facts and figures. So far, over a thousand ULFA cadres have been killed in encounters and military operations, and over four thousand have been taken prisoners or have surrendered. Yet, have the ULFA's human resources been depleted in any significant way? Have they lost their ability to recruit new cadres?' The SHS slowed down, and began again, 'True, the flow of recruits has diminished considerably in recent years, but it has not ceased completely. We've information that only last week some recruits were smuggled into Myanmar territory. How's this possible? If they're down for the count, how have they been able to attract new recruits? What does an outfit like ULFA feed on? Upon the thousands of gullible unemployed, of course, particularly from the rural areas...'

As Lahiri expected, SHS was homing in upon this contradiction for the umpteenth time—economic development was sine qua non towards ending insurgency, yet by impeding outside investment, insurgency made impossible the desired level of economic development! The pet postulate of the government and others; the favourite bogey; repeated ad nauseam from umpteen platforms; the infuriating alibi for bureaucratic ineptitude and political self-centredness; lying at the heart of the State's disinformation campaign against the ULFA; shifting the blame for the current mess in the region from a corrupt and incompetent administration and placing it squarely on the insurgents—all were huge obstacles on the road to eliminating insurgency.

Lahiri's bland features concealed the cacophony of laughter, rumbling like an active volcano within his bowels. SHS had earlier said that the issue was far more complicated than Lt Gen. had made it out to be. Yet here he was, himself stripping the tangled web to hook out a single strand—just one of the multiple causes why the insurgency problem had dragged on for so long. Lahiri noted with satisfaction that refreshments were being served even as the discussions were going on—'a time-saving device'. Obsequious waiters were laying empty cups on saucers beside each member seated at the long, rectangular conference table, pouring tea and whispering enquiries as to whether milk and sugar were to be added, placing quarter-plates heaped with pastry, sandwich, *barfi,* patties, cashew nuts etc. This being a high-level meeting, the fare, too, was expected to be high-level! He took an involuntary peek at his watch, surreptitiously scrutinized the faces of the aged, uniformed servers—present at the discussions in such a meeting—and wondered if any of them were the eyes and ears of the enemy. Did someone within the elite dozen or so, seated around the conference table and now digging into the refreshments, bought or black-mailed into whispering secrets? Or the humble clerical-level keeper of the minutes or any of the assistants seated on chairs set against walls; or the fellow at one corner ready to jump to rectify acoustics problems, if any were to arise? The ULFA had informants everywhere; within the State Police and Intelligence departments, too. Accounting for the fact that on many occasions, the Army and Paramilitary Forces were hesitant to pass on vital intelligence to the State-run forces of law and order. Even now, in spite of the setbacks it had suffered in recent months—or the loss of the support and goodwill it had earlier enjoyed among the Assamese masses—the outfit was not without its reach and resources.

SHS's monologue dragged on for some more time. Then, discovering that the focus of individual attention was veering more towards *barfis* and cashew nuts—and that his tea was getting cold—he was deftly passing on the oratorical baton to DGP, who was now having to let his own tea cool in the bone china cup while expostulating on logistical lacunae—particularly lack of manpower in the police department with hundreds of vacancies still to be filled up; the deputing of his forces to undertake other duties such as VIP security; the lack of cooperation from and coordination with the army authorities, especially in the matter of intelligence-sharing and joint operations et al. The serving of refreshments was a signal that the end of the meeting of the Unified Command, which in fact was the Un-Unified Command, was in sight. Another quick glance at his watch confirmed the fact—no concrete decisions would be taken, and the status quo would be allowed to be maintained. Having been turned down, Lt Gen.'s request for added teeth would not be reiterated but everyone knew the army would wend its own way—United Command's decision or not. In the current scenario, no one would be much bothered whether a cadre who would rather surrender should be shot dead or not; the meeting would invest upon the SHM the onus of initiating any major shifts in current policy—in consultation with the state chief minister and the officials of the Union Home Ministry.

It had been a humdrum two-hour meeting; there had been some cut and thrust of rapiers but not tipped with much venom; mostly carefully phrased bureaucratic exchange of inanities—yet, though many aspects of the long existent insurgency issue had been 'discussed'. Lahiri noted that no one trespassed into the grey area. In fact, they avoided it as they would a leprous beggar on the footpath…the P-factors—power, politics, pelf, players, people, puppeteers—the glut of ironies, and ugly, naked truths so droll to his innards. The inspector himself belonged to a Bengali family, which had migrated from erstwhile East Bengal during the British Raj to settle down in the Brahmaputra valley. He was a member of the fourth-generation, educated at an Assamese school, and could speak the language as though a native. In fact, he had assimilated to such an extent that his colleagues never considered him a Bengali. His wife was Assamese and his sons had forgotten their Bengali heritage; he, too, thought himself to be an Assamese rather than a Bengali. Yet, somewhere deep within him was an instinct which deterred him almost unwillingly from the emotional involvement with 'causes' dear to middle-class Assamese hearts; perhaps the past is so deeply embedded within one there is no escaping it. Which, of course, might not be true because the past in many others with a background like his had seemingly disintegrated into dust so they could become intimately entangled in the 'destiny' of the Greater Assamese Race. It was this lack of emotional involvement which enabled him to maintain a distance between himself and events; see issues and developments in multi-dimensional perspectives, without bias and unclouded by parochial impulses. This was an asset as far as his job was concerned; on the other hand, the nature of his job armed him with the knowledge and insights denied to most others.

Thus, more than most, Lahiri was aware that conflict hotspots in the North-East—particularly Manipur, Assam, and Nagaland—as areas of conflict everywhere in the world, were shadowed arenas where invisible combats were as real as the all too visible ones. And that they were filled with puppet-masters: some who worked with just one or two puppets and others with millions, some who made strategic places such as the state capitals of Dispur or Imphal or Kohima their puppetry stage, and the bigger ones who did so with Delhi. With no involvement, utterly dispassionate Lahiri chuckled at the all-pervading irony. Ever since had India attained independence—which was different from attaining 'freedom'—Delhi had strove to ensure those who infested Dispur, Imphal, Kohima etc. remained its puppets, not hesitating to hit below the belt when things began to slide towards the contrary. The British had understood all too well that the aura emitted by the region east of Bengal was far different from their mainland sub-continental colony, but not the ones who had replaced the British. For decades after independence, those who had trodden the corridors of power in North Block or South Block had failed to sense the different ethos of the communities peopling the North-East—never mind the Nagas led by Phizo, who had declared independence from the Indian State even while Jawaharlal Nehru was orating from the Red Fort's ramparts about the new-born nation's 'tryst with destiny'.

Incomprehension begotten by indifference, neglect begotten by incomprehension—so much so that the rest of India could watch impassively as the Chinese, in 1962, rubbed the noses of the Indian Army jawans in the mud and strolled as far down into Indian territory as the town of Tezpur in Assam, on the north bank of the Brahmaputra. However, despite the incomprehension, indifference, and neglect; despite the reality that only the Chinese aggression had made Delhi wake up and take notice, and galvanise it into compensating for its stupidity; bridge the river Brahmaputra—the only major river in India not to be bridged till then—which stood as a stark testimony to neglect of the region; build roads along the Indo-Chinese border to ferry troops; initiate conversion from metre-gauge to broad-gauge railway lines, not for the benefit of the local population but to send essential commodities quickly to those guarding the borders; despite the realisation amongst the people of North-East India in the aftermath of the Chinese intrusion that though almost fifteen years had passed since independence, they continued to remain on the fringe of the consciousness and conscience of a self-absorbed, self-serving mainland, their land precariously strung on to it by a single, 20 kilometre-wide corridor—despite all this, the communities peopling North-East India had so desperately wanted to be 'Indian' and feel 'Indian'. The middle-classes of each community, in particular, had looked towards the mainland for accolades and occasional pats on the back, their incessant whining about being ignored was, in fact, a quirky outcome of this yearning. Look how proudly they flaunted the North-East's 'glorious role' during the freedom movement; figuratively faxed to Delhi and elsewhere portraits of regional icons like U Tirot Singh, Bir Tikendrajit, Rani Gaidallo, or Maniram Dewan for recognition and acknowledgement!

The Chinese invasion had been merely one of the many disillusioning buffets—had the dragon-army not inexplicably retreated, the map of Asia as well as the Indian sub-continent would have had to be redrawn; that not too many beyond the check-gate at Srirampur—marking the boundary of Assam and West Bengal—had shed tears at the imminent loss of the entire North-East was no doubt a revelation; as had been the farewell speech made by the then prime minister Jawaharlal Nehru. But there were many other factors leading to the feeling of alienation; in every sense the mass-movement of the eighties, though it genuinely had illegal influx from Bangladesh as its leitmotif, was also a 'take notice or else' warning from a bulk of the communities populating the Brahmaputra valley. Delhi, in connivance with Dispur, had come down with a heavy hand on peaceful protesters—yet another knife-stab on an already wounded psyche. Little wonder then just three decades into the post-independence phase, 'differences' rather than 'commonalities' were aired by the agitators; ghosts of the past such as the *Yandabu Treaty* of 1826 between the British and the Burmese marauders were dragged out of closets; acquiring political power for the regional forces had been an un-stated objective. While the extremist wing of Assamese nationalism like the ULFA had raised demands for an independent Assam, the AGP—the political offspring of the mass-movement—was swept into power in the elections held towards the end of 1985. But the inexperienced youths who suddenly found themselves catapulted onto the treasury benches were mere playthings in the hands of seasoned bureaucrats of the State; also, no match for those wily veterans who treaded upon the corridors of power in Delhi.

Moreover, it had been easy to debilitate the resurgent Assamese nationalism by the masters at divide and rule—the region's ethnic history facilitated this. Assamese society was, in fact, a conglomeration of diverse tribal and non-tribal communities, bonded together by strong rulers with the sense of a shared destiny. The British had understood such a bond could be loosened by their infamous 'divide and rule' policy. Later, after independence, when in Assam the British Empire was replaced by the Congress Empire, the latter picked up a leaf from the imperialists' book and injected the politics of micro-parochial identity to destroy—for once and for all—the broader Assamese nationalism shaped through centuries. Undivided Assam suffered major dissections; the hills were the first to be ripped away. Mizoram, Meghalaya, Arunachal Pradesh—smaller communities were incited to reassert their individuality. The Congress was acutely aware Assamese sub-nationalism was anti-Congress in essence and had to be destroyed; if it had been the politics of caste in the rest of the country, it was the politics of identity in the North-East.

The roster of tribal communities which re-discovered their individual roots and shrieked for 'autonomy' grew longer by the years. It had been 'divide and rule' by Delhi at its 'best', and that enabled the Congress to continuously rule truncated Assam for almost three decades after independence.

During this period, this party embarked on a move to create a major vote bank to ensure its political hold on the region continued forever—the process had started towards the fag end of the British rule, when the Congress was invested with the responsibility of forming State governments. The party then had actively encouraged land-hungry migrants from East Bengal to come and settle in under-populated Assam, gave them land as well as the right to vote so they would be eternally grateful to the party, and exhibit it at the hustings. This had been acceptable as long as the sub-continent remained one but even after India won independence and a new nation had been wedged between the North-East and mainland India, the Congress continued to allow a stream of migrants from East Pakistan to enter and settle in this country through an intentionally porous border, thereby fattening its vote-coffers—a blatantly anti-patriotic act which the rest of India, especially the Jawaharlal Nehru-led government at the Centre, conveniently chose to ignore. The indigenous people of the North-East watched in horror and dismay as they were outnumbered by lakhs of East Pakistanis, and later, Bangladeshis—who homed in like a swarm of locusts into the valleys and hills. This, combined with the neglect by the Centre and apathy of mainland India—which often looked down at people from the North-East, as also the feel of being abandoned with nothing to do and nowhere to go—was fodder to resurgent nationalism. Nagaland, Mizoram, and Manipur shuddered with insurgency; Assamese nationalism tried to re-assert itself—the mass movement of the early 1980s demanding detection and deportation of illegal infiltrators was as much directed against the Congress as the illegal migrants, the last throw of the dice for Assamese nationalism to regain political power. From the point of view of the puppet-masters in Delhi, the movement had dangerously united the diverse communities yet again, and threatened to disrupt the exploitation of the region's rich natural resources through the mechanism inherited from the British colonialists. So, guided by Delhi, the puppets at Dispur had put on a macabre show, brutally coming down on peaceful protesters and killing and maiming thousands. Figuratively, this was the bed where the ULFA gestated and took birth—hundreds of fire-brand youths, appalled by State terrorism, took to arms, raised the banner of revolt and declared secession from India as their aim.

Such had been the vigour and stamina of the six-year-old mass upsurge for a while that it altered the political landscape of Assam; when the non-violent leaders of the movement under the banner of AGP succeeded in wresting political power from the Congress, Delhi, naturally, could not allow it to continue. Equipped with its dirty bag of tricks, the Centre was at the divide and rule game once again. The Bodo community, which had been one of the most active participants in the mass movement and played a glorious role, was egged on to demand a separate State—as were others. Insurgent groups mushroomed overnight amongst many communities—Lahiri himself had seen first-hand agents of RAW train and arm Bodo militants to destabilise the AGP government in Assam. Inexperience of the AGP leadership, the dirty-trick departments of a hostile Centre, and a servile bureaucracy long owing allegiance to the Congress and still smarting from the humiliation suffered at the hands of protesters during the mass-movement—all these combined to ensure that soon Delhi's stooges were once again ensconced at Dispur. The illegal infiltrators who were already in the State were now made eligible to vote, so the Congress vote bank would be further enlarged; in fact, the border continued to be kept open to allow even more of them to pour in. Thus, the 'historic' Assam Accord signed between then prime minister Rajiv Gandhi and student-led agitators remained a mere scrap of paper, with most of the clauses—including the all-important one of detecting and deporting aliens and building a border-fencing—remaining unimplemented. The wheel had come full circle as far as Assam was concerned. By the 1990s, it was business as usual on its political front—the upheaval of the early 1980s was a mere aberration in the continuity offered by the Congress.

But now the divisive tactics began to boomerang on the State government. History was replete with such ironies, thought Lahiri with grim inner laughter as he scraped off the last bit of *barfi* from his quarter plate. How often the ghosts of the past come back to haunt us! There were demands for separate States from almost every community, and the inevitable rise of smaller insurgency groups patterned on the ULFA—the Bodo insurgent outfits trained by RAW being the most dreaded of them all. A spate of violence, bomb-blasts, train derailment, sabotage in oil-installations, encounter killings, secret killings, extortion and kidnapping for ransom—Dispur began resembling a fortress—the region crackled with savage fury; the Indian Army, Paramilitary Forces and the State Police Force had their work cut out for them. But Delhi had the perfect antidote; as had been done in conflict zones such as Nagaland, it poured in huge amounts of money—ostensibly for economic and infrastructural development—in reality to line the pockets of vested interests, which could act as buffers between the authorities and the common multitude. Had the shadows of the ULFA and other insurgent groups not darkened the region, the Centre might not have been as munificent. Delhi's generosity continued, although it was soon apparent that rather than the people benefitting through greater development of infrastructure, setting up of industries and generation of employment, it had actually been politicians, bureaucrats, middle-men, contractors, petty suppliers and their ilk who were making hay while the sun shone. In the process, Assam—whose dwellers had once been known for their lack of acquisitive mentality as well as honesty—turned into the 'most corrupt' state in the nation. There was always the possibility the Centre would grow less generous once the ULFA problem was tackled…so who in his right mind would kill the goose laying the golden egg? Some of the lucre could be used to purchase segments of the media, including some prominent newspaper editors; corrupt influential elements of the middle-class; hypocrites amongst the intelligentsia, academicians and intellectuals who could play a role in the anti-ULFA masquerade. Delhi, in connivance with Dispur, could continue to flaunt its anti-ULFA stance and turn public opinion against the outfit even as it kept it alive. Money meant for welfare of the people could be siphoned away to create private 'armies' for many of the residents in Dispur—the 'soldiers' being culled from surrendered insurgents who could carry weapons to cow down the civil populace.

It had been, thought Lahiri—without the least desire to pass judgement for his style was only to observe and chuckle inwardly—a well-planned strategy by masters at the board of a political chess-game, which did not fail in its objective. With the passage of the years, memories of the mass movement faded from the public mind—Assamese nationalism was gradually emasculated, despite the efforts of groups of die-hards to revive it. Regional political elements became so debilitated they could not be political alternatives to the Congress any longer; in fact, the illegal infiltrators had been empowered enough so as to create their own political entities, which were growing stronger by the day even as the regional entities grew enfeebled. But the most terrible consequence had been the conditioning of the civil population to horror and brutality. News of killings of army jawans or gruesome photographs in newspapers or the electronic media of bullet-ridden corpses of insurgents failed to evoke the sorrow and revulsion of the past—a misinformed civil population, caught in a war of attrition between the State and the numerous insurgent groups, slowly but surely began losing its sympathy to the ULFA cause and longed for the peacefulness of the past.

Moreover, an entire generation of youthful champions of regional nationalism had aged by three decades. The new generation which replaced it was not fired by similar parochial urges; shorn of public support it had earlier enjoyed, its objective and ideology not relevant to the pan-Indian nationalistic ethos to which the new generation subscribed—everything conspired to reduce ULFA to an anachronism, and its aim of an independent Assam into an absurdity. It had been almost preordained, the pitting of a handful against the might of the Indian State could have had no other result. Neither Delhi nor Dispur was gracious in victory. There had been no real initiative on their part to start a process of dialogue with the insurgent leaders; Lt Gen.'s assumptions were actually baseless. After *Operation Rhino*, the ULFA had offered to talk. In fact, in January 1992 it had declared unilateral ceasefire with the Indian Armed Forces. But despite knowing that the outfit had set up bases in Bangladesh with the help of the Bangladesh Intelligence Service and Pakistan's Inter Service Intelligence (ISI), the Centre had spurned both the offers of talks as well as the ceasefire—choosing instead to go along with the policy of armed containment. Yes, Lahiri had seen it all…followed the inexorable movement of the wheel right from the very beginning; seen the erosion of values in the ULFA itself—the metamorphosis of an ideal-inspired outfit to a ragged band of extortionists seemingly more interested in money and gimmickry than fighting for a sovereign Assam; stooping as low as to now touch even petty businessmen when earlier it had bled only bigger ones, thereby further alienating itself from the people. Yet, the ULFA continued to have its uses as far as Delhi and Dispur were concerned, which explained the apparent reluctance to engage it in dialogue. Privy to secretive goings on, Lahiri knew for a fact that some political leaders of the ruling Congress had direct contact with a section of mid-level ULFA cadres; in fact, during the 2001 State Assembly elections, the ULFA had actively helped the Congress win at the hustings because of the 'secret killings' of relatives of ULFA cadres—which had taken place during the AGP government's second five-year tenure. Since then, in every election, the ULFA had been a behind-the-scenes player. A part of the money extorted by the ULFA and other insurgent outfits from the tea industry and businessmen found its way into Dispur—a convenient arrangement whereby the

ULFA left politicians alone while the latter looked the other way when money was being extorted. Yes, thought Lahiri, it was all a devious, complex game of chess which seemingly had no end.

Yet there were individuals within the ULFA in whom the flame of idealism still burned—like Lahiri's civet—though both were mere pawns in a bigger game. And Lahiri's civet was Lahiri's passion…it gave an illusion of meaning to the absurdity called life. The cups, saucers, and quarter plates had been taken away by now. The SHM was recapitulating the points made and decisions taken at the meeting. 'They're, after all, our boys,' he was saying…

At four o' clock that afternoon, in the metropolitan police headquarters at Guwahati, the DGP of Assam had Inspector Lahiri seated before him in his office.

'I understand Hiren Bora has re-entered upper Assam,' the DGP said.

So his guess had been correct, Lahiri thought sardonically. It would be his civet, alright!

'Yes sir, he has,' he replied.

'Gives us a chance, doesn't it?' the DGP asked hopefully.

'Yes sir, it does.'

'Let me not beat about the bush, Lahiri,' the DGP said, 'I don't have much time before I retire. Like any other officer. I would like to leave an abiding imprint that would become a part of police folklore long after I'm gone, if you understand what I mean.'

'Yes sir, I do,' Lahiri said.

'But abiding imprints are hard to come by, Lahiri! The Army and Paramilitary Forces lead the anti-insurgency operations...it's been a problem for our department to earn kudos, even though it's us policemen who have to work under more difficult conditions than those snotty bastards. Smack in the centre of the firing line, though far less adequately trained and armed. It's us who often earn the wrath of local villagers!'

That, thought Lahiri, was true enough. On paper, the Army and Paramilitary Forces had to function in coordination with the State Police—whether on routine patrol duty or in search and snatch (or kill) operations, the presence of the State Police as well as a District Magistrate (DM) was mandatory. But in reality it was the former who called the shots and received pats on the back. All that the police department got was blame—a breach of security, a single spark of violence, a bomb blast at a crowded marketplace or a hand grenade lobbed at a paramilitary patrol party—it was always intelligence failure or deficiency in anticipation on the part of the local police!

'Deficiency in anticipation, bah!' The DGP would have used a spittoon had any been there in the vicinity! 'I'm fed up with hearing the phrase, Lahiri. This brings me back to Hiren Bora. Bagging him...or even being the primary agent in bagging him... =would be a feather in our cap, wouldn't it?'

'Certainly sir, it would.'

That, again, was true enough. Hiren Bora! AKA Rongmon Changmai. AKA Shamshad Hussain. 'Hiru' to his comrades and the media. Inspector Lahiri had shifted through the file on Hiren Bora so many times he knew the contents almost by heart. The ULFA had lost a number of middle-rung leaders during *Operation All Clear* in Bhutan. Hiru had been in one of the camps—God alone knows how he managed to give the Indian-Bhutanese security forces the slip—escaped, and had emerged stronger and even more important to the ULFA after the debacle. The truth was that most of the aging top ULFA leaders—except the self-styled commander-in-chief of its armed wing—had become sedentary, leading middle-class type family lives in safer havens such as Bangladesh. They were passing on responsibilities to the younger cadres in the outfit more and more. And Hiren Bora had emerged as the most important, dreaded, and wiliest of them all, closer to the commander-in-chief than anyone else. After *Operation All Clear*, the ULFA had shifted its base to Bangladesh; the Begum Khaleda Zia government there guaranteed safety. The other option, Myanmar, could not be used since the Indian government had persuaded the National Socialist Council of Nagalim (NSCN) to ensure that the Kachin Independent Army (KIA) no longer afforded protection and training to the ULFA.

Yet, naturally, every player in the bigger chess game was expected to do the double-bluff; Indian intelligence agencies knew for a fact that though not permitted to set up camps, ULFA cadres were allowed by other insurgent groups to shuttle through jungle terrain between Myanmar and Bangladesh. Thus, vigilance on the India-Myanmar border had not been relaxed and the security scenario in upper Assam continued to be on the radar. The Bhutanese setback had entailed the remnants of the ULFA there to shift to Bangladesh but, later, Hiren Bora had slipped out to join his chief in the Yunan province of China. And now he was back in upper Assam—much earlier than anticipated—sent by his mentor, perhaps, to carry out a deadly retaliatory assignment, more likely to extort funds and recruits. No matter what the motive, he was within trappable range—an opportunity unlikely to occur again for a long time. Bagging Hiren Bora would be a key to creating departmental folk-ore, for sure.

'Lt Gen.'s people must be in the know,' the DGP continued. 'But they're keeping all the information on Hiren Bora close to their chests. I would like to go one up on them this time. As far as I am aware, you're the best authority on this particular cadre and have been keeping track of him.'

Best authority! Was that all the DGP could manage? Not use words such as 'passion' or 'obsession'! But then, Lahiri thought with dry humour, it was, in fact, a tribute to his own ability to conceal his inner urgings.

'I don't know about the "best" part, sir,' Lahiri said with a modesty everyone agreed was typical of the man. 'But yes, I've been keeping track of his movements and assisting the authorities in any way I can.'

'So where is Hiren Bora now?'

'In the Tinsukia tea-belt in upper Assam, most likely. We assume he is targeting the tea-sector for raising funds. Perhaps also the oil industry.'

'Most likely? That's neither precise nor comforting. What was it, a phone intercept?'

'No, sir. The outfit's into the misinformation game, just like us! Lots of misleading stuff in the intercepts...difficult to separate the wheat from the chaff. From a paid hireling. A surrendered ULFA cadre, the one who first recruited Hiru...same village. Now he's in a designated camp for surrendered cadres. Apparently Hiru tried to contact him.'

'How reliable is your informant?'

'Can be relied on, under the circumstances. A few days back I went to Tinsukia to interrogate him myself. Seems he asked Hiru to back off the moment he tried to make contact.'

'Stupid of him. If he's being paid for the job, he should have kept him hanging till we were on the scene.'

'Old loyalty, sir. Or an instinct for self-preservation. Hiren Bora is reputed to be ruthless. Also, sir, a big Marwari merchant at Tinsukia had reported to the army an attempt to extort money from him had been made. On specific instructions of the army, he did not inform the local police. Though we came to know, anyway. We're not without our own resources, sir! He did not mention Hiren Bora by name, but we can put two and two together and guess it must be him. Makes it certain the army, too, knows the civet is in town.'

The DGP found himself caught off guard. 'The what?'

'Just a figure of expression, sir,' Lahiri said quickly and gravely to cover up his momentary lapse, fearful the old coon might guess he was capable of humour. Worse still, that he might be self-indulgently passionate!

'Oh, right. Well, if we're to go one up on the army, we need someone with your experience and knowledge on the spot. I'm sending you on an assignment to upper Assam, Lahiri. Just an oral order between you and me...no paperwork...no informing anyone else even within our department, much less the army. You'll by pass all senior officers and report directly to me.'

An assignment after his own heart; so ironic that the DGP made the order sound like a request. Lahiri did not allow his face to mirror his sense of satisfaction.

'Yes, sir. I'll drop everything else.'

'Good. Any thoughts on a possible strategy?'

'A bait, sir.'

'To trap the civet, eh?'

'His family, sir,' Lahiri said hastily. 'Always the weakest link with our boys.' Seeing his superior raise an eyebrow, he added pointedly, 'Not my phrase, sir. The minister's. In the morning's meeting.'

'Yes, yes.' The DGP could not detect the unarticulated humour in the inspector's voice, so he was not amused. 'What about his family?'

'I got personal details out of my informant. As you know, sir, Hiru's from Chungijan village under the Doomdooma Police Station. Father, a farmer with a small land holding. Had always been on the fringes of poverty—still is.'

'If that was meant to be a compliment, save it for another day,' the DGP said testily. It had been a compliment, of course. Being one of the principal fundraisers for the banned outfit, crores of rupees had passed through Hiren Bora's hands. Yet his family lived as it always had, barely able to make ends meet! Said a great deal about the fellow, it did.

Lahiri took the rebuke in his stride, fished a small, dog-eared notebook out of his pocket, licked a thumb with his tongue to be able to leaf through the sheets and peered at scrawled notes through seemingly short-sighted, (though sharp, all-seeing) eyes. 'So far we've been focussing on Hiru, sir, not his family,' he said. 'I went the other way round with my informant. Since he was from the same village and had practically grown up with Hiru, he could provide intimate details. So I talked less about the ULFA and more about their earlier life in Chungijan—teenage activities, community roles, their families and all that stuff. Tried to get an idea of Hiru's personality...the kind of young man he was.'

The DGP understood the logic behind such an approach, could see through the intentional bumbling mannerisms of the one confronting him (though not the inner humour), and had full faith in Lahiri's abilities, otherwise the latter would not be sitting in the chair opposite him. The man was one of his finest intelligence officers, and had to be properly used. He nodded but kept silent while Lahiri stopped at a page and began to read.

'Hiru's family details, sir. Father, Dharmeshwar Bora, born 1948, married Indreshwari in 1977. Hiru, born 1979, so 26 years old. Sister Debeshwari, born 1981, 24 years old, unmarried. Hiru's mother Indreshwari died of gastro-enteritis in 1990, when Hiru was 11 years old. Traumatic experience for the kids, especially Hiru. Mother was taken to the nearest rural dispensary well in time, yet she died. You see, there was neither a doctor nor much medicine there!'

'Go on.' The DGP's curiosity was roused.

'With his fields to be worked on and two youngsters to raise, their father married again a girl named Dipali from an adjacent village, who was somewhat younger than him, the very next year. Here's the significant bit: on 26 December 1992, a boy was born to the new wife—Hiru's stepbrother. Named Okon, now 13, he's studying in class VIII at the Government Boys' School at Doomdooma, around eight kilometres from Chungijan.'

'So Hiru has a stepbrother half his age? Significant, you said?'

'You'll soon understand why, sir.' Lahiri took off his spectacles, plucked out a handkerchief from his pocket, wiped the lenses, put them back on and peered at his notebook again. 'We come to Hiru's educational career. Like most rural youngsters, he had his early education at the village school—or what passes for a school—usually a thatched hutment with a single teacher, some having none at all. You know, sir, one of those institutions where students have to carry their own sacks to sit on the earthen floor since the only piece of furniture is the teacher's chair! The teacher imparts minimal level knowledge, often without textbooks or blackboards and chalks, and then packs off as many of his students as he can to the primary school in the closest township.'

The DGP was taken aback. 'You almost sound angry! I'd imagined a shrug of the shoulder would have been more your style.'

'Cynicism is no deterrent towards comprehension,' Lahiri said. 'The psychology, sir! Hiru, an above average student, passed matriculation in 1995, division first, Doomdooma Government Boys' School. Got scholarship and passed BCom, Doomdooma College in 2000. That was as far as he could go, for without money, pursuing a university education or taking a specialised vocational course was impossible. In fact, it was a wonder he got that far—many rural youngsters drop out at the matriculation stage. His sister, of course, could not be sent to school, but Hiru made her literate by teaching her at home.'

Lahiri closed the notebook, almost defiantly, as if he knew the contents by heart. 'Their father,' he continued, 'though aging, had quite a few years of work left in him. So it was assumed the younger son, Okon, after matriculation, would take over the farming. Hiru was expected to find a job, earn enough to marry off his sister and get himself a wife.'

'Ah, find a job! The fly in the ointment, isn't it?'

In this sterile soil no opportunities grew! The DGP had touched upon a tale re-enacted thousands of time in the region. 'Yes, sir,' Lahiri said. 'You must understand Hiru was a leader amongst the village youth; even an elected member of his college students' union. Someone who, despite his poverty-stricken background, had earned the respect of peers; a role model to be emulated, the lad who led the *naam-prasanga* in the village *naamghar*; the chief organiser of the area's rural sports meet during *Rongali-bihu*—even the village *gaon-burrah* occasionally sought his advice. It did not take him long to realise that, outside his tiny, familiar milieu, he was a nobody. A blow to his ego, the implanted seed to his subsequent actions.

'There were no jobs in the immediate surroundings, apart from primarily menial ones. The area is rich in natural resources like oil and coal, exploited since British days. But managerial or even supervisory posts in oil or coal companies required far more than a graduate degree... The only jobs available were temporary ones...loading trucks or laying gravel on roads. True, small towns had grown up around the industries, but these had merely petty traders who could at best offer a salesman's job. Hiru discovered that even for the humblest job, there was fierce competition.'

'So he sought refuge in the ULFA, eh?'

'Not immediately, no. We aren't sure how he managed to raise some funds. No, no, he didn't mortgage the farmland to the local moneylender—perhaps from a friend, perhaps from some girl infatuated with him. He then came to Guwahati towards the middle of 2001. My informant, who did not go beyond school level, is not sure what he did here—couldn't have been a pleasant or fruitful period, for he returned to his village nine months later, with nothing much to show for his absence. My informant had, by then, been two years with the ULFA. Hiru, he told me, was easy meat! Just three weeks in Chungijan, and he was recruited.'

Lahiri, with a ritualistic air, plucked out his notebook again. 'Sometime in April 2002,' he said, and placing the notebook back in his pocket as though it contained nothing more, 'the rest you know, sir. His rise in the set-up has been phenomenal.'

'Good,' said the DGP appreciatively. 'But where's all this leading to?'

'The family, sir! Hiru had been very close to his family, the pride and hope of his parents. More than personal ego, it had been his inability to help his family which had caused his frustration. He surreptitiously dropped in at his home at least three times during the first two years after joining the ULFA. But, due to his rise in the ranks and growing importance, as also more effective intelligence-gathering on our part, for the last two years he has not been able to visit his family even once! I'm convinced he'll do so this time.'

The edges of the DGP's lips curled into a smile as the logic of Lahiri's hunch sank into him. 'You've taken necessary precautions?'

'Went to Chungijan after getting the stuff from my informant and had a quiet chat with the *gaon-burrah*. He'll be keeping his ears open and let us know the minute he suspects something brewing. We also have paid informers in Doomdooma—and, of course, in the village itself—they've been put on high alert. There is one thing, sir. If the need for an operation does arise, can't we do it on our own?'

'I would like nothing better,' the DGP said wistfully. 'Unfortunately, we can't dodge the system. The army will have to be informed, if they aren't already onto it. But I'll make sure the ones who matter at Dispur know the information for the raid came from our side.'

'Right sir. I'll be leaving for upper Assam by a night bus today itself. I'll set up base in Doomdooma and work from there.'

'Good. Knowing you as I do, I'm confident you have some specific date in mind.'

'A long guess, sir.' Lahiri said. 'Hiru was closest to his stepbrother, even closer than to his own sister. Okon worshipped the very ground Hiru walked on. So my bet would be on 26 December. That day, you see sir, happens to be Okon's birthday, when he would be turning fourteen. I will, naturally, try to get it confirmed through my sources in the area.'

'Bravo! You know, Lahiri, these days it's in fashion to tag on a designation to an assignment like the one I've given you. What do you think would be an appropriate tag?'

'I've no idea, sir,' Lahiri said, secretly cognizant of what was coming.

The DGP smiled. '*Operation Hepa*, what else,' he said.

WET PANTS

'Go to bed,' Ai had said. 'I'll wake you up when he comes… If he comes.'

His mother's face was composed, voice emotionless and impersonal. But he had heard the tell-tale quiver, a tremble which was an almost inaudible, despair-filled sigh; like one heard within a breeze-swept patch of thatch-grass. He'd sensed the sadness, the underlying longing—and the fear.

Pitai, slouched upon a rickety *murrah*, shoulders stooped, had nodded but said nothing. His father had been sitting in the same posture since twilight, brooding and silent, as though he could not trust himself to speak. Bai, too, had uttered no word, made no movement. Huddled on the wooden *pirrah*, his elder sister seemed like a mute statue in the dim light of the kerosene-lantern; but he needed no words to sense how she felt. The same sadness as in Ai, yet tinged with expectancy. At his imminent arrival.

When he comes… If he comes!

Okon had flitted away to his room.

A tiny space all of his own, walls of spliced bamboo plastered with mud, white-wash fading into dirty grey, mud-patches peeling off at places. Naked bamboo rafters, skeletal, cob-webbed, through which the thatch of the roof could be seen in daytime. But not on a night like this, with the thick, black quilt of fog outside screening off the moon.

Now, on his back, within the intimacy of a thread-bare mosquito-net, underneath a couple of thin, worn out blankets, Okon lay still, eyes closed. But sleep refused to come. The tiredness of an active 13-year-old at the end of the day had touched his limbs, weighed down his body. But not touched his mind, nor weighed down his eyelids, though tight-shut.

Sleep had touched the village hours ago. In fact, a little after sunset. Most of the villagers retired early. Electricity had not arrived at this remote rural hamlet in upper Assam, just a stone's throw away from the border with Myanmar. Kerosene for lantern or mustard-oil for *chaki* was getting costlier day by day. Thus, the sensible thing to do was to get up at the crack of dawn and retire early in the evening, making full use of daylight hours.

Yes, the outside world was asleep. But their cottage was too steeped in anticipation for sleep to come. And his mind was too filled with memories of his beloved Hirukai…

A fraternal love almost feral in its nakedness, an absence, a near-animal anguish, felt perhaps in the womb of his mother despite the two of them having gestated in different wombs; felt from infancy, he cradled in Hirukai's arms as the night's enactment in the village *bhaona* performance unfolded. The *rakhyasa* had pranced on to the *naamghar's* stage, two steps forward, one step back, terrorising the fictive village, ignoring tear-bloated importunities for animal-carcass offerings in lieu of the demanded human flesh. The epitome of evil, this ogre—the hideous mask it wore, intentionally exaggerating its vileness, arched eyebrows raised over monstrous, black, terrifying eyes; open, cavernous mouth revealing tusks and red tongue and lips splattered with human gore. The saviour was of royal blood; he wore fake armour aglitter with tiny glass pieces which reflected light; his cardboard crown twinkled with tinsel; his mace was made of papier-mâché but, consummate artist that he was, he carried it as though it had been made of iron. The spectators were mesmerised into a collective hush as he assailed the *rakhyasa*. A terrible battle raged…the universe shuddered in the collective imagination and a dust storm cloaked the earth. Then the climactic fall; punctured pouch of red paint concealed near the heart of the *rakhyasa* spouted blood. Okon's tiny fingers had tightened around Hirukai's arm, drawing courage and reassurance from the warmth of intimate contact. Some infants and toddlers had let out wails but not Okon, absolutely certain that as long as he was in Hirukai's arms no ogre—not even this gargantuan *rakhyasa*, the fattest man in the village—could harm a hair on his head.

Okon, since birth, had been Hirukai's shadow; bound together with the threads of an inexplicable passion that could not be untied even in moments of separation. *Rongali-bihu* was the festival he loved most; when spring arrived with the cuckoo's lilting call and blue orchids bloomed, the air pulsated with the throb of myriad drums; the camaraderie and excitement was infectious; young men's thoughts turned to love; some of them would suddenly break out into an erotic *bihu* song without rhyme or reason; it was the joyously crazy season. For a fortnight, Bai had pounded *bora-chaul* at the *dheki* to make delicious *til-pithas* and *ghila-pithas* while Ai grated coconuts for the *larus* which melted in one's mouth. The craziest of all was the day of *goru-bihu*; Pitai could not afford bulls for ploughing, since maintaining a pair for such a small land-holding was uneconomic. Each year, when the time for ploughing the fields arrived, he would borrow bulls from a more well-to-do villager in lieu of a part of his produce. But they had the cow and her calf. On *goru-bihu* morning, the somewhat flabbergasted beasts would moo out plaintive complaints as they were rubbed all over with turmeric paste and festooned with garlands—not of flowers but chopped gourds and aubergines! Then, with boisterous noise and ululations, the villagers would lead their unwilling animals to the riverside together and lovingly bathe them—an underlining of the reality that even in these modern times, cattle were important to rural folk of the region.

The next day would be *manuh-bihu*; Okon would be up at the crack of dawn, have a bath, don new clothes and then touch his elders' feet. He would then stuff himself with the delicacies his mother and elder sister had cooked; Hirukai would almost ritualistically dress his little brother so that he, too, could join the village *huchari-dance* troupe—*dhoti*, *chapkan* shirt of *pat* silk, a *gamocha* tied around the waist, and another like a turban around his head. Hirukai, naturally, led the *huchari* troupe although it was the village elders who could no longer shake a leg because of aching joints, who showered blessings on each of the households the troupe visited. The male-only troupe would move from household to household, being ceremonially welcomed in each with offerings of betel-nut and *paan* placed upon brass *horai*; it would dance and sing accompanied by drums, cymbals, bamboo flutes, buffalo-horn pipes and a bamboo clapper called *toka* which made a peculiar, dull '*tok-tok*' sound—the troupe would be rewarded with small amounts of cash or in kind. Also, the members of each household would kneel and prostrate themselves before the *huchari*-group as the elders, to a crescendo of drumbeats and buffalo-horn tune, sonorously sound out the blessings, wishing the family prosperity and good health throughout the Assamese New Year. Little legs would tire after a while, but Hirukai would be there to pick Okon up and carry him to Ai or Bai, who would take him home to a veritable feast of *joha-chaul* and fish-curry.

Even as he grew up, *Rongali-bihu* continued to be a joyous occasion because Hirukai had been there, teaching him new dance steps or yet another *bihu*-song—so had been *Bhogali-bihu*, the harvest festival. If Pitai's pickings in the paddy fields had been paltry, no one told Okon about it; as always, it would be Hirukai who led the rest of the village youths in building the temporary bamboo and thatch hutments called *bhelaghars*—as also the tall, community *mejhi* with wood collected from the jungles—all of which would be set alight on the morning of *Bhogali-bihu* in ritualistic obeisance to the god of fire. Hirukai would also lead in organising the fishing excursions to catch fish for the community-feast on *uruka* or *bihu*-eve; collecting enough sweet-potatoes and *kaath-alu* for roasting in the mejhi's embers on *bihu* morning.

Hirukai, in fact, had been there for almost every moment of Okon's young life. Being popular, good at studies and involved in almost every community welfare enterprise, he was a busy youth to say the least. Yet he had always found time for Okon, teaching him stuff not only from textbooks but also through practical demonstration: how to set traps for catfish, shrimp and small fish in the muddy shallows of the stream which gave the village its name. The trick was to select the right spot on a part of the river close to the bank, use a narrow-necked, earthen *koloh* half-filled with mud with a rope tied around it, which could then be lowered into the water at the spot, the other end of the rope being tied to a shrub; when a week later the pitcher was lifted, it would be swarming with life. If they were lucky, there would at least be a couple of fair-sized catfish inside, as also some shrimps and small fish—which made for equally good eating. Hirukai knew the jungle well too; born in poverty meant that from his very childhood he had had to scrounge the jungles and water-bodies to gather food to supplement their frugal meal of boiled rice. He could unerringly pick the younger cane-shoots from the jungle which Ai and Bai could convert into a delicious, bitter-sweet dish; he could tell the spots most conducive to the growth of the *kaath-alu* plant, whose tubers made food fit for the gods; he taught Okon how to gather wild fruits such as the *ou-tenga* and berries growing upon trees and bushes in the forest; also, which mushrooms were edible and which were not; and to distinguish the *dhekia* fern from similar-looking, inedible impostors. He taught Okon all this and much more; but above all he taught his brother that poverty was no hindrance if one had zest for life; that the earth—the trees, the grass, the water bodies, and the sky—afforded sustenance and pleasure to those who knew her well; that one could retain one's dignity in spite of one's penury and work one's way out of it…

They had him trapped.

Just two days back they had trapped the civet. By the side of the duck-coop. The *hepa* must have made a number of forays for many nights to try get at the ducks. Its sharp teeth had ineffectually bitten the bamboo ribs and cane strands of the duck-coop; its claws had sought to burrow through the earth. But the duck-coop had been constructed to withstand such assaults.

Pug-marks on the moist earth had given it away. Hirukai, with Okon assisting, set the wicker-trap. Must have been real hungry, the civet, to have so easily walked into the trap. As he had walked into this.

Perhaps the *hepa* had spent hours tearing at the cane strands holding it captive, nostrils quivering with feline rage. Perhaps, towards first light, it had lost heart for, when Hirukai and Okon found it, the civet lay submissive, as though having accepted its fate.

'Drown it in the river,' Pitai had said.

Hirukai was not fool enough to pick up the trap. He looped a rope at the top, taking care to keep his fingers away from the animal's fangs. Then, with Okon in tow, he set off with the civet towards the river, over the low, earthen embankments which crisscrossed the stretch of paddy fields, across the grazing grounds flanking the jungles, on to the narrow trail leading to the river.

Then, to Okon's surprise, Hirukai had turned right, walking towards the lush jungles instead of the river.

'But Pitai wants us to drown it,' Okon, guessing what his stepbrother was up to, cried out.

Hirukai chuckled. A little inside the jungle he set the trap down, took out a clasp-knife from his pocket and sliced away the cane strands bonding the door. The *hepa* knew what was good for it! The moment the trap-door opened, it streaked towards the undergrowth.

'Didn't kill a duck now, did it?' Hirukai had said. 'But mind you, not a word to anyone, least to Pitai.'

Now, who is the civet? On his right was an impassable bamboo thicket; behind him, the village pond; on his left, the fenced-in compound of Mukundakai's cottage. Given the man's temper, to be entered at one's own peril!

They had him trapped. An eight-year-old civet cat! Three elderly village boys, covering one side each and cutting off escape, absolutely certain Okon would not dare to jump into the village community pond. The village council's orders had been explicit, painted on a small signboard stuck upon the bank. No swimming, no washing clothes. A bamboo palisade all around to keep the cattle away.

So no jumping into it even if an eight-year-old's life was at stake!

Okon muttered a prayer under his breath. As though in response, the saviour hopped on to the stage. He heard a familiar voice ask: 'What's going on around here?'

Hirukai! On the way to the village *naamghar*.

Fists unclenched. Shoulders drooped. The elder boys grinned sheepishly. 'Nothing, Hirukai,' one of them said.

His stepbrother had taken in the scene and realised the implications. 'Let Okon speak,' he said.

'They want me to steal betel nuts from the old widow's trees!'

Okon saw a spark flare into fury in Hirukai's eyes, so did the three boys. The latter had tried to use the youngster. Perhaps inducements at first, now physical coercion. Okon was sharp-witted and agile. Could climb up the slim stem of a betel nut palm quicker than a squirrel.

'The old widow, eh? Don't you three know she has no one she can call her own? Her coconuts, betel nuts, jackfruits which she sells—those are what keep her alive. And the charity of our villagers. Aren't you ashamed of yourselves?'

The boys shuffled uneasily on their feet.

'Let me warn you.' A commandment as effective as the signboard beside the village pond! 'Try touching him again and you'll have to answer to me...'

Yes, the world outside was asleep. Only the creatures of the night were astir—in the jungle that grew denser the deeper one went;

in the paddy fields and grazing grounds; within the groves of bamboo; beneath the plantain copses; perhaps in the air; ghouls and demons which flitted about in the dark; the witch who lived upon a tall betel nut palm; the old ghost with flowing white beard who lived in the forest. The softest of sounds blended into and deepened the night's silence—he splash of fish in the water-soaked paddy fields, ponds and ditches; the slither of a cobra in search of prey; rats gnawing at grains in granaries; the swish of bat-wings and owls on shadowy flights; the tick-tick-tick of a gecko on the walls of the room and the familiar drone of insects around the mosquito net.

Occasionally, there were sharp bursts of sound: sudden, raucous croaking of frogs which as abruptly died into stillness; the periodic barks of the pariah mongrels of the village; the distant howling of a jackal on the prowl; the cheep-cheep-cheep of cicadas. It required the silence of the night to prove how shrill the song of cicadas could be.

Tonight, there were unusual noises, sought to be muted by those who made them. The sound of heavy vehicles bumping over unpaved rural roads, deliberately brought to a halt at a distance from the village; the wary approach of padded footfalls, voices whispering into walkie-talkies. But Okon, wrapped up in a quilt of memories, had been rendered deaf to such distant sounds…

'Come,' Hirukai had said to Okon, with the air of a conjuror about to unveil a fabulous trick. He led, the boy followed, till they passed the residential section of the village and the surrounding paddy fields to the fringe of the jungle where the sprawling bamboo grove stood. This was a cherished community property—if a villager had to re-thatch the roof of his hut and needed bamboo for the rafters, or required those precious stems to repair a broken fence, all he had to do was approach the village council. The *gaonburrah* would weigh the requirement and give the necessary permission, and the villager would cut the permitted number of stems and carry them away—but only those which grew on the fringes, for a few metres deeper, the close-growing stems formed an impenetrable wall. Thus, no one knew what lay further inside that sprawl of bamboo; but then almost everyone had heard of the *daini* who dwelt within the grove; due to her insubstantial form the witch could, smoke-like, sweep through the tiny gaps in the stems of bamboo into the grove's heart to build her hovel; mothers used the power of her spell to hush crying infants; even elders gave the grove a wide berth if and when they had to occasionally inspect their paddy fields at night for some reason or the other. But this Sunday morning Hirukai, reaching the grove, first looked around to ensure no one else was nearby, then sought out a point and began walking into the dense bamboo curtain.

'Hirukai!' six-year-old Okon had cried out in terror. 'What are you doing?'

'Come,' Hirukai had beckoned once more. 'Don't be afraid.'

The momentary terror had been wiped clean from Okon's soul at Hirukai's reassuring words. Without hesitation, he followed as his elder brother slithered through gaps in what had appeared to be an impassable wall, deeper and deeper towards the dreaded *daini's* lair but the little boy was unafraid; as though by magic, thick stems had parted at Hirukai's touch. Okon, small and agile as he was, had even less difficulty in sidling through. Some 10 metres deep in, and the shaded darkness beneath the tall, long-leaved stems of bamboo brightened into unexpected light—a small clearing where a rocky layer had ensured no bamboo could grow; a carpet of grass, mossy growths and some ferns and creepers softened the stony ground. A circle with a jagged edge surrounded by those tall, pliant, thick-growing bamboo, whose stems almost leaned together at the very top yet let in enough of the sunlight to make the halo appear incandescent in contrast to the adjacent gloom.

'Hai!' Okon had cried out, startled, eyes open in childish amazement and awe. 'The *daini's* lair!'

'Fiddlesticks!' Hirukai had scoffed. 'There's no *daini*—that's just superstitious village nonsense carried down mouth-to-mouth. This is merely a small clearing within the bamboo grove. Took me quite a while to find it.'

They sat in the clearing for some time in silence, savouring the emotional closeness a shared secret could enkindle. Then they traced and retraced the route again till the path, through the maze into the clearing, was ineradicably imprinted upon Okon's mind.

'It's our own little space, yours and mine,' Hirukai had said. 'I doubt if any villager knows of it. So keep it to yourself, will you? Not even to Bai…'

Hirukai, rather than Pitai, had taken Okon, aged six, to the elementary school around two kilometres away from Chungijan village—the very same one he had earlier attended before going on to higher studies elsewhere. The passing of the years had not witnessed any infrastructural development of the elementary school; it remained the bamboo and thatch structure of Hirukai's days, without furniture and possessing just a couple of blackboards. The single teacher was the monarch of all he surveyed (a school inspector was there at the district headquarters but had never felt the need to 'inspect' this school). The teacher acted as the *guru*, the office clerk, the accountant and the chowkidar of the institution; his sole mandate was to equip the youngsters in his charge with the rudiments of grammar and arithmetic so that those who aspired towards higher education—there were quite a few who were content with imbibing what this worthy being had to offer and aspired no further than that—could get into the primary school at the nearest township of Doomdooma, almost eight kilometres away. It was fascinating how he handled multiple 'classes' at the same time, setting an exercise for one and hopping over to another to explain something, making one class recite aloud arithmetic tables while familiarising students of another class with basic sentence structures—the thin bamboo cane he carried, a potent symbol of his authority.

One fateful morning, Hirukai had made Okon wash his pair of shorts—the better of the two he owned—and his vest; thus, the boy was dressed in his best as he set off for his maiden tryst with 'education'. His elder brother had fashioned a crude bag from a *gamocha* woven by his sister at the household handloom. Inside it had been placed a rectangular slate-board and a box of clay pencils; there were no text-books. At this level, all the text-books required were with the teacher and Okon would get the first of these only at the primary school, if he ever went there (which was covered by the State government's free text book scheme). With the bag slung across one shoulder, a brand new hessian sack (procured from a whole-sale dealer in Doomdooma by Hirukai), Okon had set off somewhat unwillingly, along with his stepbrother, for the school. Not that he really needed to trudge those two kilometres and back six days a week, the village schoolmaster framed the rules for his institution as he pleased—more often than not asking his pupils not to come on particular days because he would be preoccupied with some domestic chore or the other. The real teacher had been Hirukai, who sat with

Okon at least thrice a week for an hour or two in the afternoon, going over his lessons.

Pitai had taken it for granted that one 'educated' person was enough in the family; he expected to hand over his plough to Okon once the lad grew up even as Hiru got a job. In his opinion elementary education was all that was required of his younger son, and being able to count and sign his name would be ample. It had been at Hirukai's insistence that Okon, when eight, had sought and received admission at the primary school in Doomdooma. Hirukai, in fact, had himself escorted Okon to the school and got him admitted; it had also been his elder brother who bought him the second-hand bicycle from a grocer at Doomdooma, and taught him how to ride it so he could cycle the eight kilometres and back to school (Hirukai himself had never been able to afford a bicycle, so it had always been on foot for him). The school had more teachers; no longer did Okon have to carry a sack to be spread out on the floor to squat during lessons. The school now had wooden desks and benches; it even added to Okon's wardrobe by providing him two pairs of school uniform (under the government's free school uniform scheme for students coming from below poverty line families) each year. Though the *gamocha*-bag which Hirukai had fashioned continued to be in use despite its stained and frayed appearance, the satchel and clay pencils had been replaced by writing books. And with each passing year, the bag grew fatter with addition of text books. Most of the other students had more fancy schoolbags, a fact brought to Hirukai's notice by his younger brother. But the former had simply said, 'It's not the bag which matters. It's what's inside it that's important.' Even when Okon had gone on to primary school, Hirukai tutored him three days a week; the potential he had sensed in Okon was being recognised by the teachers, too. The boy was always ahead of the pack in his studies, despite being perhaps the poorest of the lot…

Two worlds—of the secondary school eight kilometres away with its own set of problems and posers (challenges that had to be met with the precision of grammar, mathematics, and scientific formulas), a world of predictive rationalism; and of home, with its everyday uncertainties and in-exactitudes, the constant need to eke out sustenance for each moment, the irrational fatalism exhibited by Pitai, Ai and Bai and the superstitions of the villagers—often collided in Okon's sensibility. Hirukai had been the stabilising agent; though he loved Ai and Bai and feared Pitai, it had been Hirukai with whom Okon shared occasional anxieties, sought answers to transient conundrums, and shared innermost secrets. Taciturn by nature, he was something of a loner—neither having too many friends at school, most of them anyway being from other villages, and none too many in the village either. Perhaps the love for solitude that fitted his persona was brought about by his excessive devotion to Hirukai; on the other hand, it had been Hirukai's companionship which perhaps helped compensate a chronic inability to attract friends.

Though he participated in community festivities and took part in the sports meet during *Rongali-bihu*—and even won a couple of prizes in the sprints for his age-group—he rarely joined the other village youngsters in a game of amateur football, or lesser games like *tang-guti* or marbles. Household chores, including looking after the cow and calf, running errands for Ai and playing with Bai, spending the weekdays at school and doing his homework the moment he was back before darkness set in, solitary rambles in the fields and forests or angling for fish, and helping Pitai in the paddy fields—these had been fulfilling enough for him to not yearn for more company. And, of course, the overshadowing presence of Hirukai—the fount of all practical knowledge in his minuscule world—the master of things that could fascinate a child.

Then, at the school in Doomdooma, Okon discovered something unique and wonderful, something not only leading to another obsession, but also offering a peep-hole into his own self. There was a 'library' in the school at Doomdooma—a couple of book-filled cupboards, the doors of which the headmaster always kept locked. He had no intention of letting his wards touch the books in case some were stolen, which might result in 'audit objection' next time there was a school 'inspection' and some allotted books were to be found missing—never mind that the higher authorities were least concerned with how many books there were in the 'library'. However, the very year Okon joined the school, the army—which had a base nearby—in one of its 'Public Relations (PR)' exercises, had donated a few lakh rupees for building a permanent room for the library, shelves, desks, and benches, as also to buy quite a lot of new books. An officer had taken personal interest in what books should be purchased, and after its ceremonial opening, the headmaster had no option but to allow his students—at least those who were interested in doing so—to actually touch the books on the shelves, read them in the school premises and, horror of horrors, take them home for a few days. Okon had been one of the select few who were allowed to take library books home. And thus began his slide into a different and magical world, which though created by someone else's imagination, was very much real in that of the child's.

Pitai had frowned at his youngest child's new fascination, but Ai and Bai approved, as did Hirukai. Okon would steal off with a book to the back of the cowshed and, seated on the ground with his back to the mud-plastered wall, weep dry-eyed at the plight of Tejimala, the little girl so cruelly treated by her stepmother, the antithesis of Ai who loved Bai and Hirukai as though her own, or silently laugh at the craftiness of the monkey who deprived the quarrelling cats of their share of *til-pitha*. Okon could now read in printed word tales enacted through *bhaona* in the village *naamghar*; the stories were there in books such as *Akonir Ramayana*, *Akonir Mahabharata* or *Akonir Purana*. He would occasionally read out such stories aloud to Ai and Bai, and sometimes, even Pitai would listen to him on the sly. Sometimes the books took them back far away to an antiquated time, when the *devas* or gods waged war with the *rakhyasas,* those hideous ogres forever plotting to kill and maim and destroy; sometimes to far off Ayodhya, resplendent in the glimmer of a myriad earthen *chakis* as it awaited Rama's triumphant return. They would laugh together at Krishna's childhood pranks at Dwaraka—Ai and Bai knew such stories because they belonged to the oral tradition, but pretended they were hearing them for the first time and looked suitably amazed or amused.

Then Okon had moved on to more original tales which really thrilled his Ai and Bai, but the back of the cowshed was not a convenient location for uninterrupted reading. Often, deep inside another world, he would receive summons for some chore or the other, had to wake up as if from a trance and scamper back to reality. By then, he had matured enough for occasional self-introspection; had understood that he was none too brave. That, in fact, he was quite a coward; the opposite of the other daredevil village lads who seemed to fear nothing and no one. Hirukai, of course, being the bravest among them all. Yet, one Sunday morning he had set out on his own with a book in his hand without telling anyone, had crossed—unnoticed—the paddy fields covered with mud-spattered seedlings to the community bamboo grove. He muttered a prayer as he sidled through the strands of bamboo and spent a few hours in the *daini's* lair undisturbed, reading the Assamese translation of *Uncle Tom's Cabin* titled *Tom Khurar Jupuri.* The secret tremble within him vanished as he slid into the book; amidst the quietude, his heart had gone out to the black slave who had sought nothing else but to give and receive love. Okon had silently raged at the *rakhyasa* named Simon Legree; had returned home after completing the final tragic chapter to a severe tongue-lashing by Ai and Bai who, however, listened the same evening to the strange tale which had taken place long back, and in a far off land. That day, Okon, too, learned one thing: if one wanted to do something passionately enough, one could overcome one's own cowardice and deep-rooted fears; he could sit reading a book in the *daini's* lair without Hirukai beside him…

This night, the bamboo rafters were draped with cobweb-like memories; insubstantial yet weirdly cloying on the mind, difficult to scrape off—their whiteness, darkened by the passage of time. But in his case, the latest of memories had become a sooty black, the colour of despair, while those of the earlier days had retained a pale, idyllic whiteness. Recollections triggered off throughout the day by the previous night's visit of Rajeev, son of a Chungijan villager, who now worked as a mechanic in a garage at Doomdooma. The bearer of news had come to the village, spent the day with his own family and then slipped into their house after nightfall to convey the message to Pitai: Hirukai was back in the area and would pay them a visit at around eleven o' clock the following night; to keep everything normal and not let out the slightest peep. Rajeev had left as silently as he had come. In that vast darkness, he could not be seen. Yet, given what happened later, surely there had been eyes that had seen him come and go. Or, perhaps, Rajeev himself had been treacherous! Okon almost grew disoriented with joy when Ai gave him the news; bolts of electricity seemed to pass through his body. Just an hour or so spent with his family and Hirukai would be gone—but even that would fulfil deep-rooted longings; his heart seemed to inflate like a gas-filled balloon sold during *Durga-puja,* till he seemed to be floating in the air. He had been strictly instructed to stay within the cottage lest his excitement become a betrayal. All through that day, Okon was like a *hepa* that had been entrapped in a cage. Now, recumbent on the bed within a tiny space all of his own, he was swimming in a veritable sea of memories even as he struggled to keep from drifting into sleep—the reason he did not hear those occasional, tell-tale noises which disturbed the familiar sounds of the night. Pitai, Ai, and Bai were, perhaps, too overwhelmed with their own thoughts and memories to have noticed those unnatural, unfamiliar sounds…

An environment close to nature, an impecunious existence but cocooned within a loving, caring ambience, an active life and an imagination unfurled by the power of the written word to activate innate creative impulses—all in all, Okon was growing up to be a normal, intelligent boy, though somewhat taciturn and a bit of a loner. By now, he was getting good at making up tales of his own and trying them out on Ai and Bai, though he had not been able to summon up the courage to try them out on Hirukai; he had always sought to stay in high esteem in his elder brother's estimation, and feared that the latter would laugh at his tales. Routine, normal life, day after day, induces an optimistic outlook; the optimism of childhood denies the possibility of things changing or the sky falling down. That was the reason why the gradual change in Hirukai had first disturbed Okon, and the later, sudden, and unexpected development crushed him. He could recall the day when the change had started; it had been a case of euphoria, slowly but inexorably melting first into disillusion and then into despair.

But since Hirukai never unloaded his own troubles on him, Okon was uncertain as to what had caused the change. A gradual darkening of Hirukai's temperament which Okon had never sensed before, culminating in a thunderous argument with Pitai, inducing the child to run out of the cottage and crouch for a couple of hours in the womb of the *daini's* lair, so that he was unable to tell how the quarrel had ended. He was certain that others in the family understood the cause of the change in Hirukai, but no one told him a thing. He did ask Bai but she had simply said that it was some temporary setback and he did not need to worry, for things would soon work out for the better and life would be like what it had been before. Hirukai had willed himself into trying to act as normally as he could with Okon, helping him as usual with his homework, and occasionally taking him out to set the fish-traps. But the child could see through the pretence and grew fearful that the end of a compact none of the two had needed to acknowledge was nearing its end, and that the protective arm would soon be withdrawn. Love mingled with terror, the terror and concern deepening the love till it was more than what a young sensibility could bear. Okon felt himself trapped, like that *heap,* in a cage of circumstances which he did not understand. Yet, there was no one he could turn to for elucidation and reassurance because even *Bai's* words no longer yielded comfort, and he instinctively knew for a certainty things would never be the same again. His instincts had been infallible—just a couple of weeks after the argument with Pitai, his stepbrother had put his meagre belongings in a handbag and left the house. A friend of his who owned a rundown motorcycle came to pick him up; before he left Hirukai had pulled Okon aside, put a protective arm on his shoulder as he often did in the past, and told him that he was off to Guwahati to find a good job—since there was nothing suitable for him nearby. Certainly, he would visit home from time to time, Guwahati was none too far away. And once he had settled down, he would take all of them there to show them what city life was really like.

It had been a betrayal, of course—the first of a series which would rip off the flimsy fabric of childhood's innocence—though it was not Hirukai but circumstances which had played the betrayer. Yet, to the immature Okon it had been his idol who had betrayed him. He was too young to comprehend the contradictions criss-crossing the path of life, the abruptness with which a moment of joy can prove to be merely a prelude to abysmal sorrow. Okon was clear in his mind that the change in Hirukai, and in the life of his family, had begun in a moment of unbridled joy. The results of the BA examinations were out. Hirukai was gone all day, waiting at his college for the results to be put up on the noticeboard. He had returned late in the afternoon along with a boisterous group of friends. They had cheered as Hirukai told his family that he had secured first division with honours, and offered them cheap sweetmeats purchased in the town. Pitai's eyes had glistened with paternal pride; Ai had retreated into the household prayer room to light a *chaki* before the *thapona* to express gratitude to the Almighty; Bai had wept tears of joy openly, while Okon performed his own version of a war-dance, hopping up and down and cheering madly, louder than anyone else. It had been the last occasion when the roof of the ramshackle cottage had almost been blown away with unrestrained, booming laughter by the whole family.

But then, it had not taken long for laughter to dampen into tears of actual sadness in the eyes of Ai and Bai, and gloom the colour of dark green moss to settle on the earthen floor, mud-caked walls and cobwebbed rafters as though the season had prematurely turned into one of perpetual rain. Each weekday, Hirukai would ride in silence along with Okon to Duliajan and leave his brother and the bicycle at the school, and set out on foot to God alone knew where. The youngster learnt from Bai that Hirukai was in search of a job but as one day followed another, it was apparent the township had been inhospitable to his icon; it could not cater to the aspirations of someone destined in Okon's imagination to be the saviour of the world. How could an individual change so rapidly? Within months, the glow which always radiated from Hirukai's face, had dimmed into glum bleakness—and then the terrible quarrel with Pitai, and Hirukai's abrupt departure!

Okon had not known it then… Even after his elder brother had gone he continued to cheat himself into the belief that things, as Bai had said, would be the same again once Hirukai found a suitable job in Guwahati. But the motorcycle ride had been an irrevocable severance of a nine-year-old bond. He sustained himself through the months of Hirukai's absence by recalling golden memories just as he was doing now; every night he had prayed to Lord Vishnu for his elder brother's return. The bullies in the village had begun picking on him, now that the protective arm had seemingly been withdrawn and he was coerced into performing tasks for them which he abhorred. He began to falter at school; only Bai was concerned but Pitai and Ai remained oblivious of it; the teachers of his school were least bothered that one of their better students from a nearby village was suddenly getting poorer grades. Occasionally, the boy looked withdrawn and lost; he did not lose his passion for books, and spent more and more hours unseen in the *daini's* lair—trying to escape from the reality shadowing his tiny world. But he no longer read them out to Ai and Bai or made up tales to tell them. He had never been much of a talker but now he spoke even less, answering his teachers only when asked to respond to some query or the other, and responding to Ai and Bai (Pitai himself was not much of a conversationalist) mostly in monosyllables. Had there been cheering news from Hirukai, things might have been different—but the news coming from Guwahati was not heartening, and the money sent home had been paltry. And then, as abruptly as he had left, Hirukai returned. His response to Okon's effusive welcome had been relatively cold; to his elders, he now appeared to be an angry young man who internally raged at everyone and everything. Suddenly, Okon grew afraid as he saw wild fire in his elder brother's eyes—the same wildness and volcanic rage that he had seen in the eyes of the *rakhyasa* at the *bhaona*! It was an all too brief enactment. Within a few weeks, Hirukai was gone.

Okon could remember the day of parting as if it was only yesterday. 'Come,' Hirukai had said that Sunday afternoon in the gentlest of tone, but the boy could sense the effort consciously made by his brother to hide the emotions churning within him. They had walked together—as so many times before in the past—bonded together by invisible, ineluctable strands, over the low earthen embankments criss-crossing the paddy fields…across the grazing grounds to the bamboo grove, and then into the *daini's* lair. For an hour they had sprawled face up, side-by-side within the oval clearing, recalling incidents of the past; the 'do you remember' stuff, laughing, for when one looks back, even the most terrible or shameful or embarrassing incident invariably evokes laughter. It had been, in a way, a transient catharsis for Hirukai—to Okon's inner eye, he seemed to have reverted for a moment to the Hirukai of yore who Okon loved, adored, and never feared—had become momentarily mellow as though the pent up anger had wafted away along with dredged up memories in the slight breeze blowing through the bamboo. But that was an illusion; his elder brother had suddenly sprung up, involuntarily shrugging his shoulders as though in renewed resolve, and inducing Okon to spring up, too. Hirukai put a protective arm across the youngster's shoulder.

'I'm going away,' he had said softly. 'No, no, don't ask me where I'm going or to do what. The less you know, the better.'

'For how long, Hirukai?'

'I've no idea. For quite some time, maybe. Perhaps I might never return. You will be the man of the house now. Pitai is growing old…will grow older. Look after Ai and Bai.'

'But why, Hirukai?' Angry tears welled up in Okon's eyes.

'I can't tell you. It's for a good cause, that's all I can say. I'll drop in on all of you whenever I get the chance.'

Bewilderment, anger, desolation—the *hepa* in the trap! Utter helplessness. No one to cut the cane strands! With surprising strength for one so young, he thrust away the protective arm.

'I hate you, Hirukai,' he shouted, but the wall of bamboo muted his voice, making it sound hollow and disembodied, as though emerging from someone else's mouth. The boy broke away, slithered through the crazy route out of the maze, and raced across the grazing ground and the paddy fields. The sun was low on the horizon, the air still listless. Okon fled to his tiny room and flung himself onto his bed, his tears wetting the thin, worn-out mattress. No one called out to him to come for dinner; a shroud of silence seemed to have descended on the hutment. No one lit a *chaki*, not even before the *thapona*; there was not a glimmer of light in the house, and the fire in the kitchen remained unlit. Okon cried himself to sleep. By next morning, Hirukai had disappeared from his life.

With the saviour gone, the *rakhyasas* had a field day for a while. They hopped on to the stage one by one, or in groups. The first of these appeared innocuous—a tubby, khaki-clad policeman from the Doomdooma *thana*. He sat on a *murrah*, drank the glass of water offered to him, and asked Pitai about the whereabouts of Hirukai. Pitai replied he did not know, that perhaps his elder son had gone back to Guwahati to renew his search for a job. The policeman appeared satisfied; he had not bothered to question Ai or Bai, and completely ignored Okon. He then rode off on his bicycle. The young, unsuspecting child had not guessed it was only the onset of a nightmare; he would never forget that morning when a horde of *rakhyasas* had arrived over the dusty village road upon a military jeep and truck, led by two local policemen on a motorcycle. Neither the child nor anyone else in the village could know that such a show of strength was deliberate; the people were adequately subdued by the sight—ugly, moustached ogres who, to the 10-year-old Okon, appeared to be tall as betel nut palms, dressed in camouflage fatigues and armed to the teeth. They searched their tiny cottage with contemptuous nonchalance, even rummaged amongst the clothes of Ai and Bai without the hint of a qualm, scoured the front compound and backyard with professional thoroughness though no one knew for what, probed with powerful torches the naked bamboo rafters and the thatch overhead and then, finding nothing of remotely tangible value, hauled away Pitai in their truck—ignoring the frantic pleas of Ai and Bai.

By then, quite a crowd had gathered before the cottage. There had been some protesting shouts as Pitai was roughly shoved into the vehicle, but a couple of *rakhyasas* had pointed their guns at the villagers…everyone stopped moving and grew silent. They watched impassively as the vehicles left, raising a trail of dust. Some cronies of Hirukai had cycled all the way to the Doomdooma *thana* for news about Pitai. The officer present there told them that he had no idea that a paramilitary raid had been conducted in Chungijan village (which fell in his jurisdiction); that if local police personnel had been present they must be from some other police station. But they would not find their men in other police stations either; most probably, the army personnel had taken him to their own base for interrogation—a conjecture soon confirmed by the phone call he made. The young men had returned to the village, frustrated and helpless. There had been a conclave in the *gaon-burrah's* house and quite a bit of angry muttering, and talk about meeting the local member of the legislative assembly. But the elderly and respected *gaon-burrah* had advised restraint, and suggested waiting for a while before taking further action.

Pitai had been dropped off in a jeep at Chungijan the next morning, both hurt and humiliated. Habitually taciturn, he said nothing much to Ai and Bai, or to some of the village elders who came to the cottage to meet him—merely stating that the army had asked questions about Hiru and nothing further should be done, for it will only serve to muddy the waters. Despite his worn-out clothes and unshaven features, there was a quiet dignity about Pitai; he, as his forebears, had silently tilled the land through generations. Some of his ancestors, as *paiks* of the Ahom monarchs, had fought for the realm before returning to till the earth and later merge into it. With stoicism, they had continued the tussle with unsought-for consciousness, surviving, procreating, and passing on genes to the next generation till he, too, would be with the land—not asking for much from anyone except that he be allowed to retain that dignity all through his life. The army-camp interrogation had hurt his pride; he had been treated no better than a road-side mongrel... ancestral blood had been defiled, though his interrogators who came from other climes could not understand that this could happen to an illiterate, poverty-stricken peasant who lived in a tumbledown cottage.

The first interrogation had been just the beginning; strangers, mostly local khaki-clad policemen, would drop in every now and again and ask questions—always to do with his elder son, Hiru. Twice more, men dressed in paramilitary uniforms had come in jeeps and trucks, in blatant shows of strength before the villagers, to haul Pitai away and return him next morning, looking further hurt and humiliated. The sudden, always unexpected visits by the Paramilitary Forces had utterly terrified Okon, even though they took place in the daytime. Others failed to notice it, but the child had developed a stammer which was none too pronounced when he spoke with Ai and Bai, but began to be a definite impediment in communicating with others, especially with teachers at school. Then, after a few months since Hirukai's departure, the visits by the keepers of law and order ceased; by now everyone knew what the youth had done to arouse such interest in him. He had joined the insurgent group calling itself the United Liberation Front of Assam, the third young man from the area to have done so that very same year. The loss of the army's interest in his family came from the realisation that they truly did not have the least idea as to where Hiren Bora had gone or what he had done. Although the visits by the authorities ceased for the while, Okon continued to be haunted by a nagging, persistent dread. Occasionally, he would have nightmares and wake up in the middle of the night in a cold sweat; and then be bathed in relief that the *rakhyasas* who had bared blood-spattered fangs at him had been mere shadows of a dream world, which dissolved the very moment he opened his eyes…

Paradoxically, life carried on as usual, though nothing was ever the same after Hirukai had left. Paradoxically, though the protective arm had seemingly been withdrawn, it, in fact, had not been withdrawn. Okon sensed it in the village; the bullies now left him alone, as though he was an ember in a *mejhi* too hot to touch—some of them even spoke sycophantically to him and offered token homage such as a fistful of litchis or an unripe mango. He sensed it at school when he suddenly changed from being a 10-year-old non-entity to a cynosure of all eyes—even the headmaster, who suddenly grew interested in his academic progress. Okon remembered the night Hirukai had crawled into their cottage…it had been almost 10 months after he had left, and on the very day Okon had been born 11 years ago… an unannounced visit. The young lad had been deep in his dream world when an excited and emotional Bai had shaken him awake.

'He has come.' There were tears in Bai's eyes.

'Who?'

'Hirukai!'

Okon was out of his room and into Hirukai's arms in a flash, clinging to his elder brother as if he would never let go. 'You're back, you're back' was all he could say.

'Hush, not so loud,' Hirukai said. 'They've ears and eyes all over.'

'Who? The *rakhyasas*?'

Hirukai laughed—the familiar laughter that had been such music to Okon's ears.

'*Rakhyasas,* eh? Don't worry, they're just made of flesh and blood. Can't harm a hair on your head, remember. Here, I've something for you. A pen.'

A cheap ballpoint pen of Chinese make; a chador for Bai, a box of Chinese-made incense for Ai, and a battery-operated alarm clock for general use in the house, also made in China.

It had been an all-too-brief moment of euphoria. Ai complained she had not been forewarned, so there was not much in the house to cook up a meal befitting the occasion. But Hirukai said, 'I don't have much time. They're waiting in the jungle for me. I have just one hour.'

Okon began to cry. 'I won't let you go, Hirukai. You can't ever leave us again.'

But Hirukai had left. Ai had quickly cooked some rice and sour *dhekia* curry and her stepson had tucked into it as though it was the most delicious feast he had ever eaten. Both Ai and Bai had been full of questions, but Hirukai said the less they knew the better, and instead asked them about how the village was faring and how well the paddy on their land was ripening. Pitai had said nothing, though his palpable anger and love mingled with the smoke emitted by the wood-fire in the kitchen; he refused to take the small wad of hundred rupee notes his son tried to thrust into his hands despite the latter's explanation that, as a soldier of the ULFA, it was his wages which he had saved. So his son gave the money to Ai who was more practical; he picked up the rifle which was leaning against one wall, ruffled Okon's hair, opened the door partially, peered carefully around and then like a ghost, disappeared into the darkness.

The two thousand rupees Hirukai had given Ai was a windfall. It enabled his stepmother to have a goitre, which had recently sprouted upon her neck, operated upon. She had gone along with Bai and Okon to the small government hospital at Doomdooma, and had it examined by the doctor there. Some basic tests were carried out and the doctor said that apparently it was not a malignant tumour, but it would keep growing larger and larger and be a painful bother unless immediately removed. Unfortunately, his hospital was not equipped to carry out such an operation and, anyway, he was merely a general practitioner and not a surgeon, so they would have to go to the Medical College Hospital at Dibrugarh. A village youth named Moni had taken Ai, Bai, and Okon to Dibrugarh, where they were put up by one of Ai's relatives who served as a mere peon in the deputy commissioner's office, but apparently had done pretty well for himself—considering he was the proud owner of a plot of land and a house in the premier city of upper Assam. He also had sundry urban necessities such as a TV and a refrigerator, though he commuted on a scooter, for a car might have been a blatant giveaway!

The peon, in turn, referred them to another villager who worked as an orderly in the Dibrugarh Medical College Hospital; with his assistance, Ai was examined by a specialist who, too, opined that an operation needed to be performed to have the goitre removed. But she would have to wait for a while because the beds in the general ward were booked for months, and the surgeon himself had a busy schedule. So they would need to book a bed immediately and come back when one was available. But once they were out of the doctor's consulting chamber and in the jam-packed waiting room, the orderly said he could make 'arrangements' so Ai could be operated upon by the same specialist surgeon the very next day, and then be taken to a bed in the general ward. But for that, some palms would have to be greased. He mentioned a sum which was way beyond Ai's capacity but Moni, a physically large and hot-headed young man, had marched back into the doctor's chamber, thrusting aside the protesting attendant guarding the door. What he had said to the doctor none of the others knew, but the very next day the same surgeon performed the same operation without charging any money, while a bed was made available in the general ward for Ai to recuperate. In fact, the surgeon himself arranged some prescribed antibiotics not available in the hospital pharmacy to be brought from outside and administered to Ai, who was discharged two days later with the instructions that she approach the Doomdooma doctor when it was time for the stitches to be removed; and if any problems related to this particular bit of surgery were to arise, she was free to come to Dibrugarh and consult him at any time. Moni did not go into details about what he had told the doctor later, he said that he merely informed the latter that Ai was the mother of ULFA cadre Hiren Bora of Chungijan village—and everything had gone the way it did. Thus, the four of them simply had to pay their bus and rickshaw fares up and down, about 50 rupees on the *pedas* gifted to the peon's family, and Ai could add the rest of the money Hiru had given to the meagre savings she was making for Bai's marriage—if and when it took place.

So, obviously, the protective arm had not been withdrawn.

There were two more fleeting midnight visits the very next year; the first in April just before *Rongali bihu*, and the final one in November. Each visit had brought in humble gifts and had added to Ai's savings, too, which she kept in a tin box buried in the earthen floor beneath the bed she and her husband slept upon. Each departure had been a knife-stab to Okon's childish heart; for days afterwards he walked as though in a trance, wishing Hirukai had never come to rekindle emotions forcibly suppressed. The morning after the third visit, a paramilitary unit had driven into the village. A domineering, uniformed man had yelled in Hindi at Pitai, accusing him of giving shelter to an enemy of the nation; they had once again shifted through the scanty household effects searching for only God knew what. Fortunately, Ai's tin box had escaped their gaze, but yet again, Pitai was hauled off to the army camp and then dropped off the same evening with the warning that if his son were to inform him he would be visiting them on any particular day, he would be well advised to let the authorities know.

The search operation had confirmed what many of Hirukai's former cronies had been suspecting for some time: someone from the village had been recruited by the authorities to spy on the villagers and play the quisling, but there was no proof. Most certainly, Hirukai and his group had learnt about the raid; understood the hazard of another visit not only to them but also to Hirukai's family—for throughout 2004 and almost till the end of 2005, the nocturnal visits ceased, though the money was sent through emissaries regularly. Ai was never tempted to spend any of the saved money because all of them knew the savings would be kept apart for Bai's wedding whenever the time came, which would not be too many years away. Bai was a plain-looking, shy, and introverted girl, so there would not be many suitors. On top of that, the family had developed a 'reputation' which might keep potential bridegrooms away, at least for the time being. But ultimately Bai would have to be wedded off with some semblance of dignity; she must not be sent to her husband's home as though she were a pauper—a minimum number of Assamese ornaments, at least a couple of *muga* and *paat mekhelas*, as also some furniture and cooking utensils would have to be given. Pitai's pride would not allow him to even as much as touch Hiru's money; but for Ai, the amount sent was taking her daughter just that much closer to becoming a bride.

Of course, in the absence of Hirukai it had fallen to Okon's lot to help out his family in supplementing their nutritional needs; it surprised his mother and sister how quickly he had matured. Although not yet into his teens, he brought to bear all Hirukai had taught him: setting fish-traps, scouring the jungle for wild vegetables, ferns, cane, bamboo shoots, and fruit—it was almost as if Okon was striving to be another Hirukai! 'Hirukai must be present at Bai's wedding,' he would tell Ai. 'I know he will come back for good, and it is only after that we'll get Bai married off.' Ai had marvelled at how adult-like the 12-year-old had sounded while talking of his sister's wedding; it was as if the child had become a man much before he ought to. Nowadays, because of the extra load being the 'man' in the family entailed, he had much less time for his studies, and even less for reading non-textual books. On his last visit, Hirukai had reminded Okon he needed to do well in studies, and he had promised to do his best. But this was easier said than done; a vacuum had to be filled. Pitai had aged a decade in the span of the few years since Hirukai had gone; had become sluggish and occasionally unable to work in the fields in the heat. Naturally, he began to be more dependent on Bai and Okon, even as the land produced less and less. It had been both a physical and mental decline with him; his taciturnity grew more pronounced and, nowadays, he spoke mostly in monosyllables. He almost completely stopped interacting with other villagers; it had been left to Ai and Bai to carry on with the socialising so vital to community life—despite their awareness that Hirukai's growing notoriety had erected barriers between their family and other households in the village (though no one blamed them for what had happened).

While Ai took on additional household chores, Bai began sitting for hours at the household *tator-shal*. The child Okon, with dexterity much beyond his age, had built an additional shed of bamboo and thatch at the back of the house—big enough for the handloom to be shifted to, and water-tight enough to withstand the savage fury of the monsoons. Some of Hirukai's money had been spent on buying yarn so that Bai could weave intricately designed *gamochas* and simple *paat-mekhelas*, which a wholesaler from Doomdooma would purchase at the end of every month. Yes, a vacuity had somehow to be filled, yet a permanent void seemed to have settled into the household. Okon's studies suffered but he did not care; nor did the rest of the world, which apparently was too busy with its own affairs. Meanwhile, news updates of Hirukai kept percolating into the ears of the adults. Occasionally, a friend of the family would come armed with a newspaper clipping wherein Hirukai was mentioned. The lad from Chungijan had become a very important cog in the machinery of the United Liberation Front of Assam; some of the village youths seemed to be actually proud of this, though they did not say so before Hirukai's father, mother, and sister. Above all, everyone tried to keep news of Hirukai from falling upon Okon's ears; even as the adults settled into the new life—despite the emptiness which had engulfed the house, and tried to recreate a semblance of normalcy—Okon remained the odd man out. He would often talk to Bai about Hirukai, expressing his confidence that their elder brother would come back once again to become a permanent part of their lives; he kept repeating he was sure Hirukai would be there when Bai was married off. Yes, of course, he knew Hirukai had joined an organisation declared illegal by the government. He was no child and the boys at school had told him things but he also knew that many of those who had gone the way Hirukai had had also come back and been accepted by the government. 'Do you know, Bai, they've even set up camps for them, that's what I've been told. They've surrendered, some of the boys told me, and the government even gives them food. But Hirukai doesn't have to stay at no camp since we are here.' Even though the weeks passed and Hirukai did not come back—not even making a fleeting, one-night visit—he neither receded in Okon's memory, nor was his optimism dampened. He told Bai about meeting Hirukai so many times in his dreams, especially during those terrible, terrifying ones in which *rakhyasas* with drooling jaws would come at him—only to be shot dead by the AK-47 wielding saviour…

Awash with longings and memories, Okon had willed himself to stay awake till Hirukai came this night. Although his limbs were heavy with fatigue, and it was the darkest depth of the night—when the ghouls and demons perched on the thatch-roof of the cottage were waiting for the birds to begin their pre-dawn chatter, before departing for the jungles—Okon had, for long, forcibly thrust away the languor threatening to shut his eyelids. But as the hours passed and the suspicion of being once again on the verge of betrayal crept into his mind, it grew progressively difficult to maintain resolve. Gradually, the memories, too, became blurred; with the pre-dawn light yet some hours away and it being a foggy, wintry night, heavy eyelids drooped shut and Okon slid into a dream-filled sleep. Perhaps, the disillusion during consciousness reflected itself in the subconscious—sure enough the *rakhyasas* with their echoing guffaws and blood-stained tongues manifested in his dreams but the saviour did not come; the saviour had turned his back as the laughing demons crept towards the cringing child.

Okon curled himself into a foetal crouch and moaned aloud in his sleep. It was someone else who pulled him away from his dream, from the *rakhyasas*. In a state between sleep and wakefulness, he heard Bai's voice float into his mind. 'Wake up, Okon, for God's sake wake up!' She had thrust away the mosquito-curtain and was shaking the child hysterically and vigorously. 'Wake up, Okon, for God's sake wake up!'

'What? What is it, Bai?' He was out of the blankets and up on his feet even before being fully awake. 'Has he come?'

'Hush! Listen!' Bai said.

The urgency in her voice sharpened his senses. He heard the sounds outside before being aware of the eerie light bathing the cottage; the *rakhyasas* had come yet again but outside his dream world, using high-power floodlights to illuminate the hutment. A terrifying, disembodied, artificially magnified voice was speaking in Hindi through a megaphone: 'Everyone in the house, come out with your hands in the air! We will give you five more minutes…then we fire.' Bai pulled Okon into the front room; Pitai and Ai were already there. The fear and bewilderment in the faces of the elders terrified the child, and he began to cry—the saviour had not come even in real life, even though there were *rakhyasas* everywhere out there! 'Put your hands up,' Pitai said as he unlatched the front bamboo door and pushed it open. He lurched out with his hands in the air, followed by Okon, Bai, and Ai. They made a ludicrously, hideously comical foursome—an aged couple, a girl and a 13-year-old, features of each twisted with fright, eyes bulging out in terror as they sought to see through the blinding light. Yet, no one was amused, no one let out thunderous guffaws like the *rakhyasas* of his dream; instead, paws grabbed and thrust them against one wall of the cottage, faces towards the wall, bodies pushed against the mist-dampened mud, ice-cold steel on their backs. The air reeked of adrenalin; the *rakhyasas* were in the grip of nervous frenzy. There were more barks: 'Cover the rear. You, cover me.' Sound of an already open, flimsy bamboo door being savagely kicked down filled the quiet of the night. 'Sir, no one else is inside.' 'Search the entire area. Don't let your guard down. Yes, search, search, search!'

A graveyard-like silence had descended upon the rest of the village. Others must have awakened to the noise and the light, but not a peep—no one stirred, not a door opened. A dreadful fear sank into Okon's soul as the knowledge of the saviour's impotence—of his absence—hit him. It was bitterly cold; the child was trembling though it was more due to terror than the cold. And then Okon felt the rush of warmth near his underbelly—his bladder had burst as though a grenade, and warm piss wet his half pants and then trickled down his bare thighs.

THE DAINI'S LAIR

In the early hours of 26 December 2005, much before sunrise and under the cloak of foggy darkness, Hiren Bora entered the bamboo-grove—the *daini's* lair or 'witch's grove' as Okon had named it—fringing Chungijan village. The intricate route through the maze of closely-growing bamboo had been indelibly etched in his mind, and with the aid of a pencil-torch, he had no difficulty reaching the little patch of clearing inside. Once he had penetrated into it, he unzipped his trousers to urinate into the bamboo clump. He unfurled the *endi-chadar* shawl wrapped across his upper body, revealing a semi-automatic, double action Glock handgun—which he placed carefully on the ground. The gun, and a small clasp-knife, were the only weapons he carried. Some of his compatriots preferred to augment their personal fire-power by lugging hand grenades slung to their belts, but not Hiren Bora. He had ceased to do so from the very day a cadre close to him had been blown to pieces when the grenade he was carrying had accidentally gone off.

The clammy darkness within the *daini's* lair made it an ideal place for leeches, mosquitoes and other insects; Hiren Bora rubbed his legs, arms and face with a homemade ointment given to him by a Kachin resident, which had proved to be miraculously effective in warding them off. Then, he lay down on the damp grass beside his gun and, using the small bag he had been carrying across one shoulder as a pillow and the *endi-chadar* as a blanket, fell into exhausted sleep.

It was well past noon when he woke up. The feeble rays of the winter sun filtering through the overhead bamboo canopy had not disturbed his sleep. He stood up and stretched himself like a civet after a nap. Cold, dampness, and fatigue had stiffened his sinews, and he performed a few exercises to loosen up. He took out some *luchis* made of flour and a slice of dried mango pickle—that would be his last meal of the day till he departed from the witch's lair around midnight. Ai was sure to have a sumptuous meal ready for him, since she was forewarned this time of his coming. He unscrewed the cap off a plastic bottle containing water and washed the meal down.

He had always been close to Nature. The four years as an insurgent, mostly spent within harsh environments such as the thick jungles on the India-Myanmar border, had bonded him even closer. Animal-like, without hesitancy, he went to the very edge of the clearing and defecated, wiping himself with the sheet of newspaper which had earlier been used to wrap the *luchis*. He dug out some earth with his fingers, scrubbed his palms and washed his hands with water from the plastic bottle. Such small practicalities had been drilled into him during training. Eat before you shit, so even if your hands remain impure, the germs don't enter your belly.

Now, there was nothing else to do but wait patiently. He spent some time dismantling and cleaning his handgun, each movement fluid, deliberate and calculated, using nominal effort. This had become second nature to him, the prior planning out of every action, even seemingly trivial ones. Yet, if he looked back, it had always been an aspect of his character ever since he was born; the ability to map out in advance possible hitches and consequences, and plan accordingly. His stint with the ULFA had merely brought this trait out into prominence; it had been the one significant asset enabling him to climb up rapidly in the outfit's hierarchy, till he had become the right-hand man of the commander-in-chief of its armed wing. Of course, *Operation All Clear* in Bhutan had deprived the ULFA of a number of middle-rung leaders, necessitating the upgradation of relative newcomers like himself. But even then, had it not been for certain traits in his personality—for instance, his ability to coolly, dispassionately appraise any situation and plan and act accordingly, as well as the kind of courage which is born of a sense of desperation—he may not have climbed upward so facilely. He had sensed the change within him in the last few years; now he was no longer the angry young man who had impulsively set out to become an outcast. The long months of rigorous training in a Kachin Independence Army camp within the dense jungles of the upper parts of West Myanmar had knocked the anger out of him—as also the passion, endowing him with the capacity of seeing individuals and situations objectively. It had inserted cold steel into his soul. He had been practical and a realist even before joining the ULFA; the sudden spurt of hot blood that led him to the outfit had been an aberration which, unfortunately, could not be undone. However, previously his temperament had been mellowed by idealism—disillusionment had brought forth dispassion; the need for perpetual alertness in a hostile milieu where a single false step could spell death and destruction transformed this dispassion into cold ruthlessness. His growing notoriety as an uncaring, fearless cadre induced dread even into his superiors in the outfit. He had come to Chungijan this time much ahead of the hour communicated to his family; it entailed wastage of time, but then time had less meaning for him these days, and caution, more. He was not forever reminding himself that, although seemingly yet free, he was a civet trapped in a far bigger cage, for which neither time nor caution had any meaning.

Having dismantled, cleaned and re-assembled his semi-automatic, Hiren Bora once more lay recumbent on the ground—head resting on the bag, eyes closed. For one almost always on the move, the few pauses in between were moments for recollection...

The bunch of new recruits stood at attention under the blazing sun. Sergeant Major Pradyut Basumatary surveyed the ragtag group with near contemptuous eyes, wondering how he would manage to turn these mostly scrawny, underfed youths into the fighting machines the cause demanded. He had been training batch after batch of recruits for over a decade in that same camp belonging to the Kachin Independence Army (KIA), set upon a clearing on the mountainous slopes of upper Myanmar. With each passing year, it had become increasingly difficult to draw in new recruits; also, the quality had gone down drastically. His comrades in the KIA—tough, battle-scarred veterans—commiserated outwardly but laughed inwardly at his outfit's gradual decline. Although goodwill remained, the ULFA had lost prestige with their host; as if the latter sensed they were fighting a futile cause...reflected in the increasing number of 'surrenders' and setbacks confronted by the outfit, as also the deterioration of quality and dwindling number of new recruits.

There had been a time when the ULFA had its uses as far as the KIA was concerned—their cadres much respected by the Myanmar insurgent group, their leaders able to interact on equal terms. The Assam section in that sprawling camp, demarcated clearly from the other 'guests'—which included Manipuri and Naga insurgent outfits—had then been bigger and busier, with more weaponry. Many a time, the 2nd Brigade of the KIA had requested the 13th Battalion of the ULFA based in the camp to help resist incursions by the Myanmar Army. Some ULFA soldiers had been killed in such skirmishes. Mostly, the Myanmar Army maintained its distance unless pressurised by someone in the military junta at Yangon to make forays against the KIA. Also, occasionally, some unit or the other of the Myanmar Army would march into one of the few isolated villages in the Kachin area and lift a few chickens or a pig—the KIA would then wreak retribution by ambushing the adversary. Often, ULFA cadres would volunteer to take part in such ambushes to display the group's solidarity with the KIA cause. But the biggest factor in keeping the KIA hospitable had been the cash regularly contributed by the ULFA to its coffers; during the initial stages of the 1980s when the ULFA had enjoyed the support of the bulk of the people in the Brahmaputra valley, its coffers had been replete. The KIA appreciated the percentage being offered for help and support to the group. This supplemented its own income—generated mainly through smuggling of opium, rhino-horn and gems such as jade—and enabled it to keep its armoury equipped with up-to-date weaponry purchased from China. The latter nation, typically, had been running with the fox while hunting with the hounds; its support had enabled the junta at Myanmar to cock a snook at international opinion, maintain its autocratic stance and keep democratic icons like Aung San Suu Kyi under house arrest. At the same time, it had been arming the KIA to keep the generals on their toes; such compulsions of international politics were, of course, hardly of concern to the KIA—whose leaders seemed content to remain glued to the exigencies of the moment.

Now, the ULFA's contribution had been reduced to almost one-fourth of what it had been earlier; there was no complaint from the host. The hardy Kachins were loyal to a fault, and did not forsake friendship or forget past help. It was true that once, recently, for a while the Assam section in that KIA camp had been shut down and the inmates politely requested to leave—but it had, in fact, been a tactical move, a play-acting to temporarily ward off pressure from the Indian and Myanmar regimes (agents of the Indian Research and Analysis Wing had even set up meetings with KIA bigwigs, and a great amount of cash had changed hands). But most of all, this play-acting was to ward off pressure from the Chinese, who were trying to attain respectability in the eyes of the global community. By then, the ULFA had become powerful and resourceful enough to set up camps on its own within the jungles of the Indo-Myanmar border; also the National Socialist Council of Nagalim—the Naga insurgent group more commonly known simply as the NSCN—had been a staunch ally through thick and thin, and their help and support had never been withdrawn. Once the pressure had lifted, the KIA had opened the door of the camp of its 2nd Brigade to the ULFA again, and the Assam section had once again seen activity. Although the Indian Army during *Operation Bajrang* in 1990 had raided and destroyed many ULFA camps on the Indo-Myanmar border (discovered to be deserted because the ULFA cadres had been warned beforehand) and had forced a segment of the outfit to shift to the jungles of Bhutan to set up new camps, the Assam section in the KIA camp had remained a key to the ULFA's overall operating scheme—with the KIA cadres and leadership remaining as friendly and supportive as ever.

The feeling of inadequacy was actually within the ULFA veterans such as Pradyut Basumatari—at the loss of prestige and his outfit's inability to contribute more—and also in the fact that within the depth of his heart, the sergeant major knew the tide had turned against the ULFA long ago. Yet, it was not in him to delve into the causes or envisage an alternative life for himself. He had joined the ULFA almost since its inception in 1979; the Brahmaputra valley had been ablaze with the agitation against illegal infiltration of foreigners back then. As a local leader of the All Assam Students' Union, he had been in the thick of it all, braving the batons and the bullets of Paramilitary Forces as the Union and state governments tried to crush the peaceful agitation through force—thereby inexorably leading it towards violence. He had suffered beatings and seen dead bodies being carried by truckloads into morgues at Kokrajhar in lower Assam, where he hailed from. As a 19-year-old passionate youth, he had wanted to hit back; the formation of the ULFA and recruitment by it had been perceived by him to be an opportunity to do that, and he had taken it. It had been a purely emotional response; ideology had nothing to do with it—he had not been bothered by the 'political' aspects of the issue then, even as he was not now. The magnitude of the objective which the ULFA had set before itself had not struck him then, nor had he been troubled by its seeming impossibility. A handful of callow youngsters, guided by a couple of elders having an ex-army background—with hardly any resources but bolstered by the longings of an entire community—taking on the might of the Indian State! For well-nigh 22 years, Sergeant Major Pradyut Basumatari had considered the ULFA to be his family; had given up his near and dear ones, his career prospects and dreams of marrying and raising a family, all for a cause which yet remained close to his heart—sovereignty for Assam, the land of his birth, his Motherland. An elusive dream which, at the moment, still seemed far away. Despite being a committed cadre, he had long acknowledged its un-attainability… Yet, one which, even today, he cherished and would willingly sacrifice his life for. In 1991, he had been shot in the hip during an encounter with the army in the Kakopathar area of upper Assam; a comrade had carried him upon his shoulders into the jungles to evade capture. That had curbed his mobility and, after recovery, he had been assigned to the task of breaking in new recruits and shaping them into fighters. Since then, he had been based within that KIA camp in the Hukong valley—a more or less permanent camp of hutments of bamboo and thatch, equipped with a hospital and a trained doctor—leading a sedentary life, in contrast to many of his comrades who were perpetually on the move on missions. He had become fluent in the local dialect which was not much different from ones spoken by some of the tribes of Arunachal Pradesh, and was on back-slapping terms with the KIA commanders in the camp as well as members of other insurgent outfits from North-East India. In a subtle way, he had taken on the phlegmatic nature of the very people amongst whom he had now chosen to live—their stoic acceptance of whatever lay around the next corner—the trick was to live for the moment and focus on the job at hand, rather than wallow in sadness at the dawning of disillusion or weep unshed tears at dissipating dreams.

Once again, he scanned the motley band before him, his contempt mingled with pity. These were no revolutionaries fired as he himself had once been with idealism, throwing themselves into the struggle to liberate their Motherland, impelled by some unseen gene to respond to the urges imprinted through millennia upon the brain. These pathetic specimens before him were failures masquerading as patriots; using the ULFA route to escape from their own inadequacies, as well as those of the society they had been born into. Nowadays, some took to drinks, and some joined the ULFA! Perhaps haunted by intimate, secret ghosts—you could see it in the eyes of many of them—or to fade away from reproachful glances of fathers and mothers, with meagre belongings stuffed into cloth-bags and battered egos. Yes, like most of the recent recruits, these, too, would have to be trained to withstand the physical rigours of their chosen course. But, more importantly, they would have to be subjected to rigorous mental indoctrination to make them understand that it was the cause, and not their petty egos, which was more important.

His experienced eyes picked out a face; it had more character! In his early twenties, perhaps, but more mature than the rest.

'You there, take one step forward.' Then, as the youth did as ordered, 'What's your name?'

'Hiren Bora.' An impressive voice, somewhat defiant.

'Hiren Bora, what?'

'Hiren Bora, sir,' someone behind prompted.

'Hiren Bora, sir!'

'Good. I'm putting you in charge of this group. Zaman?'

Lance Corporal Zaman stepped up and saluted.

'Get them kitted up. Then put them through the routine. Let's see what we can make of them, shall we...'

That very first morning in the KIA camp, under the blazing sun, Hiren Bora had sensed the contempt in Sergeant Major Pradyut Basumatari's gaze and tone, but was not offended because he understood the reason. His recruitment by a friend (now a 'surrendered' cadre in a designated camp) to the insurgent outfit had not been made as easy as it had been due to any patriotic posturing on his part—he sensed all too well the hawk-eyed veteran would have seen through such pretence. It had been, primarily, the hurt caused by a deflated ego which had reduced him to the ideal state of despair, where any way out becomes seductive—particularly if it enabled him to lash out at something, anything, even though not fully comprehending as to why. He recalled that his maiden job 'interview' after the announcement of the BA results had come as a jolt. The job itself had not been much—a floor manager in a car-dealer firm in Tinsukia. He had responded to an advertisement in the 'situation vacant' column of a local newspaper; had been euphoric that his worth had been acknowledged and, although there had been over three hundred applicants for the job, he had been summoned for the interview along with four dozen others. With characteristic self-confidence, he had made the trip to Tinsukia, certain he would be selected. However, much of his confidence evaporated when he reached the venue of the interview—crammed with 'educated' young men like himself, some of them smartly dressed and urbane in manners; adequately glib and superficial not only to impress the interviewers, but also to mirror his own inadequacy. In his old shirt and trousers, despite these being clean and ironed, he had appeared to be a travesty.

The owner of the car-dealing set-up had been a second generation migrant from Rajasthan, whose father had originally established it a few decades ago, having come at the behest of another third-generation migrant relative who had informed him how easy it was to start a 'business' in this part of the country. Initially, the founder of the dealership, like many other immigrants from elsewhere in the country, had made it a point to hire personnel belonging only to his own community—even if the employee had to be imported from Rajasthan! However, such a 'sound' policy received a set-back during the Assam Movement; with intimidating and potentially violent youths protesting against the discrimination against 'locals', the owner had to bid his second and third cousins goodbye and hire the 'lazy and inept' locals in their place. The rise of the ULFA was an additional inducement to employ locals—at the moment 80 per cent of this company's personnel were locally recruited—thus, those summoned for the interview belonged to the state and spoke the local language. This meant Hiren Bora enjoyed no particular advantage by belonging to the area; most of those summoned for the interview were armed with diplomas in management, in addition to their college degrees, even though the post of a floor manager in a small town car-dealing firm did not sound too ambitious! He had to wait for almost three hours before being called for an 'interview', which lasted barely five minutes. Even the fact that he was one of the most 'local' of the locals (some of the candidates had come from places as far away as Sibsagar and Jorhat!) had not helped.

Hiren Bora had returned home despondent and chastened, though not yet disheartened. There was no question of him joining a diploma course in business management; such courses cost money and took up at least six months to complete, and he had neither the money nor the time. For some time, he worked in a sweet-meat shop at Doomdooma, owned by the father of a friend, while hunting around for a job with better prospects; at the refinery, Oil India, Oil and Natural Gas Corporation and the fertiliser and natural gas concerns—everywhere, qualifications, in addition to those possessed by him were, required, as also 'experience', which was like putting the cart before the horse. How was one to get experience unless first taken into a job? He answered advertisement for school-level teaching posts and discovered, to his dismay, that he had to grease the palms of the ruling party's middle-men (with a hefty sum which would require years to recover). In fact, the demands of *dalals* had to be satisfied for any type of government job; it was a well-organised scam tolerated by those in power since it kept the grassroots workers happy—after all, a government job carried with it a guarantee: once employed one could not get fired, not to speak of the money under the table as well as a retirement pension in the bargain! Thus, a Congress *dalal* considered it was only fair he or she be adequately compensated for helping someone get a government job! Given the circumstances, Hiren Bora appeared suited for nothing, and nothing appeared to suit him; gradually, his customary, cheerful optimism dampened into gloom. As last recourse, he had thought of opening a business of his own, but to do so he needed money. When he made enquiries at the local branch of a national bank in Doomdooma, a supercilious clerk had told him some sort of collateral: a piece of land, a house or a fixed deposit—anything whose value exceeded the amount sought for—was required. Thus, the quarrel with Pitai. Hiren Bora regretted that more than anything else—his father would not even hear of mortgaging his ancestral property. If his business failed, all five of them would be without a roof over their heads! It had been the Marwari owner of the sweet-meat shop where he was temporarily working who had seen the worth in the boy; he suggested Hiren Bora go to Guwahati, where there were better prospects. Perhaps he could work his way to a business management degree by attending an evening college; he gave him the bus fare to Guwahati and a little extra money so that he could fend for himself till he found a job. Hiren Bora had initially been reluctant to accept his friend's father's charity. Also, to leave his family; but the quarrel with his father made it easy for him to make up his mind—and within a few days, he was off to the largest city of Assam and the Gateway to North-East India.

He had been to Guwahati only once before… An excursion trip organised by his school—some memories had been retained. But the city had changed beyond belief. The narrow lanes fringed by single-storey, Assam-type houses had mostly been replaced by tall sky-scrapers; footpaths swarmed with vendors and crowds; the roads were chock-a-block with traffic, the noise deafening. All the filth and squalor and human wreckage marking a decaying city were visible in this metro—Guwahati, Hiren Bora thought with disgust, must be the dirtiest city on the planet! The contrast with Chungijan was blatant; the compound of even the most humble village cottage like his own had been sprucely cleaned each day, the earthen floor swept and scrubbed each morning and evening. Here, in Guwahati, the people appeared to have been conditioned to accept the garbage littering the roadsides and shop-fronts; they were impervious to the stench and the dust which lay in the atmosphere in a perpetual haze. But he discovered that the minds of most of the denizens of the city were bleaker; apparently, the stress of having to live within the raucous urban environment had charred their souls. After a great deal of searching, he finally found his childhood friend—the one who had migrated a few years back to Guwahati after passing out from school, and who he had earlier contacted. Now, he was a changed man, far more urbane and absolutely egocentric, less friendly though not openly hostile. 'It's every man for himself here, pal,' had been his first welcoming words when Hiren Bora had finally hunted down the crowded tenement-building where he lived. 'Two weeks, that's the most I can keep you here. I'm doing this against my landlord's objections...for old time's sake. Then you'll have to make other arrangements.'

Less than a week had been all that Hiren required to discover that the metro was not much better as far as job prospects were concerned. In fact, in many ways even worse. At Doomdooma, he was known to many, at least, and could find some job or the other, no matter how humble. But in Guwahati, he was a total non-entity…merely a speck of the dust which perpetually polluted the city's air. His friend offered no guidance, volunteered no help. Hiren Bora was crestfallen to discover he was just one of the hundreds of thousand young men who had descended upon the city to look for jobs. Honesty, integrity, and willingness to work hard were no more the valued criteria. The key appeared to be specialisation—in anything, whether as an electrician, plumber, or mechanic, et al. There were institutions imparting training in such vocations, but the ultimate key was 'money' with which to pay for them. For instance, drivers were in short supply in a city where residents were setting a record in buying new cars. A number of training 'schools' had mushroomed to teach young men the rudimentary way of driving a car; these also helped the trainees to acquire a driving license without having to undertake the mandatory driving test! But then, the aspirant had to pay through the nose for the lessons as well as the bribe to be given for the license!

Hiren Bora scoured the industrial area of the city; went from shop to shop asking if a sales assistant was needed, and then a chance meeting with another acquaintance from Doomdooma guided him towards a genuine job opportunity. As the city expanded, real estate developers had thrived; residential complexes were sprouting all over. These needed 'security guards' provided by 'security agencies'. The newly-met acquaintance proved more charitable than the one who had offered to put him up for a couple of weeks, and himself took Hiren Bora to such an agency. Perfunctory questions were tossed at him—name, place of birth, date of birth, could he give some identity proof, etcetera. He had offered photocopies of his matriculation, pre-university and BA certificates, as well as an identity card which had enabled him to sit for his finals at college. The interviewer did not bat an eyelid at the fact that the candidate before him was overqualified for the job; nowadays even youths with MA degrees were working as door-to-door sales representatives! It had been the simplest of recruitments—no filling up of complicated forms or physical tests to determine his endurance and stamina, as they did in police recruitment. The head of the agency, also apparently its sole employee, liked the look of Hiren Bora—yes, an opening as a security guard was likely to occur at an apartment complex in a week or two. The moment it was available he would be informed, if he left his contact address and telephone number. The housing 'society' of the apartment building would be paying his salary directly to the placement agency; it would deduct half his first month's wages of 3,500 rupees as commission and, 10 per cent for the next three years. Hiren Bora had sheepishly explained he did not have a contact number or address; the two week offer by his earlier host in the city had expired and currently, he was living on a concrete bench in a bus stand while making ends meet loading trucks at the goods shed of the railway station.

But the newly-met Good Samaritan made a startling offer. 'Look,' he told the fellow at the security agency, 'I'll take him in till the job materialises. Here's my contact number.' Hiren Bora thanked his benefactor profusely, but the man had simply said, 'Get the job, first. Then you can not only thank me, but also pay back what I've spent on you in good time...after you get your salary.' Sure enough a week later the call had come; an apartment called Suprabhat and 3,500 rupees per month as per the agreement, and 1,750 rupees would be deducted from his first month's salary, and 350 rupees then onwards. For the first time in many months, Hiren Bora had been suffused with optimism; hope dawned within him that he could make something of his life. The builder of the apartment complex had not paid much attention to the needs of those who would be responsible for the building's security once it had been completed, the units handed over to the new owners and a 'society' formed. Thus, Hiren Bora had to share a small, cramped room adjacent to the car parking space with the two other security personnel, use a common toilet also used by servants of some of the affluent tenants, and cook in an improvised kitchen. But given the abysmal depths he had descended to once his 'friend' had asked him to leave, this seemed to be heaven itself. Another stroke of luck enhanced the newly harboured hope—the 'security agency' which had facilitated his appointment folded up the very next month, so the 'society' began paying his salary directly to him and the 350 rupees was no longer deducted every month. Through thrift as also by earning extra money doing odd jobs for the building's tenants, he could save a bit, even after sending 500 rupees home every month. Now, he could think of taking up the course in Business Management to at least give himself a fighting chance at a managerial job. A number of 'institutions' imparting crash courses in this discipline had come up in the city. Hiren Bora took the advice of a tenant who was a chartered accountant as to where he should seek admission, found the recommended institution's fees to be too steep, approached (as advised) a bank for a study loan and was refused. So he finally settled for a course in a less expensive institute, which also allowed fees to be paid monthly rather than as a lump sum in advance.

A year-long 'condensed' course, his sole option under the circumstances—yet, a giant step for a young man from a remote, backward village. But, seven months into it, disaster struck and Hiren Bora's carefully laid plans came crashing down. He had arranged, with his two security guard counterparts, to take the night-shift so he could attend classes during the day. It had been taxing, for he hardly had a few hours of sleep in the morning before boarding a bus to the institute. Also, a couple of hours had to be kept apart for extra studies and completing curriculum 'assignments'. Hiren Bora began to feel the pressure getting on his nerves; he tried to compensate by catching up on lost sleep for a few hours during the night-shift itself; after all, nothing much happened between 2:00 and 5:00 am, since both the entrance and exit gates were bolted and locked. Even if some late partygoer returned to the apartment building in the wee hours of the morning, all he had to do was honk the car horn and Hiren Bora would be jolted awake.

That fatal night, as he lay in an exhausted, almost coma-like sleep, a gate had been somehow opened and a new, expensive car belonging to an affluent and influential tenant had been stolen. Clearly, it was the work of a gang of expert car-thieve. Not only had they been able to unlock and unbolt the exit gate, but also open the door of the car without setting off the alarm, and then push the heavy vehicle out of the building without alerting the security guard. The police had arrived promptly—the owner of the stolen vehicle had clout—and suspicion of connivance with the gang of car-lifters immediately fell upon Hiren Bora. The police surmised that someone inside the building had to be involved on two counts: first, the lock to the gate had not been broken but opened with a key, so it was quite likely the security guard had let the gang in; second, it was well-nigh impossible to carry out such a heist without alerting the guard on duty, unless he was in cahoots with the perpetrators. Hiren Bora was arrested, handcuffed and taken to the police station, where he was subjected to a rigorous interrogation by the Officer in Charge (OC) and two of his underlings. The young man had told his side of the story frankly—the course he had been taking, and the lack of time to sleep which had induced him to slumber during that part of the night. As for the locks to the gate, each of the security guards had his own key. Also, the gate keys, along with some other keys, were always kept hanging on nails upon a wall in their room, so anyone could have made a soap-impression of it. Hiren Bora's earnestness of tone and credible narrative, as also the fact that he was studying in an institution even while working, may have convinced others but not these hard-nosed policemen. The first slap delivered by the OC took Hiren Bora by surprise. His impulsive reaction was to go for the bastard's throat, but the two underlings caught and flung him to the ground, and blow after blow had rained down on him...

As he lay upon the gradually dampening ground, eyes closed, body relaxed like a civet cat in repose, a cruel smile appeared around the corners of Hiren Bora's lips at the recollection of the OC. The police had to ultimately set him free, of course, since despite the beating he had refused to acknowledge guilt, and there was no hard evidence to indicate he was hand in glove with the car-lifters. But the fleshy face of that obese OC had remained etched with acid in his memory—the fat cheeks and those cruel, sadistic eyes. A routine transfer (ironically, a promotion) from the metro to a mofussil town on the north bank of the river Brahmaputra had brought the bastard within easier reach of Hiren Bora—by then, a young man in the process of building up a reputation as a totally ruthless ULFA cadre. Against the wishes of a segment of the organisation's leadership but with the full consent of the commander-in-chief of its armed wing who agreed with Hiren Bora's objective of striking terror in the heart of the establishment, the OC and three other policemen had first been lured into a nearby village and then abducted and taken to a hide-out on the Indo-Bhutan border. Hiren Bora's smile was at the remembrance of the terror upon the OC's face and the tears in his eyes as he begged for mercy. Before the horrified gaze of the three policemen, Hiren Bora had taken out his revolver and shot the OC through his forehead. One shot had been enough. His colleagues had been set free to take the tale of the OC's killing back to their compatriots—yet another episode serving to build up the Hiren Bora mystique.

THE RECRUIT

'*The Indian State is in the grip of a small segment of bourgeois politicians, bureaucrats, and profiteers. It is a tiny section of the societal structure, battening off the whole like a leech stuck to the buttocks of a buffalo* (laughter). *The gap between the rich bourgeois and the impoverished masses is widening with each passing moment—the capitalists are gaining in strength and enjoying the fruits of the so-called economic progress while the impoverished masses languish for want of food, shelter, and medicines. The bourgeois elite controls the entire societal machinery—it is they who choose who gets a job and earns a salary; it is they who control how much the poor, hard-working peasant is to get for the produce of his fields; it is they who plan how the societal and economic structure should develop, so they and their ilk can perpetuate their hold over the impoverished masses. The vast majority of the people of the Indian State cry out at the inequality and injustice of it all, and their cries must be heard...*'

Day in and day out these 'revolutionary lectures', designed to knead the lump called the human brain into an alternate shape were delivered; every morning, seven days a week, for two hours after the morning drill and one hour in the evening before dinner. Sergeant Major Pradyut Basumatari had duly conveyed his impressions of the newly-recruited batch to the commander of the ULFA's 13th Battalion. The latter agreed that these acolytes, too, like the previous ones, had to be subjected to a relentless barrage of lectures so as to subjugate dominant egos, suppress unseen demons and instil within them genuine revolutionary fervour. Thus, the lectures—day in and day out, morning and evening. Cunningly, the economic and societal inequality components of the pre-fabricated indoctrination module imparted first, since the recruits had mostly joined the ULFA due to economic compulsions and a nebulous perception of social inequality. '*Revolutionary organisations like the United Liberation Front of Assam must act as defenders of the impoverished masses...*' The monotonous voice of Lakhidhar Gogoi—called *mama* (maternal uncle) by all members of the outfit and the oldest individual in the Assam section of the KIA camp—would drone on and on. *Mama* was with the ULFA in an advisory capacity, was not a combat cadre, and acted as the official ideologue and communicator of the outfit's ideology. '*We need to avow that the bourgeois elite are an enemy and we have to combat their machination. Members of the bourgeois have structured society so as to enable them to exploit the impoverished masses. We need to act—through violent means if necessary—to dismantle this exploitative mechanism, and put power in the hands of the people. It was the great revolutionary Mao Tse Tung who said power comes from the barrel of a gun. This is why each day, we train you in the use of firearms and explosives, and urge you not to hesitate to use your arms to kill the enemy...*'

On and on and on. A month in the camp and Hiren Bora no longer had to focus attention upon the words for them to pour automatically through his ears and imprint themselves upon his brain—changing its contour, reshaping his perceptions, hardening the arteries leading to his heart till only icy cold plasma and not warm blood could gush in, gush out. '*But as committed cadres of the United Liberation Front of Assam, our job is not to be the defenders of the masses of the entire entity called India, though we will not desist from cooperating with other organisations of that country which profess ideals similar to ours. We are wholly committed to Mother Assam, and it is the oppressed masses of our Motherland on behalf of whom we must fight...*' Repetitions, weavings in and out, detours and cul-de-sacs—Hiren Bora could squat on the ground at the very front row and look at Gogoi impassively—straight in the eye—and allow the stream of words to enter into his consciousness, even as his thoughts dwelt somewhere else. He would recall the night when the organisation had picked him up—from a roadside *dhaba* between Doomdooma and Makum, the April, pre-monsoon showers had commenced and the night had been warm and wet. Yet, the air had been redolent with the fragrance of the *kopou* orchid which had started to bloom everywhere, heralding the *Rongali bihu* festival. Everywhere, there had been the throb of drums and the lilt of the buffalo-horn pipe as the villagers prepared and practiced for *huchari.* A man, wearing a helmet which made recognition impossible, had ridden a motorcycle to the *dhaba* and gestured to him to ride pillion. There had been no exchange of words; they drove south-east for an hour and a half…the rain and darkness had not allowed Hiren Bora to guess exactly where they were headed. Over slushy, unpaved rural roads, the path was absolutely bereft of human or animal presence due to the lateness of the night and the weather. Suddenly, the driver stopped in the middle of nowhere. 'Go on ahead by this path for a kilometre or so,' he spoke for the first time in a low voice. 'It will be something of a steep climb. Don't leave the cleared trail or you might get lost. You will reach a *chang*-house with a lit kerosene lantern at the door. Knock on the door. You're expected. Good luck!' His unknown escort turned the motorcycle around, and disappeared into the black of the night.

Hiren Bora, drenched and shivering, had stumbled along in the darkness over that narrow trail, with his small bag containing his meagre belongings slung across his shoulder. Coercing his brain to act as a compass, squinting his eyes to judge the direction better despite the almost total absence of light, he continued walking. He knew well why his escort had left him in the middle of nowhere to make it to the next stage of his trek on his own; a deliberate and tiny hiatus in the chain—so one link could not tell a thing about the other even if caught and cruelly interrogated. It had been a steep climb, indeed; the slush had made the ascent even more difficult. He slipped and slithered down a number of times, clawing at the ground to break the falls—his clothes, limbs, and face, splattered with mud. He could guess he must be somewhere on the Assam-Arunachal Pradesh border, the Tirap District of the latter, most likely. He finally made it to the top of what in the daytime would be confirmed to be a hillock. And then, a little further down below, he saw the *chang*-house, set some 10 feet above the ground on stilts, a small kerosene lantern flickering on the elevated corridor surrounding the hutment and sheltered from the rain by the thatched eaves. By the time he made it up the bamboo staircase, he had been breathless and panting despite his physical fitness. Hiren Bora knocked on the door. To his surprise, the man who opened it was a Naga and not an Arunachali; a taciturn, unsmiling fellow, who simply let the newcomer in, pointed towards a straw-bed covered with a hessian sheet, dimmed and blew out the lantern, and left. Wet and somewhat disorientated, Hiren Bora had flung himself onto the bed and fallen into an exhausted sleep...

Then the gradual slide towards political ideology: '*Our ultimate objective? The setting up of an independent State of Assam. A sovereign State, the indigenous population of which will control their own destiny and not have policies imposed upon them by the bourgeois State machinery in Delhi, in connivance with the bourgeois boot-lickers at Dispur. Our comrades from Nagaland, who have helped us so much, had declared an independent Nagaland decades back just after the end of the imperialist rule; we are sorry that it took our people a few decades more to realise the treacherousness of the rats who infest Delhi. But now, realisation has come and we have become aware that the proletariat masses have two enemies: the bourgeois political and bureaucratic machinery in Delhi, and the bourgeois boot-lickers at Dispur. It had been the sad reality of Assam's loss of sovereignty and the surrender of her bourgeois political leadership to their masters in Delhi, which has enabled the latter to make slaves of all of us. Assam had never been a part of the Indian State till the advent of the British. Since pre-historic times, the mighty Brahmaputra river—which flows from one end of the state till the other, and is linked to the Ganges—had enabled waves of migrants to come and settle in the fertile valleys and hills of the region. Mongoloid tribes had come from China and South East Asia to colonise the land in the form of small communities, and add to the Austric and Dravidian presence already here; from the West came Caucasoid elements, bringing Aryan customs and beliefs. Assam was the meeting-ground of two great cultures, those of China and India, while being ideally located for economic self-sufficiency. In the past, mammoth kingdoms ruled by Mongoloid monarchs had sprung up in the region—that of the Asura dynasty with powerful potentates likes Narakasura and Bhagadatta, later the Varman dynasty, with the wise king Bhaskarvarman taking the realm to its cultural and economic apex.*

'But by the time the Ahoms entered the valley from Burma through the eastern passes in 1228 AD, the region then known as Kamarupa had broken up into small principalities—the Koch kingdom of Naranarayan with his army commander Chilarai, or the kite-king being the largest and most powerful of them all. However, it had been the advent of Sukapha, the prince from the Shan or Tai tribe from Mungman or Pong, situated in upper Burma on the banks of the Irrawaddy river, which made an irreversible impact on the destiny of the people of the region and resulted in the formation of the Greater Assamese Race. Bit by bit, the Ahoms conquered the whole of the Brahmaputra valley, and by imposing a uniform system of administration, laid the ground for the political unification of the Assamese people and formation of the Assamese identity. Assam, a sovereign realm, prospered under patronage of the Ahom Swargadeos, and reached economic and cultural heights never attained before. No doubt, the wealth and power of the mighty Ahom Empire had attracted the vultures from mainland India (laughter). *Since the 13th Century, Muslim rulers had had their eyes on the valley, and made no less than 17 attempts to bring it under their sway—first came the Turks, followed by the Pathans. At the beginning, their own empire being at a fledgling stage, the Ahoms did not have to confront the invasions directly, but left it to the Koches and other petty chieftains to engage the enemy. The very first Muhammadan invasion was by Bukhtyar Khilji; later, in 1227, a Bengal governor named Ghiyas-ud-din was said to have ascended the Brahmaputra as far as Sadiya, but had to finally beat a retreat. These were followed by unsuccessful invasions of Tughril Khan in 1257 and Muhammad Shah in 1337. In the 1560s, Kalapahar—a renegade Brahmin and iconoclast, and the general of Sulaiman Kararani—invaded the Koch Kingdom of Naranarayan and ascended the Brahmaputra to Tezpur, but then had to retreat, wreaking his frustration and anger by destroying Hindu temples*

and images. The mighty Mughals, of course, repeatedly attacked the Ahom Empire but were repulsed every time, its final defeat being at Saraighat by the master military strategist, Lachit Barphukan...'

It had been the most terrible trek he had undertaken in his life. Since then, he had made even more difficult and hazardous journeys but now, he was armed and trained, and knew his way about and mostly was in the lead. Then he had been a neophyte—blindly following someone else, unarmed and helpless, not knowing where he was being taken to or what perils lay before him. Sure enough, the next morning after a wet night spent in that *chang*-house he was nursing a fever…but his inscrutable and taciturn Naga host did not seem to notice or bother. Hiren Bora was pleased to discover that the sky had cleared during the night and the sun was out; emerging from his hutment on to the veranda, he saw he was in a village—though the main cluster of dwellings was at a distance away, and the one he had spent the night in was somewhat isolated. Behind the other hutments were terraced fields of rice, but these did not extend very far…and then the dense jungles took over. Hiren Bora could make out how thick the foliage was even from such a distance. Climbing down the stairs, he went to a nearby stream for his morning ablutions, and squatted behind some bushes to defecate. He was given a bowl of sugary, pounded rice soaked in water by his host upon his return. As he wolfed down the food with obvious hunger, his host—who had till then communicated only with nods and grunts—now said in the peculiar dialect called Nagamese: 'We wait. You sleep. They come for you. You move at night.' Hiren Bora felt a sense of relief; the wait would give him hours of precious rest to recover from the cold, and for the heat to leave his body. He had flopped back onto the thatch and hessian bed, and sunk into a fevered sleep...

'By bringing the smaller tribes under their tutelage, encouraging inter-cultural marriages and other social exchanges between the tribes, the Ahoms succeeded in breaking ethnic and cultural barriers, initiated the formation of the Assamese language and imbued into the people a nationalist spirit. Since you are all Assamese, you need to know these facets of the glorious history of our people and take pride in the glory of our past. And then, in the latter part of the 15th Century, emerged the colossus named Mahapurush Sankardev—the Vaishnav saint-poet of Assam—who through his doctrine of Ekasarana Namadharma, as well as through his contributions to Assamese literature and fine arts, brought about a socio-cultural renaissance to the land. He played a seminal role in enhancing the feeling of oneness amongst the people, and formation of an Assamese identity. From the prehistoric past through centuries after centuries, and till the time the sun of the Ahom Dynasty set, the region earlier called Pragjyotisha, then Kamarupa and now Assam had retained its sovereign character—being in no point of time a part of the so-called Indian nation...'

They came for him just as the sun was setting and half-light played upon the terraced rice fields and darkening jungles. Two Naga youths barely out of their teens and dressed in camouflage fatigues, with full battle gear—including grenades slung from loops at the sides of their jackets and armed with sophisticated weapons—stood before Hiren Bora. The contrast with the dour caretaker of the *chang*-house could not be more marked; they were simple and cheerful Naga youths, ready to exchange pleasantries and answer in Nagamese any question thrown at them. Oh yes, they were cadres of the NSCS, who had come in response to a request made by the base commander of the ULFA's 13th Battalion to escort some new recruits to the KIA's 2nd Brigade camp at Death Valley. 'Heh heh, just a joke,' one of the Naga escorts laughed loudly and said, 'It's actually Hukong valley, but called Death Valley because so many die due to malaria, typhoid, diarrhoea, skin afflictions, and more!'

Make no mistake, it would be a hugely dangerous trek to Myanmar, not only because the Indian army constantly patrolled the border this side and did not hesitate to shoot on sight anyone trying to get across to the other side, but also because of the treacherous terrain and thickness of the jungles. Moreover, they would have to move in the dark because the army did not patrol at night—they would seek sanctuary in friendly villages during daytime. 'Nor is it any different on the other side because the Myanmar Army patrols it, too. Although they are not as enthusiastic in their duties as the Indians, heh heh. No, no, the route is not a fixed one...you must understand there has to be room for detours based on the information received with regard to the Indian Army's presence.'

'Who will give the information?' asked Hiren Bora.

'Why, our own people in the local villages...not to worry, not only do we have eyes and ears everywhere, we also know the general route like the back of our hands. Ah, but we need to get going, for there are others like you to be picked up on the way.'

The dour-faced Naga caretaker gave him a medium-size cloth bag of dry, pounded rice, which Hiren Bora placed in his hand bag. The NSCN insurgents threw a pair of camouflage fatigues at him, which he put on over his dirty and crumpled trousers and shirt. They also asked him to rub some dirt over his face. 'Ah, it's dark enough now, so let us make a move, shall we?' Surprisingly, the unsmiling caretaker of the *chang*-house had held out his hand to Hiren Bora—the grip was strong and conveyed warmth. 'Good luck,' he had said, and they were off.

Four more youths concealed in the same village for three-four days, awaiting Hiren Bora's arrival, were picked up as the group moved swiftly into the jungle. The week-long trek to the Myanmar border would forever be engraved in Hiren Bora's mind. The going had been relatively easy on the first night on foot, despite the ground being slushy due to the recent rains; having been brought up in an Assamese village, youths like him had no problems with wet ground and slush. It had been apparent to the armed guides that Hiren Bora was fever-ridden, but they seemed not to be bothered by this, and were unwilling to make concessions. So the young man gritted his teeth and marched along without a sound—a fact which won the approval of the Naga escorts. The night's journey had been continuous, with just one half-hour break for rest and a drink of water. With immaculate timing, they had flitted like ghosts into a village on the foothills as dawn was about to break; this was the easternmost tip of India, so dawn arrived much earlier, even as far-off places like Delhi remained wrapped in total darkness. This, again, was a hamlet unlike an Assamese village; all the hutments were *chang*-type—single-roomed and elevated, with domesticated animals like pigs and chicken kept below the floor so they could feed off the waste periodically dropping from upstairs. The Naga escorts were as fresh and lively as they had been last evening, but the recruits were dog-tired— especially Hiren Bora, whose haggard and sweaty visage indicated the will-power he had shown in staying the course.

But even though he was numb with fever and fatigue, he had not lost his sense of bearing, and could guess the route they were taking. In all probability, though he could not be absolutely sure…since the first motorcycle ride he was being directed south-east into the Tirap district of Arunachal Pradesh, so the second night's halt must be somewhere near Khonsa. Yet the very fact that the land they had crossed was relatively plain and less dense with verdure—marking for easier traversal—indicated their escorts planned to cross into Myanmar not across the border with Arunachal to that country, but continue to travel southward till they reached Nagaland. Since the NSCN had its undeniable hold upon that state, and NSCN leaders could move to-and-fro with impunity between India, Myanmar, and China through well-established routes, this was to be expected, for it would facilitate comparatively safer passage for the new recruits. Hiren Bora, however, kept his thoughts to himself; one of his escorts came up and fraternally touched his forehead, and then with his fingers pried apart the eyelids to examine one of his eyes. 'Not malaria,' he said, 'just a simple fever. It will pass.' An aged Naga woman with withered, uncovered breasts came and handed him a bamboo tube containing a bitter liquid, indicating it was an herbal potion for his fever which he should drink. Later, she brought all of them rice and pork stew garnished with bamboo shoot. Hiren Bora had never eaten pork before; it had been taboo in his village. But he told himself that from now on he would eat whatever was offered to him! Despite the fever, he felt as though he had never feasted on anything more delicious in his life...

'Yes, till the advent of the 19th Century, this land was an ethnologic mosaic given a singular identity with the strong, sovereign political leadership provided by the Ahoms. However, entering the 19th Century, the sun of the Ahom Dynasty began to set, and the period of darkness commenced for the indigenous people of this region—a pall which has not lifted till today, even though we have entered the 21st Century! Think of it, comrades, two centuries of slavery and deprival—has it not been right for us to rise up against this subjugation and servitude? The Ahoms first disowned their sovereignty as early as the 1790s when a weak-kneed monarch, unable to withstand internal rebellion and depredation by freebooters and mercenaries from outside the kingdom, requested

the help of the British. Although the arrival of the British restored a semblance of order to the beleaguered land for a while, their departure witnessed a renewal of anarchy, with internal squabbles emasculating royal authority and numerous local uprisings, bringing about civil disorder. Then, in 1816, the infamous Badan Barphukan sought the help of the king of Burma in his quest to acquire the Ahom throne for himself. The Maans, as the Burmese were called by the people of Assam, made repeated incursions into the land—killing, raping, and pillaging, ravaging what had once been a prosperous, self-sustaining society...and decimating at least a third of the population. But their success in the Brahmaputra valley soon brought the Burmese into conflict with the British. To cut a long story short, the British finally defeated the Burmese and, on 24 February 1826, Assam was incorporated into Britain's Indian Empire through the Yandabu Treaty. For a while, the Ahom king was retained as the titular head, but in 1838, this pretence was done away with—the king was deposed and pensioned off, and Assam was placed under the direct administration of the British, thereby losing the freedom and independence it had enjoyed through six centuries of Ahom rule.

'The land was subjected to the most naked form of colonial exploitation, the onerous burden of taxes on the people, leading peasants to revolt. Such rebellions like the ones at Phulaguri and Patharughat, however, were suppressed brutally. Oil, coal, minerals—nothing was spared by the rapacious British. The virgin forests of the foothills and valleys could be cut down to erect the most visible sign of colonial exploitation, the tea-gardens, which entailed that enormous chunks of agricultural land pass on not to farmers but capitalist entrepreneurs. The British took a great deal without putting anything back; infrastructural development was undertaken only to prepare the region for economic exploitation; English education was introduced to facilitate the germination of

a colonial culture amongst the burgeoning Assamese bourgeois. However, the biggest thing that the British took away was the freedom of the entire community, by bringing the region under a common administration and uniform civil code—the British irrevocably destroyed sovereignty, and entwined Assam's destiny with the rest of India...'

Having slept through almost the entire day, Hiren Bora was relieved to find the fever had left him by the evening. Although awake, he continued to lie on the thatch-bed upon the floor and watch the slanting rays of the dying sun spear into the *chang*-house through a small, rectangular bamboo-ribbed window. His four companions were still asleep; the Naga escorts were nowhere to be seen. Hiren Bora stood up, went to the open window and peered out—the *chang*-house they were in was built upon a hillock overlooking thick jungles; only the top of the vegetation was visible and nothing else… There were no human voices though the occasional hook-hook-hoo of the hoolock gibbon could be heard; all of a sudden the verdure was lit up by the burst of illumination which always announces the passing of another day. Perhaps, thought Hiren Bora, the dipping sun which was about to dive into the foliage was a symbol; a sign, so to speak, of a breaking with the past—the closing of one chapter of his life and the beginning of another. Yet, as the consciousness of the finality of the step taken seeped into him, there was no sadness; perhaps the anger and frustration within his soul had made sadness impossible, or perhaps it was due to the induced exhilaration flooding into one when fever leaves the body. No, he did not feel sadness at his enforced departure from Chungijan…leaving Ai, Pitai, Bai and, above all, Okon, behind. Instead, he was gripped with the excitement of adventure, of one stepping into unknown territory. A door had shut behind him, but another had opened ahead.

The creaking of the wooden floor as Hiren Bora walked to the window woke up the others. Minutes later, the old Naga woman entered the room, once again carrying plates of steaming rice and pork with bamboo shoots. She touched Hiren Bora's forehead and her lips parted in a wide grin, revealing a black, toothless, gummy mouth. 'Good,' she said, 'you'll be OK. Now eat.' He once again tucked into the food with the same relish he had displayed in the morning. Half an hour later, the two young escorts arrived, and within moments, they were once again on the road. Hiren Bora was not given enough time to even thank the old Naga lady, and soon he was moving silently and ghost-like in the all-pervasive darkness.

Each night, they covered approximately 25 kilometres. Fortunately, the weather held. The journey became more and more difficult as the jungle thickened; sometimes the foliage was so impassable their guides had to hack out a path with their sharp-bladed *daos*. The absence of well-worn trails meant numerous stumbles over exposed roots of trees. The new recruits were not used to travelling on such terrain; thorny *jengpat* shrubs tore at their skin and their clothes, a host of insects—including blood-sucking mosquitoes—as also leeches the size of one's fingers, added to the torment. All this made Hiren Bora ask if it would not have been more convenient to travel by day when at least some of the inconveniences of night travel could be avoided, despite the risk of being spotted by army patrols. One of their escorts had reiterated that safety was more important than convenience—the Indian as well as Myanmar Army patrolled only during daytime, perhaps precisely for the same reason as stated by Hiren Bora…and also, perhaps, because they felt less vulnerable to attacks by insurgent groups. There were two more village stops—in each, local informants briefed the guides about the latest movements of the Indian Army, location of temporary army camps and patrol routes, enabling the two Naga youths to chalk out the path they themselves should take to steer clear of the army.

The fifth day had to be spent in the open; within a small clearing beside a stream. They could not risk a fire, so they ate pounded rice soaked in the stream's clear water with jiggery, and they slept on the hard ground—with the guides taking turns to keep watch, in spite of the fact that they, too, had travelled throughout the night. This was a situation which entailed greatest risk, since an army patrol might stumble on to them if they were not watchful; also, elephant herds which did not honour international boundaries constantly migrated from one country to another, and the risk of an encounter with them was very real. Hiren Bora guessed the absence of a village must mean the party was on the fringe of the India-Myanmar border; he had no idea whether they had crossed over by now and were, in fact, on the Myanmar side. He suspected even the escorts were none too sure! However, having left the spot towards dusk, by the next morning they had reached a small but full-fledged NSCN camp built deep within the jungles— which meant they were in Myanmar. The insurgents of the camp had welcomed the visitors warmly; if they feared attacks by the armies of either countries, they displayed no sign. There was great feasting and merriment in the late afternoon, after the new arrivals had had their sleep; there was plenty of rice, beef, pork, vegetables, and rice beer. The NSCN apparently had a flourishing supply line open—the only scarce commodity was salt, but the two guides had brought with them packets of salt to hand over. When the feasting and bonhomie was over, the group continued on its way, with Hiren Bora suddenly suffused with a sense of belonging—as opposed to the feel of alienation which had gripped him when he had been amongst his own...

'Yes, apart from exploitation of the land's natural resources and utilisation of vast arable tracts to set up huge tea-gardens, the worst consequence for the indigenous people of Assam after the annexation of the region by the British was the loss of their sovereignty. The area, despite its blatant ethnic and cultural differences, was stitched to the Indian mainland, and lost its former character as a link between India and South-East Asia—only to become a remote outpost of Britain's vast Indian Empire. The British tried their best to suppress Assamese nationalism; the hanging of Maniram Dewan and Peali Baruah after the 1857 uprising was a stern warning that natives who dared to oppose colonial designs would meet a similar fate. No wonder the bourgeois stratum, which had germinated and evolved in Assamese society with the coming of the British, kowtowed to their colonial masters and acted as a buffer between them and the proletariat masses. It is a fact of history that the Assamese bourgeois class, though it began opposing British policies under the political banner of the Indian National Congress, had at no point of time been spokesperson for the toiling famers or workers, or a defender of their rights.'

'Instead, into the 20th Century and with the freedom movement becoming strong in the subcontinent, the Assamese bourgeois shifted allegiance and began kowtowing to native masters from the Indian mainland—particularly north India, and specifically Delhi. The so-called Indian nationalists of this region did their best to extinguish Assamese nationalism which now, apart from being set upon by the British was, so to speak, assailed by native Badans, too, who swore by the names of the Gandhis and the Nehrus. Thus, without a shot being fired, Delhi was achieving what it had failed to do despite repeated attempts through centuries during the Ahom rule—assuming control and shaping the destiny of this region, with the willing connivance of a section of the Assamese bourgeois. The Congress leadership of Assam came entirely from a bourgeois

stratum which derided Assamese nationalism as chauvinistic and parochial—those Badans wearing Gandhi-topis sold the soul of Assam for their own political ends. Rather than to give a clarion call for sovereignty as Phizo had done in Nagaland, these spineless traitors began licking the boots of the Congress leadership in Delhi, which in turn was controlled by bourgeois elements from north India. The Assamese bourgeois Congress leadership failed to even demand a special status for their state, let alone ask for the imposition of protective shields such as inner line permits for outsiders. In their frenzy to hang on to the coat-tails of the powers in Delhi, these Badans went on an all-out offensive against Assamese nationalism. The masses, too, hypnotised into believing that their quality of life would improve and that a new, free, egalitarian society—where there would be no discrimination based on caste, creed, religion, and economic status—would emerge, forsook Assamese nationalism for the so-called Indian nationalism.'

'It was cheating of the most reprehensible kind! Oh yes, the proletariat masses were led up the garden path by a handful of bourgeois quislings who had sold the entire community to further their own political ends. It did not take the people long to discover the magnitude of the deceit played upon them—one exploitative white master was merely replaced by a much more exploitative, unscrupulous, and malevolent brown master. For over a decade and a half, Delhi continued to bleed the region of its natural resources—they drilled more wells for crude oil, but rather than set up refineries and ancillary units in Assam, they laid pipelines to Bihar and carried away the oil to be refined there. Hundreds of thousand tons of coal was transported to mainland India to feed industries elsewhere; our forests were chopped down relentlessly... while the proletariat masses slaved away at tea plantations, the profits were enjoyed by a handful of brown capitalists from outside who had had the resources to buy out tea plantations from

white owners in the post-independence period. Like the British, the Indian colonialists kept on taking without giving anything back. There was no infrastructural development, communication remained primitive, and there were no new industries; the state became dependent on mainland India for everything—from rice to candles! There was no attempt to tackle the flood problem which annually destroyed so many lives, and so much crop and livestock; the Brahmaputra was the only major Indian river to remain unbridged. The single metre-gauge line connecting the region through a 20-km wide strip with mainland India terminated at Amingaon, from where passengers had to cross the Brahmaputra by ferry, before resuming their journey from Pandu. The proletariat masses grew more impoverished under the new, free regime; as you all have personally experienced, unemployment grew rife, most of the existing industries passed on to the hands of outsiders, and the very air of Mother Assam became unbreathable with the reek of neglect and exploitation.'

'All for what? Just to keep a handful of bourgeois opportunist dalals in power! The centuries-old pride of the Assamese people was irrevocably demeaned. The local Congress leadership coined the self-explanatory, demeaning phrase called 'the High-Command', meaning the leadership at Delhi, and would not even shit or piss without the 'High-Command's' permission (laughter). *Lakhs of outsiders flooded Assam, in places one could not even speak the local language; worse still, millions of illegal migrants from foreign countries were allowed continuous entry into the land, despite the fact that India was an independent nation now...'*

Once within Myanmar territory, the jungle thinned out close to the bank of a large and powerful river—the Chindwin, they were informed. The terrain, though less covered with vegetation, remained mountainous and treacherous. It was, in fact, a blessing that they were trekking in the night; their route—with winding bridle-paths tracing the sinuous river's contours, often overlooking gorges so deep it took one's breath away just to look down—would have appeared far more difficult to traverse had it been daytime. Yet there was a perceptible easing of tension on the faces of their guides; they had remained cheerful and talkative throughout, but Hiren Bora had sensed the underlying apprehension and caution—clearly, the threat from the Indian Army was grave! The threat from the Myanmar Army grew even less as they entered the Kachin state; it was hostile territory for the army but amicable towards those whom the KIA called its own. They traversed kilometres after kilometres of the dangerous terrain, crossing lesser rivers over bamboo bridges without seeing a single soul. They were camping on their own at sunrise and passing the daylight hours either sleeping or angling for fish, till at dawn one day, (Hiren Bora as also the other recruits had lost track of time and days) they stumbled into a Kachin village. Ramshackle hutments of bamboo and thatch—a lifestyle almost primitive to Hiren Bora as he was used to the comparative spruceness of an Assamese village. It looked as if time had forgotten these people, who yet used wood and stone implements for everyday activity and appeared to lack the slightest notion of modernity. *Chang*-houses set on bamboo stilts, the cackling of chickens and ducks, the grunts of pigs and the barking of a couple of dogs seemingly belonging to the entire village community had announced their arrival. The chief of the village had been more than gracious; his mask of gravity, which did not appear incongruous despite the indigent environment, sliding into a smile of delight as two packets of salt were gifted to him. A male piglet was killed—a precious sacrifice, indeed, on the part of the villagers—its meat along with maize-bread constituted the repast offered to the visitors. Living as they did in a mountainous terrain, the villagers cultivated maize rather than rice. The Kachin area being thinly populated, the guides told the recruits that this was one of the few villages in the region. Hiren Bora observed that the compactness of the village meant that not more than a hundred families lived within it; maize—seemingly their staple food—was cultivated in terraces dug upon the mountainside a little bit away from the hutments. Thus, the cottages, unlike in an Assamese village, were not separated from one another by sprawls of paddy fields. The villagers reared cattle, though not for milk or ploughing—consumption of milk was none too prevalent amongst tribal communities of Mongoloid descent... While the nature of the terrain entailed that the terraces be manually hacked out and tilled, the short, stocky cattle—let loose during daytime for grazing and sighted by the visitors only as they were about to leave towards nightfall—were reared primarily for meat. Hiren Bora was astonished to find that one of the hutments had a bamboo cross, fastened with cane to the outer rafter of its roof. He had had a vague notion that the people of this region, like those elsewhere in Myanmar—as also many tribes in Arunachal Pradesh—were Buddhists, but this community apparently were Christians. The two Naga guides, who also belonged to this faith, informed him that most of the population in the Kachin state were Christians—yet another reason for their antagonism towards people from other parts of their country. Hiren Bora noted the innocence of a people almost totally cut off from the modern world—the happy ambience prevailing in the community and the rows of faces wreathed in smiles, and the spontaneous hospitality with no expectation of monetary compensation. These villagers must have existed in a manner prevalent for untold centuries, being born, living, and dying in the same ancient way, without aspiring for the material advancement chased by much of the modern world. However, the villagers did have one grievous complaint, articulated by the chief in a dialect which the Naga escorts understood: units of the Myanmar Army would occasionally descend on the village and extort some livestock in exchange for leaving them in peace. The guides assured him his complaint would reach the ears of the commanding officer of the 2nd Brigade of the KIA, to whose camp they were now headed...

'Within years of achieving so-called independence from colonial rule, the people of Assam realised with dismay that only masters had changed, not the colonial ethos. Suddenly, the masses of our unfortunate Motherland found themselves without tangible political power, without a voice, without any avenue for material advancement—with even their traditional assets being seized by outsiders and infiltrators. The masses of our unfortunate Motherland soon discovered that they had to fight and demonstrate for everything even as the boot-licking so-called representatives of the people failed to articulate or address their grievances. They had to agitate for refineries and other industries to be set up, they even had to fight for the Assamese language to be made the official language of their state. The most terrible consequence was, of course, the emasculation of Assamese nationalism which, though weakened, was not dead. Then came the biggest blow to jolt awake the dormant Assamese nationalism. In November 1962, the war of words between India and China translated into actual conflict—hordes of soldiers of the Chinese Red Army overran Indian border posts in Arunachal, gunning down Indian Army jawans in thousands, and marching triumphantly into the Brahmaputra valley. The Indian establishment paid dearly for a decade and a half of neglect—because of the poor communication infrastructure, it had been near impossible to get much needed supplies in time to the Indian jawans on the border. It had been then that the head of

the Indian bourgeois establishment, Jawaharlal Nehru, made his infamous farewell speech to Assam… So easy to shed a few crocodile tears after years of exploitation and injustice! How unfortunate... our comrades of the Chinese Red Army, rather than annex North-East India and make it a part of the Great Chinese State, chose instead to inexplicably retreat and hand over this region back to the exploiting bourgeois establishment in Delhi and their boot-licking lackeys in Assam. However, the sense of betrayal unleashed by the Chinese aggression of 1962 ignited the fire of incipient Assamese nationalism, and the region exploded sometime later into a mass movement—the likes of which the nation had not witnessed in the post-independence period. The core demand was the detection and deportation of illegal infiltrators from foreign countries, but at the same time the mass movement embodied the volcanic eruption of anger of the Assamese masses at decades of exploitation and neglect. The bourgeois boot-lickers at Dispur came down harshly on peaceful agitators; hundreds were killed in firings by police and Paramilitary Forces, thousands injured. There were mass arrests and beatings and torture—it was as if Assam was a conquered nation wherein the invaders could heap at will death and agony on the local multitude. There were brave and patriotic young men who could not bear to see the Motherland and her sons and daughters writhe in agony; they realised that fire has to be fought with fire. And, thus, in the terrible flames of ordeal the United Liberation Front of Assam was born...'

After days and days of continuous night-time trekking, a fortnight after he had been picked up by the unknown motorcyclist, Hiren Bora, the other recruits, and the two Naga guides finally reached the central camp of the KIA's 2nd Brigade. The muted welcome the newcomers received was almost anticlimactic, given the violent disruption to their lives and the fact they had entered a potentially lethal phase—not to mention the dangerous trek they had undertaken to get to the camp. They were made to have their first bath in a fortnight, given a meal of rice and fish curry, and allowed to sleep and recuperate for the rest of the day and night. Other recruits had streamed in earlier; the group Hiren Bora was in had been the last to arrive. All of them were put up in a long, rectangular dormitory-type hutment with two-tiered bunks made of bamboo, and furnished with cane baskets to keep their personal stuff in. He slept for almost 24 hours at a stretch, so fatigued he had been. Lance Corporal Zaman had awoken him the following morning along with the others; he was allowed to perform his morning ablutions, and then directed to a central mess for a morning meal. Some of the new recruits had already caught fever, others carried injuries sustained during the treacherous journey—but this did not deter Lance Corporal Zaman from herding them into the indoctrination room, where they were introduced to *mama* and made to listen to his first lecture. Next, they were taken to an open spot which had a tall bamboo pole with the ULFA's flag (emblazoned with the image of a rising sun) fluttering atop it, and made to stand in three files and await the arrival of Sergeant Major Pradyut Basumatari. Hiren Bora was struck by the sheer size of that camp; set upon a hillside beside a stream which ran through a tiny, almost gorge-like valley, it was a mammoth, sprawling complex of hutments divided into many sections allotted to various insurgent outfits of North-East India—a glaring presence in the desolate wilderness with not the least trace of other human settlements nearby. No attempt was made to camouflage the camp…its size would render it a sitting duck in case of an air-strike by the Myanmar Air Force. However, no such assault had taken place, despite the *junta's* constant assurance to the Indian government that action would be initiated against insurgents taking shelter within Myanmar territory. That China had a strangle-hold on the *junta*, as also close rapport with the KIA and their associate insurgent groups, helped maintain the status quo and keeping things in a fine balance. The sergeant major had come and barked out orders; the commander of the KIA's 2nd Brigade, too, had dropped in, and having said a few words in local dialect, left with an amused smile (the smile the sergeant major so disliked) on his face. The new recruits were made to voice aloud their allegiance to the ULFA and resolve to die for Mother Assam if needed. Each of them were fitted out with two pairs of camouflage fatigues and a pair of tough shoes, and the nightmare had begun.

Never in his life had Hiren Bora imagined training could be so hard…and the trainers, so without pity. In fact, the three hours of lecture from *mama* were the only moments of the day when there was respite; their night's sleep was reduced to six hours—to bed at 10 pm sharp, and up at 4 am the next morning. The first month was devoted to building up physical fitness and stamina—hours and hours of exercise and jungle trekking; climbing up ropes and clambering over obstacles; they seemed to always be on the move except during meal times, indoctrination sessions, and while they were asleep in bed. The food, though simple, was plentiful and wholesome; the trainers knew that good nutrition was essential for building up the constitution. But neither fever nor bouts of dysentery could melt their hearts, and one had to collapse in a genuine faint to elicit a drop of compassion and be carried to the hospital.

Earlier, the training period for new recruits had been far longer, but current circumstances had forced the ULFA leadership to trim it down and put the new recruits into the field of actual action earlier. Thus, hand-to-hand combat training and sessions of martial art began in the second month itself, and lessons in weapons-handling commenced from the beginning of the third.

Not everyone was imparted training in the making and handling of bombs—this was a specialised job, and the trainees were handpicked for dexterity in the use of fingers. Although Hiren Bora had not been chosen, he had pumped out details from a fellow comrade, and soon knew what exactly needs to be done if ever the occasion required him to use this knowledge.

During the final weeks of training, the recruits were shown how to handle sophisticated electronic gadgets—which included, apart from cell phones and computers, familiarisation with GPS tracking systems and satellite radio. Having been put in charge of the group, Hiren Bora had his work cut out for him, and had to labour harder than his colleagues. Yet, this brought out the best in him, and revealed to his seniors his innate capacity for leadership. Right from the start, much of the menial work in the camp—from sweeping the hutments to taking the buckets of excrement from the latrines to be dumped away from the camp—had to be performed by the latest batch of recruits. But within a couple of weeks, the sergeant major was impressed enough to take him off menial tasks and entrust the job of whipping the recruits into tip-top physical shape. Hiren Bora proved himself not only to be a fierce fighter on the training ground, but also an ace marksman; when there was a gun in his hand, it almost became an extension of his body. Also, the others could not have felt it, but there was a wilful hardening of his heart; he could, without remorse, see the pleading look in the eyes of a recruit—weak and dehydrated from diarrhoea, as he asked to be excused from the morning's PT—and order him to do a triple round of the training ground as punishment...

'Yes, my men, fight fire with fire. The imperialistic Indian State did not hesitate to mow down over seven hundred innocent Assamese civilians who were protesting through peaceful means. This showed

that the colonial mentality of Delhi cannot be changed by Gandhian methods, and that the young patriotic generation had to take up arms. The last two decades have exposed how right we were in choosing to disown peaceful methods, and instead take up arms in a challenge to the Indian State run by the bourgeois. I ask you, has the Assam Accord been implemented so far? How many illegal infiltrators have been deported from Assam back to Bangladesh? The bourgeois-dominated Indian State does not respond to peaceful protest—it responds only to violence. Don't be fooled by recent acts of generosity by Delhi towards Assam—it is only because of the presence of the ULFA that Delhi continues to remain focused on our state, just as the existence of insurgent groups in Manipur and Nagaland keep those two states within Delhi's focus...'

Day in and day out, relentlessly; the most monotonous voice, though occasionally its pitch would rise, and *mama* would become almost hysterical as he spoke, sometimes frothing at the mouth. Now, alone within this growing darkness and deepening cold of the *daini's* lair, Hiren Bora, at the back of his mind, could hear the voice reeling off the words: *'The struggle to attain our objective would be long and hard—a sovereign, independent Assam cannot be attained in a few years or even a few decades. You must bear in mind that the British indulged in almost two centuries of exploitation before Indians could wrest their freedom back. Our movement is barely two decades old...we may have to endure many more decades and have many sacrifices to make before our dream of a sovereign, independent Assam can be reached.'*

'Do not doubt that the ULFA has many enemies, the military and Paramilitary Forces of the Indian State being not the least of them. We have enemies in the corridors of power in Delhi; we have enemies amongst the boot-licking quislings at Dispur. A large section of the Assamese bourgeois intelligentsia has turned against us—it

considers our dream of a sovereign Assam to be an unattainable goal. We have had our setbacks, no doubt; some of our leaders and cadres have lost their determination to carry on the fight, and chose to join the bourgeois brigade instead. They have given our enemies an excuse for indulging in a disinformation campaign—that the ULFA is finished, that we have run out of human and material resources. Yet we are here, aren't we? You are here, aren't you?'

'Yes, we have opted to take on the entire might of the Indian State, its military and Paramilitary Forces, its vast intelligence apparatus, its mammoth financial resources. An impossible feat destined to fail from the very start, they say? Let me tell you why it is not impossible. As I had said, it might take some more decades, but the bourgeois Indian State is too replete with innate contradictions to retain its present character, as well as its armed power. Economic inequality, which mocks at its egalitarian pretensions, contradicting linguistic and cultural differences, the diminishing power and role of the Centre and the rise of regional satraps—it is as if history is gradually repeating itself. Political wisdom dictates that one must await the ideal opportunity to strike at the enemy...you need to understand such an opportunity would present itself sometime in the future. You must understand that the break-up of the self-contradicting, unwieldy Indian State is inevitable, and that it is then that we will seize our chance...'

THE UNEATEN MEAL

He had not drifted off to sleep. He was not fully awake. Rather, he was in a sort of self-induced trance—a trick he had learned from one of his comrades in the KIA. The *daini's* lair was drowned in pitch-black darkness; the thickening fog had wetted the skin on the exposed parts of his body—his face and hands—and these now had the feel of ice; but this did not bother Hiren Bora as he lay upon the mist-drenched earth and allowed scenes from the past to flit across the screen of his memory. Not in an orderly sequence of frames following an ordered time-schedule, rather, in a seamless medley of recollections jumbled up in a mind which could—in the state of repose he was in—pick out bits and pieces, and leisurely slot them in the proper order. The cold dampness within the *daini's* lair triggered off recollections of his first feel of the cloying, perpetual dampness of the Kachin earth; just as in Assam during the monsoon season, it had rained there unceasingly for the first four months of their stay in the KIA camp. Much of their outdoor training had been done in the rain and consequent slush; two recruits had died in that period, both from an undiagnosed disease that discoloured their skin and disfigured their faces. There had been nothing the camp doctor could do—'a new viral strain,' he had shrugged his shoulders and said. Hiren Bora and the others had emerged from the training period in the right frame of body and mind; they received bad news towards the end of their training: some cadres of two camps in Myanmar had surrendered at the 4th Corps Army Headquarters of the Indian Army at Tezpur; the chief of the ULFA's *Enigma* unit had dispatched an SOS for reinforcement—Hiren Bora and a few select trainees were sent to an ULFA camp at Myanmar.

There had neither been time nor enough old hands for the newcomers to be put on training forays. Yet, the dip in morale after the surrender had to be immediately countered, and something which would attract media attention while showing the world that the ULFA still wielded clout had to be accomplished. Anti-insurgency measures in upper Assam undertaken by the Indian Armed Forces were making a tangible impact; a highly effective network of spies and informers had been set up, and older ULFA comrades had been thoroughly identified by the army and police. They would immediately be recognised by someone or the other in the vast spy network; the need of the moment, therefore, was to send cadres yet unknown to the Indian establishment, so they could penetrate the anti-insurgency shield. Hiren Bora had volunteered to be a part of the mission the moment it was broached before him and his comrades. The camp's captain had received positive feedback from the headquarters about this young man. Anyway, it would be self-defeating for a veteran cadre to head the group, since it would increase the danger of detection manifold. And so, Hiren Bora had been asked to lead the mission. The target chosen had been a safe one, keeping in mind the rawness of those assigned to carry out the assignment. Yet, it accorded well with ULFA's ideology and had sufficient propaganda value—blow up a part of an oil pipeline near Nahorkotiya. The fact that after the Assam movement and the signing of an accord between the movement's leaders and the Indian government, a couple of refineries had been set up within Assam. They made little difference to the ULFA, and one of the main thrusts of its propaganda continued to be the exploitation of the region's natural wealth by the fascist bourgeois elements of mainland India. Moreover, the blaze resulting in an explosion at the pipeline, would be bright enough to grace local and national newspapers and TV channels in the form of spectacular images!

The three-member unit had crossed over to the Indian side and taken shelter in the Lakhipathar area; they hid within the hut of a farmer who had been paid generously for his 'hospitality'. On the second night, at Lakhipathar, a linkman had made contact and had given them a hand-drawn map, with as updated details as possible of army and police patrols en route to the target. Hiren Bora, having taken a quick look at the map by the light of a kerosene lantern, noted how carelessly that route-map had been drawn. Also, that the time-frame for reaching the demarcated spot, completing the operation, and retreating to a safer zone was none too accurate since it did not allow for sufficient time needed for a secure retreat. Later, he realised that the inconsistencies and inaccuracies, as also the fact the linkman had not looked him in the eye while replying to his queries, should have been pointers. But he had not been as experienced then as he was now; the enemy had come in the dead of the night and called out to them to surrender. 'In the ensuing fierce gunfight, two of the insurgents and the only other civilian in the cottage were killed, while one insurgent managed to escape', a report in a regional newspaper read. Hiren Bora had managed to slither away to safety with just a bullet-graze upon his shoulder, along with the bag containing material required for the explosion. The contingency plan discussed with his superiors entailed abortion of the mission and a retreat to the Myanmar camp in case of any setback, but Hiren Bora had other plans. Taking unsought and unwelcomed help from people he knew to get shelter during daytime, he had his wound patched up, reached the designated target spot and set up the IED along with a timer—and was well away from the area by day-break. 'Huge Explosion At Oil Pipeline Near Nahorkotiya', the headline in the regional English newspaper had screamed the next day. The electronic media had, of course, reported the explosion even quicker, repeatedly telecasting images of the fierce blaze and thick, black plumes of smoke.

That had been the first of many exploits which accumulated with the passage of time to create the charismatic aura now surrounding the name of Hiren Bora. Towards the end of 2002, Indian intelligence agencies received reports that the small ULFA camps in Myanmar were being dismantled because security had become too tight in upper Assam for effective operations, as also due to information received by the outfit from the KIA headquarters of another possible joint anti-insurgency operation by the Indian and Myanmar Armed Forces. The number of camps set up by the ULFA in the jungles of Bhutan close to the India-Bhutan border—as also in the Chakma hill areas of the Chittagong District in Bangladesh—had been increased, and a bulk of the ULFA cadres had made their way to those camps. There had also been a tie-up with a recently-formed insurgent outfit from Meghalaya, and a base had been set up there. Apparently, the ULFA's focus was shifting from upper to lower Assam, with the principal city of Guwahati as the main target. Indian intelligence agencies had followed these developments closely but were unable to respond because both Bangladesh and Bhutan, for different political reasons, were loath to embark on joint anti-insurgency operations with the Indian Army.

However, what had not reached the ears of Indian intelligence was the presence of a single ULFA camp deep within the dense jungles on the India-Myanmar border, close to the Arunachal Pradesh—under the charge of Lance Corporal Hiren Bora (one of the rare cases where a relative newcomer to the outfit had been given a commission as well as responsibility of handling an entire camp). The insurgents in the camp had lain low for a while; ULFA activities ceased perceptibly in upper Assam while there was a comparative increase of the same in lower Assam. But during the lull in upper Assam operations in the winter of 2002, Hiren Bora had re-entered Indian territory on a single occasion. He went alone and with no specific orders from headquarters; on the night of 26 December 2002, he was with his family—handing over a little money to Pitai, and answering the hundred and odd questions thrown at him by a hysterically joyous Okon while feasting on the sumptuous spread laid out by Ai and his younger sister. By morning, he was gone as suddenly he had arrived; he had spent a week in hostile territory, now looking at the layout from a completely different perspective than the one when he had been a law-abiding citizen. He had returned to the Myanmar camp with invaluable intelligence for his superiors—that security had perceptibly relaxed, and perhaps after a couple of months' wait, operations could be resumed in upper Assam. No doubt the army had cleared the Lakhipathar area, but it had once again slackened patrolling of those jungles, so temporary set-ups were possible in that strategic spot, from where to strike at the hated enemy.

Hiren Bora's meticulously crafted report went as high as the commander-in-chief of ULFA's *Enigma* unit. The latter had been impressed enough to relay the report to the commander-in-chief of the ULFA's armed wing. The immediate outcome was the investing of responsibility upon Hiren Bora to plan and execute operations in upper Assam; according to the directive such operations needed to be less ambitious initially, given the limited resources—both in terms of men and material of the outfit in Myanmar during that point of time. But later, more audacious ones would have to be launched directly against the Indian Paramilitary Forces. The ULFA High Command had also enquired if reinforcement was required, but Hiren Bora had replied in the negative—a small group which could streak swiftly across enemy territory while launching a series of assaults was the need of the hour. The barrage of lightning strikes against oil installations and communication networks throughout upper Assam beginning from April 2003 took the Indian Armed Forces by surprise. A small group rapidly on the move seemed to be involved; the name of Hiren Bora aka Rongmon Changmai aka Shamshad Hussain kept appearing repeatedly on the intelligence radar. It was clear to all concerned that this lad from Chungijan was of a different mettle, and had already taken up the role of a mission leader. That he had made it to the India's intelligence agencies' list of most wanted of ULFA insurgents in so short a time was almost magical.

Meanwhile, the Bhutanese were getting restive (in fact, in May 2003 Bhutan's king Jigme Wanchuk, under pressure from Delhi, had called upon the people of Bhutan to expel the ULFA from their land); so insurgent activities directed from within the Himalayan kingdom had to be suspended to allow the friction to subside. This entailed greater activity through the Meghalaya corridor in lower Assam, and on the part of the small group still holed up in Myanmar. Towards the middle of May, the unit led by Hiren Bora sneaked into Lakhipathar, and set up temporary camp there to make sporadic forays. Army and civil intelligence soon woke up to the realisation that the Lakhipathar area had been re-occupied by the insurgent group, and a full-scale clean-up drive was initiated from the fourth week of June 2003— forcing the unit back into Myanmar territory. Yet, two months later it re-entered Indian territory, and with a tenacity which astonished the paramilitary and civil authorities, reconstructed the camps at Lakhipathar destroyed during the drive and commenced operations once more—playing a devious catch-me-if-you-can game. Hiren Bora split his group in two, himself leading one of them in carrying out sabotage, while the other was put to extortion and kidnapping to acquire funds for the outfit. On 25 August, just days after the Indian State celebrated its Independence Day, Hiren Bora's group blew up the rail-track between Lakwa and Safrai. The objective had been less to disrupt communication in a comparatively insignificant area— since not too many trains ran across that stretch of the mammoth Indian Railways—and more to cock a snook at the establishment by hitting a target right under their nose—the area being in tight control of the Indian Army which had bases close by.

The Indian Armed Forces had retaliated with a sustained anti-insurgency campaign with dual objectives, the first being to flush out the group responsible for the act of sabotage. But there was another ancillary aim: incidents such as the railway-track explosion could be conveniently used to conduct raids in local villages and pick up people, especially youths, for interrogation while keeping them in lock-up for a number of days—the Armed Forces (Special Powers) Act gave them the authority to pick up whoever they pleased. Such terror-inducing raids had rarely yielded much useful results or information—it was merely a part of the psychological warfare to arouse anti-ULFA feelings amongst the villagers, who would be made more than aware who their true masters were, and of the danger of giving shelter or help to the insurgents. The anti-insurgency drive had had its desired effect; it also emboldened many potential victims of ULFA's extortion to contact the civil authorities the moment any member of the outfit got in touch with them...traps were laid, and some members of the outfit had walked into them and been either captured or shot dead (though purported instructions had been to take them alive if possible, the low level officers and jawans occasionally deemed it safer to do so otherwise); others barely managed to escape. Things were getting tougher for the ULFA. The increased surveillance had coerced Hiren Bora's depleted group to go back to their hideout in Myanmar; he duly reported of the stringent security measures reintroduced in upper Assam to his superiors based in Bhutan—of the enhanced guarding of railway-tracks and oil installations, as also of the hostile ground situation where it was getting more difficult to hire informants or to get villagers to offer shelter. Apparently, by now every village had informers reporting back to the authorities!

New instructions had come from the General Council of the ULFA, most of the top guns of which were now in Bangladesh, under the sheltering umbrella of the Khaleda Zia government. Hiren Bora was informed that intelligence inputs suggested diplomatic efforts were on to convince the Myanmar *junta* to undertake another drive with the Indian Army to destroy ULFA camps close to the international border—though there was only a single camp manned solely by the ULFA, the spate of whose activities in upper Assam had misled the Indian establishment to presume there were many. Simultaneously, friends in the NSCN had conveyed the news that personnel of the India's RAW had visited KIA headquarters once more (again carrying heavy bags, significantly!), and held conferences which boded no good, so quick decisions were needed to be made. The new instructions emanating from the General Council were to disband camp and trek across the foothills along the north bank of the Brahmaputra to join a camp sited in Bhutan. But prior to that, they were to carry out one final, spectacularly savage act which would send out a gruesome message to the enemy: slaughter non-combatants! Hiren Bora, who by then had earned sufficient trust of the central leadership to be made privy to even the most secret information, knew precisely how to implement the latest instructions. Since it was now dependent on the Khaleda Zia regime for logistical support, the ULFA had abandoned its anti-Bangladeshi stance; thus, it would have to be a new type of non-combatant who must be targeted! Towards the end of November, Hiren Bora embarked on his final trip that year to upper Assam, along with two comrades. He made use of the opportunity to pay his last visit to his family at Chungijan, cleverly simulating the love he no longer felt…though he gave Pitai money (which he promptly passed on to his wife) and small gifts to his mother, sister and Okon. Then, he had re-joined his comrades and walked into a brick-kiln at Kakopathar, and shot dead 11 migrant, Hindi-speaking workers after lining them up against a wall. Within a fortnight of the savage butchery, Hiren Bora and his unit were entrenched in an ULFA camp on the India-Bhutan border close to the Manas National Park.

Not for long, however! It was somewhat surprising that the ULFA leadership had not seen it coming; on the night of 20 December 2003, the Indian Army along with Bhutanese military personnel launched *Operation All Clear*—an all-out assault upon an outfit boxed in from every side, an inevitable carnage. Heavily-clothed and heavily-armed men had materialised out of the thick mist to shoot or bayonet ULFA cadres to death as they slept in their makeshift tents. The ULFA camps were razed to the ground; having first shifted through the dead bodies and the wreckage for intelligence-relevant material, the camps were set on fire. Hundreds of ULFA cadres were killed or captured, including over a dozen of the middle-rung leaders. Some of the corpses lay within dense jungles to be fed upon by scavengers and, thus, were finally listed as 'missing in action'. Once they had gotten over the surprise, the ULFA cadres fought back fiercely and inflicted casualties amongst their adversaries; it had been an unequal contest though, and the insurgent outfit suffered such a heavy blow that it took a long time for them to recover. However, Hiren Bora and a few trusted compatriots had managed to slip across the 'chicken-neck'—to the safety of Bangladesh territory, along with some arms.

Hiren Bora would never forget that terrible night. Later, the Indian establishment had announced triumphantly that it had irreversibly broken the ULFA's back, conveniently choosing to ignore the reality that the top leadership was safely ensconced in Bangladesh; especially the most dreaded and powerful of them all—the commander-in-chief of the outfit's armed wing. Time after time, the commander-in-chief had proved his organisational skills, rebuilding the ULFA after every setback, and simultaneously creating an international network encompassing China, Myanmar, Bhutan, and Bangladesh, and having four ULFA battalions directly under his command. Hiren Bora did not see much action during his brief sojourn in Bangladesh. In the Chakma Hill areas, Chittagong, Buxa Bazaar, and Dacca— accompanied by agents of Pakistan's ISI, he was constantly shifted from one spot to another on minor assignments. But he did take one huge step in his life; at Dacca, he was summoned for a meeting with the commander-in-chief of the armed wing himself. The latter had received a great deal of feedback on this particular comrade. He, apparently, liked what he saw, for the very same day Hiren Bora was inducted into his elite band of bodyguards.

What had made Hiren Bora return once more to his native village, to a life and loves he had wilfully forsaken? As he lay within the inky darkness of the *daini's* lair, a bleak smile suddenly creased his hardened features—neither filial nor fraternal love, certainly! Love no longer had a slot in his cynical soul; the three and a half years of existence as an insurgent fugitive—constantly on the run and desperately focussed on simple survival—had swept clean memories of childhood and youth, so that the phase of his life in Chungijan appeared to be a distant, imagined dream. Ai, Pitai, Bhoni (Bai), and Okon were insubstantial apparitions conjured up by the mind. Had it been a kind of death-wish, this night's return to his native village? Dumb creature that it was, doesn't the *hepa* know a trap baited with death forever awaits it at the very next bend? Or does it know that the compulsions of the moment render it blind and oblivious? The wry smile continued to linger at the edges of Hiren Bora's lips; pretence had to be maintained! Old ties needed to be kept alive; yes, it had been the compulsions of the moment which had made him come to this bamboo-cage and wait for the night to deepen. He had been thrust into a mistrustful world where deception was the norm; only Chungijan held the people he could absolutely trust. So he had come to his native village well knowing that love and trust could be made use of. Yes, pretences had to be maintained.

Over three and a half years… So much had happened within this period! He had straddled five countries, seen and heard things unimaginable for a lad who had been born into an impecunious family and grew up in a tiny village in a remote corner of India. Three and a half years…almost an entire lifetime packed into this short span, such had been the hectic, breathless pace. Others had chosen to give up and surrender to the bourgeois-ruled Indian State. But not he—not Hiren Bora! There was nothing to go back to, even if there was nothing to look forward to.

The highlight of those action-packed years had undoubtedly been the trip to China, to the unique and wonderful city of Kunming, the capital of China's southern Yunnan Province bordering Myanmar; in the entourage of the commander-in-chief, with the aid of the KIA. Their group had taken a different route on this occasion, cutting across the loosely-guarded India- Bangladesh border at the Cachar district in Barak valley, crossing over to Manipur and then on to Myanmar. A dreaded Manipuri extremist group had guided them across the Manipur, before they made contact with their KIA escorts at Mytkyina. The commander-in-chief seemingly had a good relationship with every insurgent outfit in the North-East, and was trusted by all. Their escorts had taken them to the camp of the KIA's 3rd Brigade based near the China-Myanmar border. The cadres in this camp had been involved in more engagements with the Myanmar Army than those in the KIA's 2nd Brigade camp. This was because a small river marked the boundary between China and Myanmar at that point, and there was a narrow suspension bridge over the river much used by the KIA to go to and come from its camp within China, housing the General Headquarters of the outfit. There were constant skirmishes between the KIA and the Myanmar Army, which the former controlled and the latter tried to destroy. A couple of days spent at the KIA's 3rd Brigade camp, and the commander-in-chief and his small band was escorted over this bridge to the KIA Headquarters. From now on, there was no need for trekking on foot; a good road led to Kunming and their hosts were kind enough to lend them an old but trusted jeep—along with a driver and an interpreter. The commander-in-chief's mission was to get aid from the Chinese communist regime in the form of much needed weapons. *Operation All Clear* had resulted in huge losses for the ULFA in terms of men and material; while new manpower could be recruited and trained, the seizure of a great amount of arms and ammunitions had been a crippling blow. Also, increased vigilance and greater intelligence input within Assam saw lesser earnings for the outfit through extortion. The commander-in-chief would be meeting a Chinese official to discuss assistance to the beleaguered outfit, so it could carry on its fight against the bourgeois Indian establishment.

Hiren Bora had been enthralled. Although he had been to Myanmar, Bhutan, and Bangladesh, the ambience was too similar for a true feel of being in a foreign country. In Myanmar and Bhutan, there had hardly been much contact with the local people; he had mostly been confined to camps in the jungles. In Bangladesh, he had stayed in cities like Dacca, but the places and the people were similar to those of Assam. China was altogether different, a new ambience and a novel culture… The winding, mountainous road had given way to flat-land with long stretches of paddy—the men and women dressed in shirts and pyjamas, wide brimmed bamboo-hats on heads—working in them. They crossed small, busy settlements with quaint names which Hiren Bora had trouble pronouncing; occasionally, industrial conglomerates. The air echoed of industriousness as opposed to the lethargy which seemed to be the normal ambience in Assam; the Chinese were a busy lot. Kunming—despite its blatant urban aura, the thick, slow-moving traffic on its streets, and the smog which hung over it in the evening—was a revelation. There was a certain orderliness to the chaos; unlike Guwahati, the streets were quite clean despite the numerous construction activities in progress—an overt reminder of China's burgeoning economy. None of the stenches associated with the hated city of Guwahati, politeness everywhere as also faces wreathed in smiles, and much nodding of heads and politely uttered words—no matter that none in their group understood a word of what was being said.

The Chinese authorities, like the KIA, had been gracious hosts. Their group of four (six, if one counted the interpreter and the driver) had been accommodated in a government guesthouse overlooking the beautiful Cuihu lake; beside the lake was a sprawling park filled with tree-lined walkways and canopies built in typical Chinese style. Hiren Bora and a companion with no role to play in the negotiations had enough free time on their hands to venture into the Cuihu Lake Park, sit upon a bench under the shade of a willow tree, listening to the music being played all around them. Then, as evening descended, dancing groups in exotic, indigenous costumes accompanied by musicians appeared as if from nowhere, transforming the park into a magical realm full of music, dancing and joyous laughter. Hiren Bora was canny enough to realise the two of them were being watched and followed, but it did not prevent him from revelling in the atmosphere and letting the music—so much like the *huchari* songs he used to sing in Chungijan—flow into his soul. The food served in the guesthouse, too, had been delicious. Hiren Bora had known better than to ask what was being served. The next day he and his companion, this time accompanied by a local guide, had left the more modern section of the metropolis to venture into the old city—as different from the former as oil and water. Numerous narrow lanes, century-old, many-storied buildings perched precariously on both sides, balconies draped with washed clothes hung to dry, and ducks and chickens freely roaming on the lanes—an incongruity within the urban environment. Some of the bigger houses having courtyards had been invariably converted into family-run restaurants. Strange faces and customs, the blend of the modern and the ancient, orderliness and cleanliness—Hiren Bora knew what he would like to make of Guwahati if ever given the chance! Those wonderful days spent in Kunming had been made even more magical by the fact that the negotiations had been successful, and the Chinese authorities were willing to help out—the first consignment of arms and ammunitions would be reaching the outfit through Chittagong port within two months...

Hiren Bora did not see any future for the ULFA, its cause or for himself. That many of the remaining ULFA cadres had been demoralised after *Operation All Clear* he had no doubt; there had been murmurs in the rank and file about the bourgeois lifestyle being led by the ULFA's top-ranking leadership in Bangladesh, even as the outfit ranted against the Indian bourgeois establishment. Far too many cadres were surrendering to the Indian Armed forces; the surrendered cadres in turn were being utilised by the Indian intelligence agencies to give away information about the outfit and reveal vital secrets. The ebbing away of popular support among the Assamese masses meant that the ULFA was finding it increasingly difficult to carry out its so-called war against the Indian Paramilitary Forces; the kind of insurgent-army clashes which had taken place in the initial stage of the ULFA's birth were a thing of the past. Nowadays, if any encounter took place, it was only because the Indian paramilitary and police had been able to detect the exact location of an ULFA group on a specific mission, and had raided its hideout. There had been very few prisoners taken during such 'encounters', mostly cadavers! The outfit had suffered one blow after another since 2003; on 2 August 2004, one of the most dreaded of its leaders—the commander of its 28th Battalion and chief of its *Enigma* Unit— had been captured (though the Indian establishment had projected it as a surrender).

Demoralisation had bred desperation; the decay in ideals had brought about degeneration in modus operandi. For instance, the ULFA, along with other insurgent outfits of the North-East, had every year called for public boycott of events such as India's Independence Day or Republic Day. At the beginning, when the ULFA's writ ran across the Brahmaputra valley, the public had always kept away from the government's flag-hoisting ceremonies on these two days; thus Indian flags had been unfurled and speeches made by politicians was in empty stadiums and other arenas. But, as the influence of the outfit waned, the people began, once more, to throng to these venues during those two occasions. The ULFA's frustration was evident in the kind of strategy it suddenly adopted to stop such attendance through intimidation; on 15 August 2004, a time-bomb, planted in the Independence Day flag-hoisting ground at Dhemaji on the north bank of the Brahmaputra at the extreme eastern corner of Assam, had exploded and killed 16 school children and a spectator—but none in the VIP enclosure! Unfortunately, the utter shock which had swept across the valley at this dastardly act and the sense of abhorrence palpable even among ardent ULFA supporters had not restored sanity. On 26 January this year, a bomb planted at the Republic Day parade venue—the prestigious Judge's Field in Guwahati—had injured three, again members of the public and not politicians or policemen.

No doubt this blast was of low intensity, designed more to show the public that the ULFA still possessed clout—the Judge's Field on that day had been a top security area, yet the ULFA had succeeded in breaching security, and less to kill or injure. But public revulsion had been no less, and rather than marvel at the outfit's bravado, the people—particularly a section of the intelligentsia—had denounced its folly and lack of concern for the lives of the people. For a few months after the blast, somewhat reinvigorated by the supply of Chinese weaponry (collected and distributed among its cadres with the aid of the ISI) as well as induction of fresh blood, the outfit had embarked on a spree of attacks on Indian Paramilitary Forces and bomb-blasts at oil-installations in upper Assam. Hiren Bora had led some of these operations, but the burst of activity had failed to enthuse the people of Assam into once again siding with the ULFA's cause—the clamour was for peace to return to the region. The General Council of the outfit had finally acknowledged that the organisation's objective must not go against those of the people. A truce was unilaterally declared and recently, just a few months ago on the September 8, a People's Consultative Group—comprising of select individuals from different segments of the Assamese society who the outfit trusted—had been formed by it to hold talks on its behalf with the Government of India.

The first round of discussions between the group and the Union Government of India had taken place on October 26, but Hiren Bora had no expectation that this essay on the part of the ULFA would succeed. He was intelligent enough to understand that the leadership of the outfit had been coerced into negotiating from a disadvantaged position—the victor rarely gives away too many concessions while negotiating with the vanquished. Yet, he was indifferent to whatever the outcome might lead to; as he constantly reminded himself, despite the constant barrage of propaganda his brain had been subjected to during the period of training, he had not made ULFA's core objective—creation of an independent, sovereign Assam—his own. All he had wanted when he first joined the outfit was to lash out no matter what at; to assuage his hurt ego for the betrayal he had suffered, though he did not quite know whom to blame. The last few years of constant running and killing had eerily swabbed away the humanity from his soul, turning him into a wild beast; all he wanted to do now was to live for the present, to blindly follow instructions from the commander-in-chief, even though it might involve the slaughter of innocents...

Even the cicadas had fallen silent. The frogs no longer croaked amongst the ripening paddy in the fields. Fireflies twinkled amidst the all-embracing darkness, creating foggy pearls of moving light. Hiren Bora could hear the beating of his own heart, so silent it had grown! The bamboo no longer creaked. Their leaves rustled in the breeze no more.

The deathly, cold-drenched fog did not bother him, but he was terribly hungry; it had been quite a while now since he had last eaten. He was tempted to walk out of the *daini's* lair into his family's house, where Ai would be waiting with a hot meal. Hiren Bora fought down the temptation despite the fierce hunger.

He had told Rajeev he would enter his home exactly at eleven o' clock that night, and stay for an hour—a necessary precaution. He would actually slip into the house at 2:00 am. No one could be trusted. The three-hour gap was needed to ensure Rajeev had communicated the information to no one but Ai and Pitai. Hiren Bora looked at the luminous dial of his watch. Exactly midnight. Still two hours to go.

Once again, he was suffused with an almost overwhelming urge to leave the dank darkness and head for the comforting warmth awaiting him in what he had once called his 'home', amongst his 'family.' They must all be awake; their eyes must be turning again and again towards the face of the alarm clock—the one he had brought on his last visit, with a dial that glowed in the dark. Ai must be fretting that the food she had so lovingly cooked would become cold.

But Hiren Bora had resisted temptations stronger than these. Caution like that of a beast in the wild had become second nature to him. Caution was a key to survival. He would wait.

Then, seemingly from far away, a humming sound wafted into his ears. In a swift, feline move, Hiren Bora sat upright, ears cocked.

No doubt about it. The sound of a heavy vehicle—perhaps of two—the thick drape of fog could not muffle it away from his sharp, well-trained ears.

The sound suddenly ceased. There was silence once again.

Hiren Bora smiled, the same humourless, sardonic smile. There was no use waiting any longer! He stood up, dipped into his bag and brought out a small parcel wrapped in sheets of newspaper. Switching on the tiny, flat torch he always carried, he wrote a brief note on a piece of paper, which he stuck to the cord used to tie up the parcel. Placing the packet on the ground, Hiren Bora emerged swiftly from the bamboo grove.

The meal cooked by Ai would remain uneaten tonight. Hiren Bora entered the jungle and melted into the foliage.

BAGS DON'T FLY

He smelled not only of piss but fear and shame. A *rakhyasa* had stared straight into Okon's eyes; this brought about an uncontrollable fit of shivers. The violent trembles persisted after those *rakhyasas* had left, so Ai had to pull him to her bosom and wrap him along with herself in Pitai's *endi-chadar*. 'There, there, it's all right now, it's all right,' she had had to whisper repeatedly as she stroked his head, warming his soul with her body till the tremors subsided. Pitai slouched down on the *murrah*, utterly crushed and castrated—he vented his sense of impotence by cursing under his breath Hiru, and the day his son was born. Ai let go of Okon; she filled a *chaki* with mustard-oil, lit the cotton wick and placed the earthen lamp under the *tulsi* plant in the backyard. Unmindful of the fog and cold, she prostrated herself on the damp ground and muttered out her gratitude to Lord Vishnu that Hiru had not come tonight; she prayed he be kept safe. Bai lit the kitchen fire and heated some water, and took it in a bucket to the open, bamboo-walled bathroom in the backyard so Okon could have a bath and change into the only other half-pant and shirt he had. 'We can't let the food go to waste,' Ai said, trying to sound normal. 'You'll eat it before going to school.'

'I'm not go-go-going to school today,' Okon said in a defiant stammer. 'I don't want to go to school ever again.'

Bai's voice was calm, reassuring. 'But you must go, Okon. The results of the class final exams are due any day. Perhaps they'll be out today, who knows?'

'I do-do-don't care,' Okon said. 'I shan't go.'

He retreated to his tiny room, and lifting the threadbare mosquito curtain, climbed on to his bed. It was as if his self had sunk into a deep, black abyss, so bleak was the desolation. Once again, a betrayal. Although Okon, despite his tender age, conceded it may not have been a betrayal at all. 'I hate you, Hirukai,' he had silently mouthed out, even as his eyes filled with tears once more. 'How I hate you!' Gradually the tears dried out of their own accord; it had perhaps been a blessing Hirukai had not come—had not Ai lit a *chaki* under the tulsi plant, thanking Lord Vishnu for the same? But a niggling doubt, which in reality was a hope that kept recurring in Okon's mind—had it been a blessing, after all? If Hirukai had come and been taken, would not things have become all right again? They might have put him in the camp for surrendered cadres Okon had heard about… Perhaps, later, they would allow him to come home and things would be as they had been before. But then, what if they took him to jail instead and shut him away forever? The boy remained confused and uncertain. He did not know what to think.

He savagely warded off the yearning and desolation; and then, with sudden clarity, understood what the doubt and the hope was all about. Just a single, distant improbable possibility, one only he could surmise. He would have left at once had he only dared to; but it was now the most bewitched hour of the night—the ghouls and demons flitting about in the dark, the witch perched atop a betel nut tree and the old ghost who lived in the jungle, they were at their most potent at his hour! The more he dwelt on it, the more likely it grew—Hirukai would have kept his word unless forced by circumstances! Okon, however, would have to wait sometime longer to find out; the darkness outside was at its deepest—just the right ambience for those creatures of the night, some of whom were perhaps perched on the rooftop of their cottage. The silence outside was absolute and overpowering; the raid on their cottage had been accompanied by a great deal of noise and light, but not a household had stirred, not a villager had shouted out an anonymous yell of protest; no one had come to their house even after the *rakhyasas* had left. Fear had descended on the village; like the wintry fog, it had wrapped itself around cottages and paddy fields, and shut away past empathy and fellowship. Now, in the depth of his heart, the youngster appreciated the true value of a family; understood the crushed helplessness reflected in Pitai's stooped shoulders. His father made a most unlikely saviour, for the *rakhyasas* were too powerful. If only Hirukai had never left, if only he would give himself up like others had done and come back to be the family's saviour! Okon himself had felt the same overwhelming helplessness and anger as Pitai when a male *rakhyasa* had needlessly frisked Bai. Hirukai would not have allowed anyone to touch Bai—if only he were back!

The hours dragged on; the boy slid open the lid of the ribbed bamboo window slightly, and stole a peek outside and then quickly shut it to keep out the intense cold. The darkness had perceptibly lessened, a sure sign that the evil, bewitched hours had elapsed. Okon stealthily got out of bed and wrapped a blanket around himself, so that his upper torso and head were fully covered and only a part of the forehead and eyes were exposed. He cautiously unlatched the bamboo bar from the front door; it creaked open but the others in the cottage seemed to be too deep asleep to have heard.

Outside, it was bitterly cold and the thin blanket proved a flimsy defence. Yet, the fog—which reduced visibility to a metre or two—was a blessing, for it prevented inquisitive eyes from detecting the draped, speeding figure. Okon knew the area so well that the fog did not prove a hindrance. Within 20 minutes he had reached the bamboo grove, and was inside the *daini's* lair five minutes later. He closed his eyes for a while to adjust to the clearing's muted light; his heart skipped a beat when he opened them, and through squinting eyes, saw the hazy dark outline of the packet lying on the ground. Hirukai had come! Hirukai had been there!

He rode down his excitement—there was not a single, precious minute to waste! The paddy had ripened in the fields, no doubt, and the villagers could afford to wake up later than had it been summer. Yet, the fog might thin out, and some idiot of a villager might take it into his head to get up early and spot him. He could not take the risk; though he was bursting with excitement, he could not squander time in opening the parcel there and then—that would have to wait till he was safely back in the cottage. He slithered out as quickly as he could through the bamboo maze; the light had strengthened outside, and in spite of himself, he could not resist stopping for a moment to steal a look at the packet. It was then that he saw the hastily- scrawled note stuck to one of the cords used to tie it up. Plucking it out, Okon took a quick glance. The brief note was addressed to him. He read it, and then as instructed by Hirukai, tore it to small pieces and scattered them on the ground.

Once again, the fog proved to be adequate cover. He did not encounter a single soul on the return trip, not even a village mongrel. Noiselessly, like a ghost, he slipped into the cottage through the front door. Pitai, Ai and Bai were in the front room, waiting anxiously for him.

Since it was a tiny town clinging to the national highway like a foetus to an umbilical cord—dependent on it for nourishment and growth—Doomdooma was expectedly dusty, dirty, and noisy. The highway, as it passed through the town, was a crowded, jumbled mass of pedestrians, bicycles, rickshaws, *thelas*, scooters, motorcycles, auto-rickshaws, cars, buses, trucks, et al. It being morning, with offices and educational institutions just about to start, the mass was denser than at any other time except, perhaps, in the evening when the sides of the highway became a makeshift open market, and hordes of people jostled each other while bargaining for vegetables, fish, or poultry.

Bhogali, a tiny restaurant with stained wooden tables and a glass showcase displaying trays of sweetmeats and *nimkis*—and serving as a counter behind which sat the owner—was also expectedly dusty, dirty, and noisy—and fly-ridden in the bargain! Outside, a local bus had just disgorged its load of passengers, many of whom headed towards the restaurant for a quick cup of tea before going their way, so the restaurant was doing brisk business. Two serving boys, both in their teens, were moving about with lightning speed—taking orders, clearing empty cups and plates, wiping tables, and exchanging witticisms with the cook and the cleaner in the kitchen at the back. The dominant reek was of stale vegetable ghee.

At 8:30 am on the morning of December 27, Inspector Lahiri sat upon a plastic chair at a table at the furthest end in Bhogali restaurant, chewing reluctantly upon a cold, leathery slice of *poorie* dipped in *alu-dom,* and reflecting upon the excruciating torture his tummy was being subjected to. Yes, passion had its price! He had been paying it for the last few days, holed up in a dingy hotel infested with cockroaches and bedbugs, coordinating the raid at Chungijan. Actually, he was more of a conduit for information rather than the one planning the operation and putting the pieces in place. He had arrived in Doomdooma by a night bus on the morning of December 24, checked into the hotel, and begun sniffing around at once—surreptitiously meeting some of his contacts in Doomdooma and Chungijan, having a quiet chat with the *gaon-burrah* of the village, and also getting telephonic inputs from a colleague in the police department based at Tinsukia. By the evening of December 25, he had homed in upon a youth named Rajeev—a mechanic at a garage in Doomdooma but originally hailing from Chungijan.

Not only had Lahiri been able to confirm his hunch had been accurate, he had also been able to extract the date and the time from the mechanic—the poor, none too bright garage-hand had been flabbergasted as to how the authorities knew he was involved; had begged Lahiri not to arrest him for he had only passed on the information given to him by Hirukai, whom he feared as he did Lord *Yama*. The inspector knew Rajeev was not in any way linked to the ULFA and could assure him no action would be taken, but advised he keep his mouth shut for if Hiren Bora learned of his 'betrayal', his goose would be cooked! The DGP, to whom Lahiri had directly passed on the information, had been ecstatic; he had immediately alerted the DCP of Tinsukia District, after calling up the SHM and receiving his blessings. The DCP, in turn, had contacted the army base as well as the Superintendent of Police (SP), reiterating the order he had received that the target of the operation be kept a secret from the policemen and the jawans who would take part in the raid. Only when everything had been arranged did Lahiri drop in at the Doomdooma Police Station, identify himself to the OC, and was seated in one of the police jeeps, which rolled into the outskirts of Chungijan towards the fag end of the night of December 26.

No one in the jeep knew who he was, or of the crucial role he had played in this operation. In fact, the others had been puzzled at the presence of this short, bespectacled man with a greying moustache—who looked more like a college professor. Thus, he had not been the target of the army captain's passionate outburst after the engagement, conducted with such stealth, tension, and expectation, had turned out to be a damp squib.

'An aged couple, a girl and a boy, bah!' the army man had sarcastically barked at the Additional Superintendent of Police (ASP), who had led his own force. 'Where the devil do you guys get your information from?'

'Perhaps from the army, who knows?' the ASP had retorted. 'It wasn't local info. Sent from Dispur.'

That silenced the army man; if, indeed, it had been the army's intelligence which had led to this wild goose chase, the captain knew better than to pursue the subject any further. The ASP, however, was not one to let an opportunity slip.

'The intended target is actually around in this area,' his voice was seemingly noncommittal. 'I hope you folks know that, at least.'

On the way to Chungijan, Inspector Lahiri had kept a low profile, sitting at the rear of the jeep along with the other ordinary policemen, and not uttering a word. He did not leave the vehicle during the early part of the operation. Only when it was clear that Hiren Bora was not in the cottage, and the raiding party was preparing to return to their respective bases, had Lahiri hopped down, walked briskly towards the cottage and made a quick scan of the interior. He had seen the covered brass plate and *baan-baati* lying on the mud floor of the tiny kitchen, a *pirrah* beside them. The aroma of *joha*-rice still wafted from it; obviously, someone had taken care to re-warm the food just prior to the raid. With no one around, the inspector took a quick peek at the brass plate—rice, sour-fish curry with *dhekia* fern, pickled bamboo-shoots, and red chillies. An uneaten meal—

sumptuous, considering the indigenous environment, and the Inspector knew he had guessed rightly!

Later, back at the police station, Lahiri had asked the OC for some privacy as well as the use of his phone, since he had to make a call to the DGP. The OC, with admirable alacrity, had left his small office and closed the door. Lahiri dialled the number of the DGP's home line; it was as if despite the lateness of the hour, the old coot had been sitting at the other end beside his phone, waiting for it to ring. The receiver was picked up at the second ring and, even before the inspector could say hello, the DGP was barking into the phone:

'So, no civet, huh?'

Lahiri had been taken aback. The old coot remembered! Just one slip of the tongue, and he remembered! It had been a frustrating night; he was developing a migraine and did not need any of this. However, his voice betrayed no emotion and he replied in his habitual, thin, matter of fact tone: 'Sorry sir, the trap was empty.'

'As if I didn't know! Got a call from no less a bugger than the Lt. Gen., and an earful from the SHM. Both had been waiting this late into the night for news of the operation's outcome—you can guess how important they considered it to be! Know what, Lahiri? I've been laying my skin off to save your neck.'

'Thank you, sir. I appreciate it.'

'Told them we had solid evidence gleaned from informers. Also, intercepts confirming Hiren Bora would visit his family tonight. But when we come down to the brass tacks, it was only your bloody hunch! Would make me a laughing stock if that were to be out. So what happened? He didn't take the bait? Or did you miscalculate?'

'I'm more than certain I didn't, sir. A wily fox, our Hiru!'

'Don't mix up your fauna, Lahiri.' The DGP's voice was admonitory, but the inspector could tell he was relishing his little joke. 'You'd claimed your source was infallible.'

'I stick to it, sir. A garage-hand. From Hiru's village. Had no reason to lie.'

'Gave you the exact time, didn't he?'

'Yes, sir. Get in to his home at eleven o' clock, stay for an hour. That's why we rolled in at Chungijan only at 11:30 pm—to give Hiru unrestrained passage. We homed in at the cottage exactly at midnight.'

'To find the trap empty?'

'Right, sir. But the civet was close to the duck-coop!' Lahiri's tongue was firmly in his cheek. If the DGP insisted on playing a game, the inspector would oblige.

'Huh? What do you mean?'

'I took a look inside the cottage... An uneaten meal on the kitchen floor awaiting an unexpected guest—*joha*-rice and fish-curry, sir!'

There was abrupt silence at the other end of the line as the DGP digested this momentous revelation. His voice was suffused with excitement and elation when he finally spoke.

'The others saw it?'

'I don't think they could have missed it, sir. The army people and ours. But I'm none too sure they made any inference—they didn't have the information only you and I know of, sir. Anyway, they were there for an encounter and not to play the detective.'

'Marvellous! You've handed me my card, Lahiri. I can now throw it at those supercilious bastards... including SHM and Lt Gen.'

'Premature intervention, sir...' Lahiri left his sentence tantalisingly unfinished and the DGP pounced upon it.

'That's right. Premature intervention by the army—the force should have waited much longer before making the assault. Mind you, the entire planning for the operation had been done by the army, though based on our intelligence.'

At any other time Lahiri would have pointed out to the fallacies in what the DGP had called his 'card', but he was feeling tired and the headache was worsening. 'Right, sir,' he said tersely.

'You said you had eyes in the village too, didn't you?'

'True, sir. As we waited outside Chungijan, this paid informer told us he had seen a shadowy figure sneak into the cottage before our arrival.'

'Which triggered the raid?'

'Right, sir.'

'But there were at least two dozen pairs of eyes in the raiding party. And no one saw any figure, shadowy or otherwise, leave, did they? Yet, during the actual raid, no Hiru!'

'Right, sir, he did not turn up. Our man in the village had imagined things... a trick of the light, perhaps. It was extremely foggy that night. Or plain, simple greed. The reward money for helping nab Hiru, sir. Greed, too, can play tricks with the mind and the eyes.'

'But he must have been in the neighbourhood...from your observation. So we were dead right with our hunch! The army intervened too quickly... Yes, yes, premature intervention!'

'I'll follow this up in the morning and keep you informed, sir,' Lahiri's innards chuckled at the facility with which his boss had changed 'your hunch' to 'our hunch'! He could not quite conceal the chuckle, but apparently the DGP did not notice it.

'It's in situations like this that the Armed Forces Special Powers Act comes to our aid, what say you, Lahiri? Covers our back! Also, just an impoverished family of an illiterate farmer! Can't hit back, can they? But what about the media?'

'A midnight operation, sir. So, there will certainly be no mention in tomorrow's headlines. Hopefully, since it did not yield anything, there won't be any mention even later.'

'You expect Hiru will remain in the area even after last night's fiasco?'

'If I know my man, I'm certain of it, sir.'

'You want to stay on at the job, don't you?' the old coot laughed, though his chortle sounded incongruous given the night's setback. Lahiri might know his man, but so did the DGP!

'Yes, with your permission, sir. I think I should stick with it. Everything suggests Hiru has re-entered upper Assam with some definite objective. He's the type who doesn't like to leave a job unfinished. If he was nearby, he would have known of the raid. Even if he was not in the area, someone or the other in the outfit would inform him of it. But this raid will simply make him more wary, not drive him away.'

'Oh, you've my permission, all right. We've a lot riding on this, Lahiri. So keep at it. Good hunting!'

Lahiri had winced. Perhaps the DGP had opted to take on the role of an enthusiastic spectator—two antagonists engaged in a game of chess upon an improvised table bathed in sunshine within a park—he, the passing stranger scanning their moves, taking sides, willing one of them silently along in an irrepressible yearning for vicarious excitement. Not a word of chastisement from him despite the failure of the operation; not a phrase of recrimination. Lt. Gen. must have been extremely acerbic, and the SHM must have been habitually polite but the kid gloves surely had hidden fists of iron… Yet, not a rebuke! Oh yes, the old coot, too, was enjoying himself, alright!

He had shaken hands with the OC, and told him he would be around for a while. He also requested the OC to keep his presence in Doomdooma as secret as feasible, while firmly declining his offer to fix a room for him in the local dak bungalow. He had not, of course, explained that stealth, camouflage, and anonymity were key to every hunter's strategy, so it had been by design that he had chosen to stay at the seedy, bug-infested hotel rather than the dak bungalow. Small townships like Doomdooma had not yet gotten over their rusticity; the folks retired as early as possible—the constant 'load-shedding' by the electricity department spurring them towards that end. Thus, Lahiri, choosing to walk back to the hotel instead of a proffered police vehicle, traversed a stretch totally devoid of any human presence; even the street-mongrels—very much a part of any urban conglomerate—had chosen to take refuge elsewhere rather than be out there on the cold, fog-bound highway. The main door of the hotel had been shut; he had had to hammer upon it for almost five minutes before he was let in by a grumpy old waiter, who also doubled as the night watchman.

The bed lay unmade as he had left it; the room, unswept. It was now a virtual mortuary of dead cockroaches and bedbugs (since he had earlier purchased anti-cockroach spray and anti-bedbug powder, and applied both liberally). Preparing to go to bed, he fervently hoped the precautions he had been taking were enough to have kept his identity concealed from interested parties. The civet had not entered the trap; there were other traps to be laid. Now, it was more imperative than ever he keep himself as anonymous as possible. He must continue to present the persona he had assumed to the world at large (meaning the world in and around Doomdooma)—a travelling salesman working for a garment company with headquarters in Kolkata. That he could also speak Bengali fluently and possessed a Bengali surname went well with the persona; indeed, last afternoon he had even visited a local clothes shop armed with a catalogue, enquiring if the owner would consider placing an order. The upscale nature of the clothes illustrated in the catalogue he carried as well as their exorbitant prices had expectedly ensured that the small-town retailer said 'no, thank you'. But pretence had to be maintained and the silly charade played out, for there were eyes everywhere and a stranger staying for some days stood out like a sore thumb in such a small township. It was, he constantly reminded himself, a necessary imposture. If Hiren Bora learnt that a senior police intelligence department officer was staying on for a prolonged period of time in Doomdooma, he might leave the area. Yet, as he secretly admitted, he himself had quite enjoyed the imposture—an overgrown child indulging in cloak and dagger stuff—a kind of make-believe adventure that livened up his drab life. Otherwise it had always been a cerebral essay with him—collate information and come to a conclusion. But now he was on a secret assignment and could actually play at being a secret agent!

What had caused him to be different, he did not have the faintest idea. His father had not been the philosophical type; however, that college lecturer (later promoted to an Assistant Professor) was all the time sighting a deeper moral design in everyday happenings, and never grew tired of inflicting his insights upon his children—all seven of them, three brothers and four sisters currently spread out across the country. Lahiri could remember some homily or the other enunciated by his father at least three-four times per day. In fact, just an hour before his heart conked out and he could no longer comment on the orderliness of the universe and the clockwork precision with which everything ran smoothly and punctually, he had been communicating a profound cliché to his wife. But his spiritual beliefs had, in fact, been conventional and trite.

Lahiri's mother (still alive and living in Kolkata with her eldest son) was armed unassailably with blind faith—two sessions of prayers, in the morning and night; she had not needed to lie upon her bed at night and think about death, for the next destination was heaven which lay just beyond the outer rind of the ozone layer. An aroma of smug, middle-class morality had always wafted like a spicy, garlic-impregnated smell from the kitchen in the air of the house. Neither his mother nor his father asked questions; if she had doubts, the all-knowing father was an encyclopaedia to be referred to. Lahiri suspected his brothers and sisters, too, never asked questions of the uncomfortable type; they had been happy enough to stay within the warmth of materialistic cocoons—buffered by their stoicism as well as inherited (or, perhaps, just imitated) spiritualism, against being cast into the quagmire of doubt by the vagaries of destiny. Lahiri had been the odd one out; an accidental entity fated to wallow in questions to which conventional answers seemed superficial… He did not know why.

He had experienced genuine despair, burrowing worm-like into his mind and soul. Ever since that sudden, startling moment of 'enlightenment' at the existential situation, a mental pendulum in his head had been swinging between exhilaration and depression, though no one could tell. Merely looking at him, he appeared an extraordinarily ordinary man who would not attract a second glance in a crowd. The out-of-the-blue, momentous insight had knocked whatever worldly ambition he might have harboured till then; explained why he still remained a mere 'inspector' while many of his colleagues—less intelligent and perceptive than him—had climbed up the professional ladder and were currently ensconced far higher up. He had not told his wife; his colleagues had been somewhat perplexed and had invested him with the tag of being a bit 'eccentric' though brilliant. But he had actually turned down offers of departmental promotions just because he had not wanted a desk-job, and preferred to work in the field!

Suddenly, late in the night, snuggled within the stained sheets and blankets on the bed of a rundown hotel, Lahiri was suffused with an admixture of exhilaration and sobering self-loathing. The migraine, a continuous throb upon his temples, did not distract him from the introspection. From a distance he had watched a prematurely aged man and woman, a girl feeling naked and vulnerable in the glare of the floodlights despite the clothes she wore to protect herself from the cold, and a young boy, stark terror unmistakeably stamped upon his stunned, tear-filled eyes and wide mouthed face, emerge from the house and stand frozen with hands raised in the air. A scene which should have evoked pity rather than excitement—had the nature of his job turned him into an uncaring hunter, oblivious of all else but the scent of the quarry? A terrifying thought, indeed. Not one to deceive himself, Lahiri believed he knew the answer...but rather than be afraid or contrite, his belly began to rumble with cynical, bellicose laughter. The seeming ambiguity of his perceptions mocked at his coerced passion as well as his bent towards the aspired-for shield of uncaring, pretended dispassion. He had felt pity, yes. Yet, he could not hide from the truth that he had been secretly glad it had not ended so quickly and tamely, glad the game was far from over. A rush of adrenalin abruptly lifted him up, up and up; he felt as though he was not within bedsheets but floating in a windy, vast, and empty space. Sleep became impossible. He got out of the bed to let the cold wash over his body and cool the heat. But December in upper Assam could be terribly cold indeed, and he began to tremble and had to clamber onto the bed and into the blankets to stop the shivering fit. The cold and the tremble had driven the headache away; suddenly, though it was almost daybreak, his mind felt clear and decisive.

He had stopped trying to get some sleep; instead, he attempted to think logically.

Why hadn't the civet entered the trap? Lahiri was almost sure he had been spot on in his hunch—as he had told the DGP, the creature had come near the duck-coop! So what actually happened tonight? Had the civet sniffed the damp, foggy air and been warned away by the hunters' hostile smell? There was, of course, another possibility. It was not beyond Hiru to feed the garage-hand false information and then watch the forces embark on a wild goose chase. To test the security network, as it were. So there was a slim chance that the *hepa* had not come to the duck-coop in the first place. But Lahiri discounted this possibility the moment it came into his calculations—it could not be the correct conjecture because of the uneaten rice and sour-fish curry! Surely, Hiru would not arouse false expectations in his family just to test the waters?

As he mulled over the night's happenings, in a sudden burst of clarity, he knew exactly what had happened—a thread of authentic information warped with a tiny twist of disinformation! 'Will be at his home around eleven o' clock.....stay for an hour or so', Rajeev had said. The uneaten meal was indication enough a visit had been envisaged—the disinformation lay in the conveyed timing! Rajeev and the family had been told Hiren Bora would be coming at least two-three hours ahead of the hour he would actually come! A precaution his civet was most likely to adopt—something Inspector Lahiri should have taken into account, given Hiru's reputation for meticulous planning.

But then, the moment preparations for the raid were set into motion, Lahiri had been sidelined into the role of a minor player; had he been at the centre he would have planned the entire operation in a different way. Trapping a civet required patience and persistence, traits for which these army blokes were not well-known. Not such a large force, no heavy vehicles. Sound carries a great distance at night—those trucks and jeeps were like barking village mongrels keeping the civets and foxes away. Just half a dozen heavily-armed, hand-picked men on a single jeep to be parked at least two kilometres away from Chungijan, and a silent hike through the cultivated fields now lush with tall ripening stalks of paddy, making for a good place to conceal the assault force, and lie in wait for hours if necessary. Should have told the DGP how he would have gone about it, Lahiri thought, and put another ace in his hand.

But then, having been foiled once, would the *hepa* return for a renewed go at the ducks? Lahiri could not tell for sure. These mindless animals were known to keep trying night after night to get at the poultry, but Lahiri was uncertain. The simile itself was wrong—this civet was no mindless jungle cat!

And that was when his experience and instinct came into play—familiarity with human psychology garnered automatically and almost unknowingly through decades of professional life. He had studied Hiren Bora's profile and followed his movements; he instinctively sensed an egotistic spark in his quarry—Hiru's compulsion to finish something he had set out to do. Deep in his heart, Lahiri felt that Chungijan would somehow be once again the arena of action; that the civet would take another shy at the duck-coop. Lahiri would, of course, need to look at the police department's latest intercepts for a hint—any hint—of what Hiru's next course of action might be. But he was certain of one thing at least: he must continue to focus on the family if another trap was to be laid. Let others hunt for Hiren Bora where and however they might, but Lahiri would stick to Chungijan. And, in particular, to Okon!

The anti-bedbug powder had worked its miracle, for there had been none of the stings of the previous night causing his skin to break out in red welts and induce an itch which no amount of scratching could alleviate. Yet, his mind filled with speculations, Lahiri could not sleep. He had been wide awake at six o' clock in the morning when, as instructed, a disgruntled serving boy had knocked on the door and brought tea in a cup chipped around the rim. Although the sun rose in this region far earlier than the rest of the country, Lahiri discovered it to be very dark outside—the dense fog not allowing the sunrays to burst forth. He remained in bed for another hour or so and then went to the toilet for his morning's ablutions, trying with the fingers of his mind to shut close his nostrils to the stink in the lavatory.

Fortunately, the toilet was separated from the bathroom section by a half-wall, so the stench was less on that side; no geyser for hot water, naturally, just a tap, a discoloured bucket and an equally discoloured mug. Lahiri did not hesitate; a cold-water, early morning bath had been a mandated requirement of his morning's regimen ever since he could remember. It could not be otherwise this morning despite the bone-chilling cold; an exercise at self-flagellation proving he knew not what. This was followed by a half hour of physical-cum-yogic exercises. By eight o' clock he had emerged from the hotel after politely telling the server boy he would not risk a breakfast there, and hunted around for a restaurant. He discovered that Doomdooma was not spoilt for choices as far as eateries were concerned. Finally, here he was at Bhogali Restaurant, chewing its leathery *poories* while waving the flies away.

He had time to kill so he ate slowly; not ordering a cup of tea till the *poories* and *alu-dom* had been consumed. However, a half hour stay was the best he could manage without attracting undue attention. He suspected the chap behind the counter had been frowning in disapproval the final five minutes—in such a restaurant you are not supposed to linger during their busy period but depart the moment your empty cup and plate is snatched away by an overeager server boy. Lahiri left the restaurant at 8:45 am, sauntered along the national highway bisecting the town and, on his way, picked up an Assamese daily from a newspaper kiosk. He continued to walk along the road till he was within sight of the Doomdooma Government Boys' High School. Since it was winter, the school actually started at 9:30 am, even though it was slated to start at 9:00. A large tree with a wide trunk and sprawling branches looked to be a promising spot. Lahiri stood under it so he would be out of sight of anyone passing along the national highway, and opened the pages of the newspaper.

Okon thrust the package towards Ai with an air of triumph, forestalling any remonstration from his elders. 'I knew he would come!' he said, voice breathless. 'He did come! I knew he would come!'

'What is it?' Pitai's anger had been diluted by curiosity.

'Haven't opened it yet,' Okon replied as he handed over the package to Ai. His mother tore away the newspaper wrapping and Okon exploded with a delight he had not experienced for a long, long time. It felt as though a *jadugar* with his magic wand had, at one go, swabbed away the pain and heartbreak nursed through the years! Suddenly, the previous night's terrifying and humiliating incident felt as though it had taken place eons ago!

A school bag! Brand new, not a second-hand one purchased in a flea market! Blazing scarlet in colour! Although the light within the cottage was dim, the bag appeared to glitter like a diamond to Okon's eyes, illuminating the interior with its lustre.

Ai rummaged through each of its many pockets and extracted an envelope. It contained 50 hundred rupee notes. She gave the envelope to Pitai who, after taking a cursory look at the contents, handed it back to her. Ai rummaged some more, but found nothing else. 'Nothing else,' she needlessly remarked as she passed the bag to Okon. 'Not even a letter!'

'Perhaps he didn't have the time to write one,' Bai spoke in her usual calm voice. 'He had assumed he would be meeting us, so why write a letter? Where did you find it, Okon?'

'Near the bamboo grove. A hole in a tree-trunk which only Hirukai and I know of.' The half-lie had to be told because to Okon, Hirukai's words were commandments—'It's our own little secret, yours and mine. So keep it to yourself, will you. Not even to Bai...', Okon remembered those words as if spoken only yesterday.

And the terse note, too! The one addressed to him which Hirukai must have written in a hurry. He had been instructed to tear it up...so it needed to be taken as another secret between Hirukai and him—his elders did not need to know. He also remembered how he had nagged Hirukai for a new school bag after he joined the school at Doomdooma—the crude contraption stitched together from a *gamocha* by Hirukai having become the butt of the jokes for his schoolmates. 'It's not the bag which matters. It's what's in it which is important' had been Hirukai's comment, he recalled. It had made him ignore all those jibes till his schoolmates, too, became bored with the subject—he persisted with the cloth bag despite Bai having to patch it up every now and then. Hirukai, certainly, had not forgotten! A brand new, scarlet-coloured school bag, he clung to it as though a trophy he had fought hard for. Suppressed emotions welled up inside him once again; he turned his head away so that the others might not see the tears moistening his eyes.

'I'd better put this away,' he said, trying to sound normal. 'Then feed the cow and the calf, and let the ducks out. Ai, the meal you cooked for Hirukai... I'll eat it before I leave for school.'

Bai smiled. She could not, after all, look into the future; was not an oracle able to foresee distant tragedies, so the significance of the moment had escaped her.

'Thought you were not going to school today?' she half teased.

'Of course, I shall go. You yourself said the class exam results might be out today.' With a bounce in his stride the others had not seen for a while, Okon was off to his room to stash the bag away, and then out of the front door to complete the morning chores before leaving for school. At around 7:30 am, he ate the cold rice and fish curry prepared the previous night, and by 8:00 he had stuffed all his books into the new school bag and heaved it onto his back. He then bid Ai goodbye (Pitai and Bai had already left for the fields to reap the paddy), pushed the bicycle from its perch at the backyard cattle-shed and climbed onto it, and set out for school.

Out in the open, upon the unpaved road linking the village to the national highway—which winded through paddy fields golden with ripening rice-plants—Okon felt exposed and vulnerable. He sensed peering eyes everywhere following his movements; eyes on the roadside that he could see, but which were inquisitive rather than accusing, yet disconcerting nonetheless; eyes inside dark depths of thatched cottages peering through bamboo-ribbed windows; from within the paddy fields, momentarily shifting focus scythes to stare at the passing cyclist; perhaps wondering, suspicion-filled eyes which grew wider at the sight of a blood-red school bag whose colour seemed to explode like a bomb in the misty, mellow, morning light. The comparative loneliness of the path increased his unease; the *rakhyasas* were everywhere, that's what he had heard in school. Perhaps they were watching him now with their terror-striking, demonic eyes, and would grab him at the very next bend! Also, nestling in the depth of his heart was just a tiny flicker of hope—somewhere up ahead, Hirukai might be waiting on the roadside for him. He would fling himself down from the bicycle and hug his elder brother in a tight, unending embrace. Oh yes, he must not forget to thank Hirukai for this most wonderful birthday gift!

But nothing happened. He met neither *rakhyasas* nor his saviour on the way. As he hit the national highway, his speed increased due to the smoother macadam surface of the road. Reaching the crowded township he manoeuvred adroitly through the morning rush, hopped off the bicycle at the school gate (students were forbidden to ride their cycles within the school compound), and parked it at the space earmarked for bicycles. 'Hey, Okon,' a classmate had shouted, 'looking like a *modar* flower, aren't you?' But it was simply friendly teasing without a hint of jealousy or rancour. By now, the entire school knew better than to get on the wrong side of the brother of Hiren Bora!

Okon walked regally to his classroom, the brand new, scarlet coloured school bag on his back indeed blossoming like a *modar* against the contrasting shabbiness of the old school uniform he was wearing. At school, the feeling of being watched grew more pronounced; of course he was being watched by a dozen or more pairs of eyes—but he failed to notice the one pair of bespectacled eyes which had looked up with sharp surprise when he was hopping off his bicycle at the school gate.

Standing under the tree, feeling utterly foolish, Lahiri had had to admit to himself that the failure of last night's raid put him at something of a loose end. As the DGP had so tellingly pointed out, the raid itself had been based initially on a hunch. Of course, satellite radio and cell phone conversations and short message text intercepts, as well as feedback from informers on the ground, had confirmed the target's presence in the area. But it had been Lahiri who had brought logic into play; a long shot, no doubt, yet buttressed by the laws of probability. It took a great deal of legwork, intelligent investigation, and deduction to home in on the garage mechanic Rajeev as the likely conduit—the information he provided seemingly changed possibility into a near certainty. But the trap had been found to be empty; for all he knew, the *hepa* had not even gone close to it!

Once an idea enters into one's head, it spreads in the brain like a parasitic fungus usurping the entire space. It becomes so obsessive and certain that it leaves no room for other ideas, or scope for mulling over other scenarios. That is exactly what had happened to Lahiri; a basic mistake an investigator with his experience should never have committed. He had been absolutely certain Hiru would be there at the house; though he had tried to sound confident during his telephonic conversation with the DGP and wheedled out the latter's permission to continue the hunt, Lahiri realised there was no alternative course of action (a plan B, so to speak) he immediately had in mind. He told himself he had been quite right in being certain Hiru would be there—the latter's presence in the area during Okon's birthday was too much of a coincidence not to have assumed otherwise—yet, so obsessive had he been with the notion that he had not planned what he would do if he was proved wrong…something admittedly most unprofessional of him, but then he was growing old and cynical!

Indubitably, the anti-climax created an opportunity for an attempt towards another climax; oh yes, he was secretly excited the game was far from over—there were new moves yet to be made, and new strategies to be chalked out. But he had not a clue how to go about it now or where exactly to start—a bit of irony that had his kidney guffawing, though there was more of sarcasm than cynicism in the laughter. Logically, if Hiren Bora had been unable to visit his family last night, he might not take another shy. Then the heart of the inspector's strategy would be plucked away—Okon could no longer be of any significance, no more a centre-piece in this game of satanic chess. In other words, Okon could no longer be a bait. Then what on earth was Lahiri doing at this unlikely spot on the side of the national highway, ludicrously half-hidden behind a wide girthed tree, face masked like the stereotype private detective of pulp crime-fiction by a newspaper—waiting to see if the boy would come, his innards rumbling with laughter now directed at himself?

He did not expect Okon to come. Last night must have been a horrific experience for the youngster; the years in the service had gradually sensitized Lahiri to the plight of the innocents caught in a hostile environment not of their making, victims of circumstances they could not control. However, when he encountered an innocent and comprehended his or her plight, his inner laughter ceased as though at a command from the ghost of his authentic self. Despite his cynicism, he did experience more than a drop of sympathy—the lights, the sounds, the terror magnified a trillion times in a tender imagination; the boy must yet be in bed in a state of trauma, crying his heart out. The laughter within Lahiri was actually a tacit acknowledgement that he had come to the spot since there had been nothing immediately to do after last night's fiasco. Perhaps, this morning's walk along the highway was an interlude to help clear his mind so he could think up something new. He continued to wait under the tree with its wide expanse of branches and leaves; a stiff breeze tinged with a hint of rain flayed at the pages of the newspaper, so he had to firm up his grip—the breeze drove away the remnants of the morning fog. That he could not turn the pages of the paper did not matter (made difficult by the breeze, and he had no intention of drawing undue attention to himself by doing something comical), he had not been reading, anyway.

Intent on trying not to draw overt attention to himself, Lahiri almost missed him! By now, the opposite side of the road was awash with boys in uniform— some on foot, some on bicycles, and a few riding pillion on scooters and motorcycles driven by family members. Within that mass of similarly dressed youngsters, it may have been all too easy to have missed a particular face—even for a trained, sharp-eyed observer like Inspector Lahiri. Had it not been for the scarlet school bag contrastingly aflame within the crowd of schoolboys, Lahiri's attention may not have been attracted towards the owner at all—especially considering the speed with which the boy on the bicycle had moved, alighted, and put his cycle at the stand.

Okon! The inspector felt a peculiar thrill streak across his body, he did not quite know why though. The boy, after all, might no longer be relevant to the hunter! Lahiri had not had a good night's sleep for some time now—first those blasted bedbugs, then the aborted mission… That was why it took him a couple of minutes before it hammered on his brain. The bag, of course! On his last visit to Doomdooma on a reconnaissance mission—just like this morning he had observed Okon on his way to school from a similar vantage point—there had been no, apparently brand new, scarlet school bag which could be strapped on to the back. Just a dirt-stained, home-made sling bag made of cloth—an insignia of poverty.

There could be no other explanation. The bag must have been a gift from Hiren Bora to his beloved brother on his birthday! The corollary, too, was self-evident—Hiren Bora had definitely been present somewhere around Chungijan last night! Lahiri tried to control his growing excitement (which had apparently wrung the neck of the imp in his innards, for it stopped chuckling), and willed himself to think logically. Had Hiru gone to visit his family after the raiding party left? But then a police picket was posted at the village until morning. Informers in the village had been instructed to be on the lookout. Also, for all he knew some policemen may have stayed back within the cottage itself. Surely Hiren Bora was shrewd enough to appreciate the risk he would be taking to try and get to his house after the raid?

Then, had he paid a visit to his family ahead of the time he had fed to Rajiv, perhaps even a day earlier? Two factors contradicted such a supposition. First, a youth in the village paid to keep watch was definite Hiru had not visited his family before the arrival of the raiding party. More significant was the uneaten meal—confirmation that Hiru was expected only that night but had not come!

Inspector Lahiri was cautious to a fault; a trait eliciting humour amongst his colleagues, yet, also the reason why they so trusted him. Despite the obvious conclusions staring him in the face, despite the excitement coursing through his blood, he would not conclude any inference to be definite. There were too many alternative explanations—even the possibility someone else had gifted the bag to Okon. He had to be absolutely certain!

He took off his outsize spectacles, rubbed the lenses with his handkerchief and put them on again. Then, with determined steps, he walked into the school and threaded his way through the students as they headed for their respective classrooms. Lahiri had an informer at the school—he might be able to provide confirmation.

An hour later, Lahiri was seated in a private bus to Tinsukia. Strangely enough, this infuriatingly warped town with its confusing maze of narrow streets, though located almost at the eastern tip of Assam, wielded great control over the state's economy—in particular the wholesale trade of commodities like potato, onion and pulses. Most residents dwelling in the heart of the town were traders who had migrated from other parts of India, particularly Rajasthan, Uttar Pradesh, and Bihar—which made it a happy hunting ground for ULFA extortionists. In fact, though no one acknowledged it officially, the rumour had it that the town's traders, with very few exceptions, had earlier been paying a fixed sum to the ULFA every month— deposited with a handful of traders who, in turn, handed it over to operatives of the outfit. Sometime back, sensing the general public's feelings against the extremists, a section of the traders had tried to wriggle out of paying the 'protection' money, but Hiren Bora had soon taken care of it. A ring-leader among the defaulters had been selected to be made an example of—a motorcycle borne youth, helmeted, with a dark visor covering his face, had driven up to the trader late in the evening as he and his son were pulling down the shutters and closing it. Before the terrified gaze of the young man, the rider had pulled out a revolver from his jacket pocket and riddled the trader with bullets, There had been no trouble for a while after that. However, the tightening of paramilitary vigil in upper Assam—combined with the abrupt decrease in ULFA activities in the area—had changed the situation again, with the traders once more emboldened enough to discontinue the payment of 'protection' money.

Lahiri took a rickshaw from the bus stand to the office of the DSP; he was not there to meet the SP—senior officers were not of slightest use to him on this occasion, but a colleague of his from the Intelligence Branch. He had earlier been posted in Guwahati, and who he knew well and trusted. They had lunch together at a nearby eatery. During the course of the meal, his colleague briefed him on the latest intelligence on Hiren Bora. Surprisingly, this top ULFA cadre was travelling alone this time and not leading a group, though he may have a unit holed up somewhere in a safe house while he carried out a preliminary reconnaissance—before giving them the go ahead for some operation or the other. But his colleague doubted it. In his opinion—one which Lahiri placed full value on—Hiru had come alone on a purely extortive trip. Some of the intercepts received by the army as well as civil intelligence strongly suggested this, he could vouchsafe it himself for he had waded through quite a lot of the recent ones. Lahiri, of course, knew about the Tinsukia trader affair, didn't he? That a businessman had alerted the army to an extortion attempt by an ULFA cadre…and that too, one with Hiren Bora's reputation. Tells you a great deal about the changed environment as far as that insurgent outfit was concerned, doesn't it?

And the Lajim Tea Estate episode. Oh, Lahiri had not been told about it yet, had he? Seems Hiren Bora made an attempt to extort money from the tea-garden management who, however, appeared to have been ready for such an attempt and alerted the nearby army base when the man was inside the garden. Imagine, Hiren Bora managed to save himself by the skin of his teeth! 'The army,' so said the colleague, 'as is becoming too frequent nowadays, did not tell us about the Lajim episode. No wonder, considering they did not succeed in catching their man. That's why the Doomdooma *thana's* OC could not tell you about the Lajim thing...he doesn't know about it, you see! But we have our resources, don't we? No matter what the army tries to keep from our ears, we always come to know!'

The significant aspect in both the Tinsukia and Lajim incidents was that Hiren Bora made the extortion attempt all by himself, reinforcing the conclusion that this, too, was a solo trip. Travelling alone, in actual fact, was safer and also facilitated mobility. Lahiri's colleague could tell that Hiru was aware of the tough security measures as well as the eyes and ears which had been placed everywhere; that he had ventured into the lion's den indicated the dire financial straits his outfit must currently be in. But Hiru was a cunning son of a bitch, a veritable fox ('a civet,' Lahiri had silently corrected his colleague), the way he managed to slip in and out of every trap set for him. That fiasco last night, for instance—a blooming red herring—made one wonder from where the devil they got the tip-off. Some stupid army moron, most likely!

'So you feel as I do?' Lahiri quickly interrupted, sipping a cup of after-lunch tea. 'Hiru will remain in this area till he carries out whatever he has come for?'

'Certain of it. He has always been a persistent little bastard—I should know! Trust me, tea-gardens are his most likely target this time. You can't carry out kidnappings or bank heists alone, at least not in the current tight-security environment.'

'Not the oil industry? Or coal?'

'Less likely. Both of those have heavy security presence. But tea-gardens are isolated and possess laughable security, though some of them have tried to train their own garden-hands. Yes, your man appears, to me, to be after those bloody brown sahibs in tea. And he'll bloody well stay in this area till he collects enough moolah, trust me.'

'Increases his chances of being trapped?'

'Hope so. But tell you what, he has not used any of his communication devices the whole of today, not even to inform his superiors about last night's raid at his home. Oh, of course, you know that he knows about last night's raid, else I would not be fool enough to sit here talking to a stupid moron, ha ha. Yes, not a beep out of him.'

'Gone into a hole, do you think?'

'Yep, I think so. Although we can't be certain how long he'll remain incommunicado, his higher-ups have enough trust in him to have given him a free hand.'

'If what we hear correctly, Hiru is now amongst the 'higher-ups' himself,' Lahiri observed.

'That's true,' his colleague said. 'What about you? Anything you might have come across that may give us a hint as to what he would do next?'

For one moment, Lahiri was tempted to talk about the school bag and his suspicion that Okon was somehow in touch with his brother. Yet, with a willpower honed through years of experience, he resisted the impulse…more because he was uncertain about the facts and less because he distrusted his colleague.

'No,' he said shortly.

'Well, that's it then. We don't know where Hiru is, what he plans to do next. In fact, we know nothing new about him at this moment. If he continues to maintain silence, it'll make our task more difficult. And yours, if I may add.'

'Mine?' Lahiri asked with the look of befuddled innocence, characteristic of his features. 'What makes you think I'll not be returning to Guwahati this evening itself?'

His friend and colleague let out a knowing smile. 'You've made this personal, haven't you?'

'Perhaps so,' Lahiri answered, taking off his spectacles, rubbing them with his handkerchief and putting them back on again. 'One needs one's dose of adrenalin every now and again, doesn't one?'

If you want to make secret contact with someone, do so in a crowded place—a tenet Lahiri had religiously followed all through his professional career. Also, do not use the same place twice, if you can help it. The road-side market in Doomdooma was jam-packed in the evening with shoppers; such was the noise and bustle that his contact had some difficulty in locating him. When he finally did, Lahiri drew him to one side towards a kiosk selling tea in plastic cups. He ordered two cups of tea, paid the required amount and then guided his contact to a relatively secluded corner.

'Let me confirm again,' Karuna Saikia, teacher of class VIII of the Government Boys' School at Doomdooma, said avidly. 'There's a large reward involved. So I get paid for what I tell you now, don't I?'

Looking at the fat, greasy, greedy face, Lahiri felt uncharacteristic anger flaring inside. But then, as always, the innate consciousness of futility acted like a bucket of water and he slipped facilely into indifference. 'Not immediately,' he replied. 'You know what government procedures are like. Formalities have to be observed. Moreover, although there's a reward on Hiren Bora's head, it becomes disbursable only after he is caught. Information leading to his arrest and all that stuff, you know.'

'Meaning I don't get paid now?'

'Not now, certainly. And the final outcome will determine whether you get paid at all.'

'That's unacceptable. I'm taking a huge risk, you know?'

Before Karuna Saikia's stunned gaze, Lahiri's features changed; though the spectacles remained in their place, the eyes peeping through them suddenly seemed to have the gleam of a tiger on the hunt. The habitual bemused expression was abruptly replaced by one of purposeful severity, and there was cold steel in his normally thin voice. Such was the dramatic, schizophrenic metamorphosis that a streak of fear stabbed into Saikia's heart.

'Listen,' Lahiri said in an ominous tone. 'You'll do as I say, reward or not. You don't know who I am. You've no idea who you're up against. We're out to trap a dreaded terrorist. You fail to cooperate and I'll have you locked up. The Armed Forces Act gives us special powers. Do I make myself clear?'

Although the evening's chill had already set in, beads of sweat appeared on Saikia's forehead. He nodded with exaggerated, supremely comical vigour to signify he understood.

'Fine. Tell me what you learnt this morning?'

'You were right. Okon's bag is new. A classmate confirmed the boy brought it instead of his old one just this morning.'

Lahiri concealed his rising excitement, keeping his voice tough though.

'Did you take a look at it?'

'Yes, as you instructed. When the kids were out on the playground—during the break. Made in China!'

'That's none too important. These days this area is crammed with cheap, China-made goods. Did he tell anyone how he got it?'

'No. A classmate asked, but got no reply. No one dared press him for an answer. He seemed extremely proud of the bag. Not unnatural, of course—his family's poor and he's a young boy.'

'But your tone implies you've an idea where he got it from?'

Karuna Saikia laughed—a nervous titter. 'Oh, everyone knows. From his elder brother Hiren Bora, who else? You know, Okon has changed since Hiru left to join the ULFA. He used to be a bright, normal kid, I remember. Now, he's a loner who keeps his own company. But, this morning, I saw something in his face and gait but couldn't quite place what it was. He seemed genuinely happy. And do you know what it takes to make Okon happy?

Hiru, who else? You smart guys can keep playing your cat and mouse game, but you failed to nab him in last night's raid. How do I know? Why, the whole world knows what you guys and the army were up to last night! But let me tell you something, bags don't fly! Hiru must have been there all the time you smart guys were playing your games—and got in touch with Okon. Threw dust in your eyes, he did!'

A trace of venom tinged Karuna Saikia's unexpected outburst. Lahiri noticed with contempt how the muscles on the fleshy face wiggled due to the vehemence with which the man spoke. His defiant words, no doubt, were prompted by a latent animus against authority, as well as disappointment that he would not be immediately rewarded for his toil and trouble. Lahiri, however, remained indifferent.

'Bags don't fly, eh?' he said without rancour. 'You may be right about that! Now, if you really want a slice of the reward money—it's a huge amount, mind you, more than you can dream about—you'll have to work for it. Talk to the boy. Cultivate him. I would've done it myself, but he will not trust a stranger. You're his teacher! Tell him about the surrender-offer being made by the government to insurgents. Tell him about those boys who have ceased their rebel activities and been re-absorbed by society. You get what I mean?'

'Certainly. I'm no fool. You want to use the boy to try get at Hiru?'

'Use him?' Lahiri's voice lost its severity and became sardonic. 'We're all using each other all the time, aren't we? I'm counting on you. Your help is of the essence if we're to prepare the bait and see what we come up with.'

'Prepare the trap, you mean?'

'No, the bait first. Brainwash the boy, Saikia. I can't be absolutely certain we've chosen the right bait, yet we need to give it a go. Tell him you were approached by a police officer with a surrender offer for Hiru. But only him. As far as the rest of the world is concerned, you don't know me. Never heard of me. Not that I fear you might spill the beans to anyone. Hiren Bora is ruthless.'

'How do I contact you?'

'You don't contact me, I contact you. And don't worry about the money—if the *hepa* is trapped, you'll get your reward. I personally guarantee it.'

'Thank you,' Karuna Saikia said with genuine gratitude. 'But don't you want my cell phone number?'

'Not really,' Lahiri replied, 'I already have it.'

Bags don't fly—a dribble of wisdom from the mouth of a lout!

Lahiri lay within the warm womb of the bed. He was tired; his limbs felt heavy—a reminder every night that he was not getting any younger! But the weight of the conundrum was heavier on his mind, making sleep impossible. Anyway, more and more these days, he used these moments (before drifting off into uneasy sleep) for reflection and tonight, despite the languor touching his limbs and the fact that he had had practically no sleep for the last 48 hours, would be no exception. No, not on thoughts related to professional or worldly matters, nor in meaningless burrowing into the past to dig up chortles or sighs but a scrutiny of the future in the context of the vacuity of the present. He had performed the daily ritual of calling up his wife; she had then been watching a favourite soap-opera on TV so he had kept the conversation short—yes, yes, he was all right; no, no, he couldn't exactly say when he would be back. Poor, aging woman; unfailingly, every afternoon and night she would escape into a fantasy fabricated by someone else. He thought about calling up his sons but then decided against it. He felt a spasm of pain in his stomach…the food he had been consuming in the past couple of days was taking its toll! Reluctantly, he got out of bed to hunt for a couple of Zentec tablets as well as an Alzolam sedative pill from his bag, and downed them with mineral water before quickly climbing back into the bed to escape the chill.

Of late, at home or elsewhere, these were insidious moments—of lying awake trying to slide into sleep—the all-too-familiar empty black screen which unfurled before closed eyes and the sinking feeling at the pit of his stomach. There were those fortunate ones unbothered at that imminent nothingness; could delude themselves by prostrating before clay figurines or, like his wife, fill the vacuity with inane images. But not he; perhaps the wages of being too intelligent—a tragic-comic condition eliciting mirth in his innards and depression in his mind. If scepticism was a sign of intelligence than intelligence itself was a curse; how he wished he could ward off the feeling of futility with those inane images or submit (like her) to the cheating placidity induced by blind faith. He had discussed his mood swings with a friend of his who worked in the forensic laboratory, and had been recommended anti-depressant pills which could be bought over the counter. Lahiri had tried them but discovered that the artificially induced exhilaration led to even greater depression after the medicine's impact had worn off. He had ultimately found his own panacea; fought of the sense of futility by willing himself into passion and focussing on those pinpricks—case after case pursued through all these years with an obsession which ordinarily amused, but occasionally alarmed his colleagues in the department. It had been this pastiche passion which had inspired the DGP to set him after Hiren Bora—his obsession for the moment, his goal—Lahiri's civet!

He chuckled audibly. He shoved those dark thoughts away and focused on the issue of immediate concern; he had mastered the trick to perfection! The black cavern of his mind began filling up with a single image, which grew bigger and bigger till it no longer seemed a void. They were not that different after all, he and Hiren Bora! The hunter and the quarry! Both were loners. However, Lahiri hunted both day and night while the civet was a solitary creature which hunted only in the dark of the night; Lahiri could imagine the beast holed up somewhere during daytime, moving towards his objective only at night. But in such a hostile environment, the dark of the night was hardly an effective shield. So far his reputation for ruthlessness had proved to be a far more effective shield for Hiru—even those who would give him away hesitated to do so because they knew retribution would immediately ensue. How else could he move with such impunity through a veritable minefield, throwing dust in the eyes of his hunters?

The boy Okon could be the key to a conundrum—the only key he had, Lahiri acknowledged ruefully. How did he get hold of the bag? There must be some unseen string linking the two stepbrothers, though Lahiri could not fathom what it could be. Of course, the family, including the boy, could be picked up and grilled; something those idiots in the army would have done had they suspected such a link… But it would surely shoo the civet away, defeating the very purpose! Fortunately, Lahiri was the sole individual to have latched onto this lead involving the brand new scarlet school bag—he could pursue it and discover whether it led to anything more concrete, and then get in touch with the others. If it led to yet another empty trap, only he (and the DGP) would be aware of it. The third person in the know, Karuna Saikia, could be trusted to hold his tongue. So, for the moment, Lahiri—like his civet—would hover around in this area, the trapper keeping his eyes on the bait. The sedative was beginning to take effect; the tiredness in his limbs, too, acted as a soporific. Lahiri felt his eyelids grow leaden and, in a few moments, slipped into a dream world filled with bags which flew...

MOVEMENTS ON A CHESSBOARD

Inspector Lahiri had been wrong on at least two counts in his assessment of Hiren Bora. First, he had been wrong in his supposition that the flame of idealism burned in the heart of this rebel and he was passionately committed to the ULFA's goal of a liberated Assam. He could hardly be at fault; the single-minded commitment, more than most cadres, that Hiren Bora had shown striving to further the ULFA's 'cause' could not have made other assumptions possible. Even his superiors in the outfit had been misled into harbouring a similar misconception, and he had not deemed it necessary to correct them. Only Hiren Bora himself could look with dispassionate eyes into Hiren Bora's soul and sense the uncaring despair layering it like a sheet of frozen ice.

But then even he, himself, could not explain the rapid degeneration in his nature and his unsuspected capacity for brutal violence. Had Inspector Lahiri known about his quarry's true mental state, he might have been able to offer an explanation—given as he was to approaching things from a cerebral perspective. Often innocence, when traumatically disillusioned, slides rapidly into extreme cynicism. As for his capacity for brutality, who knew what primitive gene lurked in one's body? For generations Hiren Bora's family had fought as *paiks* for the Ahom *Swargadeos* during times of war—who knew what had been infused unknowingly into his blood? Inspector Lahiri did not know; his ignorance had somehow inserted in him the teeniest tinge of an undesired sense of empathy towards this man. This, in turn, had induced a sense of guilt. Hiren Bora, on his part, did not feel any guilt whatsoever for all that he had done in the last three years; he, in fact, felt almost nothing.

Second, ruthlessness was no shield! Lahiri imagined that Hiren Bora had been able to move with such ease within an inimical environment because those who sheltered and helped him were afraid of the repercussions if they did not do so. But Hiren Bora knew different. A reputation for ruthlessness no longer counted in a milieu fraught with unending violence; people had grown inured to the killings and raids, bomb blasts, sudden halts and identity checks by the forces to a point where they seemingly ceased to care. Also, the ULFA no longer commanded respect or inspired dread; especially after the Dhemaji bombing, the outfit's relationship with the people had touched rock bottom. This, in turn, had emboldened targets to defy its diktats.

On this trip he had gone to Tinsukia and met one of the petty traders, who used to earlier collect money from the business community and hand it over to the outfit's representative. But the conduit had flatly refused to carry out his assignment any longer. Not that he did not want to, for the percentage he received for his service had been more than generous. But, of late, the business community was resisting all sorts of extortion drive—it had become the target not only of the ULFA, but of some smaller insurgent outfits which had lately sprung up. Not to mention the pseudo-insurgents as well those who came to collect 'contributions' towards festivals and the like. The business community of Tinsukia had become fed up! At the same time, the administration had begun to take action against members of the community for 'abetting' the outfit; though no one had been incarcerated so far, the prospect of being arrested for aiding and abetting enemies of the nation was all too real… So, sorry, he was helpless! Hiren Bora had sensed that the man was speaking from his heart; threatening him with his gun was of no use. At great risk, he had contacted a couple of the bigger Tinsukia traders directly. One of these had informed the army of the extortion attempt as he had been instructed to do; luckily, an ULFA informant tipped Hiren Bora off and he had to leave Tinsukia in something of a hurry.

The grease which helped the mechanism of this society slide smoothly was money; greed rather than fear of reprisal had enabled him to evade traps set for him so far. Greed itself was a possible ally of those who wanted to bring him down. In order to survive, he had to pander to greed with hard cash; neither past friendship nor love for their motherland but sheer cash had motivated those who had helped him on this trip. In fact, greed was an obstacle on the path of those who wanted to nab or kill him, for the only carrot they could dangle was what they might possibly give in the future, rather than on the spot cash. On the other hand, it was the fear of State reprisal—the ruthlessness of those men in uniform rather than fear of Hiren Bora's ruthlessness—which had impelled some to betray him, though he had been able to avoid pitfalls so far.

But getting his hands on a large sum of cash had become a problem. It had been a frustrating trip so far. Perhaps this was because it had not been planned properly, something which Hiren Bora was not used to. For instance, if he had some back-up support, they could have robbed a bank in the area; but he had come alone! The request for monetary assistance had been made by Sergeant Major Pradyut Basumatari, who was still in the KIA's 2nd Brigade camp. Although there had been far fewer new recruits from the upper Assam side for some time now, the ULFA had still retained a full-fledged training camp and crew. The commander-in-chief of ULFA's armed wing (the only senior leader of the outfit not to lead a sedentary life but be astoundingly mobile and active), on his way back to Bangladesh from yet another meeting with Chinese officials—this time at the KIA's 3rd Brigade headquarters itself—had spent the night in the KIA's 2nd Brigade camp along with his entourage. Hiren Bora was present when the Sergeant Major had told the commander-in-chief of his sense of shame that the ULFA was no longer putting much into the KIA's kitty despite enjoying their hospitality. Hiren Bora was supposed to have departed for Bangladesh the next night along with the others, but had been instructed to stay on and see what he could do to help out. With his trademark self-confidence, he had set off on his one-man mission—taking the Khonsa-Changlang-Jaipur route along with a small group of NSCN cadres, and separating from them in Arunachal Pradesh before crossing into the Assam border.

He had not entered the once familiar territory in upper Assam for some months now. And since he had come unprepared, he needed some feedback on the ground situation; he tried to contact Kalpanath—the person who had first recruited him to the ULFA but later 'rejoined the mainstream', and was cooped up in a designated camp for 'surrendered' cadres near Tinsukia only to be shooed away with the warning that the environment was not at all conducive to any mission of whatever nature. Within a week of his re-entry into Indian territory, Hiren Bora realised Kalpanath had been correct in his assertion of the ground realities: the writ of the Indian Army and Paramilitary Forces ran over the entire area, and security was so tight it was difficult even to traverse 10 kilometres without risking running into a military or police patrol. The mood in the villages had turned hostile towards insurgents; the army raids and deaths in fake encounters had roused public temper—the ire, ironically, being directed against outfits such as the ULFA rather than the ones who had conducted the raids. The authorities had set up a close-woven network of informers; Hiren Bora was, of course, the most recognisable face in the area. Had it not been for his ingenuity and resourcefulness, he might not have survived that week without getting caught—especially after the failed attempt to extort money in Tinsukia.

He had not carried much money on him on this trip, in the expectation that he would have to carry much more of it back. He soon realised he himself was running out of money—a vital commodity if he was to pay off the people willing to offer him shelter. Much to his chagrin, he found himself being reduced to the level of extorting money from petty traders at smaller townships such as Makum to remain afloat. With some money on him, he went after a bigger fish: an attempt making him understand that on this trip, under the present circumstances, a different strategy was required.

Lajim Tea Estate was one of the easternmost tea gardens in Assam, located on the bank of the Lohit river; its proprietor was a Marwari tycoon who lived in Kolkata. The manager and assistant managers were all Marwaris, recruited from Kolkata (most probably relatives of the tycoon), and so Hiren Bora had thought, would be suitably amenable to arm-twisting. Over-confidence had made him just a bit careless; he had not taken into account Marwari ingenuity; had sauntered through the garden and into the manager's office, unaware that he had been spotted way back and a well-practiced drill had been set into motion. The manager, who could not speak Assamese but was fluent in Bengali (a language which Hiren Bora had picked up in Bangladesh), was courteous to a fault as he asked the intruder to be seated and enquired as to what his business was. Hiren Bora, with matching politeness, had introduced himself, and asked for a donation of 50 lakh rupees for the ULFA's cause.

If the name rang any bells in the manager's head, his poker face did not show it. He smiled an oily, servile smile and said that they never kept even one per cent of that amount in the garden, so it would be impossible to meet such a demand immediately. Hiren Bora, of course, had undertaken such negotiations with tea-garden managers numerous times before; he also knew that though this garden's boss lived in Kolkata, a sizeable amount of money was required for the workers' salary and purchase of plantation inputs. Thus, the garden would have an account in a bank at either Doomdooma or Tinsukia—operated by the manager himself. He, therefore, replied that he was in no hurry; he 'knew' it would take at least a day to withdraw the sum from the garden's local account, so he would return in two days to collect the amount—which should be in thousand rupee notes and put in a bag for easy conveyance.

This was a mistake on the part of the manager. His easy acquiescence and his courteous offer of a cup of tea to his guest, and Hiren Bora was up on his feet the very moment the offer of tea was made, his semi-automatic in hand. He circled around the manager's desk, and standing behind him, grabbed him by the hair and plucked him out of the swivel chair upon which he had been sitting. The manager was thin and pale; his face grew even paler when the man behind him put the barrel of his gun against the back of his neck. 'Let's go out together, shall we?' Hiren Bora said grimly, the ice in his voice sending a chill down the spine of his hostage. Sure enough, as he had suddenly suspected, at least two dozen male garden workers—armed with spears and bows and arrows—had stealthily circled the office bungalow. He also guessed that the nearest army and police outposts must have been alerted by an assistant manager or someone else at least half hour ago, so he did not have much time (actually, only a nearby, mobile army base had been alerted, an officer having some months ago come to the garden and met the manager to instruct him to report only to the army if any extortion attempt was made, since the local police could not be trusted).

The tea-garden workers were bewildered that the manager frantically signalled them to go away, though no sound emerged from his throat. Hiren Bora dragged him to a jeep stationed outside, and asked him to drive across the narrow garden path towards the river. He made him stop the vehicle at the fenced-in boundary of the garden, took the keys from him and asked him to run back as fast as he could to his office. For a moment he contemplated shooting him as he set off on a desperate, grotesquely funny scramble, but then decided remorse would set in more readily if he shot him in a leg instead. He proceeded to do so with stunning accuracy, and even as the manager lay writhing in agony on the ground, clambered over the barbed wire fencing into the forested track leading to the river bank; it being winter, the river was relatively dry and narrow and easier to cross. As he had expected, a dinghy of the type always to be found unattended on river banks in this part of the country, was moored on the water's edge to help him make his journey across.

Once on the other side, he lost no time in racing towards the thinly-forested section of the land; by then not only Lajim Tea Estate, but the entire area must be crawling with police, military and paramilitary personnel. Hiren Bora knew precisely how much he was worth to the authorities, though it did not induce any pride in him. They must have known by now that he had left the tea-garden on the Lohit side; the obvious inference would be that he had crossed the river somehow, so army or CRPF camps in this area, too, would soon be in on the hunt if they had not yet done so. He moved with unrelenting pace till reaching a trail he, along with NSCN compatriots, had used before. It was astonishing how much ground he covered despite the jungles growing denser the more he progressed. And then he was in a familiar village comprising of a cluster of *chang*-hutments and small spreads of wetland cultivation of rice, and had met the headman who could be trusted absolutely.

Here, at least values such as friendship and loyalty still held true, and there could be no question of cash payments; they did not conceal him within the village itself but took him back into the dense jungle. There, on a tall hollong tree which was covered with liana and parasitic orchids, the NSCN had built a *machan* at almost the very top, concealed from the ground by the leafy canopy created by some of the lesser trees. Hiren Bora had been provided with a bottle of fresh water as well as some dry ration. He had climbed agilely up the overhanging rope, and once he was inside the tiny shed bound securely to a forked branch, had pulled the rope up.

He knew that on the tree, within the *machan*, he was totally helpless and dependent on the trust he had reposed on the headman and a couple of other villagers. If he was betrayed he had nowhere to run; however, he was not the kind of person to worry needlessly about what might be, so he had taken advantage of the period of rest by curling up and going to sleep within the sleeping bag already there. It had been only the pangs of hunger within his belly which finally woke him up; he ate first, drank water, then defecated from the tree-top—using water from the bottle to clean himself. The prolonged sleep, the height, the artificial gloom created below by the dense verdure—all of it had been disorienting; he did not know how long he had slept or what day it was. He went back to sleep; it was of a lighter type…he would wake on and off between dreams startlingly vivid. Once he had even opened his eyes, and thought he had heard voices yelling in Hindi which floated up from far beneath him.

Clearly, since all communication had been cut off from the world down below, the headman had left it to his guest to choose his time of descent. With typical caution, Hiren Bora waited till his stock of water and food had finished, before letting down the rope and sliding to the ground. He ventured into the village again only after taking his time surveying it, and then contacted the headman who informed him that he had been in the *machan* for two days and three nights. Oh, yes, those men in uniform had come and searched the village—it was a pity they did not have the resources to search the top of every tree in the jungle, ha ha! Hiren Bora had embraced the headman in a bear-hug before taking his leave. Having crossed the Lohit once again, he hid during the day and trekked only at night; though he did spend half hour at the small market in Talap to buy a cheap, Chinese-made school bag—an inducement for Okon, if one was needed. Three days later, he was close to Chungijan village, concealed within the clump of bamboo that he and Okon had christened—the *daini's* lair.

Alone in the *machan*, within the sound-filled depths of silence, he had thought about the situation he was in and how to adapt to the changed environment. A new plan of action was needed now. Thus, it had been the exigency of his situation rather than familial ties which had taken him to the *daini's* lair; that he had entered it on the very day Okon had been born 13 years back was a quirky but convenient coincidence! However, things rarely work out the way one wants, especially for someone like Hiren Bora, and the kind of life he was currently leading. He had thought he would talk directly with Okon once he was with his family, but betrayal by individuals he hoped he could trust had put paid to that. Someone other than him may have acknowledged the impossibility of carrying out what he had set off to do, and returned to Myanmar and reported to his superiors about the ground realities in upper Assam—but not Hiren Bora. The persistent streak within him (which Lahiri had sensed) made him ignore such realities; he had come to get his hands on some money and he would do so—even if he had to take advantage of a child's innocence and his absolute faith in him. He had left the *daini's* lair having written hasty instructions to Okon as to what he should do, and had put the note as well as the packet within the bamboo grove. A gap of a few days was required for the heated hunt to cool off; there must not be the slightest hint of any activity on his part if the sense of urgency among the enemy were to subside. Most importantly, he must remain totally incommunicado from his compatriots so that if he was lucky, the enemy might be led into believing that he had, indeed, left upper Assam and retreated to Myanmar.

The dawn of December 27 found him at the *Highway Dhaba* located midway between Doomdooma and Talap; the owner was a strapping Bihari whom Hiren Bora knew well and had had dealings with in the past. The part of the national highway near this *dhaba* was normally full of parked trucks. However, the drivers and handymen of these vehicles did not stop only for food at that joint for; in truth, the limited menu served was barely eatable! The actual *dhaba* area was none too big, but behind the outer Assam-type make-shift building there was a large, rectangular structure indicating that the joint also provided for overnight accommodation to wayfarers. Passing travellers, which included the truck drivers and handymen as well as horny youths primarily from Doomdooma and Talap, rarely spent a night in the hive of tiny rooms constituting the rectangular structure. Rather, they paid for being serviced by the five ladies who had their quarters within the complex as well, spending at most a couple of hours before going on their respective ways. The Bihari had no fear he might be picked up by the police for carrying on an illicit and immoral business; he had the local constabulary in his pocket. At the same time, he had always got on quite well with the army men—who also dropped by occasionally, to partake of the fare offered by the *dhaba* (at a discount, naturally). The Bihari also had no problems, so far, with insurgent groups such as the ULFA; live and let live was his philosophy. Not only had he paid a reasonable sum as 'protection' money to the outfit, but also sometimes allowed cadres—who had to spend months in the confines of jungles away from the company of women—to relax for a while in the backrooms.

He was aware of Hiren Bora's reputation; when the insurgent slipped into the *dhaba* at the break of dawn (his *dhaba* remained open 24 hours a day, seven days a week), the Bihari had no hesitation in offering him shelter for a few days. Hiren Bora had candidly informed the Bihari that he did not have enough to pay him, but would clear the amount once a planned operation had been executed before he left for Myanmar. The *dhaba*'s owner told him he had no trouble at all with such an arrangement; all he wished was to be left alone to continue his business, and remit money to his family back at Bhagalpur unfailingly every month. Hiren Bora spent three days and two nights in a backroom of the *Highway Dhaba*; during the period he contacted no one, nor did he venture outside for even a single moment. But he did mate thrice in an unemotional, feral manner with one of the ladies—courtesy of the house. Her name, most likely assumed and not her real one, ironically, was Savitri. She was a kind-hearted woman who laughed easily and had taken a fancy to Hiren Bora, though she did not give a whit to his ideology or profession. On the afternoon of December 29, she had breathlessly run to the cramped cubicle Hiren Bora had been hiding in, and had informed him that the Bihari at that very moment was talking to a couple of men who had come to the dhaba on a motorcycle. She had eavesdropped on the conversation and found out that the strangers were asking the Bihari if he knew about Hiren Bora's whereabouts; the latter, in fact, had told them Hiren Bora was at the back of the complex at that very moment. The Bihari would wring her neck if he found out that she had come to him; it was fortunate she knew who Hiren Bora was, though he had not told her his name. She thought the men were waiting for back-up to arrive; he had to leave and leave fast! She had thrust away the 1000-rupee note he had held out—saying he probably needed the money more than her—and slipped into an adjacent cubicle so the Bihari would not see her if he came through that narrow corridor.

Hiren Bora, with typical, nonchalant composure, left the *dhaba* complex from the back along with his meagre belongings, past the stinking rows of make-shift urinals and over the low boundary wall into the paddy fields, which afforded some amount of cover. On the way he bought some basic provisions for a few days' stay and some other items from the Doomdooma market, and was within the *daini's* lair just before daybreak on December 30. That the package he had left behind on his previous visit was no longer there evoked no surprise in him. He knew Okon like the back of his hand—he had had not the slightest doubt his brother would respond to his summons!

Okon, too, had no doubt he would do as Hirukai had asked him to—unbothered as to why. His elder brother had instructed him to keep the contents of the hastily scribbled note close to his chest, so he had told no one, not even Bai. Pitai was oblivious of Okon's changed mood, but both Ai and Bai immediately noticed the joy which radiated from his face now. Such joy was much more than a reaction to the gift he had received from Hiru; they suspected something was afoot but tactful questions had elicited nothing, and they did not wish to press him with insistent enquiries since it might destroy his newly-displayed effervescence. They had no inkling that Okon harboured a hope beyond their wildest dream; a hope resulting from a conversation one of his teachers had had with him at school.

That afternoon, during the break, his class teacher Karuna Saikia, who taught mathematics, had threaded his fat self through the mass of boisterous students crowding the playing field fronting the school—the teacher, like Inspector Lahiri, considered a crowded place to be the best spot for a private conversation as well. Okon had not joined his classmates who were playing football with a tennis ball; instead, he was sitting alone on the low boundary wall. But Karuna Saikia had observed carefully that there were other students sitting on that boundary wall, too, so his approach towards the boy would not be noticed.

'A word with you, Okon,' Saikia said in a conversational tone, not needing to keep his voice low because of the surrounding noise. The boy had immediately sprung up from his seat.

'Yes, sir?' he said.

'I shan't beat about the bush. It's about your elder brother, Hiru.' Saikia's crafty eyes did not fail to notice the slight flicker of concern in the child's innocent features. 'Has he been in touch with you?'

'No, sir,' the boy was too quick with his answer. Saikia noted there was no follow up question from him.

'Never mind. This is between you and me. A senior official of the police department from Guwahati met me the other day and asked that I talk to you. In case Hiru tries to get in touch with, you tell him of the surrender offer that the government is making to those who have strayed from the path that you and I follow. Do you understand?'

'Yes, sir.'

'You, of course, know Kalpanath? He is from your village.'

'Kalpakai? Yes, sir.'

'He surrendered and is now in a camp till he is cleared of all the criminal charges against him. He would be returning to Chungijan in time for the *magh-bihu* feast just a couple of weeks away. No harm has come to him. No harm will come to Hiru either, if he surrenders. Tell him that. The senior police officer will extend his stay by a few days just in case Hiru chooses to surrender.'

'Yes, sir.'

Karuna Saikia continued to watch Okon's features carefully, noting with satisfaction that the boy had not denied the possibility he might meet his brother. The lad was absolutely incapable of dissemblance; the more he scrutinised the flushed face before him, the more certain the class teacher grew that he was concealing some secret. But he could not prise the truth out of him; he was already treading on dangerous ground even talking like this to Hiru's brother.

'Right. If you want, I'll take you to this police officer. He'll confirm what I've told you. So, any chance you might meet Hiru, come and let me know. And don't forget to convey my message. You do want him back at your home, don't you?'

There was a pitifully eager look in the child's face. 'Yes, sir,' he said, 'I do.'

On the evening of December 28, Karuna Saikia received a phone call from Inspector Lahiri. 'Did you talk to the boy?' the inspector had barked.

'Yes, I did. I have conveyed the message.'

'So? Your observations?' Inspector Lahiri clearly valued the crafty intelligence of his adjutant!

'Based on instinct only, you must understand. I'm almost certain he has been in touch with his brother. His face betrayed some secret...but knowing him as I do, it would be near impossible to get it out of him.'

'Good job. Even if it's a long shot, we need to exploit it. Did you ask him to get in touch with you if something develops?'

'I did. Sure, I'll take you to him if the opportunity arises. As for the reward amount, you must understand I'm doing this more as an act of patriotism than for...'

However, Karuna Saikia discovered he was talking to empty air, for the man at the other end had hung up!

A *bordoishila*—as a tropical tempest with terrifyingly fast and furious winds was called in Assam—had been unleashed in Okon's mind at the offer conveyed by the grotesquely obese school teacher. Throughout the day he could not focus on anything else, and was reprimanded by a teacher who took classes after the break. Ai noticed his absent-mindedness while he was performing his evening chores and taking his meal—but then, Okon was no longer the Okon of yore! No one, of course, knew or suspected that although the imminent prospect of meeting Hirukai had put dancing shoes on his feet, yet, to request his brother to surrender was daunting since the child did not know what the consequences would exactly be. Although he had only just turned 14, he had to make an adult decision. Perhaps they would, like Saikia sir had said, keep him for a while in a camp to clear him of all charges and then let him come home. On the other hand, they could also put him in jail and keep him there forever—and young Okon would die little by little if that happened. The decision was far harder than Saikia sir thought it to be; Okon wanted Hirukai's return more than anything else in the world, but could those *rakhyasas* be trusted? He had agonised over the issue through half the night and realised he needed to talk to someone else to clear up the confusion and ambiguity in his mind.

There was only one individual on this earth, apart from Hirukai, who Okon could open his heart to. Pitai, of course, was almost oblivious of what went on in his household; nowadays, after his morning stint in the fields, he would spend the rest of the day almost all by himself, giving only monosyllabic replies to comments or questions thrown at him by Ai or Bai. Since the departure of Hirukai for joining the ULFA, whatever communication existed between Pitai and the villagers had almost ceased; he no longer went to the village *naamghar* for prayers or to attend the periodic conclave of village elders. Ai, Bai, and Okon would go every Friday to the *naamghar* for the weekly *naam-prasanga*; but nowadays, there was an unseen screen shutting them away from the rest of the villagers who, however, treated them with the utmost deference and always offered them seats on the floor at the front at the *naamghar*. Even the village youngsters kept their distance from Okon, which he did not mind in the least, given his introverted nature. The boy, though he loved his mother, could not share any secret with her—least of all one which involved Hirukai. He knew she would become emotionally upset and spill it out to Pitai.

However, Okon could talk about the most intimate things with Bai; she might not be able to replace Hirukai in his estimations, but in some ways she was actually more close to him than his elder brother since the element of adoration was missing from their relationship. This was why having to keep the secret of Hirukai's message had been troubling him so much; had Hirukai not strictly enjoined him to keep it away from Bai's ears, Okon would have told her everything—including the existence of the *daini's* lair. But the message had clearly commanded Okon to tell no one else, 'not even Bai'! The child, therefore, tried to lighten some of his load of guilt by telling Bai about what Karuna Saikia sir had told him. Then there was the other reason—the urge within him to discuss the issue with someone before taking such a serious decision, even though he had already made up his mind.

'Saikia sir has been talking to me,' Okon told his sister. It was evening. The sun at a distance was on the verge of setting. Both were seated on *pirrahs* at the front courtyard of their compound.

'What about? Have you been neglecting your studies again?'

'No, no. He has been talking about Hirukai,' Okon protested, not looking towards his sister but at the bamboo palisade marking their compound's boundary. Village cattle were wending their way home from the grazing grounds, leaving a trail of dust in their wake.

'Saikia sir? Hirukai?' Bai was genuinely startled. 'What has Saikia sir to say about Hirukai?'

'That an important police officer had approached him. Wanted to give us a message. If Hirukai were to ever make contact with us, we're to tell him the government is offering him a chance to surrender.'

'Surrender?' Bai was unable to comprehend the implications of what Okon had been saying.

'Yes, like Kalpakai. He's safe in a camp, you know. Will be free by next week and come for the *uruka* feast at Chungijan.'

Bai did not immediately reply, but mulled for a while over what she had been told. Then she said, 'There's something not right about this, Okon. Why through Saikia sir? The policeman could have talked directly to us. God knows they have come so many times…even those terrible army men, to our house!'

'I don't know,' Okon said, avoiding Bai's eyes.

'Also, Hirukai's in terrible danger. No one can be trusted. See what happened when he told Rajeev to let us know he was coming? They were waiting for him, the army and police people! He had somehow come to know, so he did not turn up. I don't think he will try to come again. He knows there are informers everywhere, even in the village.'

'Maybe. Perhaps. But what if he were to meet me somewhere else? Without actually coming to our house? Should I tell him about Saikia sir and what the police officer said?'

Bai looked sharply up at Okon, but the boy was avoiding her eyes. 'Are you up to something, Okon?' she asked.

'What do you mean?' Okon asked with all the innocence he could muster. But Bai, clearly, was not convinced. 'You watch out now,' she said with a degree of rebuke. 'Hirukai can take care of himself and make his own decisions. Also, there is no way he is coming back here after what happened the night before last. So you won't get a chance to convey the message, right?'

Okon pursued the theme no further. Bai was shrewd and they were treading on dangerous grounds! The conversation had proved to be fruitless; the weight of having to make a crucial decision remained heavy on his mind.

Inspector Lahiri checked out of his hotel on the evening of Tuesday, December 27, immediately after his meeting with Karuna Saikia at the Doomdooma market. The food in the hotel, of course, had been terrible, but that was not the reason for the shift to the dak bungalow located not too far away. The cockroaches and bedbugs had been routed, so that, too, was not the cause! Actually, he had not anticipated a prolonged sojourn at the small township. If he remained much longer at the hotel, his cover was at risk of being blown. After all, he had no idea how many more days he would need to stay. The three-night stint in a seedy hotel of a one-horse town like Doomdooma already appeared too long—especially for a travelling clothes salesman, given the limited number of garment shops in the market. Moreover, his recent behaviour had not quite fitted in with his assumed persona. After all, even the most credulous would hardly expect a clothing salesman to return to his hotel at an unearthly hour as he had done the previous night!

Another equally compelling reason had been that the telephone in the hotel was out of order, so for any calls Lahiri had to make (he was committed to report to the DGP every day) he had to go out and use a nearby public call office—a matter of great inconvenience as well as another reason to arouse suspicion. He, in every sense of the term, belonged to the old school of intelligence officers—never mind that with the latest electronic technology even landline calls could be intercepted. It was a part of his modus operandi never to use his cell phone while calling the DGP or any of his contacts; cautious to a fault, he, in fact, did not use his cell phone to call anybody apart from his wife. So he had rung up the OC of the local *thana* from a PCO in the market after the chat with Karuna Saikia, got his room at the dak bungalow booked and the chowkidar there alerted about his imminent arrival.

The fellow at the hotel counter was surprised at the sudden departure of his salesman guest—the sole resident of the hotel for the nonce—he had helpfully pointed out he would have to pay for a full day since check out time was noon. Lahiri had curtly told him it was alright and he would pay for the extra day; his business at Doomdooma having finished, he would be leaving for Tinsukia by a night bus. He had shifted bag and baggage (meaning a medium size worn out suitcase, which he could easily carry) to the dak bungalow on foot—an old, Assam-type bungalow which had seen better days. He would be its only occupant for quite some time now, so he was informed by the old chowkidar—with Tinsukia having a host of overnight-stay facilities everyone, including government officials, preferred that town to Doomdooma. The chowkidar was the cook, too. But meals had to be ordered well in advance and a payment made so he could purchase the required groceries from the market, and keep it in his custody till the time to serve arrived. Everything, Lahiri had noted, was as satisfactory as it could be under the circumstance—he was armed with anti-cockroach spray and anti-bed-bug powder, the linen and blankets on the bed were relatively clean (cleaner, in fact, than those of the hotel!), there was even a mosquito-repellent plug-in despite the mosquito-nets draped over the bed, and the chowkidar cum chef's cooking was a revelation (being far better in taste and quality than of the hotel or Bhogali restaurant). All in all, Lahiri had no reason to complain about the shift in venue. The most important thing, of course, was that he had a working phone in the room, as also privacy (though the dak bungalow was relatively small, the compound containing it was inordinately large; also, as the chowkidar had already repeatedly informed him, he was the sole tenant in the bungalow for the time being).

Now that the plot-line had taken a different turn, necessitating a longer stay than he had envisaged, it was imperative he remain cooped up in the room of the dak bungalow (no matter what the chowkidar might think), unless some essential task required him to venture out. In a small town like Doomdooma, a stranger who stays for even a day catches the attention of the locals—one who stays on for many days (even if it might be in the dak bungalow) without any apparent and definitive purpose rouses suspicion! Lahiri was all too aware of the need for caution on his part; he reminded himself that the ULFA, too, had its eyes strewn about in most unlikely places. One hint of the prolonged presence of a senior inspector of police intelligence in Doomdooma might destroy any possibility of ensuring that the civet stays within its home range. He had to let things take their own course; he was no longer in control of the situation… Now, all depended on how others acted.

He, therefore, spent most of the time reading newspapers bought on his behalf by the chowkidar. He also spent a great deal of time meticulously trimming his moustache with a pair of small scissors he always carried in his toiletry pouch. The trimming ritual was almost therapeutic; it helped to take away his thoughts from the job at hand and focus them on strands of harmless hair which needed to be chopped mercilessly down. It also required artistry, the touch of a sculptor giving shape to his unique creation!

He, of course, was all too aware of a civet's trait. Although it instinctively knew its fangs to be ill-equipped to tackle bamboo or the steel-mesh walls of duck-coops, it would come night after night for yet another attempt at possible entry. But then, was his simile born merely of a childhood memory? Perhaps, even now his quarry was on his way back to Myanmar—thanking his lucky stars he had managed to elude two moments of almost certain capture, and not wanting to test his good fortune any further. Something at the back of Lahiri's mind continued to insist that this was not so; this was not the way Hiru would behave. His colleague at Tinsukia had also agreed with him on this… Hiru would not go back empty handed! Who knew, the *hepa* might even return to the duck-coop from which it had been chased away! Hiru had been in touch with the person most cherished by him; yes, there could no longer be any doubt that somehow Hiru had managed to contact his brother—the odds were a thousand to one. Lahiri would have been the first to acknowledge its improbability—though thwarted once, would Hiru make another attempt to meet his family?

Yet, there were no other options but keep track of the Hiru-Okon link; Lahiri must bank on Hiru's persistent nature, and hope the yet unidentified link to Okon held the key. Having shifted from the hotel to the dak bungalow he had gone out only twice: first, for a quick trip to the *thana* for a brief chat with the OC to enquire about the manpower he had under his command and the kind of weapons they carried; and the second to Chungijan under the cover of darkness. He had entered one of the cottages and paid the village youth named Bhodiya (his in-house informer, so to speak) 300 rupees to follow Okon wherever he went and keep him under observation at all times. On his earlier visit, he had equipped the fellow with a cheap mobile phone; though signal reception was poor, at least contact could be maintained.

Other than these short-duration bursts of activity, Lahiri had been almost inert. A call from his colleague at Tinsukia late in the afternoon of December 29 pulled him out of his somewhat pessimistic inertia. The man had just learned that Hiren Bora had been spotted by the police at a *dhaba* this very afternoon. But the idiots who had spotted him, rather than tackle him on their own, waited for back-up to arrive, thereby allowing Hiru to make yet another escape. The fellow seemed to have nine lives of a cat, Lahiri's colleague had commented. Just minutes later he received another call—from the OC of the Doomdooma *thana*—with the same information that a man most likely to be Hiren Bora had managed to give the slip to the police at a point midway between Doomdooma and Talap.

The inspector had been thrilled. Only one inference could be drawn from the latest encounter—Hiru was not on the retreat. If he had planned to go back to Myanmar, he would have been well on his way by now and would not have taken the risk of spending a couple of nights at a *dhaba*—which Lahiri knew had a bad reputation, where betrayal and discovery had been almost inevitable. When he called up the DGP there was exuberance in his voice, which surprised the veteran policeman.

'We're still in with a chance, sir,' he told his superior. He explained about the new bag which Okon now carried to school. He had definitely established that the bag had been gifted by no one else but Okon's elder brother. This irrefutably indicated Hiru had been near Chungijan on the night of December 26, and had somehow made contact with Okon. He mentioned in details the steps he was taking to keep Okon under observation, just in case his brother tries to contact him. He also conveyed the latest information about Hiru having evaded arrest at a *dhaba* (something the DGP already knew), strongly hinting that he would remain in the area and, perhaps, make another extortion attempt. Lahiri desired to stick with Okon in the hope Hiru might try and get in touch with him.

'It's the slimmest of chances, sir,' he conceded. 'But I don't see any other direction for us to push toward. Nor do we want to lose this opportunity, for the fellow might not enter Assam again for God only knows how long. As I told you, sir, the bond between the two brothers is strong. So the possibility of Hiru wanting to meet him at least once before he leaves is within the realms of possibility.'

'Look, Lahiri, I trust your judgement,' the DGP barked. 'So proceed in whichever manner you think fit. The bag...a fine bit of sleuthing on your part!'

'Thank you, sir. You understand, of course, that bags don't fly!'

'Are you underestimating me, Lahiri? However, try not to let too many in on this. You know, it's the barking of the village pariah mongrels which keeps the *hepa* away!'

Lahiri could not quite see the point his superior was trying to make, but emitted a titter all the same as though he could appreciate the humour. 'Just one thing, sir,' he concluded. 'The army has been unreasonable about sharing information with the civil administration. It had not informed us about the extortion attempt at Tinsukia or the incident at Lajim. The response in both cases had been initiated entirely by the army, and our policemen—even those of the anti-terrorist commando force—were not called upon to assist.'

'Well, the abortive December 26 night operation did not help! So what are you suggesting—no more quid pro quo?'

'Exactly, sir. They know nothing about the bag or that Hiru was near Chungijan on December 26 night. If anything tangible emerges from this, and we do get an opportunity to apprehend our man, we can act on our own without involving the army. I have made enquiries at the Doomdooma *thana*. We have the resource for it.'

The DGP chuckled. 'You're a man after my own heart, Lahiri! Go ahead and keep the buggers out of the picture, if things do reach that stage. I'll take care of any repercussions at this end.'

The army encampment at Dangori was not a permanent one, but a make-do establishment set up for strategic reasons, manned by an elite, rapid-action, anti-insurgency squad of the 4th Rhino Battalion. Although the heavily-guarded complex comprised of temporary structures of bamboo and thatch—which meant not much of a hassle if it were to be shut down for strategic reasons and shifted elsewhere—the encampment was equipped with the fastest heavy-duty vehicles owned by the army, and the latest arsenal of weaponry and communication equipment. The canvas tent, housing the monitoring wing, had someone at the instruments 24 hours of the day; there was very little insurgency-related information which did not reach this little tent.

Just beside it was a small hutment—the spartanly furnished office of the commander of the squad, Major Harekrishna Bhagat. On the night of December 29, though the clock on the wall showed it to be almost 9:30 pm, the major was still in his office—along with a man in civvies, an intelligence officer from the Research and Analysis Wing of the Union government of India; he currently went by the name of Ravi Arora. That he had five other identity cards for appropriate occasions was a different matter altogether!

The RAW officer had arrived an hour earlier. Accompanied by the Major Bhagat, for a while he discussed immediate developments vis-à-vis Hiren Bora with army intelligence personnel attached to the squad, shifted through the copies of documents considered relevant for some more time, and then went to the major's office for a well-deserved shot of whiskey. Glass in hand, he leaned back in his chair and put up his legs on the table behind which the army officer was seated.

'Bloody shame!' he said.

'Yes,' conceded the major. 'Gave us the slip twice in a matter of a few days. But then, the idiots who were his targets were late in getting in touch with us.'

'That's a matter of opinion,' Arora said smugly. 'You're supposed to be a rapid action squad! Moreover, no anti-insurgency police commandos were with you when you responded... So no independent witnesses to back-up your assertion.'

'If it's a question of our words against theirs, I'll let it be that way.'

The RAW officer was unfazed by the contempt oozing out of the major's mouth. 'Look, I'm here to help, not antagonise you,' he said. 'You underestimate me in citing wrong figures. The ULFA alpha male called Hiren Bora has given the security forces the slip at least four times during the last few weeks, not twice as you claim. First was the extortion attempt at Tinsukia.'

'Yes. We set a trap for him. But somebody warned him off.'

'Does that absolve you from being blamed, I ask you? The army on that occasion did not seek the local police's assistance... did not even inform them! So you cannot blame their intelligence network for the leakage. Face it major, it's someone from your own intelligence network who tipped Hiren Bora off, so you're the chap I would blame.'

Since the army officer chose not to reply, Arora continued. 'The second occasion was the raid on the night of December 26 at Chungijan village. Your superiors are already chagrined at the way the raid was conducted. Too many men, too many vehicles, too much noise—just to nab a single person.'

'But the target did not show up!' Major Bhagat objected.

'How can you be sure? He may have come. More subtlety on your part and he may have even walked into your trap. That's what your superiors are perhaps discussing at the moment in the army cantonment in Guwahati!'

Arora drained his glass and refilled it from the bottle on the table. 'You botched up on the third occasion, too—once again, you failed to nab the fellow in the tea garden despite getting an early alert. The manhunt you launched after his escape was so much money and energy down the drain. Not too good a show, I must say.'

'But this afternoon's incident. It was the local police all the way!'

'That's right. But then the *dhaba* is merely a stone's throw away from here. So the fellow was literally under your noses, yet you couldn't sniff him out, could you? Yeah, had those police idiots contacted you, I'm sure you could have been there quicker and perhaps nabbed your man. But then you don't call the police when situations like the Lajim type come up, do you? So why should they bother to inform you?'

Major Bhagat once more lapsed into sullen silence. 'Let me tell you what the problem is, major,' Arora continued. 'It is complete lack of trust between the agencies meant to undertake anti-insurgency measures in a coordinated manner. Too much rivalry, too little faith in one another's capacity to hold on to top secret information, too much treachery, too many betrayals. But then, I've not come here to wax eloquent on the shortcomings of our system. Rather, I come as a friend.'

'What are you getting at?'

'Wait. Just a moment. Have your orderly call your man who led the raid at Chungijan.'

Soon afterwards, a young captain entered and saluted the major. If he was startled to see a civilian in the room with his legs atop the commanding officer's desk, his face did not betray it. Also, to his surprise, it was the civilian who popped a question at him.

'Tell me, captain… During the raid at Chungijan, did a man not dressed in police uniform accompany the police team?'

'Yes. A mousey, bespectacled man. I must say that I had been surprised to see him.'

‘Thank you, captain. You may go.’ This time, the young officer’s salute as he left the room included both the men in its ambit.

‘That would be Inspector Lahiri, top sleuth of the Special Intelligence Branch of the State Police Department. Based in Guwahati. If my information is correct, he has been sent on a specific mission by the DGP himself. In fact, again, if my information is correct, he was the motivator for the raid at Chungijan. Thus, his presence in the raiding party!’

‘How does that matter to us?’

‘You guys are not very high on the ability to infer things, are you? Look, if Lahiri had come in connection with the raid on Chungijan, he would have returned the moment it was over. But he stayed on! Apparently, he is convinced Hiren Bora has not fled to Myanmar but is determined to complete what he had come to do. I would not have known about all this had I not had a mole within the police intelligence at Tinsukia. Lahiri had known my man for a long time and trusts him. What he did not know was that the fellow also works for me. For a regular payment, of course. Lahiri came to him for the latest information on Hiren Bora’s movements, as also to confirm that the bugger would stay on in the area.’

‘I ask again, how does that matter to us? A parallel investigation by the police department...it happens all the time. At least they had the courtesy to engage in the Chungijan raid with us in the lead.’

‘A courtesy they’re not likely to repeat, if the *dhaba* encounter is anything to go by! But there is more than meets the eye to the fact that Lahiri has decided to prolong his stay. I know the man. He is meticulous in what he does and doesn’t miss a trick. I’ll bet you a fiver he knows something more than he is divulging.’

Major Bhagat raised an enquiring eyebrow. ‘You want us to keep an eye on him, is that it?’ he asked, almost incredulously.

'Exactly! Use local resources. Try and learn what he's up to and then step in at the appropriate time.'

'Tell me, why this act of goodwill towards us? I've not laid eyes on you till this evening!'

The man—who at this point of time called himself Ravi Arora—smiled, finished his drink and stood up. 'Let's just say I hate these local bastards and leave it at that, shall we?'

On the morning of December 30, a tall and powerfully-built man parked his motorcycle in front of the small hotel where Lahiri had stayed for a few nights, and entered through the door. He did not take off the helmet he was wearing, nor did he lift up the visor. Finding no one at the desk, he banged loudly upon it. Minutes later the clerk on duty at the counter, clearly irritated, emerged from the backroom.

'Hey, what the devil are you playing at?' he asked angrily.

The man removed his helmet, and the clerk blanched. Everyone at Doomdooma knew Gohain! Decades back he had joined the ULFA, but had later surrendered—thereby becoming a dreaded member of the group known as surrendered ULFA, or SULFA for short. He was feared by all and sundry, something he used to his advantage.

'Sorry, Gohain-da. Didn't know it was you.'

The SULFA man called Gohain thrust a photograph at the face of the clerk. 'Seen this man?'

'Yes, of course. He stayed with us for a few nights. Checked out last Tuesday evening. Seemed to be in a bit of a hurry. Let me get the register so you can see for yourself.'

'No need. Did he tell you where he was headed?'

'For Tinsukia, he said. Would be catching a night bus, he said.'

Gohain shrugged his shoulders and was about to turn and leave when the clerk at the counter spoke again.

'Hey, Gohain-da, is there something in it for me if I give you some useful information?'

Gohain grinned. 'Depends on what that information is.'

'Well, the truth of the matter is that this fellow said he was leaving for Tinsukia on Tuesday evening. Yet I can swear I saw him the very next day near the bazaar. Mind you, he paid for a full day although he left in the evening. Made me curious, it did! So I followed him when I saw him next, and where do you think the fellow goes to?'

The clerk paused for effect. Gohain played along.

'Yes, where to?'

'The police *thana*, where else? Made me more curious, it did! Being my off-duty morning, I waited for the fellow to leave the *thana* and then followed him. Where do you think he went?'

Again the clerk paused for effect and once again Gohain played along.

'Yes, where to?'

'The dak bungalow! The idiot thought he could pull the wool over my eyes. Clothes salesman, my left toe! One of those bloody intelligence chaps... Could make it out the moment I laid my eyes on him.'

Gohain pulled out a 100-rupee note from a wad in his pocket and handed it to the grateful clerk. 'Thanks,' he said with a suavity which did not quite match up to his notoriety. 'It's the dak bungalow for me, then.'

It had been the chowkidar who alerted Lahiri about the presence of a motorcyclist who was keeping an eye on the dak bungalow from the shade of a tree on the opposite side of the main road. The old man had read significance in the fact that the OC of the police *thana* had arranged for the guest's accommodation. He had also been mystified because the man remained cooped-up in his room, venturing out only twice all these days. Despite being old, the chowkidar was a person equipped with sharp eyes—he had spotted the motorcyclist while trimming the hedges near the compound walls. Had his guest not been something of a mystery, he might not have told him that he was apparently being watched.

Lahiri was alarmed, though he tried not to show his concern to the watchman. However, he wrongly assumed that the man outside was an ULFA linkman deputed to keep a watch over him. If this was at Hiren Bora's instructions then, thought Lahiri, his *hepa* might be as good as gone.

EYES

From the very moment he entered the *daini's* lair, Hiren Bora was at work. He had less than an hour before the early birds among the village folk woke up. The probability was none too great, but Hiren Bora was not willing to take even the almost-zero chance; one of these might choose to saunter through the thick fog towards his patch of paddy, and get close enough to the bamboo grove to hear noises emanating from within—reporting the same back to others in the village. They might simply think someone was poaching upon the community bamboo patch without taking permission, and come to investigate. But that would be of little help. It had been extremely dim in the clearing; even the beams of his small, flat torch could not provide much light. But then, he was like a *hepa* with eyes trained to see its way in the dark!

With unerring instinct his hands had curled around one bamboo stem after another till he found what he wanted; a young and thin plant, hardly much past its sapling stage. He cut it down with a knife and spliced it into eight thin, bendable strands with ends like arrow-heads. These, he bent into an arched shape and stuck the ends with some difficulty upon the hard, humid earth so that he soon had the skeleton for his shelter. He took out a square of light, thin plastic purchased in Doomdooma, which when unfolded provided enough material to cover the bamboo framework. He secured the edges of the plastic to the ground by driving small bamboo stakes into it. He could relax a bit after having completed the crude, makeshift structure, since there would be no more activity involving sound. It was large enough for a grown-up man to recline on the ground in a fully stretched-out posture; Hiren Bora grunted with satisfaction—the *daini's* lair would be his place of stay for the next few days and nights, and he needed to be as comfortable as he could under the circumstance. The shelter would prevent his getting dew-soaked at night, while the sleeping bag (Chinese-made, also purchased yesterday evening) had warmth enough to protect him from the fog-ridden cold of December nights.

Although the leaves of the bamboo rustled continuously, there was, in fact, very little breeze coming in through the heavy shield. Even if a stiff gale had been blowing, his shelter would be able to withstand it because of the protection offered by the thick bamboo growths. It would not be of much use, of course, if there was a spell of heavy, tropical rain—but this was the end of the English year and the season was winter, so the chances of heavy downpour were minimal. The moment such uselessly futile thoughts flitted into his mind, Hiren Bora knew it would be a long day and a long night for him. Because of the Bihari's treachery, he had had to return to the *daini's* lair a day in advance of what he had planned; he had summoned Okon on December 31; it was a Saturday, so a half-day at school for the boy. He would be able to make the tryst in the latter half of the day, and then have the entirety of Sunday to carry out his assignment as well as report back to his elder brother. He had grown accustomed to thinking and planning ahead like this; but he, too, was no stranger to the fact that sudden twists more often than not disrupted well-thought out strategies. The ability to adopt a phlegmatic attitude towards whatever happened had also become his second nature.

But stoical acceptance had its limits, Hiren Bora thought ruefully! This mission had been one frustrating episode after another; moreover, periods of inertia where he had had to lie low had been far more than days of activity. Those spent upon the *machan* or at the *dhaba* had been a sheer waste of time; even the days of activity had not moved him an inch towards attaining this mission's goal. True, time no longer held much meaning to Hiren Bora; a prolonged, almost nomadic, rootless existence numbs one to the sense of passing time. But then, he had not quite grown immune to the ennui which days and days of inactivity can bring; this was the way of youth and, despite having matured beyond his years, he could not contradict the impulses of Nature beyond a point.

Not one to cheat himself, Hiren Bora acknowledged his patience indeed was being stretched thin on this trip. What he refused to admit was that his disconcerted mood was as much due to the feel of guilt lying deep in his core: here he was, making cynical use of the one person whom he could absolutely trust and who had the deepest faith in him! He told himself it had been unavoidable; there was no feasible alternative since, seemingly, all his other resources had been compromised. It would be, of course, a last desperate throw of the dice; if this attempt did not succeed, he would make his way back to the KIA camp in Myanmar and confess to Pradyut Basumatari that he had failed. He told himself he was not putting Okon in any jeopardy; the boy would simply be a conduit for communicating with the intended target…that in his state of mind, he was displaying the slightest of qualms at having to use Okon was pointer enough that the environment can never totally obliterate basic, gene-imparted traits.

A few hours inside the *daini's* lair and Hiren Bora began pacing about like an animal in a cage; with a sudden start he realised he could not stay cooped-up in such a small space for much longer, and needed to engage in some form of activity. He also direly craved for a cup of tea, but lighting a fire within the confines of the clearing was unthinkable—the light emitted by a small fire could be kept hidden from other eyes, but not the smoke and the aroma. Thus, any cooking he had to do would be only after darkness when the sharp-nosed villagers would be safely in their cottages! Also, he might have to stay for a few days within his lair, so defecating in the clearing was out of the question, for the smell might grow unbearable—such fatuous concerns, such silly thoughts! What he needed was a bit of self-induced excitement; he had not quite felt like this for a long, long time. Suddenly Hiren Bora stopped pacing, and plucking out a half-filled polythene pouch from his handbag and the large, by now almost-empty plastic water bottle, began moving through the bamboo maze.

Reaching the end, at the edge of the paddy fields he stopped—his sharp eyes scanning the area around him. The sun was up, the fog-screen had completely lifted and he had to shut and then reopen his eyes to get them adjusted to the abrupt brightness. There were figures, male and female, at a distance, but no one close by—the villagers within the paddy fields were focused on reaping the golden ripe harvest, and so, were less likely to be attracted towards any movement this far away. Also, if he shuffled along the fringe of the bamboo grove, the darker background would help to shield his movements from the sharpest of eyes; a long way back during training it had been drilled into him that he must wear dark-coloured clothes and never white during missions. So the clothes he wore now blended well into the background.

Hiren Bora moved along the outer perimeter of the bamboo spread. Arriving at its edge, he veered sharply away from the paddy fields towards the jungle, cutting through a narrow trail and then turning towards a point where the greenery gave way to the Chungijan stream. Once again, he surveyed the area around him with eyes which missed nothing. Before stepping out of the verdure onto the un-forested bank, he scooped up the clear cold water and washed his mouth, and refilled the water bottle. For one moment, he thought of having an invigorating swim in the stream but decided the risk was too great. Then he dug into the polythene pouch for his favourite meal of *luchi-bhaji*, made a paper-boat (he recalled doing something similar with Okon when he was very young) of the newspaper wrapping, and watched it sail down the stream. Next, he defecated, and washed his hands after rubbing them with soil scooped up from the ground.

Any one observing would not have known that every sense of the man was on full alert—the way he lolled on the grassy stream-bank with closed eyes. But there were unsought, disturbing memories, and all too soon he jumped to his feet and began making his way upstream along the bank. Oh, he would feed on dry ration during the day, but he was determined he would make a feast of it at night when he would be able to light a small fire and cook. For the next couple of hours he inspected various fish-traps set up by the villagers, taking just one fish each from those having them and placing it in the polythene pouch. When the sun reached the zenith of its climb across the sky, Hiren Bora made another meal of a packet of pounded rice he had in his pocket. Then he moved once more into the jungle in a purposeful way, gathering an *ou-tenga* fruit growing wild, as also soft cane strands and red chillies. To his delight, he chanced upon a ripening jack-fruit which had miraculously managed to survive an onslaught from the birds and herbivorous creatures of the wild.

He began his return journey to the *daini's* lair when the sun was quite low on the horizon; the fields were empty, the villagers had departed. Once inside, he waited till the sun had set and the fog rolled in to enhance the darkness. He then lit a small fire and cooked up a meal of rice and fish in sour *ou-tenga* curry. It had been a cathartic trip—the day's journey through a memory lane. The uneasy restlessness he had experienced in the morning was no longer there; it had been replaced by the sense of tranquillity only one with no conscience and ignored memories can experience. Taking out a pad with the ULFA logo as a letterhead, he began writing out the extortion letter...

Almost miraculously, there had been no nightmare last night—no *rakhyasas* with hideous features, arched eyebrows raised over monstrous eyes and cavernous mouth splattered with human gore disturbed him in his sleep. Perhaps, this was because the saviour was close by (though concealed), and only he knew it. Perhaps, it was also because of the strong possibility (at least in Okon's mind) that the saviour could be cajoled into remaining close by forever, and not go away again. Nothing can be more seductive than optimistic joy; Okon was too young for self-introspection, but even he could understand that the seed of hope planted by Hirukai's note and Saikia sir's words had sprouted, and its tendrils had curled around his mind and soul. He would keep his tryst, speak from the heart with the saviour, and things would again be the same as they had once been.

He woke up at the crack of dawn on Saturday, completed his chores and was off to school on his bicycle at the usual time. At a distance away from the cottage, he stopped, somewhat undecided. He hopped off the bicycle, placed it on its stand, and then looked in the direction of the paddy fields and the jungle beyond. It was a powerful, natural impulse; he knew the mentor of whom he was but a shadow must be inside the *daini's* lair by now. He could simply skip school and go straight to the place whose secret only he and Hirukai knew, and fling himself into the latter's arms. They would lie upon the ground as they used to before, and look up through the bamboo chimney at the tiny patch of blue which seemed further away from that angle; they would talk their hearts out; of the things each had seen and done; and then Okon would talk about the offer conveyed by Saikia sir and would beg his icon to say yes. The child had no doubt Hirukai would agree; he could appreciate the hardships his elder brother must have gone through—a simple yes on his part would end the ordeal and deprivation for ever and ever!

Involuntarily, he shook his head. Hirukai's words were commandments; he had asked Okon to meet him this afternoon at the *daini's* lair once school was over—the afternoon it must be! The boy had no idea why his brother wanted to meet him despite the risk this entailed—the needless 'be careful no one sees you' caution in the note implied that Hirukai had not underestimated the danger. The reason to him seemed clear—his elder brother, too, had been yearning to meet with and embrace him in a bear-hug, though he did not understand why he had been asked to go in the afternoon when the risk would be greater. He could have been at the bamboo copse early in the morning with the fog at its thickest; but then, surely Hirukai would not want him to miss school—most likely the reason for 'afternoon after school'! Yes, Hirukai's words were commandments and the question of him going to the *daini's* lair right now did not arise. Okon took one lingering look across the paddy fields, hopped on to the bicycle and began pedalling towards the main road to Doomdooma.

But now, a frown of perplexity rumpled his young features. The section of the road where he had come to a stop contained nothing but paddy fields on either side; there were very few trees and no cottages. So one could see a long way across the length of the road both left and right—the frown on Okon's features had been caused by the fact that he had spotted through a corner of his eye another cyclist coming by the same road. There was, of course, nothing peculiar about two cyclists riding at the same time over a *kutcha* village path. However, the odd thing was that the other cyclist had also suddenly come to a stop for no apparent reason in the middle of nowhere, and stood gazing like Okon at the jungle on the horizon!

On the move again, the boy took one quick look backward—yes, the other cyclist, too, was now on the move! A wave of panic swept over him as his intelligent mind grasped the implication, and the perplexity upon his features hardened into concern. Eyes were watching him! Has someone else come to know? Or had Bai somehow guessed what he was about to do and sent someone to follow him? This appeared implausible—but the person behind him was no mirage, he followed him right up to the macadam national highway and was still on his tail, no longer making secret he was shadowing him.

It took him back to the days immediately following Hirukai's departure to join the ULFA. For many months Okon had sensed the presence of watchful eyes—observing the cottage, tracking their every movement, Pitai and Bai as they walked together to work in the fields, Okon as he made his way to school. But sometime later, the mostly unseen eyes had disappeared altogether. But here was a pair now! Okon understood this was no coincidence. But then, was he not Hirukai's acolyte? Could he not take care of a simple pair of eyes?

The fellow seemed to be an ass, the way he had stopped

when Okon stopped. He should have simply ridden on and Okon would not have suspected a thing! So, apparently, it would not take much to turn him into a bigger idiot! But first, his identity must be uncovered; he had stayed too far behind to make identification possible, and Okon did not want to keep looking back since this might alert the man that he had been spotted.

He continued to pedal on at a steady pace, the one shadowing him doing the same. As always, he had left home having given himself more than ample time to reach school, so there was no need for hurry. The early morning traffic on the road was not much, and those on bicycles were mostly students—so it was not difficult for the boy to keep track of the other's whereabouts. Then, as they entered the outskirts of Doomdooma, Okon suddenly burst into a frantic pace, something not immediately spotted by the person trailing him because by now, students on bicycles had become sizeable in number; by the time he woke up to the realisation, Okon was already out of sight behind the bend on the road as it snaked into the township.

Reaching the crowded roadside market area at the centre of the town, Okon took a quick look behind to make sure he had lost his man, hopped down from the bicycle and placed himself behind a small *ghumti*—whose owner sold everything from betel nut to biscuits. Sure enough, five minutes later the person following him appeared in a tearing hurry, a bewildered look on his features. He did not tarry at the market place but shot like an arrow towards the school.

It was Bhodiya, the village wastrel! The man who, according to village gossip, had not done an honest day's work in his entire life, yet could afford a mobile phone; the man who, Okon knew, had once asked Pitai for Bai's hand and had barely managed to escape a fist on his face from an irate father.

The youngster emerged from his hiding place and slowly pedalled towards the school. Bhodiya had stationed himself quite openly under a tree on the opposite side of the road fronting the school gate. A look of enormous relief appeared upon his features as he spotted Okon entering the school compound and parking his bicycle.

There was no sense of triumph in the boy at outwitting someone—rather, he was deeply troubled. He had to think up a way to keep Bhodiya from following him, and he had to do it soon.

Unlike the quarry, the hunter (the trapper, rather) was not trained to wait for frozen time to thaw and the earth to start moving on its orbit again. Although Lahiri did not know it, even Hiren Bora had had a sudden fit of restlessness, coercing him into engaging in pedestrian activities for the impatience to subside. In the inspector's case, the restlessness was more pronounced. No doubt, he considered that patience was of essence on such a mission, and felt he was patient enough for the job. But then, he had not slept well the past few nights; also, the fact that he did not have the power to influence events and had to let things take their course while he waited was extremely unnerving. He had doubled the time undertaken for physical and yogic exercises, and discovered these were overrated as far as their ability to calm frayed nerves were concerned. There was a definite danger that his moustache would be an unwitting victim of his restlessness; never had that growth received such prolonged and unsought for attention!

He had called up his wife more than he normally did, which roused concern even in her that something was amiss, though he assured her all was well. The DGP had sensed this was a period of lull and stopped calling, with the instruction that Lahiri get in touch with him only if he had something new and worthwhile to communicate. Karuna Saikia did not have much to report; Okon had been attending school as usual the past couple of days, flaunting his new school bag. Lahiri had spoken just once to Bhodiya; the fellow had started keeping an eye on the boy as instructed to do, but there did not seem to be much abnormal activity in the offing. A few more days of such inactivity, Lahiri ruefully thought, and his passion would turn into ditch-water!

Two minor developments troubled him, and between spells of trying to work out the crossword and Sudoku puzzles in various newspapers, he had mulled over these. First was another call he had received from his friend and colleague from the Tinsukia office, asking if any new developments had occurred on the Hiren Bora front. Lahiri could not quite place what it was, but something in the manner in which his colleague phrased his queries had disturbed him—it had seemed to be far deeper than mere curiosity; there had almost been a tone of interrogation in the manner in which the probing questions had been asked. An instinct had prompted him not to divulge anything to his colleague during the last meeting at Tinsukia; at that time he had accepted the latter's questions about his thoughts on Hiren Bora to be quite natural. But the latest, unexpected phone call raised a question mark in his mind, though he could not explain to himself what the question itself might be. Second was the motorcyclist who had parked himself opposite the dak bungalow. He recalled that when his attention had been drawn towards this unknown person by the chowkidar, he feared the worst: that Hiren Bora had learnt of his presence, and had sent someone to confirm the same. However, when on Saturday morning the motorcyclist returned and parked himself at the same spot, Lahiri began to wonder. If this was an ULFA linkman, he should have departed once the confirmation had been made; that he had come again meant the man had been sent to keep an eye on him. Lahiri could not fathom why. While he could put up with enforced inertia, questions for which he had no answers were like painful needles that poked into his logical mind.

He needed to quell the rising restlessness in him; he also needed to test the waters, though he doubted it would provide much illumination. Summoning the chowkidar to inform him that he was going out on a stroll and would be back shortly, Lahiri walked purposefully out of the dak bungalow's gate, sparing the motorcyclist not as much as a glance. He moved along the highway towards Okon's school; it being ten o' clock, classes had already started, and apart from the vehicular traffic, there were not too many people on the road.

Lahiri crossed the road—not that he really needed to, but because it enabled him to look right and left as though watching for oncoming traffic. Sure enough, the motorcyclist had followed him on foot, coming to an abrupt stop when Lahiri turned in order to make the crossing. The inspector walked along the opposite side till he was almost at the school gate. And, sure enough, Bhodiya was there—under the same tree which had offered its hospitable shade to Lahiri on the earlier occasion—his bicycle beside him! The inspector took a quick look at his watch and made an even quicker about-turn; he was more than cognizant of Bhodiya's lack of intelligence—the fellow might wave at him the moment he recognised him! He was pleased to note he had caught his shadower by surprise; the man, too, made an almost desperate about-turn and headed back to his motorcycle.

Half an hour later, having first gone to the market and entered a Public Call Office (PCO) booth and made a call to his wife—an on-the-spur, amateurish attempt to camouflage the real reason for his departure from the dak bungalow, on the assumption the motorcyclist did not know the phone there was in perfect working order. Lahiri returned to his room none the wiser as to what the fellow wanted. Something rummy was going on, but for the life of him Lahiri could not guess what it was!

Although quite alone and eminently noticeable as he squatted on the ground underneath the wide-trunked, leafy tree, there had been nothing incongruous about Bhodiya—someone seated on the roadside with little to do was a common sight in rural areas! The youth also possessed the rustic's ability to stolidly sit at the same place for long periods without doing anything; for an idler like Bhodiya, being paid to merely keep watch on a boy was simply icing on the cake.

However, this morning he was cursing himself for being stupid. Bhodiya, naturally, was blissfully oblivious that the level of his IQ qualified him for a perpetual ownership of that title! This was the third morning he had followed Okon to school; it had been alright till the blunder on the village link-road. How the devil was he to guess the boy would all of a sudden come to a stop in the most unlikely of places, and hop down from his bicycle only to gaze across the paddy fields? It had surprised him into making an abrupt stop, too, whereas he should have simply carried on, knowing as he did Okon was going to school. Then he had made another stupid mistake: instead of waiting like an idiot for Okon to continue on his way, he could have hopped down into the paddy fields, unbuttoned his trousers and pretended to pee! A man in dire need of unloading his bladders—a credible enough reason for someone stopping on the road!

Stupid, stupid, stupid! The boy's subsequent actions…the sudden acceleration of pace and total disappearance from view till his reappearance a while later at the school, indicated only one thing—Bhodiya had been exposed!

He did not know how the fellow who was paying him to shadow Okon would take this piece of news. He would have to report to him details of the day when the fellow called him as usual in the evening. For one moment, he considered keeping mum about the morning's mistake. But then, 'wiser' counsel prevailed—these fellows were omniscient and could always make out when a fellow was bluffing. Best would be to tell the truth and leave the rest in the hands of God!

Bhodiya continued to luxuriate in the warmth of the winter sun immersed in personal daydreams; with some money in his pocket, not only would he be in a position to enjoy himself during the coming *Bhogali-bihu*, but also buy a village damsel (the one he had been eyeing for some time) a propitiating gift. Pity such an assignment came only occasionally; he must tell the fellow that he wanted it to become permanent—the village snitch who would be paid a regular salary! It was the kind of job that suited his temperament. In earlier times it had carried a certain degree of risk, but with those blasted idiotic 'freedom fighters' at the end of their tether—such a job carried no more than even a whiff of danger.

Bhodiya was adept at indulging in this kind of reverie; he could have sat at the spot and dreamt on for hours, but the longer ring of a bell (signalling the end of school) brought him out of his dream. He jumped to his feet and stared fixedly at the hordes of boisterous school boys pouring out like bees swarming out of a hive. It would have been difficult to locate a particular boy immediately in the swarm, but Bhodiya was not perturbed. For the last couple of days he had been following Okon to school and home; he had had no problem picking him out because of the bright scarlet school bag slung on his back—which blazed like a *mejhi* on *uruka* night. All he had to do was wait for Okon with his tell-tale bag to appear at the gate.

Almost half the students had emerged and gone on their way; Okon had not yet come, but Bhodiya was not unduly worried. The boy may have been asked to stay behind by some teacher or the other, and would be coming out soon. Then, after 10 minutes of wait, with almost the school entirely empty and no sign of the scarlet school bag, he began to get a little nervous. It needed another five minutes and the gradual emergence of the teachers for Bhodiya to break into panic. Leaving his cycle behind, he ran into the school compound and searched around—Okon, certainly, was not inside.

Stupid, stupid, stupid! Dim-witted though he was, even he could make out that Okon had deliberately given him the slip—an outcome of the blunder he had made in the morning. Racing back to his bicycle, he pedalled furiously towards Chungijan, quite aware he would not be able to locate the boy. Oh, what would he tell the fellow when he'd call up in the evening? He had been paid only half the promised money as advance; having lost that kid this afternoon, he might well kiss the rest of the amount goodbye...

The young boy was not merely racing at a furious pace upon his bicycle, he was literally flying through the air! He felt light as a fluff of cotton ball plucked off a *simul* tree by a gust of wind, as though pure, unalloyed joy can enable one to defy the pull of gravity by casting off ballast-weight from the mind and heart. The past few days had seen him sitting, so to speak, on an emotional see-saw;

when Rajeev had first informed them Hirukai would be paying the family a visit, Okon had been ecstatic. So strong had been the feeling of anticipation, he would have compressed time itself—if feasible—so that the hours in between could be quickly shuffled through as though they were the pages of an uninteresting book. And then the sudden deflation of expectation on the dark and fearful night when the *rakhyasas* had come. Although it happened just a few days ago, it seemed so remote; the night when, for the first time in his young life, a *rakhyasa* (an authentic and not the imitation one from the *bhaona* at the *naamghar*, the fattest man in the village) had stared straight into his eyes from a close range. It had felt as though his soul had shrunk, quivering—so terrifying had been the gaze. That night, he had thought he could never ever climb out of the desolate depths Hirukai's presumed betrayal had flung him into.

Yet, the very next morning, there had been renewed ecstasy—not only at the sight of the school bag the colour of the *modar* flower, but also at the possibility of meeting his mentor once again. His heart had been singing a *bihu* song the past few days. And then this morning, as though to bring dark clouds into his patch of sunlit sky, he had sighted Bhodiya shadowing him. He understood the implications; somehow, someone suspected the link between himself and Hirukai and had set the dog after him. He had been alarmed. All morning, he could not concentrate on what the teachers were saying in class; time and again his eyes strayed towards the road where he could spot the devilish figure waiting for school to end—all the while considering his options. He could, of course, not go to the *daini's* lair at all, but that would be disobeying his mentor's instructions. Hirukai would be expecting him and he could on no account disappoint him; he had to go. Also, there were powerful urges within him which had to be satisfied.

It had been all too easy to fool the idiot Bhodiya; during the break he had searched the back of the school building and found what he had been looking for: a discarded rag. The moment the final bell had sounded he wrapped his school bag with the cloth; none of the boys who boisterously poured out of the building noticed what he was doing nor did anyone care. He had raced to the bicycle and was amongst the swarm emerging out of the school gate at the very beginning, keeping himself right in the middle. Then he had simply ridden away as fast as he could; one triumphant glance at his shadower and he knew his ruse had been successful. Bhodiya was still under the tree, peering at the group of students, trying to locate a school bag blood red as the setting sun!

His heart started singing again at the ease with which he had befooled the idiot. But the very next moment, he refocused his mind on to the serious business of reaching the *daini's* lair without being spotted by anyone else. He did not have the least doubt Hirukai would be there waiting for him; he also understood the terrible risk his elder brother was taking to see him, particularly after the raid the other night. But then, had he not always been Hirukai's shadow? More than the school bag, it was the thought that Hirukai would take such a terrible risk just to see his face and hear his voice that induced joy in him. Being but a child, Okon, instinctively, reduced situations to essentials in order to not dwell on the complexities which were the enemies of hope. Yes, he will not allow Hirukai to get away from him now that the chance has been offered. He would, without qualms, exploit his elder brother's love for him in order to bring him back to the family; he would tell Hirukai how much suffering Pitai, Ai, and Bai have been undergoing ever since he had left, as also of the vacuity in his own heart. He would use every weapon in his arsenal to sway his brother. Okon was confident that Hirukai—so kind, gentle, and loving—would respond positively to his importunities, and life would revert to what it had been before.

The group of students thinned away as he neared Chungijan and suddenly, he was alone on the highway. He looked back… the road was straight as an arrow and he could see a long distance back—there was no one else on a bicycle following him. On reaching the *kutcha* road leading to Chungijan, Okon did not turn right and take it; instead, he continued on ahead for another two kilometres till he saw a scrub-patch on to the right of the road and a narrow foot-trail, used mostly by cowherds and their cattle. He, of course, knew the area like the back of his hand; the bumpy foot-trail was not fit to ride a bicycle on, especially an old, rickety contraption like the one owned by Okon. So he hid his machine as well as his school bag within a thick growth of scrub, and began walking at a fast pace over the trail. That way he would be able to get to the jungle without having to cut through the paddy fields, and then wend his way unseen across the fringes of the vegetation till he reached the bamboo grove and the *daini's* lair.

He was at the bamboo grove within half an hour; it took him just two minutes to slither through the maze. He allowed his eyes to adjust to the lesser light. He had been absolutely certain that Hirukai would be within the *daini's* lair; but even then, his heart skipped a beat and he let out a gasp of incredulity as he saw the ragged, igloo-like structure his brother had built. The crude shelter alerted Okon to at least one thing—his elder brother did not plan to stay within the *daini's* lair only for a night, but a longer period. It indicated Hirukai was perhaps making the bamboo grove a place where he could hide as he planned out another operation. It also indicated something that should have depressed him—it had not been only love for Okon which had brought his elder brother back to the *daini's* lair! But this hardly bothered him now. He would be meeting his idol, perhaps even more than once—that was what really mattered!

Okon peeped into the shelter; Hirukai was not there, nor any of his stuff. He straightened up, perplexed. Had something spooked Hirukai? Had he left the lair? A couple of minutes later, in reassurance, Hirukai walked in through the same way the boy had just entered. Okon emitted a whoop of delight and embraced his brother in a fierce hug.

On the scale of trust, Okon would perhaps have scored a perfect 10 just a few years ago, but not any longer—Hiren Bora trusted no one nowadays. No doubt, even more than Ai or Bai, he knew the child's mind and the manner in which he would react to any situation. But then, he had not met him for over two years now; he did not know about (though he could guess) the terrible pulls and pressures the child must have been subjected to. Such pressures could destroy faith and slaughter sentiments, and irreversibly twist the brain like a piece of cloth wrung by a conscientious *dhobi* till aspects such as trust and loyalty muddied the ground.

So he had not waited (he had instinctively known Okon would come at the instructed hour) within the witch's grove for the boy's arrival, but outside, hidden in the jungle's foliage. Early that morning he had set out on his foraging excursion to gather fish, fruits, and ferns for the day. As the time for Okon's probable arrival neared, he stationed himself at a point beside a tree from where he could see the paddy fields. This had been to ensure there was no one with his brother if and when he came to meet him, or that he was not being followed. The *daini's* lair was like a cage—there was but a single exit; if others came with the boy, Hiren Bora would be trapped. That was why he had stayed outside, with his gun and his bag, at a vantage point to take a previously surveyed escape route if the need arose.

A sudden noise among the bushes had startled him into full alertness; he dropped instantly to the ground, cat-like and silent. To his amazement, he saw Okon moving stealthily by him almost at a touching distance—the clever boy had not come across the paddy fields, but taken a circuitous route across a trail through the jungle to lessen the chances of being seen. Hiren Bora did not call out, but waited for a while to make sure no one had been on Okon's tail. Then he left his hiding place and re-entered the *daini's lair,* to be greeted with a wild whoop and a hug.

It was imperative that he dissemble! His soul was like the ash-strewn hearth of a *mejhi* after the festivities were over, cold and black to the touch. Even the flame of love blazing from the boy's body could not reignite the dead charcoal residue; yet he must dissemble. His hands being full of the gun, bag, fish and other edibles, he could not respond by embracing Okon.

'Hey, let me put these away,' he said, laughingly. Okon matched his laughter with his own and released him. Hirukai stored away his things as well as the morning's haul of fish and other edibles; he washed his hands to get rid of the smell of fish, and then turned to Okon.

'Come,' he said, 'let me hold you.'

The two brothers clung to each other for what seemed to be an eternity, not talking, allowing the warmth of their bodies seemingly to fuse disparate souls. Hirukai deliberately allowed Okon to take the lead, letting his brother go only when the latter had un-wrapped his arms, so that he could look at a face and hear a voice the way he had been longing to do for years.

'You've caught fish!' Okon exclaimed excitedly. 'Remember, Hirukai, how we used to set those traps?'

'Of course, I do. These, however, aren't from any trap set by me. Filched them from some traps I found. You know, just a fish from each that won't be dreadfully missed.'

Okon laughed delightedly. 'You found *kaath-alu*, too!'

'Yes,' laughed Hirukai, 'I light a fire only at night, so no one can smell food being cooked. Except the *daini*, naturally, but she seems to be on a vacation!'

Okon laughed again. His eyes were dancing, his entire body laughing. 'Had I known, I would have brought something,' he said.

'Oh, that's alright. I'm doing fine. How's Ai? And Pitai?'

'They've never been the same since you left. You must come back, Hirukai, for their sake.'

His elder brother did not reply. Instead, he asked, 'How's your Bai?'

'She is heart-broken as well. Pitai and Ai are on the lookout for a groom for her...now that we have some money for the wedding. Ai has already put in an order for ornaments with an artisan from the village. But Bai says that she won't get married until you return.'

Hirukai nodded, noncommittally, though he continued to smile for his brother's sake. Okon was using every weapon he had, innocent of the fact that he was so easy to see through. For one brief moment, a faint glow—like that of a *chaki*—lit up inside the insurgent, to be snuffed out all too quickly through sheer will power.

'I might drop by and talk to her, who knows?' he said. 'Tell me, how was it the police were waiting when I wanted to come to you last Monday? Did they get the information out of any of you?'

The very moment Hiren Bora asked the question, he realised he had made an error of judgement. Dissimulation was difficult, alright! The exuberant smile on Okon's features disappeared. In fact, he seemed about to break out in tears.

'How can you even think that, Hirukai? God alone knows how much we've been harassed since you left. They took Pitai away to the army base so many times! Yet he did not tell them anything, not even of the times you visited us. Do you know the *rakhyasas* slapped Pitai when they were asking him questions? Last time they came one of them even touched Bai, though their leader immediately stopped him.'

A flame flared up in Hirukai at those words, but it was not of love or passion but fierce hatred. Okon saw the saviour's face harden; watched with growing anxiety his beloved Hirukai turn into a stranger, his features transform to those of a *rakhyasa*. There was an abrupt sinking feeling in the boy's heart; suddenly and instinctively, he knew that this time there would be no lying face upward on the earth and exchanging of memories! Hirukai scowled and spat contemptuously on the ground.

'Wh-wh-what's th-th-the matter, Hirukai?' Okon stuttered.

With a fierce exercise of resolve, Hiren Bora composed himself, relaxed, and smiled. He made his voice as gentle as he could and said, 'Nothing, Okon. I'm truly sorry I brought all this upon you. Perhaps, after you grow up, someday you'll understand.'

It had not been the kind of meeting Okon had dreamt about, but this in no way lessened his determination. 'It's alright, Hirukai,' he said, finding his natural voice. 'You know how much we all love you. Even the people of the village speak of you in the highest terms. You've broken all our hearts by leaving like that. You know, when you had gone, I felt empty inside. So many years have passed, but the emptiness is still there. It will be filled only when you come back and take care of the family.'

Spontaneous words of a child, unfeigned feelings! No longer could Hiren Bora look his younger brother directly in the eye. 'Did you like your school bag?' he asked, changing the subject.

'It's beautiful. Ai and Bai just love it. And the boys at school, they're jealous now. Keeps asking me where I got it, but I don't tell them, do I? You brought it all the way from China, didn't you?'

'Yes,' his brother lied. 'I bought it at the central market at Kunming in China.'

'You must have had some wonderful experiences these last few years. Oh, Hirukai, come back to us, please! We can listen on and on for hours about the far off places you've been to and the things you've seen.'

The insurgent continued to wear his feigned smile. 'Yes, Okon, I'll come back, I promise you. I do want to come back. But before I can do so, there are certain things which need to be taken care of.'

'No, come back now. Please, I beg you not only for my sake, but of Pitai, Ai, and Bai. This is the right time, Hirukai. Karuna Saikia sir has been talking of it to me.'

'Saikia sir?' the menacing tone threatened to seep once again into Hiren Bora's voice, and he had to make a conscious effort to keep the smile on his lips.

'Yes. He told me to pass on some information if you ever got in touch with me.'

'How did he know you would be seeing me?'

'He didn't, Hirukai. I can swear on the name of God to that. He knew you had come home on previous occasions. He is sure to know you were supposed to have come last Monday... Since everyone else knows, I'm sure he, too, must've known about the raid on our house. So it was only supposition on his part.'

Hiren Bora had long been aware that Karuna Saikia, mathematics and class teacher at the Doomdooma Boys' School, was recruited as a police informer just after the youth from

Chungijan had joined the ULFA—the obvious reason being that Okon also studied at the school. But Saikia's name had not cropped up adversely on the ULFA radar till this moment.

'And what was the information Saikia sir told you to pass on?'

'That the government is renewing the surrender offer. A senior police officer from Guwahati came to meet Saikia sir to assure him no harm will come to you if you surrender now. They will clear you of all criminal charges and you can come home to us again.'

Hiren Bora marvelled at how mature the boy before him, just turned 14, sounded as he relayed what he had been told. Karuna Saikia, the fat, oily son of a bitch! He had tried to use his little brother to get to him.

'Did he tell you who this senior police officer was?'

'No.'

Although he tried not to reveal it to his brother, Hiren Bora was concerned. A senior police officer from Guwahati was in the Doomdooma area even when he himself was present here. Surely, it was no coincidence; the insurgent was wily enough to connect two and two as far as the raid the other night was concerned. But what bothered him more was that he had not been informed of it. No doubt he had tried to remain as incommunicado as possible during this trip, but even then, there had been times and places where he could have been contacted. Yet, he did not know of the presence of the officer or his identity! It confirmed what Hiren Bora had long suspected; deep fissures had appeared in the ULFA intelligence network and there was no one who could be trusted any longer.

'Anything else?' Newly imprinted instincts had taken over and, almost unconsciously, Hirukai's voice had become intense.

'H-h-he t-t-told me to t-t-tell you...' the stammer was back in Okon's words and he could not finish what he had begun saying, and instead, broke down in tears. Hirukai put his arms around him and held him tight till the sobbing ceased and Okon was his old self again.

'The police officer would be staying on for a few more days in case you give yourself up, that's what Saikia sir wanted me to tell you. You remember Kalpakai, don't you? He surrendered and Saikia sir says he'll be back in Chungijan for *bihu*.'

The lad's innocent face did not match the significance of the connotations his word carried. The senior police officer would wait for a few more days in case Hiren Bora decides to surrender! So they were working under the assumption he was still in the area, despite the secrecy and silence he had maintained. Of even greater gravity was the use of Okon to convey the message. Had they just done that in the off chance the boy might come across his elder brother? Or did they have some reason to suspect Okon might be in touch with Hiren Bora?

'Tell me, Okon, has someone been following you lately?'

The question slashed at him like the lightening-fast strike of a cobra; he could not help but flinch. His mind raced over the implications if he told Hirukai he was being shadowed by Bhodiya. He understood what had made his brother ask the question and why he was so anxious about the answer. He suspected if he let out the truth Hirukai might chuck up what he had planned to do and leave the *daini's* lair this very moment. That would be the death of hope! Okon quickly turned his face away. 'No,' he said, stooping down and pretending to look at the fish his elder brother had brought in. 'I've seen no one try to follow me. Also, I've been taking precautions. Trust me, Hirukai, not even Pitai, Ai, and Bai know you're here, and that I would be meeting you.'

'Where's your bicycle? Also, your school bag, since you've come directly from school?'

The questions were shot at him, as though from the barrel of a gun. The harshness of Hirukai's voice was disconcerting, yet Okon tried to ignore it.

'I'd hidden the bicycle in some bushes, since I wanted to come through the jungle. Also, the bag...since it is heavy and would have slowed me down.'

Hiren Bora was satisfied. Okon had been a worthy acolyte; the master knew his pupil could take care of himself despite his tender age. 'I want your help, Okon,' he said.

The fog had lifted hours ago, yet it seemed to sweep from some unseen place into Okon's heart and dampen his ardour. So it had not been merely to see Okon and hear his voice that Hirukai had summoned him! Hirukai wanted him to do something for him! So no talking for hours as to what each had seen and done, no re-forging of a bond which, at one time, had seemed even death could not sever! It was to be strictly business! But then, Okon would have given his life for Hirukai, such was his love.

It was pretence on both sides now. 'Of course, I'll help you, Hirukai. Just tell me what I have to do.'

Hiren Bora did not immediately reply. He dipped into his polythene pouch and rummaged for a medium-sized sweet potato he had collected that morning. Unclasping his jack-knife, he cleaned up the outer red skin so it would be mud-free, sliced it into two halves and passed one slice to Okon. The boy could not guess it, but it had been a conscious gesture on the part of his brother—a practical and deliberate elbow prod to memory, of shared love and loyalty.

'You must understand, Okon... You don't need to do this if you don't feel up to it,' Hirukai spoke slowly, confident as to which way the puppet at the end of a string would jerk. 'I'm not forcing you into helping me. Nor am I putting you in any real danger. It's a simple job, really.'

'I'll do it, Hirukai,' Okon spoke with a measured passion far more mature than his tender years might have indicated. 'But just spare it a thought, I implore you. You can give up all this right now. Karuna Saikia sir has assured me nothing will happen to you.'

'Let me promise, Okon... You help me out with this, and I'll give myself up.' There was no inflexion in his voice to indicate to even a seasoned interrogator he was lying, less to the boy before him. Moreover, joy and hope were effective blinkers—as effective as overconfidence!

'You will, Hirukai? Promise?'

'Yes. I swear by the *thapona* in our *naamghar* that I'll surrender before *Magh-bihu.*'

Okon felt as though a huge weight had been lifted off his shoulders. His heart began singing *bihu* songs again. Hirukai noticed it, and was pleased. He brought a sealed envelope out of his bag and handed it to his younger brother.

'Go to Gandhasai Tea Estate tomorrow morning and give this letter to the manager of the bungalow. Think you can manage that?'

Gandhasai was a small tea-garden some six kilometres west from the point where the Chungijan link road met the national highway. Some of the children of the garden's workers studied in the Doomdooma Boys' School. Okon had never been to Gandhasai, but knew he would be able to get to it without any difficulty.

'Of course, Hirukai.'

'Actually, the manager is also the proprietor, and being an Assamese, you'll have no problems talking. Just tell him to read the letter and to send me a reply through you.'

'That's all?'

Hirukai smiled. His younger brother had lost none of his childish innocence, despite everything. 'Yes, that's all. Bring me the reply tomorrow itself as soon as you get it. You'll have to find an excuse as to why you need to go to school on a Sunday and cannot help out with the reaping.'

'Oh, I've already done that. For this afternoon... and for tomorrow, in case we could meet again.'

Hiren Bora was impressed. Perhaps he had underestimated his little brother! 'Watch out for eyes,' he warned gravely. 'Take care no one follows you. The trickiest part will be within the garden. But I've weighed the risks. All the proprietor is required to do is reply. If I know the tea-planter's mentality, it would be a verbal reply. I don't think he'll raise an immediate alarm. However, I'm sure you know what you have to do in case he does raise a ruckus.'

'Run like the devil?'

'Yes, that's my boy! You should be able to get back to me by noon with the reply, so I'll wait till then. If you're not here by noon, I'll assume something has gone wrong and leave this place as fast as possible.'

So deep was Okon's devotion to his mentor, he seemingly did not even notice that the latter was willing to throw him to the wolves and disappear if anything went wrong. 'I'll be with you before noon, I promise,' Okon said.

'Here, tuck this letter under your shirt and go. It's starting to get dark already. I'll wait here for you tomorrow. I remind you again...watch out for eyes that follow you.'

'And you remember the promise you've made!' Okon said, as he walked out of the *daini's* lair.

Bhodiya sat upon the upper branch of a tree overlooking the approach road to Okon's cottage and its compound. One could well mistake his stolid laziness for patience and perseverance, qualities of utmost necessity for the true stalker. However, on the contrary, Bhodiya could sit in the same spot and same stance for hours at a time, simply because he liked to sit and was averse to any form of exertion not essential to the job at hand. He, therefore, would not have minded sitting on the tree for another couple of hours had not the son of a bitch given him the slip in the morning! But, because he had lost him, Bhodiya was in a state of anxiety alien to his temperament—in other words, he was waiting impatiently for Okon to return home.

Bhodiya did not own a watch so he could not tell what time it was. He had been given a cell phone but all he could do with it was to receive calls and get the battery charged at a shop in Doomdooma whenever it threatened to run out. He did not even know that the date and time could be read on the screen of the infernal gizmo but then, of course, he could not read English either! But darkness was approaching, so the hour must be closer to five. Where in hell was that son of the devil? He had been out of Bhodiya's sight for over four hours now, and yet to return. Having lost him at school, Bhodiya had harboured the teeniest of hope the son of devil had merely come back home. Thus, having ridden back to his cottage and filled his stomach with pounded rice and jaggery, Bhodiya had climbed up this tree and taken up his position. He, of course, had known of the tree and the comfortable branch long ago; he had not dared climb it when Hirukai was there. But after he left to join the outfit Bhodiya would often climb the tree and sit upon the branch, well concealed from anyone passing below him. It was great fun to watch Okon's Bai as she swept the courtyard or washed clothes in the backyard; a pity his parched gaze could not quite reach the bathing-shed at the back—how lovely would it have been if he could only watch her having a bath!

To tell the truth, his sojourn on the branch this afternoon had not been at all unpleasant. Okon's sister had emerged twice out of the house; one, a long-ish stay while sweeping the compound, the other,- a shortish one to open the *nongola* gate to let the cow and calf in after their stint of grazing, and tether them inside the cowshed. The girl's father may have rejected him as a suitor, but there was no bar to him enjoying the sight of her—covertly, of course, for she was also Hirukai's sister!

As for Okon—there had been no sight of him, so even he could conclude the boy had not yet returned to the cottage. So what on earth was he going to tell the fellow who had hired him? That he was such an idiot who could not even keep a slip of a boy in his sight? The fellow's evening phone call was due soon. Bhodiya dreaded having to tell him he had lost all traces of Hirukai's brother.

Then he sighted the son of an adulterous mother, racing over the path, hopping down before the gate of his cottage, entering and putting the bicycle away. Well, that was that! He could now go home with the comforting knowledge that the son of the witch of the forest was sure to receive a severe tongue-lashing from his parents for returning so late, if not a cuff on the ear or two!

At around 6:00 pm in the evening, the call from the fellow came. Bhodiya told the exact truth. He had made a mistake in the morning and had been exposed. The boy had knowingly given him the slip and went missing for around four hours. Now he was back at home.

The fellow had asked just one question. 'Are you definite it was deliberate?'

'Yes,' Bhodiya had replied.

'Fine,' the fellow had said. 'Just pick up following him tomorrow from where you left off today.'

Contrary to Bhodiya's expectations, Okon did not receive a tongue-lashing. In the morning itself, before leaving for school, he had told the others he would be late returning home. The school was putting on a special pre-*Bhogali bihu* show and Okon had been chosen to be a member of the school *huchari* troupe, so had to be present for practice. That, too, was the excuse offered for leaving home the following day for school, of course—despite it being a Sunday and Pitai and Bai needing his help with the paddy—for rehearsal, what else? No one raised a word of protest; they all knew how diligent Okon was as far as doing his duties in the house was concerned. Ai and Bai were genuinely happy Okon had seemingly cheered up of late, and even actively taking part in the school's extracurricular activities. Okon himself was surprised at the ease with which he could lie to his parents and sister; he would stop doing so and explain once his objective had been attained—he was certain the others would understand and concede that he had acted for the best.

After having been seen off by Hirukai, Okon retraced the route to where he had hidden his bicycle and bag. He put the letter given to him by Hirukai carefully in a pocket of his bag and rode back home. He felt sad rather than exhilarated; dreams are always more delectable and exciting than reality. The tryst with Hirukai had not gone the way he had dreamt it would. And those instructions for going to Gandhasai with the letter—Okon knew what it implied; he had read about it in the papers, heard about it in school and elsewhere. Why would Hirukai need to carry out another extortion attempt if he did intend to surrender?

After a dinner taken slightly later than normal due to his delayed return, Okon went to bed. Half an hour later, having judged that everyone in the household had fallen asleep, he surreptitiously lit a candle, opened the envelope and read the letter. As he expected, it was an extortion demand addressed to the proprietor-cum-manager of Gandhasai Tea Estate. Okon replaced the letter and carefully re-sealed the envelope.

There was a hard grimness in his features which would have astonished those who knew him. Hirukai was within reach, something unlikely to happen for a long, long time if he were allowed to get away—which he would do, no matter how the attempt at the extortion of the Gandhasai owner went. It had been a revealing afternoon…the young lad was intelligent enough to have seen through his elder brother's pretence, and taken his promise of surrendering before *bihu* with a pinch of salt.

Alone, within the confines of the threadbare mosquito-net, he came to a decision.

Under no circumstances would Okon allow Hirukai to get away this time! *Occasionally, the saviour, too, needed to be saved!*

There were no terrifying dreams that night either.

At 7:00 pm on the evening of the December 31, the SULFA member called Gohain called up Major Harekrishna Bhagat of the 4th Rhino Battalion's rapid action squad, exasperation in his voice. 'Look,' he said, 'a friend of mine and I have been taking turns watching this fellow. It has been a day and a half now. He hasn't stepped out of the dak bungalow all this while except for the one short trip to the market I'd told you about. That trip, too, I guess, had been just a ruse to check me out.'

'So?' Major Bhagat asked curtly.

'Look, let's call it a day for the time being, shall we? He doesn't seem to be planning to go out anywhere tonight either. I and my buddies are celebrating, you see? Welcoming the New Year and all that! We can come back and resume tomorrow morning.'

'The hell you can! It's still too early for you to leave your watch. At least till midnight, as I'd told you. So shove your New Year's Eve plans up your you-know-what!'

'Look, but...'

'Are you rummaging for trouble, Gohain?'

'No, of course not!'

'Then keep watch. Report tomorrow morning, as usual. Now, if you'll excuse me, I've my own New Year party to go to.'

Gohain swore under his breath. There was nothing he could do. Ever since his surrender, these army fellows had used and abused him, and treated him as their lackey. They had enough on him to have him arrested once again, and put him behind bars. That was the trouble! But then, there had been benefits, too. They had allowed him a free-run as far as bullying the residents around the area was concerned, especially the business folk. It had been a kind of symbiosis, a financially profitable one for him. So there could be no question of upsetting the apple-cart. He would have to do as ordered, like it or not.

He hated these bastards in the army... Oh, how he hated them!

He would have got his own back, of course, had the fellow inside the dak bungalow been up to something. Sent in a distorted report, inserted a slice of false information. But there had been absolutely nothing to report, that was the problem.

Gohain swore again and called up a friend on his phone. 'Get the booze here,' he ordered. 'We're having our new year bash in front of the dak bungalow!'

Artificially incubated passion was not an antidote against boredom—Lahiri made the discovery within the confines of the ancient dak bungalow (perhaps a hand-me-down structure from the British era, as denoted by the presence of a false-chimney). In fact, induced boredom due to having spent the entire day in the room with its wall-to-wall carpeting and the decaying, slightly mouldy smell had gradually quelled the restless feeling he had experienced in the morning, killed the sentience that something was wrong, and lulled into sleep his curiosity at being kept under surveillance. Not even the information conveyed by Bhodiya could rouse excitement—perhaps it might have, had the idiot dealt with specifics. Instead, he had allowed the boy to dodge him. Lahiri almost chuckled audibly at Bhodiya's explanation as to how he had been duped. Thus, there were almost four hours when Okon had been out of sight! No doubt it was significant; the trick played by the boy upon his shadower had been deliberate. Logic demanded it be associated with a possible link between Okon and Hiru; logic also entailed Lahiri be thrilled at the significance! Could Okon have gone to meet his civet? Unfortunately, Bhodiya had lost him, so Lahiri did not know. He was not a person who would come to a conclusion based upon mere speculation. He had conveyed nothing of this to the DGP during the evening's chat, had not mentioned about Bhodiya's report, and simply told him he was still awaiting developments. He had also kept away from his superior the information that he was being watched. He would tell him only when he knew what it was all about.

Dinner was served by the aged chowkidar-cum-chef precisely at 8:00 pm. The fellow, like Lahiri himself, belonged to the old school, courteous and punctual, ready to sacrifice his own interests to that of his guests of whom— he had confessed to Lahiri—he did not have too many. He belonged to the tea-worker community; had once worked as the bungalow-orderly in a European tea-garden. That was where he had learnt to cook as well as he did. His sons and daughters were still in the tea-garden; he would join them when the government decided to retire him from service.

Wondering how the aged fellow had survived retirement for so long, Lahiri courteously informed him that he was off for an after-dinner walk and would be back within the hour. He needed to get the boredom out of his system and his sense of humour back—perhaps, also his passion! Walking out of the gate, he saw his 'shadow' on the opposite side of the road, seated on a motorcycle—but now three or four fellows had joined him, and there were two more motorcycles. The group had been drinking directly out of a bottle they were passing round, and smoking cigarettes, talking boisterously all the while. At this rate, thought Lahiri, there would be no New Year welcome party for they should be down and out much before the clock struck midnight! Sure enough the conversation came to a dead stop the moment Lahiri stepped out of the dak bungalow's gate, and began strolling down the road towards the market. One man in the group separated and followed the inspector at a discreet distance.

Western influence had penetrated even to this remote corner of the country, to a village posturing as a township—Doomdooma had decked itself up to greet the 'New Year', even though, according to the Assamese calendar, it was the 1st of the month of *Bohag* which ushered in the New Year for the indigenous communities. Many of the shops, both permanent and of the makeshift type, had remained open and, perhaps, planned to do so till the onset of the next year. Restaurants such as Bhogali and some of the shops had put up yards of colourful fairy lights; yes, thought Lahiri, such glittering trinkets as well as the fact that it was night helped to camouflage daytime's squalid dirtiness. The State Electricity Department had been munificent because it was a special night of the year; normally, such rural townships would be plunged in darkness by now but today, the power situation had held. Doomdooma looked almost pretty; quite a few people were still lingering about the central area—almost all youngsters—some girls among them. Apparently, the older members of the community preferred to stay indoors during the 'revelries'! It was all too depressing; for a fleeting moment Lahiri sensed a touch of loneliness. He attempted to compensate by buying a sweet paan from a shop and stuffing it into his mouth—a luxury he accorded to himself only once in a blue moon. It did not fill the void, but it did help him to stay on for a few extra moments in the open...out of what, ironically, was turning out to be a cage!

He retraced his steps to the dak bungalow almost reluctantly. The same reluctance, however, was not visible in the gait of his escort, who was in something of a hurry to rejoin his compatriots. The chowkidar had retired for the night; the atmosphere was quiet, apart from the moments when a vehicle raced across the trunk road. The mist was beginning to roll in from the surroundings…there was no sound of cicadas; perhaps, the periodic noise of passing trucks had driven them off to quieter environments where they could trill to their hearts' content. The quietude deepened the tiredness of his mind. In the ordinary course of things he would have taken a sedative and drifted off to sleep, but this was New Year's Eve; his sons would call up at the precise hour of midnight (if the network permitted, that is)—as was the fashion these days, he would have to ring up his wife who would be watching the New Year's Eve special show on some TV channel or the other, joining the chorus of chanters as the countdown began, no matter that she was alone—so no respite for him till the passing of midnight!

The depression was mounting; he would have taken an anti-depressant but that would prevent him from going to sleep. So he wilfully brought his thoughts to bear on his *hepa*. Where the devil had Hiren Bora disappeared to? Since the escapade of December 29, there had been no information on him. Neither his colleague at Tinsukia nor the OC of Doomdooma police station had the slightest information as to where Lahiri's civet might be holed up; he may well have crossed the India-Myanmar border. It had only been a scarlet-coloured bag which had yet kept hope alive in Lahiri's heart. Perhaps he had made a mistake hiring an oaf like Bhodiya for so important a job; but then, it was not easy finding a snitch among the villagers, and one with more intelligence was less likely to take such a job. Had he been embarking on a wild goose chase? There could very well be other answers to the riddle of a bag which had flown! The trouble was that he was losing out on credibility; even the DGP had stopped asking if anything was developing, when nothing seemingly was. Just one more day, Lahiri decided firmly. I will give myself just one more day. I will head back for Guwahati on January 2...

THE GANDHASAI AFTERMATH

Had one sat like Bhodiya on his favourite tree that early in the morning, one would not have been able to see the cottage—so thick and heavy was the winter fog. Dark, unmoving, it draped the mud-caked walls and the thatched roof…the small hutment looked like a bagged corpse in a morgue! The wall of grey-black vapour appeared almost alive; it swallowed up the cottage, making it and the people inside vanish as though they were of no significance. Yet the lead player in this minuscule drama (just one amongst the 'trillion-zillion' being played out in the cosmos, as Lahiri might have put it) was within. No doubt, the cold fog had entered his soul and induced, yet again, the desolation he was all too habituated to these days, but it could no longer enter his mind and befog perception; Okon had, by now, grown absolutely certain as to what he had to do. No matter what happened in Gandhasai tea-garden, *under no circumstances would he allow Hirukai to get away this time!*

He had hardly slept last night, willing his internal alarm clock to awaken him at a bewitched hour even though it was pitch-black outside, and the ghouls and demons still flitted about in the gelid, misty air. There was a recklessness within him brought about by desperation and determination—such was the craving passion powering his self that he was ready and outside the house 15 minutes after waking up. Everything was blinding but he did not care. He thought he could hear those spirits—damned to wander about for eternity—wheeze by him in the darkness, but he did not care. He could summon up courage from his coward self to ignore them, although he did silently keep mumbling a spell Bai had once taught him.

He groped his way to the back of the cottage and pulled out his bicycle from its perch; it was deathly quiet so he could not afford to make the least noise. He silently removed the bamboo poles on the *nongola* gate, reinserting them once he had pushed his cycle outside. Since Gandhasai was not too far away, he had not really needed to make such an early start. But he had Bhodiya to account for; he could not take the slightest chance of being followed again. It would, he thought, require more than a man of Bhodiya's calibre to keep watch at such an hour of the morning when the old man of the forest and the witch of the *daini's* lair were still perched on the thatched roof of the cottage—perhaps watching him with avid eyes as he pushed his bicycle up the village path. Yet, the stakes were too high for him to take any risk, no matter how improbable it might seem!

He instinctively followed the contours of the road, half-guessing as to when he should make a turn, continuing to push his bicycle even after he had passed the residential section of the village and the road now snaked through the paddy fields. The fog here was even thicker, so the question of hopping on to the bicycle did not arise, and he had to keep pushing it on. It had been an almost impossible trip this morning; the thin blanket he had wrapped himself in could hardly protect him from the bitter cold. Also, his legs were exposed; but, weirdly enough, he did not feel the cold… The envelope given to him by Hirukai burned in his shirt pocket, warming him inside—the compass which directed him almost unsighted across the route he had to take. By the time he reached the main road, the fog had begun to dissipate a little, though even now, it was as thick as a fluff of cotton. He turned towards his right and pushed on for another couple of kilometres, before veering off the road towards a familiar thicket.

Laying his bicycle on the ground, he made a meal of some pounded rice and jaggery he had brought along with him. He knew there was a streamlet flowing close by…he went to it to defecate and clean himself. Then he waited for the fog—now much thinner, though still dense enough to camouflage the advent of the morning—to lift completely. Bhodiya must be completely befuddled, he thought…but there was no laughter in him at this realisation. As the light grew brighter, he guessed from experience the time to be around nine o' clock. He pushed the bicycle on to the main road, and hopping on to it, began pedalling towards Gandhasai—looking back time and again to ensure he was not being followed.

He knew what he was doing was not right. He knew what Hirukai was doing was not right. Brought up within a highly moral and devout atmosphere, his guilt felt like a blow to the solar plexus delivered by a village bully. Yet, he moved gamely on. The brew of guilt and shame in his mind was thickened by fear of the possible consequences of what he was being made to do by Hirukai. How would the manager of the tea garden react when he received the letter? Would he call out to his workers to catch Okon, or phone the police? The boy understood if anything went awry, his sole option was to run—he was very good at running! But then, there might be someone who was faster! What if he were caught? Hirukai had not given much weight to the possibility that he might get into trouble…he had simply told him to run—that was disheartening. It had been bad enough that his elder brother was having him deliver an extortion letter…that he might be willing to let him fend for himself if something went wrong was even worse!

But there was no alternative; this errand was a must if Hirukai were to stay on in the *daini's* lair so that Okon could persuade him to surrender. It did not assuage his feel of guilt, but it did arm him with an alibi: he could tell his conscience why he was cycling towards a stranger to deliver an extortion letter. And, no matter the outcome, he needed to be back at the lair by 12 noon. If he was late and Hirukai was gone, all the caution and shame and guilt and fear would have been so much fog in the air!

The tea garden was located by the side of the main road, but the gate of entry had to be reached by a *kutcha* path, which had the plantation on one side and paddy fields belonging to another village on the other. A large signboard—GANDHASAI TEA ESTATE painted in bold letters upon it—stood at the junction where the *kutcha* path met the main road. Reaching it, Okon turned left and began cycling towards the entry gate. This was unfamiliar territory; he had never travelled by this path before. He was disconcerted by the inordinately large number of people who were using the path, given it was a Sunday. Then he remembered that not too far away was a *haat* which displayed its wares only at the end of every week; villagers would frequent this Sunday-market to either buy things for themselves or to take their own domestic produce—jackfruit, betel nut, ducklings and so on—to barter. This explained why there were so many people making their way over the path, but it was hardly comforting. As typical of rural folk, every passerby stared at the unfamiliar countenance of Okon as he pedalled furiously on. If there was trouble, they would surely be able to give a description of the boy to the police!

The distance to the main entrance of the tea garden over the path was around two kilometres; a burly garden *sirdar* with a stick in his hand was on guard-duty at the gate. Okon pedalled on for a kilometre more, till he reached a likely spot where he could hide his bicycle as well as make a stealthy entry through the barbed-wire fencing into the tea-garden—a spread of plantain just beside the path to his right. He stopped, surveyed the area around him closely, and finding no one within sight, darted into the spread. He did not enter it too deeply, just enough to ensure the bicycle could not be seen by anyone walking on the path. Emerging from the thicket, he crossed the unmacadamed road and scrambled across the ditch that ran along the garden fencing—dry because it was the dry season—and crawled into the tea garden territory under the barbed-wire boundary-fencing, taking extreme care to keep the barbs from touching his skin. He had been told if those rusty barbs were to lacerate and draw blood from anyone's flesh, a person would be sure to get tetanus!

Up on his feet again, he dusted himself and closely surveyed the area before him. Gandhasai was a small, compact and well-maintained tea garden. Like every youngster in such a tea-growing region, Okon, too, was familiar with tea-plantations. Even then, the beauty of Gandhasai took his breath away—despite there having been no rain for a few months and the shade-trees and bushes being layered by a coat of dust. The boy knew this was the off- season for tea-plantations; the bushes would flush profusely only when the showers arrive around March or April, yielding the first teas. Understandably enough, there was not much activity going on within. The section he was in was devoid of human presence, though at another section some distance away, he could see a band of male garden-hands pruning the bushes.

The garden's factory was a relatively small one, as was the solitary bungalow set not very far from it. As Hirukai had said, this tea-plantation was managed by the owner himself, with the help of the *bormohiri* and *sirdars*. There being no manufacture now, the factory stood desolately empty—as also the area around it. Okon knew where he needed to head towards; the narrow paths of this well-maintained garden were clear of grass and weeds, and Okon raced across the crisscrossing paths—moving unerringly towards the small, solitary, Assam-type bungalow.

Kamal Duarah lounged upon an easy-chair in the lawn fronting the bungalow of his tea garden, enjoying the warmth of the sun and sipping a cup of tea. He normally never indulged in late nights; the New Year's Eve party last night at the Planters' Club had been an exception. He had really let his hair down; one of the few aberrations in his otherwise routine life. It had been two o' clock at night when he left the club; but habits drilled into him for over two decades could not be overcome, and despite having had just a couple of hours sleep, he woke up as usual at five o' clock in the morning—nursing a hangover. There were a number of garden chores to be done and the *sirdars* would be awaiting instructions from him; but today, he would have his *bormohori* handle them. He called up the man to tell him so. The next few hours he spent awake under the quilt, luxuriating in the sentience of idleness only extremely busy and hardworking individuals can appreciate—not even summoning his bungalow-bearer for a cup of tea. It had been past nine when he mustered up enough energy to get out of bed, put on a dressing-gown over his pyjamas, and emerge from his room into the lawn and ask his bearer, Kurmi, to bring him his morning cuppa. The restful hours awake in bed had drained away the effects of the hangover, and he could enjoy his cup of tea and the surrounding quietude.

Although he was a bachelor in his early forties, he had thus far resisted importunities from his well-wishers that he get married; in truth he had been wedded to his tea garden! Gandhasai had been opened up by his great grandfather in the early part of the 20th Century; the family garden had been handed down from generation to generation till around 15 years back—when the death of Duarah's father had forced him to leave a well-paid job at a Kolkata firm. He had to take up the mantle of running Gandhasai and looking after his mother, who lived in their ancestral home in Dibrugarh. The tea industry in the late 1980s was in doldrums; rising cost of inputs and falling prices of manufactured tea had made things difficult not only for small planters like Duarah, but even for some of the bigger tea companies. During his father's days, their tea garden had slowly but surely become a liability rather than an asset. With declining production and sales and mounting debts at the bank, his father, at one time, had actually contemplated sale of Gandhasai but there were no buyers! Kamal Duarah, after taking over the property, had put his heart and soul into trying to reverse the garden's fortunes and retain the family's legacy. By dint of a frugal lifestyle (one of the many reasons he had not married) and cutting down on the garden's expenditure while increasing output, he had clung on till the tide began turning in the tea-industry's favour. Prices, both in auctions and private sales, rose phenomenally because demand was outstripping supply. By the turn of the century he had been able to clear debts, modernise the factory, pay his workers more and build up a nest-egg with the profits as a buffer against another crisis—which might come upon such an agro-based enterprise any time!

It had been his good fortune that the shadow of insurgency had not fallen upon Gandhasai; he understood it was less a matter of luck and more about the ULFA's ideology of not touching local entrepreneurs who were going through hard times—such had been the organisation's ability to pry out information that it knew Gandhasai's assets and liabilities to the rupee. But now that the hard days were over, he expected the arrival of a dreaded extortion letter any day. In fact, he had been expecting one for the last couple of years—the debilitation of the outfit's set-up in upper Assam was responsible for his not getting one thus far. But at the club, the grape-vine had it that the scourge was beginning again—the manager of Lajim Tea Estate had recently been shot at by an extortionist! Yet, when the letter actually came, he did not expect it would be delivered in the manner it had been delivered. He had anticipated something more dramatic, going by club accounts of planters who had been imposed upon—a terrifying knock on the door at the dead of the night and the muzzle of a gun at his temple. Instead, here was a young boy, perhaps not more than 12 years old, who seemingly materialised out of the thin air and held out an envelope for him!

A mere letter, within an envelope having a rising sun embossed upon it! The courier was merely a young lad. Had he wanted he could have simply called out, and the boy would immediately be seized and handed over to the police. Yet Kamal Duarah felt the chill of naked terror bring goose-pimples to his skin; he lost his voice and could not speak for a moment. The manager at Lajim had been shot in the leg as he was running away from the insurgent, but who knew where the gun had actually been aimed at! The poor fellow had resigned from his appointment and left Assam for good! With trembling hands, Duarah opened the envelope while the boy remained standing and on full alert. The letter was couched in the politest terms; the demand was for 20 lakh rupees. The owner would be given a day to get the amount out of the bank, and tomorrow night, it would be collected by someone from the ULFA. The consequences, if the authorities were contacted, would be disastrous for the owner of Gandhasai Tea Estate. The letter was signed by one Hiren Bora. It rang a bell in Duarah's mind. The same name had cropped up time and again in club-conversations, always spoken of in almost hushed tones. The insurgent who had shot the manager of Lajim Tea Estate, too, had been Hiren Bora!

Many years back, a bureaucrat based in Tinsukia had come to his garden, requesting him to inform the authorities if there was any extortion attempt. The administration, he was told, would come harshly down on a tea planter who made payment to the ULFA or other insurgent outfits—such actions constituted treason. Another time, a police officer had come with a similar kind of caution, while the club had regular visits from paramilitary personnel enquiring if any extortion notice had been served. Duarah, therefore, knew better than to send a reply in writing.

'Would you be meeting Hiren Bora again?' he managed to blurt out.

'Yes,' said the boy tersely.

'Tell him I can afford only half the amount. It will be ready by tomorrow evening.'

'I'll do that,' said the boy, vanishing into the tea-bushes—leaving only the extortion letter to show it was not all a dream.

Hirukai was not within the *daini's* lair when Okon reached it well ahead of noon; the boy, of course, had not expected him to be there, nor was he surprised when his brother entered the clearing a few minutes later.

He was also not surprised when his elder brother did not embrace him after stowing the stuff he had been carrying inside the makeshift shelter. Instead, he asked with eager impatience,

'Yes, what did the manager say?'

Okon kept his voice even. The determined decision he had arrived at last night removed the stutter from his words.

'He has agreed to make the payment. You're to collect the money tomorrow night. But he would be able to pay only half the amount you asked for.'

A smile lit up Hirukai's face. To the boy, that smile seemed more grotesque and repulsive than the thunderous laughter of the *rakhyasa* in the *bhaona*! It needed all his willpower to keep up his dissemblance.

Having received the reply he had been seeking, Hiren Bora no longer felt the need to keep up the pretence! Okon sensed the indifference; it roused sensations far, far bleaker than he had felt when his elder brother had disappeared from his life.

'Good job, Okon,' Hirukai said, patting his brother on the back. Like the previous afternoon, he once again brought out a sweet potato, scraped away the earth off its skin with his knife, sliced it into two, and passed one half to his brother. The two of them sat down on the ground, chewing on the sweet potato.

Perhaps it was the bitterness within him which made Okon throw caution to the wind. 'You don't trust me anymore, do you, Hirukai?'

Hiren Bora was startled; he suddenly realised that Okon thought he was being taken for granted; half-heartedly, he tried to make amends. 'Of course I trust you, Okon. With my life.'

'No, you don't. That's why you're never here when I arrive. You think I might bring others with me, don't you?'

'Certainly not,' Hirukai replied. 'I was confident you would not bring others knowingly. But what if, unknown to you, someone was following. As I'd told you, there are eyes everywhere.'

'Well,' Okon said defiantly, 'I didn't want to tell you of it... didn't want to alarm you unduly. But I had been followed.'

The face before him hardened into granite; the boy had never seen such a look on Hirukai's features—not even during those days when despair had wracked him prior to his joining the ULFA. Yes, how quickly can human bonds untangle—the boy was so benumbed he could not feel a thing, did not flinch as he would have done before at Hirukai's wrath!

'You...you lied!' It was as though a volcano had erupted; the earth shook, such was the force of Hirukai's anger. 'I'd asked you, and you lied!'

'I told you,' Okon said calmly. The absence of a stammer should have acted as a warning to Hiren Bora. But he was too full of himself to have noticed such petty details. 'I didn't want to alarm you unduly. Don't worry, I shook him off. No one knows you're here.'

'Who was it? A policeman?'

'No, Bhodiyakai from our village. Everyone knows he's a snitch for the police.'

'Bhodiya? The village idiot!'

Okon told his brother how he discovered Bhodiya had been following him and the manner in which he outwitted his pursuer. 'And this morning, I left much before sunrise and hid in a thicket till it was time to go to the garden. Bhodiya couldn't have followed me.'

Despite himself, Hiren Bora was both reassured and impressed by the way his brother had been carrying out his part of the bargain. He could well imagine the courage Okon had mustered to walk out of their cottage at that foggy and dark hour of the night. As quickly as it had risen, his anger subsided. He suddenly stood up, signalled to his brother to do the same and embraced. Okon hugged him as though he would never let go!

'I'm sorry, Okon,' the affection was seemingly back in the words but the boy was not taken in. He could no longer be taken in. 'These hours and hours of waiting have been getting on my nerves. I'm sorry I grew angry. I should have known that I could trust you completely.'

'It's alright, Hirukai. I understand.'

'Now it's time for you to go. Don't let a word out to anyone about meeting me, not even Bai.'

Seemingly, an inner eye had opened within Okon—he could almost see into the future. Yet, he had to be absolutely certain—after all, he was Hiren Bora's brother!

'But you'll be here till tomorrow evening, won't you? Can't I come and meet you again, Hirukai?'

'No,' his brother said sharply. 'No more risks. We've taken enough of them already. Forget I will be here tomorrow. Forget I was here ever! Spend the rest of this day at home. Go to school tomorrow. Do you understand, boy?'

Okon seemed crestfallen. 'Yes, I suppose so,' he said. 'You'll have to spend an entire day here, won't you? It would be foolish to put you in danger.'

'That's right.' His body movements indicated how impatient his brother was to see Okon leave. Yet the boy could not depart without reassurance; a final effort to placate his unruly mind that the course he had opted for was inevitable, that there was no alternative.

'I suppose I can wait a few days longer,' Okon let out a small laugh and said. 'Then there would be no more of this.'

Hirukai was puzzled. 'More of what, Okon?'

'No more need for secrecy, Hirukai. Your promise, remember? To surrender before *bihu*, after handing over this money to your companions. *Bihu* is less than a fortnight away.'

The clear hint was there in Hirukai's overtly quick, perfunctory answer, at the fact that he looked away when he made it. 'Yes, yes, I promise. Now you really must go.'

Okon had sensed enough. He felt a calmness rarely experienced in recent days. It was inevitable. He was doing the right thing, for Pitai, Ai, Bai, and himself.

Above all, for Hirukai!

The boy quickly left the *daini's* lair. Hiren Bora indifferently watched him go—an insubstantial ghost from an equally insubstantial past!

Okon flitted quickly through the trail fringing the jungle, uncaring as to whether he might be seen. There was no requirement for secrecy any longer. Rather, speed was the need of the moment. Reaching the place where he had hidden his bicycle, he did not tarry but pulled it upright, and pushed quickly on towards the main road. Once upon it, he flew. Faster and faster and faster. A decision had been made. Time was of the essence!

He did not take the turning from the main road towards Chungijan village. Instead, he sped onwards towards Doomdooma. The heavy load of decision-making had been lifted off his young mind; it made him light-headed and giddy. The reaped stalks of paddy on both sides urged him on; the mile-posts showing the distance seemed to flash by one after the other, such was his speed. Then the paddy disappeared, there was a bend in the road, then houses, shops and kiosks. Okon knew where he had to go. Past the small market, past his school, a left turn a kilometre ahead and there was Karuna Saikia sir's cottage with its big compound. A man was spreading un-husked paddy upon bamboo mats in the front courtyard.

Okon hopped off the bicycle. 'I need to speak to Saikia sir,' he panted out. 'It's urgent.'

'He's sleeping at this hour, boy. Don't you know it's a Sunday?'

'Wake him up. Tell him Okon Bora wants to talk to him.'

It is easy to tell when passion is genuine. The passion in the boy's voice alerted the man of the urgency of the moment. He went inside. Minutes later, the fat frame of Karuna Saikia waddled out of the doorway. The greedy leer which abruptly appeared on his face on sighting the boy showed he, too, was aware of the moment's significance.

Okon gestured with his eyes towards the man who had followed Saikia on to the courtyard. The teacher waddled over to where the boy was standing and whispered,

'Yes, Okon, What is it?'

'I know where Hirukai is, sir.'

Sunday, 1 January 2006, dawned gloomily, foggier than ever. Uninspiring!

New hope, Inspector Lahiri mused sardonically, is supposed to fly in and roost upon a spot in the heart on the first day of the new year and rouse optimism, never mind that it is of the English calendar! But there was not the slightest trace of hope or optimism within him as he continued to linger in bed, sipping the cup of tea the chowkidar had brought him, and thumbing through the newspapers which the man had bought at his bidding from a vendor in the market. With so much time on his hand he, had had an opportunity to thoroughly read a newspaper from page one till the end— something which had not been possible in the normal course of his life. Usually, he would have just time enough to glance at the headlines and only read items of professional concern to him. But now, he could even go through the advertisement columns, the tiniest insertion of 'Situation

Wanted', 'Situation Vacant', 'To Let', 'Accommodation' and what not—simply amazing how much material a single newspaper could carry and how many lives it could touch!

The inspector knew all too well it was not merely an item topped with a headline which constituted a story; there were umpteen untold stories within the pages of a newspaper, invisible, but only to the imagination. Lahiri however, had never allowed his imagination to take control of his mind; for an investigator, allowing the imagination to hold sway was fatal as far as objectivity was concerned. He dealt with facts and evidence and hard data. No doubt there was leeway for speculation but that, too, had to be based on circumstantial evidence and not merely upon a whimsical fancy. For instance, in this particular instance the evidence available had led to speculation of something quite probable—a link of some kind between Hiru and Okon. It had been a permissible hypothesis just as his earlier hunch had been, for it was based on circumstantial evidence. Lahiri's utter lack of optimism rested on the reality that nothing much had happened in the course of the last few days to indicate his hypothesis would be proven to be true. Yes, Okon had intentionally given Bhodiya the slip; but surely the bright youngster—being the brother of a dreaded ULFA militant—had been tailed before, and would have been by now able to spot if anyone was shadowing him. As for the ruse played upon Bhodiya, it may well have been merely an act of childish one-up-manship; there had been nothing to hint at anything else.

He had come to Doomdooma a week ago, basing himself on a promising hunch. He had expected to return within a day or two and had told his wife so, but bait had been kept dangling before him—fooling him into hoping that his civet would reappear, so another trap could be set. Time and again, he had told himself to be patient, for patience was a sine qua non for the successful hunter. He had been patient—for almost a week, his liver reminded him laughingly. He thought he had prepared bait, but the *hepa* had not taken it! For all he knew, Lahiri's civet was far away by now, safely couched within some camp in the Myanmar jungles, singling out some other duck coop to try and break into.

There was nothing much to look forward to, nothing much to do—the reason that kept him uncharacteristically in bed long after he had awakened. Karuna Saikia had nothing to report, Bhodiya could not tell where Okon had disappeared to last afternoon; the DGP had maintained telephonic silence, as had the OC of the Doomdooma Police Station. Lahiri had to coerce himself into finally getting out of bed and having the mandatory bath and yogic exercises; the chowkidar seemed to be a mind-reader, for he brought the breakfast at 9:00 am—one hour later than the time Lahiri had had it the other mornings. If the old fellow had been bamboozled by the odd behaviour of his guest—the man seemed to prefer his own company, and ever since he came to the dak bungalow, had remained mostly confined to his room—he had tactfully refrained from pointing it out. He could not, of course, have known his guest was bored to the bones; also, a tad ashamed of the silly charade he had played out after arriving at Doomdooma—a travelling salesman, bah, straight out of a cheap thriller. He had got a childish kick out of it though!

But such bathetic play-acting had proved futile, for he had become the object of unwelcome attention—if the lookout posted opposite the gate of the dak bungalow was any indication. The fellow (or, perhaps fellows) had been a mystery; Lahiri had been tempted over and again to go up to him and find out who he was. As he had acknowledged earlier, an ULFA linkman would have vanished after confirming his presence. The outfit, of course, knew who he was; and anyway, it could have got confirmation of his presence from other sources instead of keeping so obvious a lookout for so long.

Then, this morning, the chowkidar had added another element to the mystery: the motorcyclist stationed opposite the dak bungalow was not there any longer! Needlessly, Lahiri had gone out to the bungalow's veranda to confirm it for himself; well, it did give him something new to mull over… Had the fellow been a victim of the New Year binge he and his friends had been indulging in, and nursing a gargantuan hangover this morning? Or was it testimony to the unpalatable reality that, apparently, no one was interested in Lahiri any longer! He might as well prepone his departure for Guwahati and catch a bus this evening itself. When the chowkidar came at 1:30 pm with his lunch, Lahiri sent him to the bus station to purchase a ticket on a night bus to Guwahati...

However, Inspector Lahiri had missed the mark in supposing he was no longer the cynosure of any eyes. In fact, he had been so of quite a number of pairs! Not being omniscient, he did not know how pieces on the board had been moving and what new alignments had been made. He could not know, for instance, that the disappearance of the lookout at the dak bungalow gate had been the direct consequence of the unobtrusive appearance of one Ravi Arora at the Doomdooma Police Station the previous evening. He had met the OC and introduced himself.

If the OC was impressed that no less a person than an officer from RAW had condescended to call at his humble *thana*, his demeanour did not reveal it. 'What can I do for you?' he asked politely, though Arora was quick to note that he did not affix the question with 'sir'. Yes, he thought grimly, neither the army nor the local police have any regard for RAW!

'There is a State Special Intelligence Wing officer from Guwahati staying in Doomdooma the past few days. Do you know of it?'

'Of course, I do. He had dropped in at my office on the 26th of last month, and told me who he was and why he was here. He rode along with my force when we conducted the raid on Chungijan that night. I also helped him shift to the dak bungalow.'

'Right. Today is December 3. Do you have any idea why he has stayed on?'

'Not in the slightest. Nor am I interested. He would tell me himself if he needed to.'

'Wise of you! Too much stuff on your plate, isn't it? So why unnecessarily put your nose in somebody else's affairs! Now, tell me, has he made any further request to you?'

'Nothing specific. Just asked me if I could garner enough special police commandos and fire-power at short notice if there was a need to, and I replied in the positive.'

'Fine. Now here is what you need to do. If any request does come from this man, you will call up Major Bhagat of the army camp at Dangori. Immediately, do you understand?'

'No, I don't,' the burly OC said stolidly.

The RAW man was taken aback. 'You've seen my identity card?' he asked.

'Yes.'

'Still you refuse to obey me?'

'Yes.'

The OC was a local man. The kind of boot-licking ethos which the RAW official normally encountered among the police was not visible upon this officer.

'But why?' he asked, flabbergasted.

'I'll need instructions from my superior officer,' the policeman said obdurately.

Arora grew visibly angry, but the OC would not budge.

'All right,' the RAW officer said. 'If you want instructions from your superior, you'll get it. Just give me your phone.'

He called up the superintendant of police's office at Tinsukia. 'I would like to speak to the SP please,' he barked at the man who picked up the phone.

'Sorry, sir. The SP has gone home.'

Arora called up the SP at home. The OC, seated nearby, could distinctly hear the SP addressing the RAW officer as 'sir'.

Arora put the phone down. The two men sat in silence till. A couple of minutes later, the phone rang. The OC picked it up.

'Is this the Doomdooma *thana*?'

'Yes.'

'This is the SP speaking from Tinsukia. I believe you have one Ravi Arora with you?'

'Yes, sir. He is sitting in front of me.'

'You will be acting as he has instructed you to. Is that clear?'

'Yes, sir.'

The caller rang off. 'You didn't have to go as high as that,' the OC said somewhat petulantly. 'A call from the deputy superintendent at Tinsukia would have been more than enough!'

The RAW officer had next rung up Major Bhagat and informed him of the developments. 'It's as I suspected,' he had said, not bothered the OC was sitting just next to him. 'They plan to act on their own.'

'I see,' the major said. 'But are they going to act at all?'

Snotty army bastards, Arora thought! 'We've no idea yet,' he said, making no attempt to hide his displeasure. 'But you major, of all people, should know the advantage of being forewarned and at the ready. By the way, you can call off your dogs. From now on, you will get your inputs from the horse's mouth.'

'And allow them to have their New Year fun in peace, you must be joking! The dogs must be kept on leash, you know. I'll call them off tomorrow morning.'

'Fine. You also need to go through your chain of command. Up the ladder.'

'Isn't it premature?'

'No, I think it's high time. We must prepare for every contingency.'

'How high?'

'Up to the Lt. Gen. He must be kept apprised on the latest, so he's not caught on the wrong foot if need for intervention arises. I'm sure the general will give a piece of his mind to SHM. The minister, in turn, will blast the DGP. It's a dog-eat-dog world, isn't it, major?'

'You're telling me,' Major Bhagat had replied laconically as he put his phone down.

Lahiri felt depressed that afternoon. He understood why! It had been a letdown; he had faced similar failures before, so he was familiar with the sensation. The trap lay un-sprung; ember eyes remained hidden away, ivory fangs were shadowed by the foliage. Ironic, inner laughter could no longer swab away the sadness transient failure brought, nor could he climb out by focussing on the object of obsession because at least the moment's chapter was ending. There might be other traps to set and other bait to use (in his heart he had been so foolishly certain that the curtain would be drawn on this one this time!). Certainly, there would be other *hepas* to hunt, too; but an episode without an ending was ending, and that was depressing. Bhodiya had not called, Karuna Saikia had not called, the DGP had not called—even the unknown fellow stationed for so many hours opposite the gate of the dak bungalow seemed to have given up on him!

A sudden, raucous pht...pht... sound distracted him; the noise of an old scooter with a defective exhaust pipe! By now, Lahiri had grown accustomed to the noise made by passing vehicles, and could almost instinctively judge the type and distance. The increased volume indicated that the scooter was very close by, probably within the compound of the dak bungalow. Karuna Saikia had such a scooter!

Less with any real hope and more out of curiosity, Lahiri got up from his chair and walked to the balcony. Yes, it was Karuna Saikia alright, seated upon his scooter—a gargantuan travesty looking like an elephant on a bicycle in a circus (or an outsize mushroom growing on a scooter), his body straddling almost the entire vehicle. But clinging precariously at the very rear, was a boy. Okon!

The pendulum swung sharply. *Operation Hepa* was very much on!

THE BAG

Sudden laughter rumbled in Lahiri's belly; no longer was it guffaws by any individual organ but a cacophonous symphony—liver, intestine, kidney, gall-bladder et al, engaged in maniacal chuckle… Not benign (though sardonic) but an almost hysteric, shrill outburst of triumph—silent yet powerful enough to shake the dak bungalow as if it had been struck by an earthquake. Gone was the feel of a slide towards depression; he had to hold on to a railing on the veranda to seemingly save himself from falling—explosive joy at being vindicated jeered at his professional dispassion. The veranda being shadowed by the eaves of the roof, neither Saikia nor Okon had seen him yet. Lahiri stumbled back into his room and fell upon a chair. Using enormous inner strength to get a hold on himself, he picked up a newspaper and pretended to be reading. They must not sense the triumph within him, nor must they be allowed to hear his silent laughter.

There was a knock on the door; it was open and the curtains were parted, so those who stood there could see him seated inside engrossed in the newspaper. 'Come in,' Lahiri called out gravely, carefully folding the paper away and looking up through his bifocals. The wooden floor-board of the bungalow creaked as Saikia waddled in, Okon following hesitantly behind. The boy seemed terrified; Lahiri's heart went out to him but he could not yet take off his mask of severity because of Saikia's presence. 'Oh, it's you, Saikia,' he said, appearing surprised. 'Some new development?'

'Sir, this is Okon,' Saikia said. Unlike Lahiri, he made no attempt to conceal the triumphant elation within him. 'Hiren Bora's brother. He claims he knows where his brother is hiding.'

Lahiri tried to turn his face away because it was nearly impossible now to camouflage the jubilation; he knew the crafty fat fellow had heard the laughter. 'Is that so?' he said, looking at Okon and not Saikia. 'Where's your brother at this moment?'

But it was Saikia who answered. 'He wants to make a deal before he tells you that.'

'Naturally. Yes, Okon, what is it that you want?'

'He wants an assurance that no harm would come to his brother. Also, that he would be put in a camp and not in jail. Finally, he wants all cases against him to be closed and for Hiren Bora be allowed to live again in Chungijan.'

'Why don't you let him speak for himself?' Lahiri rebuked. He turned towards the boy and asked in a gentler tone, 'Is that what you want, Okon?'

The boy nodded.

'Does your brother wish to surrender?'

There were tears in the young boy's eyes, nervousness in his gait. 'I-I asked him to, b-b-but I don't t-t-think he's going to,' he stuttered out.

'So you want to show us where he is hiding so we can take him into custody?'

The boy nodded again. Fear shackled his voice, yet he managed to stammer out, 'Please, n-n-no harm should come to H-H-Hirukai!'

Lahiri's inner laughter echoed away. The stark, unmasked fear, anxiety and confusion in the boy muted triumphant chuckles, and allowed compassion to smother them. There was no escaping inborn impulses, Lahiri thought ruefully; the sinking sensation as one fought those monsters comes only in the loneliness of the dark. Otherwise compulsions and emotions of the moment make one stuck, glued to life till the final, defining breath—an existential requirement if one were not to put a noose around one's neck when the sentience of absurdity sinks in. True dispassion was only for the sages!

'I swear on my heart no harm will come to your Hirukai,' Lahiri said, using a phrase the child would readily understand. 'I can also promise he will be allowed to stay in a camp for boys who have surrendered. But as for getting the police cases against him cleared, it will take time. So you'll need to be patient. But let me tell you that there have been many instances when the government withdrew cases against boys who surrendered.'

'Like Kalpakai?' the innocence in the boy's face was overwhelming; it annihilated every trace of inner laughter.

'A boy from Chungijan on the verge of release,' Saikia intruded.

'Yes, like Kalpakai. Let me assure you, Okon, I'll do everything in my power to ensure your brother is released and can stay with you. But first, you'll have to trust us and tell where he's hiding.'

'In the *daini's* lair,' Okon said.

'In the what?' Karuna Saikia was the first to respond.

'The *daini's* lair. A bamboo thicket...the property of the entire village. There's a clearing inside only Hirukai and I know of...' Lahiri's gentle approach had had a soothing effect on the boy—he could now pour his heart out without much of a stammer. He spoke about how much he wanted Hirukai back in the house; how they had waited for his visit that night; about the raid and the next morning, when he found the packet and the note in the *daini's* lair; the joy he had felt in being gifted a school bag; about meeting Hirukai for the first time in two years, and of carrying a letter to Gandhasai tea garden and carrying back the reply to him.

'Hirukai would collect the money from Gandhasai tomorrow night,' Okon said. 'But who knows…he might leave the *daini's* lair tonight itself, after it grows dark, and wait somewhere closer to the tea garden. So we don't have much time to waste.'

Inspector Lahiri was impressed. This had not occurred to him! Listening to the boy's tale, he had complacently assumed Hiren Bora would not leave his hideout till the next day, so a midnight raid would be appropriate. But his civet had time and again proved to be a sly creature—always one step ahead of those trying to capture him. Okon, being his shadow, had instinctively pre-divined what Hirukai was most likely to do!

Almost two o' clock in the afternoon! The winter sun set early and it would take at least a couple of hours for the team to be readied for the raid and to reach the spot. Yes, there was no time to waste!

Going to the veranda, he called out to the chowkidar, who responded with alacrity. Two chairs were brought out from another room and placed on the veranda for the teacher and the boy to sit in. Lahiri gave the chowkidar money to get them something to eat from the market. He then went to his room and made a call to the Doomdooma station.

The man on duty there said the OC was at home and not in his office. Lahiri made an exception to the rules he had set for himself, and called up the OC on his personal cell phone. The *hepa* was almost at a sniffing distance from the trap. There was no need for taking the precautions his cautious nature normally demanded.

With extreme brevity, he explained to the policeman that a possible hideout of Hiren Bora had been located; the insurgent might not stay very long at the place, so it was imperative a raid be made on it as early as possible— before darkness sets in. The raiding party has to be a small one—comprising of the OC, half a dozen anti-insurgency commandos, a magistrate as required by the law and Lahiri himself—so it does not take much time to form one. Lahiri was a little put off by the OC's repeated insistence that he needed to know where exactly the hideout was located, but warded him off by assuring that everything would be spelt out in good time; for the nonce the location has to be kept from members of his force, since there was no risking a leak at this crucial moment. All the OC needed to do was to be at the dak bungalow with the raiding party and the vehicles within the hour.

He next rang up the DGP and gave him an update. Some of Lahiri's suppressed excitement rubbed off on to his chief.

'The *daini's* lair? The phrases keep getting better and better. But a *hepa's* cage would have been more appropriate. The bamboo bit is ironic, eh what, Lahiri? Cane and bamboo cage, if you get what I mean.'

'Yes, sir,' Lahiri replied, not telling his superior about the madhouse laughter which had raged in his innards because he had already seen the irony of the connection.

'Great job, Lahiri,' the DGP continued. 'It's the dream break we've been waiting for. Do the brass-*wallahs* suspect anything?'

'I'm certain they do not have a clue! We won't make the same mistake twice, sir. I've asked the OC to arrange for a small group so we can sneak up on our quarry.'

'Quarry, eh? Excellent choice of words, Lahiri, I should think! I'll wait for your next update. Best of luck. Or, should I say, happy hunting!'

The OC of the Doomdooma *thana* reluctantly picked up the phone and rang up Major Harekrishna Bhagat, and apprised him of the latest dramatic developments. 'But he wouldn't divulge the exact location,' the OC said. To the major's ears he sounded unacceptably smug, but he controlled his irritation and thanked the policeman, telling him he would get in touch again if the need arose. He summoned his orderly and told him to ask the fellow from RAW to go to the control room on the double, while he himself hurried there.

'I've just got a call from the OC at Doomdooma,' he told Ravi Arora. 'You were right...the Special Intelligence bugger has unearthed something. Just hope it's not another red herring! But we have a problem. He wouldn't tell the OC the exact location Hiren Bora is holed up at. If the bastard waits till the last moment to reveal the destination, we won't have time enough to intercept.'

Arora did not seem unduly perturbed. 'Go up the ladder again, major,' he said. 'Always up the ladder in situations such as these!'

Within half an hour since the OC rang up Major Bhagat, the DGP—who despite it being a Sunday was himself holed up in his office—received a phone call from no less an authority than the State Home Minister. 'Lt. Gen. was in touch with me a minute ago,' the SHM told the DGP. 'Tell me, have you sent someone to upper Assam on a fishing expedition?'

'I have absolutely no idea what you're talking about, sir,' the DGP protested.

'Cut the bullshit. Lt. Gen. never has his facts wrong. Seems you sent one of your intelligence people after a notorious ULFA cadre currently operating in upper Assam. Apparently, the man was successful in finding out where this boy is hiding.'

The DGP remained silent as he searched for a plausible rejoinder. But caught totally be surprise, he did not have any words at the moment, despite knowing the SHM would take his silence as admission of culpability.

'Seems this was an assignment worked out solely between you and your operative,' the SHM continued. 'The Home Department has its ears to the ground, yet no one had any inkling. Neither did the army. You failed to inform me... I head the Unified Command, let me remind you.'

'It was a rogue operative, sir, I assure you,' the DGP, desperately finding his voice, blurted out. 'He had acted on his own, without informing me or any authorisation on my part! In fact, sir, I came to know of it only after an abortive raid near Doomdooma, and since then have brought him under control.'

'You came to know of it, brought him under control, but even after that failed to inform me! In fact, no one else apart from you, neither in the police department, Home or the Indian Army seems to know about this rogue!'

'My apologies, sir. I was meaning to inform you.'

'When? After the operation was over? Anyway, let's not beat about the bush, shall we? Lt. Gen. says that there is no time to lose and he wants an answer pronto. Where's this ULFA boy hiding? We want the exact location.'

Once again, the DGP was at a loss for words.

'Look, you've had a fairly decent career,' the SHM said. 'Don't mar it just before your retirement through some misplaced sense of school-boyish honour.'

The SHM's voice remained courteous, buttery smooth like the voice of any politician should be. But the threat underneath was unmistakable.

'I can't tell you the exact location because I, too, was not told of it,' the DGP said, trying at least to partially salve his conscience. 'All I know is that it is beside Chungijan, the village from where this ULFA boy hails.'

'I'm sure that should be good enough for these army blokes,' the SHM said. 'Now, as for this maverick operative of yours, I want punitive proceedings started against him at once. Suspension followed by a departmental enquiry. We can't permit indiscipline in the forces, I'm sure you'll agree.'

'That's true, sir.'

'I'm an elephant, my dear man,' were the SHM's parting words. 'I don't forget. So a copy of the suspension letter on my desk tomorrow, and the report of the departmental enquiry by next week.'

Individual destiny is guided by the man (or woman!), the moment and the milieu—a hackneyed observation, yet perfectly true. In Hiren Bora's case, the man himself had been exceptional. Within a more favourable moment and milieu, he might have achieved great things. He possessed qualities which went towards making a natural leader, the courage to attempt the seemingly impossible and endurance to suffer in the try. He was highly intelligent, armed with the ability to observe closely and plan out his course of action beforehand. His misfortune was that he had been born at the wrong moment and in the wrong milieu; after all, there could have been nothing worse than to have been born in a penurious family in a remote part of the country, yet be endowed with character, intelligence and ambition.

If he had only given himself an opportunity to dwell on this, he would have been the first to acknowledge that human existence is chock-full of such quirky placements… As Inspector Lahiri, too, would have; had his luck been more favourable, he might have overcome the handicaps of the moment and the milieu, so that the man emerged shining like a mirror reflecting summer sunshine. Inspector Lahiri (given his philosophic bent of mind, and also because he harboured a somewhat romantic notion of this particular ULFA cadre) would have considered that Hiren Bora's predicament lay at the core of the malaise besetting the human condition, and that it was tragic. But the latter, because he nowadays lived for the moment and could not afford the luxury of philosophic speculation, would have dismissed a notion projecting him as the protagonist of a tragic drama as bullshit.

On the contrary, in the frame of mind he was currently in, he might have considered a jester in some comic pantomime to be more appropriate to describe himself (had Lahiri not tried to cheat himself through pastiche passion—and not kept his ears deaf to internal laughter—he, too, may have used a similar analogy). However, there could be no doubt that a vast difference lay between what the country lad had been three and a half years ago, and what he was now. So Hiren Bora, if only moved by a desire to, could have viewed his existence from a far wider angle. Interaction with different people and exposure to other climes and cultures had broadened his mental horizon; conversations with individuals such as Lakhidhar Gogoi as well as greater access to journals and books in places like Dhaka (and the time to read them) had enlarged his grasp on international politics, and enabled him to acquire a global perspective.

Earlier, during the days of training and indoctrination, Hiren Bora and the other new recruits had been made to peruse a great deal of material about revolutionaries of the world and the way they had changed the course of mankind's destiny, though the individuals chosen were mostly of communist ideology—Lenin,

Mao, Che Guevara, Fidel Castro and the lot. Initially, he had accepted such individuals the way those foisting the books on him wanted to—'people's heroes' who had revolutionised the manner mankind visualised ideal human societies. Later, he had been able to judge them in a more personal, yet objective manner… Alone within the jungles tolerating mosquito and leech-bites, in some jungle camp bunked upon a bamboo bed, within a safe-house in hostile enemy territory, Hiren Bora had had time to reflect upon these figures of history and pass his own verdict: he had deemed them all to be failures! The Soviet Russia of Lenin's dream lay fragmented; capitalism was burrowing into the body of communist China like a maggot into a buried cadaver; capitalist imperialism held sway over most of Latin America despite the bluster of individuals like Hugo Perez; Castro's Cuba was just a small dot on the Atlas, precariously clinging to an ideology not quite matching the aspiration of her people.

The transient nature of dogma ensured that revolutionaries and their revolutions were impermanent—like everything else in the universe; martyrs appeared to Hiren Bora to be mere jackasses willing to sacrifice their lives for what they deemed to be a 'cause'. Those celebrated 'comrades' with their ideologies and causes were the truly tragic figures. They were, of course, extreme examples—individuals who became icons to generations and millions. Yet, the pygmy revolutionaries (the world was so full of them!) with eyes focused on less ambitious causes were no less tragic. Oh yes, irrevocably destined to be the tragic hero, big or small, the universal revolutionary! But not him—Hiren Bora, the boy born in poverty but today feared and respected by so many! Secretly, he had never thought much of his compatriots within the ULFA; in particular, the top leaders, since he himself had seen the way they lived nowadays. All except the commander-in-chief, whom he regarded highly only because the commander-in-chief had a high opinion of Hiren Bora. Perhaps it had been this latent contempt for people like Pradyut Basumatari and Lakhidhar Gogoi which had made him resist conversion to their cause; resist, in fact, ideology of any kind. He was all the time laughingly reminding himself that he was a rebel without a cause! He did not know (nor did Lahiri) that there must have been an intrinsic flaw in his character; some unseen aberration inserted into his lineage none could guess when. Only this could explain the otherwise inexplicable rapidity of change to his nature which had (though he did not see it that way) reduced him to the level of an animal within the span of a few years. Had Lahiri but known of this, he would have been tickled to the bones at the accidental aptness of his civet metaphor!

Perhaps it had been this bestial instinct which had made Hiren Bora so uncomfortable the past couple of days; the *daini's* lair, from a strategic point of view, was undoubtedly a bamboo cage—surrounded on every side by thick growth of the plant. One of the primary rules in selecting any hiding place was to have at least two exits so that the option to use one or the other is available in emergency situations; the *daini's* lair only had one. If, God forbid, they came looking for him and covered the single exit, he would be in a trap just like that *hepa*—the one he had uncaged seemingly not so long ago—and not far away from where he was hiding now. Only, he doubted whether there would be someone stupid enough to open the door to the trap and let it go so it could try and kill other ducks at other times.

Moreover, one rule he set himself was never to be forced into taking action; never to lose control of events—for therein lay danger. Yet, in this case, he had been coerced into coming to the *daini's* lair for a final toss of the dice; the thing had gone beyond his control, which boded no good. Also, he reminded himself, when he had told Okon he trusted him completely, he was not speaking the truth. Nowadays, he trusted no one—his prescription to remain safe and alive. Not that the boy would betray him or disobey instructions given to him; on that account, Okon was absolutely trustworthy. But these years had made his elder brother aware of the perils and pitfalls orbiting around the tiny world of the little boy—a world darkened with betrayal and treachery. Those avid eyes were everywhere; canine noses constantly sniffed the wind. Hiren Bora was certain someone must be keeping Okon on the radar in the remote hope the boy would lead them to his brother; the reason why he had been stepping out of the trap whenever Okon was due to come and meet him.

The boy had been marvellous the way he had tackled Bhodiya; but the man was an idiot, and there might be others with more brains. True, Okon had paid his last visit and Hiren Bora remained safe; but his brother knew he would be going to Gandhasai only on the night of January 2; the probability that the young, immature boy would not be able to resist the urgings of love and make another visit to the *daini's* lair tomorrow was too great to be risked. Already, Hiren Bora had broken too many of the precautionary rules he had set for himself; it had been his strategy to always be on the move, and rarely stayed at a single spot more than a night. Had Lahiri known of this, it would have reinforced his contention that his simile had been apt—if one observes the behaviour of wild animals, one notes they rarely remain at the same spot for long; that they are constantly on the move, even if it be within their individual home range. Only domesticated beasts were mostly sedentary. Yet, this had been the third day he had spent in the bamboo-trap; he needed to leave the place now and find himself another hideout from which to make the Gandhasai visit.

But he would have to wait for darkness to set in; it would be too risky to make his move in daylight because there were farmers out there, still reaping the ripened paddy from the fields. The jungle trail could provide him with cover for only a short distance before he hit open terrain. And who knew, if his luck did not hold, he might come across someone inimical on that trail itself!

He had hours to kill yet, but this was not the only reason why he began to dismantle the igloo-like structure he had erected and cleaned up the *daini's* lair. It was a part of his nature, this compulsion to keep things orderly— above all, not to pollute Nature. That clearing was a beautiful spot; finding it had been one of the highlights of his life…the way the sun-beams filtered down through the small, natural chimney formed by the tall, slanting bamboo stems was nothing short of a miracle. To leave it sullied would be sacrilege. Deliberately, with practiced ease, he un-wrapped the polythene sheet from the framework, folded it, and put it into his bag. He uprooted the cut strands of bamboo and threw them amongst the plants on one side of the clearing, where they would rot and provide food for new-grown saplings. With his boot he levelled off the makeshift fire-place he had built to cook his dinners, and cleared away other visible tokens of his presence as best he could. It was, he knew, impossible to remove all trace; but Nature was a miracle-worker; when the rains came around April, the light grass would grow again like a carpet over the rocky clearing, and erase any sign he had ever been there.

He looked at his watch. Not yet three o' clock! The gloom within the clearing was a bad indicator of the light outside. Moreover, the nagging unease at having to prolong his stay in the *daini's* lair was building up in him, and he wanted some release. He wriggled his way through the maze and emerged outside. The sky was a clear, startlingly blue; the light had not faded, so there was still time before he could depart. The paddy fields closest to him had been cleared of the ripe rice grains, so only the half cut strands of stalk remained. Then, his memory was jolted by a sight and his mind went back to a forsaken past. Some young men of the village were gathered together at one spot of a paddy field, building a *bhelaghar* as well as *mejhis*; of course, *Bhogali-bihu* was just around the corner! Hiren Bora remembered the fun and games of those days… For a long while, he watched the village lads at work. Then, forcibly, he drew his eyes away and re-entered the clearing amongst the bamboo.

The sun had been dipping down on the horizon. Perhaps another hour, and he would be ready to leave. He doubted if he would ever enter the *daini's* lair again; his decision never to visit his family again had been taken this morning itself. After feeling just a pang of remorse at seeing his young brother walk out, Okon, Ai, Pitai, and Bhoni belonged to the past and should forever be kept there, he had finally decided. He could not hide from himself that his brother's fervent importunities had got under his skin; he had spent hours last night weighing his options: a life in a village, or even at a township—he doubted, after what he had experienced and what he had become, that he could once again go back to that kind of a life. Disillusion, frustration, indoctrination, an environment of perpetual violence—these would bring out the beast in even an idealist, let alone a rebel without cause like him. No, he must continue to allow himself to be moved by those unseen demons and go on his chosen course; it was a compulsion, there was no alternative...

Lahiri and Okon waited for the raiding party at the open space fronting the dak bungalow. The inspector had asked Karuna Saikia to leave after promising he would recommend the school teacher for a part of the reward money in case all this resulted in something positive. The fat, oily bastard had actually been relieved—his services were no longer required, and he had scooted off on his rickety two-wheeler. It was not that Lahiri wanted him to vamoose before the others arrived in order to protect his information source; the OC could simply question the chowkidar to find out about him (though Lahiri doubted if the policeman would waste time on such small fries). The main reason he had asked Saikia to go was because he just could not stand the sight of him; to a person of his generation, to whom a school teacher was the most respected individual in the community, the sight of one descending to such depths was repugnant.

He kept looking at his watch and at the sky; for a moment he considered walking to the *thana* because it was so close by and his suspense would be lessened, but then gave up the idea since it might decrease his authority before the policeman. Beside him, Okon, too, was in a state of nervous frenzy; his bladder grew full and he had to race down towards a boundary wall to relieve himself. At that precise moment, two jeeps roared into the compound—one of them being driven by the OC himself in order to make room for the entire party.

Okon stopped urinating halfway and ran back to Lahiri. The OC, in the lead vehicle, opened the door at the front and the inspector jumped in, pulling the boy up so he could squeeze in at his side. 'Chungijan,' he said, anticipating the policeman's query. 'Where's the magistrate?'

'In the other vehicle. We had some difficulty locating him... which is why we're a bit late. It's a Sunday, you know.' The policeman was not the least bothered that, with the inspector sitting beside him, he could not call up those army sons of bitches at once and tell them about the destination—even if it was not a specific location. That would be his excuse if later enquiries were made on this particular raid. He was already feeling guilty about having betrayed Lahiri's confidence—a double betrayal would be too much!

There was something about the OC's manner which disturbed the inspector, but this was not the moment for counter-questions or speculation. The two vehicles drove at a fast speed; it being a late Sunday afternoon, the road was almost deserted. Within 10 minutes, they reached the junction where the *kutcha* road to Chungijan met the main road.

'Go for a kilometre and stop before we hit the actual village,' Lahiri instructed as the OC turned right, on to the *kutcha* road, raising a cloud of dust—much to the discomfort of the occupants of the vehicle behind them. Half a kilometre ahead, just before they reached a bend on the road, the policeman slowed down and Lahiri looked at him, perplexed. The reason was apparent just as they took the bend—an army truck was blocking the path, with soldiers standing beside it waving at them to stop.

'Damn!' Lahiri said under his breath. He looked at the OC. The man was staring straight ahead with that stolid gaze of his. Lahiri understood.

Flanked by two soldiers in full combat-gear, Major Harekrishna Bhagat, with Ravi Arora just behind him, strode up to the lead vehicle.

'Inspector Lahiri, I presume,' the major barked out. 'May I request you to get down?'

Stretching out across Okon, Lahiri pulled at the door lever to open, nodded for the boy to hop off, and followed suit. The major and his men were tall and strong of build (though Ravi Arora was a trifle shorter). The inspector, facing them, looked even more diminutive than usual, and with his bespectacled eyes and kindly face, hardly menacing. Yet the major could sense the force pulsing out of the man, the fierce desire to protect his turf and, perhaps, the boy beside him. Could it perhaps also be the quarry?

'This is outrageous!' Lahiri burst out, though he knew the battle was already lost.

'Hardly that, inspector,' the army man laughed and said. 'On the contrary, it's your actions which have been outrageous. Thought you could hoodwink us, did you?'

'It's not a contest, Major Bhagat,' Lahiri peered with his eyes at the army man's name-tag and said. 'If I guess correctly, we're after the same target. But did you have to bring your entire battalion with you, huh? That's why we tried to act on our own in the first place.'

His sally hit home. The army man lost his cool and would have retorted with anger if Ravi Arora had not stepped in. 'Look, we're losing valuable time arguing. Inspector Lahiri, you've earned our gratitude in getting us this far... but now it's time the army takes over.'

'Not if I can help it.' Such intransigence—coming from the short-statured, bespectacled man—would have seemed ludicrous had not the occasion itself been so fraught with gravity.

'Oh, but you don't understand,' Ravi Arora said suavely. 'You're in no position to dictate terms. In fact, we shan't even allow you to participate in the operation. You see, Inspector Lahiri, your department itself has put you under suspension. But I sense you've not been informed.'

Lahiri took out his cell phone and called up the DGP. 'For heaven's sake, Lahiri, do as the army blokes say. And keep me out of this, will you?'

Lahiri had not even put in a question, but that had been reply enough! 'Fine,' he told Arora. 'But you've made a mistake coming with so large a force. The villagers may have already seen you. Who knows, someone or the other might even now be racing to warn Hiren Bora!'

All the while Okon had been standing stock-still, petrified with terror, sensing his bladders filling up again. The *rakhyasas* surrounded him; the reek of adrenalin was terrifyingly familiar. But at Lahiri's words, he summoned up a supreme effort and said,

'No. That can't be. No one but I know where Hirukai is hiding!'

'Right, boy,' Arora said with a triumphant air. 'Come, show us where your Hirukai is holed up.'

Okon said nothing, but looked up expectantly towards Lahiri. The inspector shrugged helplessly and nodded.

'You promised!' Okon reminded.

'Yes, I did.'

Okon led the soldiers up the road and then, just before reaching the point where the residential part of the village commenced, turned and climbed down from the road into the paddy fields. He moved on across the narrow, elevated paths crisscrossing the fields for a few hundred metres and then pointed, his words directed only at Lahiri. 'There. You can see it from here. The bamboo grove over there. It's the *daini's* lair. That's where Hirukai is hiding.'

'Well, then that's as far as you chaps are going!' Major Bhagat barked out. 'It will be a purely army operation from now on. No, not even the commandos of the Special Anti-insurgency Police Task Force!'

It was a deliberate snub, but Lahiri and the others had to grin and bear it. The army personnel were already on the run, advancing swiftly through the reaped rice-stems, taking up positions and crouching around the *daini's* lair. The youths who had been busy constructing the *bhelaghars* saw the advancing troops and began running for their lives towards the village. They, in turn, alerted others—soon, most villagers learned about the raid and poured out in hordes to see what the excitement was about...

On hindsight, Lahiri had been struck by the anti-climactic ending to the hunt. All of a sudden, time had seemingly decelerated; everything appeared to move in slow motion. The couple of army men left behind to ensure that the police party and villagers did not get any closer (civilian deaths or injuries would complicate what was a simple 'encounter') gestured menacingly but in a robot-like, lethargic way. Their silent gestures were ineffective; the villagers inched ahead as if they had seen the eyes of a snake and could not help themselves. The army men had to request the police personnel to help in keeping the crowd under control. The villagers made not the least sound; babies being held by mothers did not wail…except for the rustling of half-cut rice-stems as bodies brushed past, them there was no noise. There was no breeze; the sky retained its pristine blue, and not a cloud was present to cast a shadow on the fields. The first hint of forming mist was there in the dampening stalk-tops; another hour, it would thicken into cold black fog and come swirling slowly in to drop the curtains on this petty drama. The heavily camouflaged army *jawans* in full combat-gear were traversing the paddy fields with infuriating lassitude; to Lahiri's transformed vision, they appeared to take an entire epoch just reaching the bamboo copse. At a leisurely signal from the troop commander, they came to a stop and crouched within the half-cut paddy stems, with only the gun barrels and helmeted heads showing.

A scene in slow motion; everyone was an actor, bit players and extras awaiting the emergence of the star player who, funnily enough, was not the star in actual fact! A scene being shot for one of those films made in Mumbai his wife was so fond of; the setting was perfect—the bamboo grove and the dark and brooding jungles beyond made for a dramatic background, and the sun was low and menacingly red on the horizon. Who was the director—the major or the RAW son of a bitch? Who would be yelling 'lights, camera, action!'? But there would be no dishum-dishum fight of the type to be seen in those films; it would be a tame denouement. Confronted with such heavy fire-power, Hiren Bora had no choice but to surrender. Lahiri would not want it to be otherwise...

The light had dimmed perceptibly within the witch's grove. It was time to leave, to walk out of the *daini's* lair, out of the lives of shadows from the past. Hiren Bora bounded up with characteristic determination and athleticism, and was about to pick up his gun and bag when he heard the voice slither like a snake through the winding maze. The thick bamboo growth encaging him had muted the voice to an extent, but its import was unmistakable.

'We know you're in there! Come out with your hands in the air. Do not carry anything. I repeat, come out with your hands in the air. Do not carry anything.'

Hiren Bora did not flinch as he heard the voice on the megaphone. Had he, subconsciously, been expecting it—even desired it? He did not know. Nowadays, he did not know who he really was. Nowadays, he did not know what he really wanted. He did not know what he felt at the knowledge that he had been trapped in a cage. Nowadays, he did not really know what he felt.

It was not Okon. He knew with absolute certainty it could not have been Okon. But his brother, without doubt, must have been an indirect cause. Those bastards out there were cunning. His younger brother was intelligent and resourceful, but no match for those bastards. They must have shadowed him without his knowledge, and discovered the *daini's* lair.

Leaving his bag and gun behind, Hiren Bora slid through the maze almost till the mouth of the bamboo grove. He peeped through two bamboo stems. It was a panoramic view—the villagers gathered at a distance, the ruddy sun casting a malevolent eye on the landscape and, above all, the dozens of army bastards crouched within the paddy-stalks. Hiren Bora was a realist. The odds were too many, and he was no martyr to a cause. Perhaps Okon would get his wish, after all!

He retreated into the clearing. Once more, the voice reached him muted through the bamboo. 'We will give you five more minutes. Then we will fire. Come out with your hand in the air. Do not carry anything.'

There was no help for it. He climbed quickly up a bamboo and slung his gun upon a stem as hidden away from sight as possible. He slid down and once more wriggled his way out of the maze, and emerged into the open.

He did not know it but, of course, his fate had been decided a couple of hours ago, in a control room at a temporary army camp. Taking him alive was never an option, as Arora had pointed out. First, there were too many people, especially amongst the anti-insurgency forces, who wanted Hiren Bora dead. Second, given the stupendous number of cases against him, the legal ramifications would be too complicated and troublesome, whereas simple elimination would remove, so to say, all the hassle. Finally, experience had shown that many members of the ULFA—even ruthless killers, since they have been adorned with the 'freedom fighter' halo—had been pardoned by the government, and roamed free today.

The sharp-shooters had been selected personally by Major Bhagat.

Hiren Bora walked out, proud and erect—his empty hands held high in the air. Two shots rang out, one piercing the heart, the other the skull. Birds, returning to their roosts in the jungle and the bamboo copse rose up in the air in raucous terror.

Hiren Bora toppled to the ground, dead. *Operation Hepa* had ended, though not in the way Inspector Lahiri had envisaged.

All the while Okon had been in a daze; his bladder was full but he was oblivious of the fact. The crowd around him had become sizeable; Pitai, Ai, and Bai had come and were standing close to him, their eyes fixed in a hypnotized gaze at the *daini's* lair. Was he hallucinating? For this was no paddy field but the floor of the *naamghar*; he was cradled in Hirukai's arms, waiting—like the others in the audience—for the enactment to commence, drawing courage and reassurance from the warmth of physical contact. The audience was there, too, but why were they so quiet when they should have been loud and boisterous as usual, rendered silent only when the actors hopped on to the stage? He felt disoriented; but where was Hirukai? He was not seated on Hirukai's lap, certainly. Nor was his big brother anywhere in sight. It could not be; he could not be watching the *bhaona* at the *naamghar* without Hirukai! Only the short-statured policeman with those funny looking spectacles was beside him; what was he doing in that village *naamghar*?

There was deep terror within Okon's heart and in the pit of his stomach; that terror had first sunk in when Hirukai had left for good and the *rakhyasas* first came to rip their house apart and humiliate Pitai. That terror would not go away; this kindly policeman with his reassuring manners could not make the terror go away—only Hirukai could. That terror at the pit of his stomach had caused his stammer; made him wake up sweating at night because of those horrible nightmares—far more frightening than the old man of the forest or the witch always perched on the thatch roof of their cottage at night. That terror had traumatised his soul and played tricks with his brain.

For what was this? Not only one *rakhyasa* with tusks for teeth, monstrous, black eyes and red tongue and lips splattered with human gore—but scores of them! Waiting for the saviour to prance onto the stage—two steps forward, one step back. Ah, here he comes! Okon's heart leaps. The audience lets out a collective gasp of astonishment and falls silent. But what is this? The saviour of royal blood is not garbed in glittering armour but an old, dirt-stained shirt and trousers! But what is this? He does not move two steps forward, one step back—like actors in a *bhaona* do—but walks out steadily. But what is this? He does not carry a gilded mace on his shoulders but walks out with his hands held high in the air.

Then the final bit of insane incongruity. The concealed pouches of red colour should have burst near the hearts of the *rakhyasas*, yet the shirt front of the saviour suddenly blossoms red like a *modar* flower (or like his school bag)—and then another adorns his head. The saviour falls, to Okon's bewildered eyes it seems that it is the *rakhyasas* who break out in a macabre dance, replete with bat-like flaying of the hands and grotesque swaying of bodies. The boy looks at the bespectacled policeman for an answer, but the eyes behind the bifocals are inscrutable, glazed and hard.

Okon feels the rush of warmth at his underbelly as his bladder burst as if it's a grenade, and warm piss trickles down his thighs.

Arup Kumar Dutta is an Indian author and freelance journalist. He writes short-fiction, long-fiction, non-fiction, newspaper editorials, articles and columns, satirical pieces et al. His works of fiction like *The Anagarika's Swansong, Red—Camellia Green* and *The Ahoms* have received critical acclaim, as have his 15 non-fiction books like *The Brahmaputra, Unicornis, Cha-Garam—The Tea Story, The Final Frontier, The Roving Minstrel* etc. His 17 juvenile adventure novels include *The Kaziranga Trail, Blind Witness, Smack, Lure of Zangrila, Revenge, Save the Pool, Oh Deer, Footprints in the Sand, The Counterfeit Treasure, A Story About Tea, The Crystal Cave* etc. Among the awards he has been bestowed with are Shankar's Award, Journalist Welfare Foundation Award, Kamal Kumari National Award and The Life Time Achievement Honor Award by AWIC, the Indian Chapter of International Board for Books for Young People. Between 2004-2008, the Government of India appointed him Director, Jawaharlal Nehru Indian Cultural Centre, Jakarta, and Indian Cultural Centre, Bali, with the rank of a Counselor in the Indian Embassy, Jakarta, Indonesia. In 2018, the University of Dibrugarh conferred D. Litt (*honoris causa*) on him while the Government of India honoured him with the Padmashri. His website is www.arupkumardutta.com.